CHASING
The HEIRESS

Books by Rachael Miles

Chasing the Heiress

Jilting the Duke

Published by Kensington Publishing Corporation

CHASING *The* HEIRESS

RACHAEL MILES

ZEBRA BOOKS
KENSINGTON PUBLISHING CORP.
http://www.kensingtonbooks.com

In memoriam
Harold Ray Hawkins (1938–2015)
A big-hearted man

ACKNOWLEDGMENTS

No book makes its way to readers without the kindness of many people. My agent, Courtney Miller-Callihan at Handspun Literary, never fails to offer smart direction and good sense. At Kensington, I remain grateful for Janice Rossi's cover design, Anthony Russo's illustration of it, Erin Nelsen Parekh's cover blurb, and Kimberly Richardson's and Jane Nutter's helpful promotions and advice—but most of all, for my editor, Esi Sogah, who wields her pen with precision and grace.

Thanks to Adrianne Busch and Richard Porter for your help with my author photograph. Richard normally photographs wild and peopled places, and I'm grateful he agreed to pretend I was just another landscape.

Cathy Maxwell and Jodi Thomas offered priceless support. Cathy Blackwell, Celia Bonaduce, Michelle Carlin and the indefatigable Stephanie Eckroth were ever available to read and to critique. Carey Adams, Diane Kendall, Brian and Sue McFadden, Lowell and Veronica Rice, Ashley Stovall, Tony Walker, and Allison Whitney offered love and support in a difficult year, as did Micki Bragalone, Ana Katherine Curry, Beth Haga, Tricia Heaney, and Paul Wackym. I am grateful for my family (those I name here and those whose names I hold in my heart): my sister Lynn, my mother Mary, and my uncles—David, Larry, John, and Sam Wagliardo—who, when there was nothing more I could do, sent me home to write. As always, my deepest thanks to Miles, who reads everything well.

Chapter One

"Do you have her?" Archibald Pettegrew, Lord Marner, already knew what the answer would be, and he ground his pen into the desk pad before him, crushing its tip.

Ox looked at the ground, hat in hands, his hulking frame braced against his employer's displeasure. He shook his head. "We've watched all the stages to London for three weeks. We thought we had her in Shrewsbury, even snuck into a garden party to snatch her, but it weren't your lady."

"She's not my lady, you fool." Marner crumpled the letter he had been writing. "But she must be found."

"She can't have gone far—not on foot. She has no money, no friends. None of the farmers on their way to market remember seeing her, and none gave her a ride. We asked at all the tollbooths for a dozen miles." Ox's tone was more frustrated than conciliatory. "If she's between here and Shrewsbury, she can't stay lost forever."

"That's what you said two weeks ago and again last week." Marner rose from his chair. Placing his hands firmly on the desk, he leaned forward over the broad expanse of wood. "What if you were wrong? What if she didn't head to Shrewsbury? What if she had traveled to one of the other market towns and from there to London?"

Ox ran a broad hand across his jaw. "On this side of the canal . . . nearest market town is eight miles northwest across rough country—hills, forest to the south, then there's the river, and even if she could have gotten that far, she didn't cross at the Montford bridge. No, we have her pinned. And soon she'll bolt."

Marner wasn't appeased. "What if she crossed the canal? A child could swim it at most places."

Ox swallowed. "Well, then, she would have been noticed, a sodden woman walking alone in a fancy dress."

"Widen your search. Check every inn on every road from Ellesmere to Bridgenorth." Marner shoved the chair back from the desk and walked to stand in front of Ox. He pointed his finger in sharp angry motions in the bigger man's face. "I need her. Here. Now. Not in a week. Now." His finger punctuated each word.

Ox recoiled slightly, then bristled and stood to his full height.

"'T'ain't my fault. If you'd given me my way," Ox spit his words, "she'd be here. In the churchyard, next to your aunt. Dead and buried with a nice tombstone to mark her grave. Simple, clean. A fall from a horse, a broken wheel on a carriage, a swim in the river turned drowning. No one would have said nay. You'd have your precious estate, and I'd be paid."

Marner turned away, pulling his rage under control. He knew better than to push Ox too far. "She ruined everything."

"I told you to keep her away from the old lady." Ox frowned. "She's a sly one. You knew that the moment she came here."

"I can still set it right. Then it won't matter how she dies." Marner's anger turned cold, hard. "But first you need to find her."

Chapter Two

Colin Somerville woke, heart pounding, the heavy thud of cannon fire fading with his nightmare. Heavy brocaded curtains hung over the carriage windows to his left. Feeling suffocated, he shoved the curtains apart and breathed in gulps of crisp September air. Beyond the window, the sun fell gently on the green rolling hills of Shropshire. In the near distance, open pastures with grazing sheep gave way to enclosed land, where turnips were growing. He fell back against the seat. He was in England, not Belgium. It was only a dream.

Judging from the position of the sun, they should reach Shrewsbury by dusk. He rubbed his face with his hands, pressing his fingertips into the tight muscles at his forehead and temples. To calm his heart, he used an old trick his brother Benjamin had taught him. He focused on naming the various scents in the air—wool, newly harvested wheat, dirt loosened to pull the turnips, and water. Likely the Severn.

His companion, Marietta, grew restless in her sleep. He stilled. She curled her hand under her chin and nestled farther into the down-filled pallet tucked into the well between the two carriage seats. Colin had bought her the thick pallet that morning at Wrexham. The gift had cost him more than he could easily afford, but her widening smile had been worth the cost. Since then, she'd spent the day sleeping, her back to one seat riser, her swollen belly pressed against the other.

A line of bright sunlight from beneath the window curtains shone above Marietta's head like a nimbus. But unlike the Madonnas he had seen at Rome or Venice, whose faces were lit with an internal glow, Marietta—even in rest—looked weary. The dark hollows in her cheeks, the deep circles under her eyes, the bluish undertone to her lips, all reminded him of the El Grecos he'd seen at Toledo. He thought of his sister Judith's confinements—she had never looked so ill, not with any of her four boys. If Harrison Walgrave had sent him to bury another woman . . . He pushed away thoughts of Marietta dying, reminding himself instead of how Walgrave had presented the mission.

"It's straightforward." Walgrave had held out the address of a cottage in Holywell and a miniature portrait. "Escort the widow of one of the Prince Regent's Habsburg cousins from the western coast of Flintshire to London." The portrait revealed a pixie face with auburn hair and emerald eyes. A sweet face. An innocent face. His gut had twisted. Leaving the items in Walgrave's hand, Colin had turned to the door.

"Find someone else. I'm not your good soldier anymore."

"It's not that easy. I offered Barclay and Sundern. But Prinny wants you. Apparently your work at . . ."

Colin had paused, his hand on the doorknob, waiting for the word "Brussels." The churning in his stomach turned into a wave of nausea.

". . . Edinburgh has not gone unnoticed. The prince regent considers this a personal favor." Walgrave had tossed the miniature at him, and Colin had caught it automatically.

"And be charming. Prinny specifically mentioned your wit and charm. I didn't tell him you've become a scowling misanthrope."

Colin resisted the sudden urge to throw the miniature at Walgrave's head and storm away. "Perhaps you should have. I'd rather be sent into the worst hell in London where I can scowl as I please than play nursemaid to a spoiled Habsburg princess."

Walgrave had raised one shoulder in a half-shrug. "Since I could not dissuade Prinny, I at least made it worth your while." He held out an official document on heavy parchment.

Colin read the contents, then folded it, all without comment. Walgrave waited silently until Colin held out his hand for the address. "After this, I'm finished. No more missions. No more death. No more lies." Walgrave had nodded his acceptance.

It had taken Colin two days to travel to Holywell, two days in which he had steeled himself to smile and be charming. But ultimately the princess had charmed him. Heiress to a mining magnate, Marietta had caught the eye of a visiting (and impoverished) member of the Habsburg royal family. Though she had been impeccably trained at the best finishing school in Paris, when Colin arrived, he found her teaching the housekeeper's parrot to curse in five European languages. "Don't call me Princess," she whispered, casting a grim eye to the housekeeper, hovering at the edge of the terrace. "Or she will raise my rate."

It had taken three more days to separate Marietta's possessions into two groups: those which the carriage could carry and those which would have to be shipped from Liverpool around the coast to London. Most difficult had been determining exactly which clothes she could (and could not) do without for her first week at court. Then, just when he had thought that they might set out, she had insisted that his coachman, Fletcher, accompany her trunks across the inlet to ensure they were well stowed for their London journey. All told, he had been gone from London for more than a week before he bundled Marietta, her paints, her embroidery, her knitting, her books, and a handful of magazines into the carriage and set off on their trip. But somehow he had not minded. Marietta was sweet, resilient, and companionable, anticipating the birth of her child with real joy.

He shifted in his seat, but his legs—outstretched on the backward-facing seat to give Marietta more room—felt like leaden weights, long past numb from a lack of circulation. He moved one foot down into the small space remaining between Marietta's feet and the carriage door. The blood began to move agonizingly into one set of toes.

He unfolded his map and began to recalculate their trip. Holywell to London was two hundred and eight miles. Even a mail coach, traveling at seven miles an hour, could travel the distance in thirty-two hours, and his brother's third-best carriage was able to clip along at ten. But the princess needed substantive food, frequent stops, a real bed at night, and opportunities to shop at any tempting village store they passed. Their first day, they traveled only to Wrexham. Twenty-six miles in six hours. Their second day would measure little more. He had already promised she could spend the night—and morning—in Shrewsbury. Using his forefinger as a measure, he counted off the miles from Shrewsbury to London. The return would take a sennight, if he were lucky.

Marietta moaned and tried to shift her weight. Why—he berated himself for the fiftieth time—hadn't he borrowed a better carriage? One with ample seats, thick comfortable bolsters, and better springs. If he were to play escort to a pregnant princess, why hadn't the Home Office informed him? Had they intentionally withheld the information? Or had they not known?

He forced his attention back to the map. If Marietta gave birth on the road with only him and Fletcher for midwives, he would kill someone in the Home Office. He wasn't yet sure who. Perhaps the lot of them, but he would begin by strangling Harrison Walgrave.

The carriage began to slow, the springs creaking into a new rhythm. Colin waited for Fletcher to offer the usual signals: two slow taps for an inn, a fast double-tap for a crossroads, and a heavy heel-kick for danger. But no taps, kicks, yells, or pistol shots alarmed him, except perhaps the nagging absence of any warnings.

Colin tapped on the roof and waited. No response. His senses grew more alert, listening, but he heard nothing beyond the normal sounds of a country road.

Even so, he shifted his second foot—still numb—from the opposite seat to the floor and slid several inches toward the middle of the bench. There, Colin moved a cushion aside to reveal a built-in pistol cabinet that had been added by his brother, the Duke of Forster.

His movement wakened Marietta, and she began to speak, but he held up his finger before his lips, then touched his ear. *Be quiet: I'm listening.* Her green eyes, always expressive, widened, and she nodded understanding. She pulled the thick feather comforter up over her belly, as if to hide.

The door handle moved slightly as someone tried to open the door. Luckily Colin had bolted it from the inside. Their highwayman grew frustrated, pulling against the door handle several times.

Reacting viscerally, Colin wrenched the pistol cabinet door open. But before he could withdraw the pistols, the window glass shattered inward. Marietta recoiled and tried to push herself up as the curtains were torn away, wrenched outward. Colin moved to protect Marietta, trying to place himself between the princess and the broken window. But his feet found no solid purchase, just a river of down shifting beneath his weight. Losing his balance, he fell back hard onto the seat.

Two hands in long leather gloves, each holding a pistol, reached through the window frame into the carriage.

As in battle, everything slowed. Both pistols pointed at a spot in the middle of his chest. At this range, he had no hope of surviving. And he felt more relief than fear.

Colin held out his hands to show he was unarmed. He could see nothing of the highwayman. Only a dark duster and a mask.

The guns didn't fire.

One pistol shifted to the opposite seat. But Marietta wasn't there. Seeing her on the floor, the highwayman repositioned his sights.

Realizing in an instant this was no robbery, Colin flung himself between Marietta and the barrel. He heard the cock of the trigger, saw the flash of fire, and felt the hit of the ball in his side. Black powder burned his flesh.

Dark smoke filled the cabin, and he choked, coughing.

His ears rung from the boom of the gunshot, but he saw the flash of the second pistol firing along with a shower of sparks from the side and barrel of the gun. He felt Marietta's scream. He pulled himself up, half standing, one hand against the carriage roof to steady himself. His side stabbed with pain at each expansion of his lungs.

Marietta tried to rise behind him, choking as well. She pulled against the clothes on his back, but he brushed her hands away. When the smoke cleared, his body would stand between Marietta and their assailant. He would die. But after Belgium, he felt dead already—what would be the difference?

Marietta beat the backs of his legs. Small burning

embers burned on Marietta's pallet. Some of the lit sparks from the pistols had fallen onto the down-filled bed. He assessed the dangers automatically. Once the embers ate past the woolen cover and fire caught the feathers, the danger would spread quickly.

Still on the floor, Marietta pushed herself backward toward the opposite door, kicking the smoldering bolsters and pallet away from her. With each kick, she further entangled his feet. He couldn't reach her, at least not easily. And he couldn't reach and load a gun without stepping from his defensive position in front of her. Thick smoke burned his eyes.

With neither sound nor sight to help him, he had to choose: the dangers of the fire, growing with each second, or those of the highwaymen who could be waiting outside. Tensing, he unbolted the door, pushed it open, and leapt out. His leg hitting wrong, he fell and rolled into the ditch beside the road. He raised himself cautiously. The highwaymen were gone, having attacked, then left. Not robbers then.

He pulled himself to standing. He should worry about Fletcher and the postboy, Bobby, but there was no time. Smoke from the feather-stuffed pallet billowed from the coach. He could see Marietta's legs, vigorously kicking the smoldering bed away from her. She was alive, but trapped against the locked door on the opposite side of the carriage.

Ignoring the pain below his ribs, he pulled hard on the pallet, dragging a portion through the coach door. Already, the smoldering feathers were breaking through the wool in patches of open flame. He heaved again, releasing all but a third from the coach. Flames began to dance across the pallet.

If the pallet broke apart before he could remove it, he'd have to sacrifice the carriage, and then he could offer little protection to Marietta. He pulled hard once more, and the pallet fell onto the green verge next to the road. Then, to protect neighboring crops and livestock, he dragged the pallet, flames licking at his hands, into the middle of the road, where it could burn without harm. Once carriage and countryside were out of danger, he hunched over, hands on his knees, and tried to breathe without expanding his lower rib cage.

After a few minutes to recover his breath, Colin looked up at the carriage. Fletcher remained at his post, his body slumped forward.

Colin climbed the side of the coach, gritting his teeth against the pain. Blood oozed through the hair at the back of the coachman's head. Pressing his fingers to the older man's neck, Colin felt the beat of the artery. Alive.

Listening and watching for trouble, Colin weighed his options.

They needed to move, to get off the open road. But for that, he needed Fletcher conscious. At least he wouldn't have to explain to Cook how her man had been killed on a quiet English road after surviving a dozen campaigns against Boney.

Still unable to hear, Colin retrieved a water flask from under the coachman's seat. Tenderly cradling the older man's head, Colin washed the blood away. The wound was a long gash, slantways from the back of Fletcher's ear toward the back of his head. He pressed his fingers against the gash. Long but not deep and worst at the curve of Fletcher's head where the weapon bit hardest through the skin.

Fletcher moaned.

Colin lifted Fletcher's chin. "Pistol shot. Can't hear." Colin picked up the fallen reins and held them out. "Can you drive?"

Fletcher took the reins in one hand. Then, raising his eyes to Colin's, Fletcher held out his other hand, palm down, as one does when indicating a person's height.

"Bobby?" Colin looked around for the postilion. Fletcher's nephew had grown up on the ducal estate. The loss of Fletcher or Bobby would devastate the household.

Fletcher nodded yes, then scowled. Leaning forward, he braced his elbows on his knees and supported his head with his hands.

"I'll find him. Stay with Marietta." Colin took the rifle and the cartridge bag from beneath the coachman's seat, loaded the gun, then placed both on the bench. Fletcher put his hand on the gun.

Colin leapt from the coach, gritting his teeth against the pain as his feet hit the ground. Then, walking back along the road, Colin began looking for the boy, searching through the overgrown verges and dreading what he might find. A child's body bleeding and broken after a fall from the carriage. *Let him be alive . . . and, if wounded, with wounds that can heal.*

Colin turned at the curve.

About a tenth of a mile beyond, he saw the boy's body at the verge of the road. Colin ran to the boy and knelt beside him, checking his wounds. No gunshots. Colin felt his relief like cool water on a parched tongue. Bobby's arm was twisted before his chest, as if he had been flung from the coach-top or dragged down from it. But Bobby was alive. Fletcher, Bobby, Marietta, all alive. At least their deaths wouldn't weigh heavy on his conscience.

The boy struggled to lift himself up and began to speak. But Colin shook his head, pointing to his ears. "Can't hear."

Bobby pointed to his ankle. Colin felt it. No obvious broken bones. "Can you stand?"

The boy shrugged and held out his uninjured arm for help. Ignoring the arm, Colin lifted the boy to his feet. Luckily Bobby was still small and lithe, not the strapping youth he would be in another year. Colin supported Bobby's weight gently as the boy tested his ankle, gingerly at first, then with more pressure. When Bobby tried to step fully on the ankle, he recoiled in pain.

"Let me help." Colin wrapped his arm around Bobby's waist, avoiding his injured arm. The two walked slowly back to the carriage. There, Fletcher and Colin helped the boy to the seat next to Fletcher, and Bobby took up the pistols.

When Bobby was settled, Colin motioned for Fletcher's attention. "Where's the other one? The one the stable master insisted would care for the horses?"

Hit me, Fletcher mouthed, demonstrating a blow to the back of his head.

Colin's strength suddenly faded. "How far to the next inn?"

Fletcher held up two fingers, then three. Two to three miles.

Colin moved slowly to the open carriage door, calling out in case Marietta's ears had recovered from the pistol shots. "Marietta, there's an inn within the hour."

He stepped in front of the open door. Marietta was seated on the floor, leaning against the backward-facing seat riser, her legs bent at odd angles. Her eyes closed, she held one hand to her chest; the other cradled her belly. At her shoulder, blood seeped through her fingers, covering her hand and staining the front of her chemise. Blood pooled on the floor below her.

Colin's chest clenched. He swung himself into the carriage, yelling "Fletcher! Drive!" as he pulled the door shut behind him.

He pulled off his cravat and tore it into strips to make a bandage, then crawled beside her.

To stage an attack and steal nothing . . . not robbery.

Murder. He needed to think. But first he needed to slow Marietta's bleeding.

The carriage began to move, first slowly, then faster, and faster still.

Lady Arabella Lucia Fairbourne plunged her hands into the wash water, reaching for another dish. By pure luck, she'd found work as a scullery maid at an inn—and with it servant's lodgings. A place to hide.

Several times in the last fortnight, the innkeeper's wife, Nell, had offered her the easier work of waiting on guests in the dining hall, but each time she had refused. The dining hall was too public. Someone might recognize her.

She pulled her hands from the water and examined them, first on one side, then the next. Fingers puckered, cuticles split, palms roughened and red. Her hands looked like those of a woman who worked for a living. The hands of a scullery maid doing hard but honest labor. She smiled. She was exhausted, but free.

She preferred useful labor to idle luxury, even if that work was washing dishes rather than caring for the wounded in her father's regiment. Others would consider working in a tavern kitchen a reversal of fortune, but then, they had never lived in her cousin's house. She pressed her palm against the seam of her dress on the outside of her leg. She felt the comforting thickness where she had sewn in the papers her great-aunt Aurelia had entrusted to her. "Take this letter to my old love, Sir Cecil Grandison." Aurelia's frail hand had patted Lucy's gently. "He'll understand what to do."

A curl of jet-black hair tickled her cheek. Drying her fingers against the rough wool of her skirt, she tucked the curl back under the edge of her soft mob bonnet. At a secondhand clothier, she had traded her best walking dress for an ill-fitting servant's dress dyed a somber blue, and she'd bought the shopgirl's silence with a pair of embroidered slippers barely worn. Lucy the scullery maid looked nothing like the lady her cousin's men sought.

She dried the platter with a soft cloth. From the windows far above her head, a soft light suffused the kitchen. Evening. Her favorite time of day. Guests, servants, and family all fed, the kitchen cleaned for the night, and Alice, the cook, leaving her alone to finish the washing. Even so late in the day, the autumn sun would be out for another hour or two, allowing her some time in the inn's private garden. Separated from the public yard by a high wall on the courtyard side and thick hedges on all others, the garden made her feel almost as safe as she felt in the kitchen.

But feeling safe was different from being safe. The roads were still too full of her cousin's men to try another move. Only that afternoon, she'd seen the one called Ox ("Oaf" she thought would be more appropriate) looking around the stable yard while his horses were changed.

He hadn't seen her. She had been looking out of the window of the attic room she shared with Mary, the cook's helper.

Ox had seemed preoccupied, almost as if he wished not to be noticed, keeping to himself rather than joking with the other stablemen as he typically did. Had they given up on finding her? Certainly no one would expect her to be so close. After all this time, she had hoped that they would have moved the search to London by now. She watched, heart pounding, until he mounted a horse and rode away.

Garrulous Mary noticed all the men in the stable yard, and it was easy to learn anything she noticed. Ox hadn't spoken to any at the inn, save for calling for a new horse.

He hadn't even haggled over the price, Mary had added with surprise.

Lucy placed the last dish in the drying rack. She let the water drain from the sink as she wiped her hands on a rag. Perhaps she should stay another week.

From the hook beside the garden door, she lifted a long black knit shawl Nell had loaned her for her evening walks in the kitchen garden and wrapped it around her shoulders.

Behind her, she could hear raised voices and shouts coming from the dining hall. Footsteps ran toward the kitchen. Alarmed, she stepped outside, pulling the door quietly shut behind her. She put her ear to the door, hearing muttered curses, and the kitchen being searched. She pulled the shawl over her head and slipped to the side a few feet—into a darkened corner where the garden wall met the house. There a trellis covered with roses climbed the face of the wall, creating a small declivity where she could step out of sight. She had found it weeks ago when she'd examined the house and yard, looking for places to hide should she need them.

The door opened, the light from the kitchen creating a tall shadow on the ground. She remained very still.

"Lucy!" One of Nell's sons called into the garden from inside the house. "Lucy! Alice!"

She did not move or answer. She would not show herself until she knew why she was wanted and by whom.

"What are you doing, boy?" Alice's voice joined Ned's. "Lucy's done for the night. Leave her be."

"B-b-but there's a duke in the yard. His carriage was attacked by highwaymen," Ned stammered. "Ma said to find you and Lucy."

Not Ox or her cousin. She stepped out from beneath the roses and returned to the kitchen, as if responding to Ned's call. If there were wounded, she might be of use.

* * *

"Oh, my, oh my." The innkeeper paled when he opened the door of the carriage to see Colin sitting on its floor, cradling the body of a woman covered in blood and in labor. "My wife, Your Grace, we need my wife." Flustered, the innkeeper shut the door.

The door opened again immediately. This time, a round-faced woman with kind eyes who was clearly used to taking control when others hesitated silently assessed Marietta and Colin for a moment.

"I'm Mrs. Newford, Your Grace. Nell, you may call me. You needn't worry. We can care for you and your lady." Then she turned to issue instructions to her husband and the servants behind her.

And Mrs. Newford was right. Within minutes, she had helped Colin out of the coach, wrapped Marietta in a cloak to keep her arm from moving too much, and transferred the wounded princess carefully to a litter.

Colin had not interfered, admiring the skill with which Mrs. Newford marshaled her troops. Wellington would have done well to have had her as one of his adjutants.

The boys—Nell's sons—carried Marietta's litter not into the inn itself, but into an adjoining two-story lodge sharing the rear courtyard. Unlocking the main door, Mr. Newford revealed a hall with six doors. "Three rooms en suite on each side. Two bedrooms joined in the middle by a sitting room. And the same upstairs."

His round-faced wife hurried in ahead, opening the door of the first room on the right and motioning her sons to place the litter on the bed. A maid with black hair turned down the bed linens, then stepped out of the way.

Colin moved to raise Marietta off the litter, but Mrs. Newford shooed him to the end of the bed. "Leave it to Alice and me. We know what to do." The two women shifted Marietta's weight, lifting her slightly so that the boys could pull the litter free. Their efficiency made him grim: he had neither protected Marietta nor participated in helping her now.

"The bullet needs to be removed." He pointed at Marietta's shoulder, still weeping blood. "Do you have a surgeon and a midwife?"

"I am the midwife." Mrs. Newford patted his arm. "I have delivered all the babes within five miles for the last twenty years, excepting those at the manor house."

At that moment Marietta cried out in pain. Another contraction pulled her forward over her belly.

Mrs. Newford stroked Marietta's hand, cooing softly. "Nell is here, lass, Nell is here. This is a safe place. You be in a safe place." Marietta fell back, eyes closed, her chest rising weakly in shallow breaths.

"We should wait to remove the bullet until after the babe is born." Nell turned back to Colin. "Let me dress your lady's wound and attend her labors. My boys will draw you a bath. There's nothing for you to do here. 'Tis woman's work."

At Nell's capable management, Colin felt his strength drain away. The room began to sway, and he gripped the back of a nearby chair to keep his balance. "I have also been shot."

Nell looked up sharply. Her gaze moved from his face to his beige pants, which were mottled with blood, not all of it Marietta's. "Lucy, help His Grace into the drawing room and care for his wound while his bath is drawn. If need be, call the surgeon. Alice will help me with the lady."

The dark-haired maid came forward from the dark corner of the room behind him. He was used to servants seeming to be part of the walls, but something in her manner suggested she had been hiding, present if needed, but out of sight if she wasn't.

As she walked toward the adjoining room and her eyes

met his, he could see why she might hide. No one could ignore the depth of those dark eyes, the clearness of her skin, or the richness of her mouth, and all framed with curls of black hair slipping out of the confines of her bonnet. Suddenly, he imagined burying his fingers in that thick hair, kissing that beckoning mouth until she pressed her willing body against his.

He shook himself: after Octavia, he had avoided all women. Perhaps the blood loss had made him nostalgic.

Marietta cried out again, reminding him where he was and why. He felt his face return to a scowl. It wasn't like him to forget his duty at the sight of a pretty face. Oh, but what a face.

The dark-eyed maid pushed open the door to the drawing room and stepped through, holding the door open for him to follow. The evening light from the windows revealed a fireplace, a table and several chairs, and a connecting door open to another bedroom beyond. In silhouette, she was shapeless. A disappointment and a relief. The attraction was just an illusion of his weakness.

He moved to follow her, but stumbled at the edge of the rug.

She was at his side before he could fall, lifting his uninjured arm and placing it over her shoulders, then wrapping her own arm around his side for support. She was careful, he noted, not to touch the wound in his lower side, but slipped her hand under the tails of his coat and grabbed the waistband of his trousers to hold him upright and tight against her. She fit under his arm neatly, and he tensed at the feel of her body, so soft against his side. Despite her unappealing shape, she was still too appealing by half.

Aware of his weakened state, he allowed her to direct him. She moved him efficiently to a wooden armless chair next to the table. She arranged him so that his uninjured side was next to the table; then she brushed his coattails out of the way and helped him lower into the chair. She lifted his arm onto the table. "There, a little support if you need it."

Over the dark-headed maid's shoulder, he watched as Alice shut the adjoining door, muffling the sounds of Marietta's labor. Tightening the muscles in his jaw, he steeled himself against her cries. Marietta would have had the babe soon anyway. At least here she had a midwife, and an accomplished one at that. No, it wasn't the birth that made him anxious, but the gunshot. The gunshot was his fault.

He waited for the maid to notice the closed door, to realize that they were alone together. But, disappointingly, she seemed unaware of him in anything but that remote way that nurses are aware of their patients.

A tap at the hallway door drew her away. Despite her unappealing shape, her bearing was elegant, her spine straight, her carriage graceful. Perhaps a governess in disgrace.

At the door, one of Nell's sons held out a tray covered with linen. The maid set it on a low table to the right of the door, then turned back to the innkeeper's son, conversing in low tones. He could not hear the words, but she was motioning with slender hands. She wanted something large, with a handle, and something small, in a jar or bottle, kept up high. He watched her, mesmerized. When the blond boy left, she kept the door ajar. Ah, he thought with satisfaction, she *had* noticed being alone with him.

Bringing the tray to the table, the maid lifted the linen to reveal bread, a substantial portion of Stilton, and a small pot of honey. Beside it stood a decanter of dark liquid and a glass.

"Mark will return with bandages and salve. Since his mother and the cook are helping with your lady, he put together the tray himself. If you wish something more substantial, I can prepare it while you bathe."

No "sir" or "my lord." But he made no comment. Everyone else at the inn had made the mistake of calling him

"Your Grace." He hadn't corrected them, anticipating the error would spread to his advantage. What had made this maid realize the truth?

"Later. I'll eat later." His stomach turned at the thought of eating.

She covered the food and unstopped the decanter. She poured, filling the glass almost to the top.

"Drink this."

An imperative. Interesting. Suddenly, he wished to challenge her, to see her mettle.

"What if I refuse?" He accompanied the question with his most high-born glare. It was a gaze that never failed to succeed in getting him whatever he wanted from tenants or innkeepers and other servants. It only failed with his family—and of course he would never use such a look on a woman of his class. "And we are not equals, miss. I expect an appropriate courtesy from a maid—for myself and my . . . companion."

"Then, *sir*, if you choose not to drink, it will hurt a great deal more than necessary when I clean your wound. But it is, of course, *sir*, your choice." The sternness of her tone was belied by the hint of a smile that danced at the corners of her mouth.

It was a retreat, of sorts—but with no hint of surrender. This maid grew more interesting with each minute.

He took the glass from her hand and tasted it. Whiskey, and a good one. His bill would be exorbitant. But, for now, he didn't care. He held the whiskey in his mouth, feeling the warmth on his tongue and the back of this throat. He swallowed and felt the alcohol warm his throat and stomach, hoping it would dull both the sounds of Marietta's labor and his own pain.

* * *

Lucy could hear the muffled sounds of the woman's labor as she examined the man. He'd stood emotionlessly as Nell and Alice had cared for his lady. Now, leaning on the table, his eyes closed, his body still, he seemed undisturbed. Who was he? A relative? A husband or lover?

But if he were, why was he so still? If *she* were his, in labor and shot, she would want him to be torn with fear or trepidation. She would want him to pace, to look anxiously at the door, to wonder if she would live or die. Was he even aware of the danger his lady was in?

A rush of anger flushed her cheeks. James would have refused to leave her side. He would have glared at the midwife until they had let him remain, watching over her, even to the end. But, this man, this man . . . he was no better than Archibald or one of her cousin's reprobate friends. She stopped herself, surprised at the strength of her emotion. It was unlike her to harbor such uncharitable thoughts.

This man was a stranger. He had been shot, his lady shot, his babe endangered. One could never predict how a person would react to such events. Men who seemed brave, even foolhardy, froze in battle; men who had seemed fearful turned hero under fire. All that mattered was that he had been shot, and she was his nurse.

She examined him once more, seeing him with the eyes of compassion. His face was drawn, his eyes still shut. But lines of pain extended from the corners of his mouth. Remorse pulled at the edges of her heart. Had she been recently from the wars, she would have realized the damage to his tailcoat was from a gunshot—just as she had realized immediately that he did not have the bearing of a duke. But after living in her great-aunt's house in almost daily contact with her cousin Archibald, she had allowed her experiences with his circle to color her responses. She'd counted this man as just another shiftless younger son, too improvident to buy a new cloak once the old one was frayed. It was ungenerous of her.

The subtle clench of his jaw reminded her of her purpose.

She knelt at his side, examining the holes in his clothing, front, then back. "Below the ribs, on the very side of your body. In fact, if the bullet had veered just an inch or so farther out, you might not have been hit at all." She touched his back gently to smooth out the material, revealing another patch of torn material. "And, it's gone all the way through. Lucky."

"I feel far from lucky." His voice, though hard, was barely more than a whisper.

"Of course." She put her hand on his shoulder in commiseration. "But no bullet to dig out is a bit of luck—for both of us." The dark wool hid how much blood he had lost.

The double-breasted tailcoat fit snugly across his strong shoulders, then narrowed smoothly beneath the buttons into the flat planes of his stomach. A row of four outer buttons held the garment tight against the right side of his body, mirrored, she knew, by four inner buttons on his left side. All four outside buttons would have to be undone to reach the inner ones. Her fingers brushed the superfine. The material was fine, well woven. A shame it was ruined.

"First I'll need to get you out of these layers of clothes." Her patient agreed with a slight nod.

The hole for the top outside button was tight, and she had to slip two fingers under the material to hold it firm. She felt the lean firmness of his chest against the backs of her fingers. Her fingers fumbled. It had been a long time since she had undressed a man. But his quiet patience in the face of pain pulled at her heart.

Forcing herself to think only of the buttons, she released the second, then the third. Only one more. But a fold where his trousers met the jacket obscured the button. *Objectivity*, she reminded herself. *You are his nurse. It isn't proper to notice the fit of his trousers. Or to notice exactly where you are having to put your hand.* But she did all the same.

She glanced to see his eyes were still shut, then, breathing deeply, she reached for the fourth button.

His hand caught hers. "I can do it myself."

"You allow your valet to undress you." She looked up, her hand still in his. His eyes were open. The blueness of his eyes startled her, as did their heat.

"My valet is not a woman, and certainly not a beautiful one. If you were to undress me, I would want you to have seduction in mind."

She pulled her hand away and stepped back, looking to the door that separated them from the woman in labor. Lucy had spent sufficient time in birthing rooms to know something was not right. The mother was too quiet. But the man did not know. Perhaps a first child for him or the first birth near to him? To be kind, she should distract him from the other room, make him focus on his own wounds. But kindness always seemed to get her into trouble.

"It's not my child. I'm not such a libertine that I would find your beauty attractive if it were." While she had paused, watching the door, he had undone the inner buttons to his tailcoat.

"It's not my place to question, sir." But she felt relieved somehow.

He tried to pull his shoulders free from the tailcoat. But it was too carefully tailored to his form. A line of blood trickled down the front of his pants.

"Wait! You make it worse." She held the bottom edge of the tailcoat steady, then slipped her hand between it and the waistcoat at his shoulder, and edged down close to the wound. She stopped at the point where the layers of clothing stuck together. "The blood has dried to your shirt and waistcoat and glued them both to your tailcoat. If you pull one off, you tear the others from the wound, and bleed again."

"Perhaps I do need help." He grimaced, then smiled wanly and offered a slight shrug. The pain made him wince.

"Perhaps you do." She returned his smile automatically, but tried to ignore the sense of warmth it spread in her chest. "And don't shrug if it causes you pain," she remonstrated.

He gave a small laugh, then grimaced. "Or laugh."

"Yes, no laughter or shrugs. Now let me work." She pressed her hand against the tailcoat, holding it against his chest, as she inched the material of the waistcoat up from it. She tried to ignore the warmth of his skin, the feel of his muscles, below the material. Once the tailcoat lifted, she moved to his side, and repeated her action on the exit wound, separating the fabrics, keeping the waistcoat from lifting with the outer tailcoat. But her progress was slow.

"Your clothes are ruined, sir. It would be easier to reveal the wound if I cut the tailcoat off, then the waistcoat and shirt . . . with your permission of course."

"Yes, that would be best," he agreed. "Under the shirt you will also find part of my cravat. I tried to stop the bleeding."

"A wise decision. I need some scissors from the kitchen. I'll be back in a few minutes." She turned to leave him just as the woman cried out loudly.

"Wait. Don't leave." He grabbed her arm, and she turned back to see him swallow as Marietta screamed again. A look of such regret and sorrow passed his face that she wondered how she had thought him unfeeling before.

"Do you have scissors in your valise?" She covered his hand with hers.

"Yes." He released her arm, but slowly. Good, she thought, the alcohol was doing its work.

"Then I can use those . . . with your permission, of course."

He nodded agreement, and she brought his valise from the second bedroom and placed it, still latched, on the floor in front of him.

"Where will I find them?" She knelt before him behind the valise.

"There's a dressing box at the bottom. You'll need to unpack to reach it."

Chapter Three

Colin watched his nurse unlatch his valise, then carefully, even gently, remove items. His spare waistcoat and trousers were on top, then an extra shirt and cravat, then the dressing box. From among his toothpowder, hairbrush, and various ointments and salves, she withdrew the scissors. Her hands, reddened and broken at the nails, seemed out of keeping with her manner.

"You are the scullery maid?" he observed, somewhat surprised.

She paused, following his eyes to her hands. "Oh . . . yes, sir." Her pause intrigued him. She was not what she seemed, except luscious—such deep eyes, such rich curls. His body felt languid with blood loss and whiskey. He found his responses to her both unaccountable and irresistible.

"May I begin?" She stood before him, moving the valise out of the way.

"Yes." He gave himself into her care, noticing that she did not warn him that her ministrations might hurt.

Behind him, the scissors chewed the fabric of his tail-coat. She stopped. "These were meant for cutting hair, not cloth. They will work fine on your shirt, but for this coat, I need something better." She walked to the table that had held the decanter of whiskey, the bread, and cheese.

"Ah, this should do." She came back with a large kitchen knife, testing the sharpness of its edge with her finger. "I'll cut this way"—she demonstrated with the blade facing her—"though you might feel the back of the knife on your skin, I will not cut you. The blade will be facing me."

As a man used to lies and betrayal, he knew he should object. He should tell her to find better scissors, to ask for Fletcher or Bobby to attend him while she worked. But he didn't. Either he trusted her (and there was no reason for him to do so), or he wished to die. Perhaps both.

At his back, the material pulled against his shoulders as she cut from the top down. When the coat separated into two pieces, she set the knife on the table at his elbow. He released his breath, breath he hadn't realized he had been holding. She pulled the half on his uninjured side free. The tailcoat was damaged beyond all repair, but she still laid it carefully on the table.

She moved to his wounded side. She held his coat at the wrist, the cool skin of her fingers brushing the tender flesh on the inside of his wrist. She lifted the material slightly at his shoulder and pulled it down toward the floor, barely moving his arm. She placed the other half of his tailcoat neatly on top of the other.

Having removed the tailcoat, she stood back, examining him as if she could see through his clothes to his chest beneath. Her gaze felt warm on his chest, and he wanted her never to stop looking at him.

"Next, the waistcoat." Once more, the blunt edge of the knife pressed into his back, separated from his body only by the thinness of his shirt, until the garment released. Then leaning over him at the front, she began to undo the waistcoat's eight buttons. He breathed in her scent, soap and lemons, and let it soothe him.

On the last button, her hand brushed the trousers covering his loins, and he stiffened in response. But she seemed unaware of her effect on him, and he was oddly grateful. If she had realized his arousal, she would have stopped and called for the innkeeper's sons or one of the other servants.

With the waistcoat cut apart in the back and unbuttoned in the front, she slipped her hand down his body once more, and he reveled in the slight press of her hand against his shirt. As one hand held the bottom layer against his chest, the other gently lifted the top layer off. He focused on the movements of her hand, more like a lover's caresses than a nurse's ministrations.

Then only the shirt was left, a thin fabric between his chest and her hands. He shuddered with desire.

"If you are cold, sir, I can leave the shirt over your shoulders, and work only on the wound."

The fabric was stained crimson where the bullet had entered, and his stomach turned, temptation fading as he remembered Marietta's face pale with pain. "No, take it off."

Using the scissors, she cut around the blood-soaked fabric, leaving circles of superfine glued to his skin. To remove the rest of the shirt, she split the side seams and those in the sleeves, allowing her to lift the shirt off his shoulders.

Colin found her efficiency and knowledge intriguing. Where had she come from, this scullery maid with cracked and reddened nails? And why, with her intelligence, had she not found more lucrative employment? She was nothing like a maid. Too confident, not aware enough of her place. It was a puzzle. He liked puzzles.

Another cry of anguish from the other room pierced his heart.

The maid placed her hand on the bare skin of his

shoulder, offering comfort. "I'm sure your . . . the lady will be fine." He felt each finger as a warm coal.

The last time a woman had touched his bare flesh had been in Brussels, and he felt again the suffocating guilt that had plagued him for months. "Her name is Marietta. I should have expected trouble." He spoke without thinking. "I should have anticipated . . ."

"No, you should not have." She stopped his objection with a hand to his chest slightly above his heart. Whether she had intended it or not, it was an intimate gesture. "The last highwayman on this road was hung at the crossroads five years ago. And you couldn't find a better midwife than Nell—I predict we'll be hearing the hearty cries of a newborn child within hours."

He took her hand, turned it upward, and kissed her palm, returning her intimacy with a lover's kiss, soft and seductive. "You are very kind, my lady."

Their eyes met. A moment passed, then two. He watched her eyes widen, heard her slight intake of breath, but she left her hand in his. No ring. Perhaps when all this was over, when Marietta and her babe were safe, he would return to this pretty dark-haired maid. If she were interested in leaving the kitchen for his bed, he could keep her well as his mistress. For the first time in months, the idea of a future held some interest. He did not question why—or whether in the morning, without the warmth of the whiskey in his blood, he might feel differently. He merely allowed himself to enjoy the possibility. Anything to keep his mind from the pain in his side and the trauma in the next room.

A tap at the door turned her into his nurse once more. At the door, Mark held a basket, and she looked through it quickly, selecting several small jars and some cloths. She named each jar as she set it on the table.

"Lavender water to clean your wound. Calendula ointment to heal it. Laudanum to ease the pain." She poured another glass of whiskey and added twenty drops of laudanum. "Drink some more. I must work on the wound."

She extended the glass, and he wrapped his fingers around hers, wanting to touch only her. She slipped her fingers out from under his.

While he drank the whiskey, she turned her attention to the circles of material glued by blood. From the second adjoining bedroom she retrieved a pitcher of water and the washing bowl left for guests. Pouring the water into the bowl, she wet a cloth and pressed it to the circle of fabric, soaking it inch by inch. Patiently, she repeated the action over and over. Soon, the water in the washing bowl was red with his blood. When the material at his front released, she repeated her actions on the back wound, until the fabric released there as well.

"Are we done?"

"It depends. Sometimes the bullet will carry bits of thread into a wound, and, if left there, they can fester." She wiped her hands on her apron. "But inspecting the wound will hurt. I could call the surgeon." She hesitated, looking toward the door to the hallway

"But you don't trust him." Colin predicted.

"No. He's inexperienced and . . ." She began clearing the table, folding the remains of his clothes into a neat pile.

"And you are more experienced?" He watched her face for confirmation.

She looked away. He had discovered a truth about her, and one she was unwilling to share.

"So, tell me, scullery maid: how do you know of wounds? It's only fair if I'm to let you operate on me rather than call the surgeon."

She looked relieved. The surgeon must be particularly bad.

"My father was in the army. I grew up in the camps." She moved the water basin to the table near the door, keeping the pitcher of clean water on the table beside him. "Until my mother's death, I helped her with the wounded."

"Wasn't that dangerous for a girl?"

"My father's men watched out for me, and most of the time I dressed as a boy." She created a clear space on the table, then moved her healing salves to the front. "It wasn't a bad life . . . between engagements, that is."

"During engagements was different."

Her face shifted at the memory, grew sad and distant; then she shrugged, pushing off whatever hell she'd remembered. "One wouldn't expect it to be good."

"Where were you?"

"Everywhere. My father was in the First Royal Dragoons. We were at Frexadas and Santarem and Badajoz and Pamplona and a dozen places in between."

"So my chances of survival are at least as good as those of the men in your hospital."

"Better." Her voice lightened and grew animated. "Here, I have fresh water and salves and a bed for you to sleep in that isn't just a folded blanket on muddy ground."

She stopped abruptly, realizing that she had given away too much. He could see it on her face. But suddenly he didn't care about her boxy figure or her broken cuticles. She must have appeared an angel to the men she'd cared for.

"Do your worst." He turned his palms up as if in surrender.

She reached for the whiskey. "Then drink, sir." This time the *sir* sounded more like a term of endearment. "I put enough laudanum into the whiskey to help with the pain, but not enough to make you sleep . . . not yet, at least. I might need you awake."

He took a deep gulp.

She poured the remaining alcohol over her hand. Her fingers felt the bullet hole gently. When she pressed the wound apart with her fingers, the stab of pain prompted a sharp intake of breath. But he nodded for her to continue.

"You have tweezers in your kit as well?"

He nodded and watched as she lifted them out of the case. On his back, he felt a splash of alcohol and a sting, then something against the inside of the wound. He suddenly felt inexpressibly tired.

"I can see several pieces of thread, but I think I can get the whole string from here." Her fingers probed the wound again, but this time the pain seemed more distant. More alcohol. Less sting. He drank another gulp.

She returned to the wound at his front. She folded a towel and placed it in his lap immediately under the bullet hole. Then she poured more alcohol over the wound. The whiskey ran down his belly and soaked into the cloth.

"That's a waste of good whiskey."

"Not if it saves your life. Stomach wounds, even one with as little damage as this one, can kill quickly."

"Is that meant to be encouraging?

"Actually, yes." She picked up a small decanter and poured its liquid into the wound on his front. "Now that I can see it, it couldn't be a better wound. Bullet missed your ribs and your organs. You must lead a charmed life."

He'd heard that before. It hadn't made him feel any better then. "What is that?"

"This is the lavender water. It cools wounds and helps avoid the heat of fever." She repeated her action at his back.

The water felt cold on his skin, and he shivered.

A tap at the door drew her away. Leaving the door open, she stepped into the second bedroom and returned with a blanket, wrapping it around his shoulders. She was observant, this nurse of his.

"There. That should be good." She returned the tweezers to his dressing box. "The boys are bringing in your bath. After you bathe, I will dress your wounds with the calendula salve."

"Are you going to aid me in the bath as well?

She looked up, startled, before she noticed the mischievous smile on his lips. "I'm sure Mark and Edward will be adequate help if you find yourself . . . incapable."

Lord, he liked this woman, unwilling to be cowed, even when embarrassed. "Does this make us friends?" he teased.

"Why, sir?" Her inflection on sir was distant, even suspicious, as if their camaraderie and attraction had slipped out the open door. Then he remembered that her beauty had likely made her a target of unscrupulous visitors to the inn.

"The midwife called you Lucy. I would like to call you Lucy as well . . . a former officer to an officer's daughter who cared for him when wounded." He'd never thought to ask a servant for permission to use her given name. But somehow it seemed appropriate.

The suspicion in her eyes faded. "As an officer to an officer's daughter . . . certainly, sir, you may call me Lucy."

"Then, Lucy, you must call me Colin."

The boys entered the room carrying a large bath basin, then pitchers of heated water to fill it. One stoked the fire, grown low in the fireplace, with new wood.

"Mark and Edward will help you with your other clothes."

He was no longer alone with her, and he felt strangely bereft. Somehow the weight of the last months seemed lighter with her beside him, so he gave her his most innocent smile. "If you can help me out of my boots and stockings, I can manage the rest."

Her brief hesitation pleased him, for it meant that she was tempted, and tempted meant she felt the desire between them. If he were a gentlemen, he would have let her go, and then asked the boys to help him with his boots and stockings and pants. But he did not want to be a gentleman. He wanted her with him. An officer's daughter would understand the sacrifices he had made—still made—and his regrets.

She shook her head, clearly amused, and indulging him. "Certainly, sir, I can help you with your boots."

Even his valet cursed the snug fit of Colin's boots, but Lucy removed them skillfully. Whose boots had she removed often enough to be so proficient?

At his stockings, she took a deep breath as if drawing in courage, then untied the knee bands on his leggings. His legs were well muscled, so he wore no pads to give his legs more definition. But to remove his stockings, Lucy had to push the pant legs up, then draw the stockings down. There was no way to do it without her hands tracing the line of his muscles.

He felt her touch as a drug. But he closed his eyes, telling himself it was the effect of the laudanum. Never before while on a mission had he found himself so distracted by a lovely face. He had been right to tell Walgrave he was finished. Too much could go wrong, had gone wrong, when one lost focus. And he couldn't seem to focus when the dark-haired maid was near him: it was a warning—he was sure—that he should no longer be in the field.

When his legs were bare, he opened his eyes to find her examining him. Were her eyes dark with arousal or some other emotion? Was that look of deep consideration a function of desire or just the concern of a nurse for her patient? He couldn't tell. His mind felt fuzzy.

"If I asked you to share my bath, would you agree? You are very beautiful, Lucy." He felt the syllables of her name in his mouth like silk—soft sounds, warm sounds.

"Does this strategy usually work?"

"What?" He feigned innocence.

"Taking a bullet to seduce the scullery maid."

"I haven't tried it before. Is it successful? I could make it worth your while." He stumbled over the words. But even through the dizzy haze of his mind, he knew those were the wrong words.

Her back stiffened, and she drew back.

He stammered an apology, but she reached out her hand toward him. He held his breath, waiting for her touch on his arm or chest, but instead, she touched his forehead.

"We need to get you into the bath."

She walked away, and he realized she was swimming before his eyes. Exhaustion, he assumed. He'd had less laudanum before this, so he must be exhausted. So tired, so cold.

She returned from the hall with both of the young men. He could hear her telling them what to do—light a fire, warm his bed. He did not correct her or insist on telling the boys himself. It felt good to let someone else make the decisions. His ministering angel would take care of him. He allowed himself to drift, to let consciousness go.

Damn, and double damn. Fever. And a blazing one. She was sure she'd cleaned the wounds well, but cloth could be trapped deeper in the wound than she could reach. And it had been at least an hour before the wound was cleaned. Likely, the fever was the result of being wounded and the aftermath of the attack on the road.

She tapped on the door to the bedroom where Nell and Alice cared for the laboring woman. Marietta, he'd called her. He had not offered his surname or the woman's, but Lucy believed him when he said that the child wasn't his.

Alice opened to the door and stepped into the hall.

"Should I call for the village women?" Lucy offered.

Alice frowned and shook her head. "No. We won't be needing the help."

"I helped at other births; this one seems wrong."

"Nell sent for the doctor, but he is tending to the manor born, and unless he hurries, he will not arrive in time. The lass won't last the night, but we're hoping she can have a look at the babe."

"Is it likely?"

"Och, sometimes she's light-headed and a bit mad; others she's frantic. In between she drifts, here and other places. But her heart is fading."

"What of the child?"

"Josiah has gone to the village to fetch Jennie Osborne to wet nurse. Her own babe was stillborn, and her man's long gone. Then, when His Grace travels on, Nell will ask him to take Jennie along." Alice listened for a moment at the door. "What of him?"

"I cleaned the wound, but he's already feverish and a bit delirious. The boys are helping him with his bath, then I will bind the wounds."

"Stay by his side. He's highborn, and we don't want no trouble that we left him alone when he was all sick-like. Should I send the doctor, if he comes?"

"No, the doctor will want to bleed him, and he's lost plenty of blood already. If we can, we should let the fever run its course."

"That's what Nell would do." Alice nodded approvingly. "You know where she keeps her herbs."

"I already have them."

"Good."

Marietta moaned, and Alice turned back to the door. "Let us know if he worsens."

Once the boys had Colin undressed and in the bath, she returned to the room. His back was to her in the bathtub, so she stood inside the doorway. The boys had bathed barely conscious men before, and they moved efficiently. The smell of soap reassured her, as if it might clear away the poisons already causing his fever.

When she'd returned to England after her father's death and moved into her great-aunt's house, she'd hoped she would never have to care for another bullet wound again. Colin was handsome in that way that all the young officers had been handsome, and in many ways they hadn't been. She could easily imagine him at a ball dressed in uniform, a jacket of vibrant madder red with gold-braided epaulets at his shoulders and polished leather Wellington boots. The white of his cravat crisp, the folds sharp. She could imagine dancing with him to a rousing country dance or to the more scandalous steps of a Bavarian waltz. She could not—did not—wish to imagine him as he would have appeared during the campaigns: his jacket faded to a ruddy brown, his epaulets tarnished, his boots scuffed, his white cravat turned grey or red, his face gaunt with the weariness of a siege or a long march.

His offer to share his bath had been unexpectedly tempting. She was no maid. Everyone in the camp had known that she and James were to marry, and she never understood why they hadn't. He kept saying he didn't wish to leave her a widow, that if he died it would be easier for her to find a husband if she had not married. But each day she had seen the young men of England dying, and she wondered just how many would be left if she ever returned.

Perhaps James, like her father, had had some presentiment of his death. She had agreed to marry in part to relieve her father's mind and in part because James had been her friend for years. When she'd returned home, alone, with neither fiancé nor father, she'd told her great-aunt Aurelia she wished never to marry; and Aurelia, whose own love had died in the Seven Years' War, had patted her hand and told her she would never have to. And then Aurelia had died as well.

The boys were ready to lift Colin from the bath and carry him into the adjoining bedroom. She stepped into the hall to keep from shocking them. No one who hadn't been in the wars understood what she knew: that bodies lost their secrets when wounded or dead or maimed beyond recognition. Artillery was a cruel killer, blasting off a man's arm and leaving him to bleed to death. Somehow, tending Colin's wound had made the images come back fresh, just when she had started to believe they had faded for good. The memories isolated her, reminding her again how different she was from all the women of her class, and even from many of the men.

When they were finished, the boys opened the door to the bedroom, signaling she could wrap the wounds. Now the drawing room lay between her patient and Marietta's labors. Perhaps it would be enough distance to muffle her cries. If the alcohol and laudanum were doing their work, he would have forgotten about Marietta's labor. She did not wish for him to remember. She did not want to see that sorrowful look cross his face again. There would be time enough for sorrow tomorrow, of that she was certain.

When she entered the room, he was already in bed, his face slightly flushed, she hoped only from the pain of moving from the bath to the bed.

"Ah, my Panacea has returned, my goddess of healing." Lines of pain creased at his eyes and mouth.

She crossed the room to feel his forehead. Hot. "You're feverish. And Panacea is the goddess of cures, medicines. You need Aceso, the goddess of recuperation."

"Aphrodite's sister?"

"Yes," she said, arranging the lavender water, the calendula poultice, and his scissors where she could reach them easily.

"Then you are also my goddess of love!" He held out his hand as an orator does when making a speech.

She shook her head, laughing. "Mark, get the whiskey for me and the basket with the bandages. I left them in the drawing room." Then, turning back to Colin, she asked, "When I get to your back, can you sit up for me? Or will you need the boys to help you?"

"Let me decide when you get there." He closed his eyes.

Mark returned with the basket. "Do you want me to pour?"

"Yes, please. Half-full." She removed the bottle of laudanum from her pocket, and she counted out another twenty drops. "Drink again for me, my lord."

"Colin." He did not open his eyes. "I will not drink unless you call me Colin."

She turned to Mark, lifting both palms up in question, mouthing, *Fever*. He responded with a shrug that said, *Whatever the highborn want, however foolish.*

"Then, *Colin*." She emphasized his name as she had emphasized sir. "You must drink this. The laudanum will keep your wound from hurting as I bandage it, and afterward it will help you sleep." He took the glass from her hand, but didn't drink.

"Do not want to sleep." He was growing restive. "Need to keep watch."

"What if I keep watch for you? I'll stay right here while you sleep." She placed the back of her hand on his forehead, testing his temperature again. "I promise: I will not leave until you wake up."

He caught her hand and kissed it. She looked around, concerned that the boys had seen his familiarity. But they were gone. Relieved, she let him keep her hand in the warmth of his. Such a little human contact seemed to comfort him.

"If you stay, I'll sleep." He opened his eyes, so blue, so tempting.

"If you act like a gentleman, I'll stay," she chided.

"I'm always a gentleman," he promised, but his dimpled half smile undercut his words.

"Then be quiet, and let me dress your wound."

He stopped arguing, but didn't sleep. Instead, he watched her. She couldn't tell if he was alert or just staring. When she finished filling one part of the wound with salve, he held the bandage to it, while she treated the other part. Then, when she needed to bind the poultice against his skin, he sat up to allow her to wrap the bandage around his waist.

When she finished, he fell back, exhausted from the effort.

"You really do look like an angel," he insisted.

"Then you haven't been to church lately," she countered. "Angels are either imposing men with swords or infant putti with wings."

"No"—he clasped her hand again—"they are dark-eyed, dark-haired beauties named Lucia. Saint of Lights. Saint of the blind because of her beautiful eyes . . . and yours are beautiful, such color. I can imagine you with a nimbus of stars."

She started at her real name, but he didn't appear to notice, only kept talking. He was drunk on spirits, laudanum, exhaustion, and fever. She realized she was still sitting on the edge of the bed, facing him, his hand clasping hers. "Colin," she spoke gently. "Let me get a chair to sit by you. There's one by the wall."

"Only if you kiss me, Lucia, my star."

She knew she could wait: he would be asleep in minutes. If someone found her sitting on his bed, it would create trouble, and, as Lady Fairbourne, she didn't wish to force this man into marriage. Besides, she didn't even know if he were free to marry. Marietta's child might not be his. But that didn't mean he didn't have obligations to another woman. She turned his hand to see if he wore a ring.

"No wife, no mistress, no fiancée." He was clearly more alert than he appeared, or he was slipping in and out of consciousness. "So you have no fear. Kiss me."

One quick look over her shoulder to the hall door told her it was shut. The door to the adjoining drawing room was ajar, but pulled to the jamb. She would hear if anyone approached.

And she wanted to kiss him. For all the wrong reasons, and none of the wise ones. He was handsome and funny, and the only man she'd ever kissed was James. As soon as she reached London, she would start the new life she and her great-aunt had planned. She would dispense her great-aunt's funds with discretion and good sense, holding herself apart as her great-aunt Aurelia had done. And who would she kiss then? The fat country squire with more land than teeth? Or the thin parson with patches on his elbows? Before she began that life, she wanted one last kiss. Colin wouldn't remember, and if he did, she could simply hide in the kitchen until he was gone or until she disappeared herself.

She leaned forward and pressed her lips softly against his, in the kind of kiss that she always shared with James—gentle, sweet. For a few moments he met her softly, tenderly on that ground.

But when she thought the kiss was over and began to pull away, he shifted the ground underneath her. His mouth opened against hers, pressing, still sweet but teasing her lips to open to him. He bit playfully the edge of her lip, then when she relented, he teased the roof of her mouth with his tongue.

Then he shifted the kiss again, from sweet and playful to something more, something tinged with such desire that she had not imagined she could feel for a man she had known less than a few hours. Still she wanted more, more of whatever passion this kiss evoked. She had thought herself experienced, but with one kiss Colin showed her a glimpse of a world beyond what she knew.

He raised one hand and pulled off her bonnet, allowing her curls to fall freely around her face, and he caressed her hair, twisting it between his fingers, and pulling her head closer to his lips. She knew she should stop the kiss. He was influenced by the effects of fever and laudanum. Without it, she told herself, he would not be so bold.

She touched his chest to push herself away from him, and he wrapped his hand around her hand, holding it to his chest firmly. But when she pushed once more, he released her with a groan.

"Ah, what sweet kisses! You truly are my angel, Lucia."

"You, sir, are quite drugged."

She slipped off the bed and moved to the chair. She felt his forehead, still hot. She would wait a while. If his fever rose higher, she would wash his face with cold water to bring it down.

For now, she would watch. His eyes were closed, but as she took her hand away from his forehead, he opened his eyes and caught her hand once more.

"No, it's you, Lucy."

His hand, with hers still clasped in it, fell to his side. And he slept.

He was caught in dreams, and they were the stuff of madness. Blood and the flash of cannons and men dying around him, as he slashed with his sword the monsters that came at him from the dark. He was back in the room in Brussels, waiting for the woman who had been his lover. He knew now that she had betrayed them all; the information she'd sold had sent hundreds of men to their deaths. She believed she could seduce him once more. Her gown was red, and he thought of Mary Queen of Scots at her execution.

She kissed him. "Not a Judas-kiss, *ma chère*, I'm here to save you." And his body responded to her kisses. He tilted her head back, kissed her once more as he had the last time they had met. She lay a set of papers before him, "These, *ma chère*, will ruin your family, especially your brother. His woman is a traitor. *N'est-ce pas?*" It was a different sort of game from before. In the dream, she walked to him confidently, her body visible under the red chemise, brushed his chest with her hands, kissed his neck, pushed him back onto the bed, and he wanted her, despite everything she had done. He still loved her. He kissed her again, passionately, let her feel his arousal, aroused her, brought her to pleasure. Then, as she lay sated in his arms, sleeping, he lifted the pillow.

The scene shifted. He wandered the hell that was Waterloo, demons following him on every side. The battle was over, but the dead looked at him with accusing eyes. He couldn't escape the dreams, but he could feel the hands of his angel, cool on his body, and hear her voice singing him the way back, songs from his childhood, lullabies he hadn't heard since his own infancy. Then the dreams started to make a place for her. She was with his men, when he ordered his men to retreat, and when he searched for Benjamin, she held his hand.

The fever wasn't abating, and he was too, too hot. She bathed his face and chest with cool water, infused with lavender to help him sleep and thistle for the fever.

Sometimes he was clearly in his childhood, playing with other boys she assumed were his brothers, but most often he was back in the war, calling his men back from some engagement. "Retreat, retreat," the words repeated on his lips. At one point, he wept over the loss of his men and, at another, called out for someone named Benjamin.

She understood such dreams. And she sat beside him, washing his face, wishing the water could wash away the dreams as well.

In the camps she'd never had the luxury to wait with one man. She'd always had to leave them to their dreams and

demons, but with Colin, she could remain. And he seemed
to know she was with him. She could do for him what she
had never been able to do for the others: hold his hand,
whisper reassuring psalms, sing songs from her childhood.
If he died, he would not die alone. But she willed him to
live, imagined she could pour her own life into him through
the palms of her hands as she held his hand or washed his
chest.

He was a beautiful man, all lean muscle, but with scars
as one would expect from a soldier. She tried to imagine
how he had suffered each one. The diagonal line across his
chest was easy, the point of a sword coming too close. He
had been lucky; it wasn't a deep cut. And it had healed well.
The stab wound at his shoulder had been more severe, and
she wondered if it pained him even now.

She knew time passed because it was light, then it was
dark, then it was light again. Mark or Andrew would bring
fresh, cool water, and she would bathe Colin until the water
was no longer cool; then she would ring the bell, and they
would bring her another bowl.

They brought her a tray with bread and cheese and soup,
and on the second day, though he was still feverish, he was
less delirious, and she was able to feed him, spoonful by
spoonful, some of Alice's hearty soup.

She changed his dressings, pleased that his wounds
weren't red or oozing. She pressed her hand to them; they
were only a little warm. She hoped it meant he was improving, but she continued bathing him with the lavender and
thistle water, and rubbing Nell's healing salve into the wound.

But he was still lost in his dreams, mumbling and crying
out, sometimes in pain. And she would sing to him again.

In the mid-morning of the second day, a tap drew Lucy's

attention to the door to the adjoining dressing room. When Lucy opened it, she found Nell, looking weary and worn.

She bent her head toward Lucy's and spoke softly in her ear. "The mother died."

"Alice feared she would." Lucy rested her hand comfortingly on Nell's upper arm.

Nell put her own hand over Lucy's for a moment. "It was the illness," Nell said, using the midwife's term for labor. "It brought on apoplexy, then her heart failed. She would 'ave died, shot or not." Nell straightened and paused, looking past Lucy at her patient. "If he lives, he might want to know that."

If he lives. The words clutched at Lucy's chest. "I will make sure he knows. His fever has not broken yet."

Nell crossed to the bed and touched Colin's forehead with the back of her hand. Then she looked at the collection of materials Lucy had gathered. A bottle of laudanum sat on the table next to Nell's basket filled with jars of various remedies. Seeing Lucy's manuscript book, she opened it, finding pages of recipes for salves, poultices, and other antidotes.

"These are good ones," she offered approvingly, her finger tracing the various ingredients. "Though I'm not sure you could get some of the ingredients for these two anywhere near here."

"The book was my mother's, and I have added remedies since her death." Lucy watched Nell turn the pages, stop and read, then move on to another page. "I helped with the wounded in the wars."

"I thought you were a lady running away from her family."

Lucy looked up, startled, and saw Nell waiting for her reaction.

"Ah, yes, I thought so, love." Nell closed Lucy's book, but held it. "But never you worry. I will keep your secret.

Anyone so happy to wash dishes has no need to return to what place she come from."

"How did you know?" Stunned, Lucy sat back down in the chair beside Colin's bed.

"First off, you don't talk like a serving gel. You try, but you miss. And my boys have told me about your nursing, and this"—she pointed to the recipe book—"shows you know the herbs almost as well as any midwife." Nell paused, placing her hand on Lucy's shoulder. "And then there were the men in the yard yesterday."

"Men?" She forced herself to stay seated. She had not seen them; she had not even thought to be watchful. She had been too caught up in saving Colin.

"Disreputable lot. I mistrusted the look of 'em," Nell continued. "Shifty."

"What did they want?" Lucy tried to keep any hint of panic from her voice.

"To know if we had seen a flighty young miss, running away from the man her guardian chose for her to marry. Said she was a bit empty-headed and could not be trusted out on her own."

"What did you tell them?" Lucy's breath caught in her chest.

"Well, I dinna lie. I said I had not seen such a miss." Nell patted Lucy's shoulder. "You will be safe here as long as you wish."

"I need to get farther away. My cousin, he would destroy your trade if he thought you had helped me knowingly, perhaps even unknowingly. But I dare not take the coach."

"No matter, Lucy. We could find a hay wain if you would like. Or mayhap the gentleman can carry you away when he has recovered." Nell handed her the recipe book and walked past her to the door. "I have greater faith now that he will."

"Nell," Lucy called out. 'The story the men told you. It is not true."

"They never are."

In the evening of the third day, she fell asleep in her chair. When she awoke, something in the room had changed. He was quiet. She felt his head, cool to the touch.

She almost wept, but she was too tired to move. He would live.

She placed one hand on his chest, and he covered it with his own.

"Have you been here the entire time?" His eyes were still closed.

"I didn't wish to leave you." She brushed the tips of her fingers down the side of his face and down his jaw.

"I had dreams." A look of pain and sorrow crossed his face.

"I know," she consoled, brushing the hair at the side of his face with her fingers. "But they were just dreams."

"Not all, not all." His eyes opened, still that depthless blue, and met hers, catching her breath. "Were you singing to me?"

"It seemed to soothe you," she confessed, suddenly shy.

"Don't leave." He moved his hand to his side, taking hers with him.

He was asleep again. He fell in and out of consciousness, but it was a healthy drifting, not the fevered one from before. She began to think she might retire to her room to bathe and sleep, but she didn't want him to be alone. She drifted into sleep as well, still holding his hand.

Chapter Four

Colin was dreaming, a sweet dream from his infancy. Judith, his elder sister, carried him on her hip through the hay meadow on their father's lands. The day was bright, and the path to the pond well beaten down. In the near distance, he could see the pond and the ducks. Once more, he felt his childhood joy at the birds, black and blue and brown. Clutched in one hand, he held the stale end of a loaf of bread to feed them.

With his other hand, he played with the golden tresses that fell heavy along Judith's back. He'd wrapped the soft hair between his fingers, twisting and turning it, tracing its length with his thumb over and over. Then it all began to fade: the ducks, the pond, Judith. He tried to will himself back to sleep. But the dream was lost.

In the stable yard below, the yells of the groomsmen announced the approach of a coach. And he was awake. Nothing left of the dream but the soothing sensation of hair curled against his fingers. Strange. He flexed his fingers. More silken curls.

He opened one eye, then the other. Lucy had fallen asleep while watching over him, still sitting in the chair, but leaning forward to rest her head on her folded arms at the edge of his bed. Her hair—a rich black—curled in waves around her face, escaped from her mob bonnet. His fingers were entwined in one of her wayward curls. He withdrew them unwillingly. It was unusual for him to find such comfort with a woman. Passion, yes. Amusement, certainly. But comfort, no. She was a rare one, this scullery maid—kind, witty, honest. She reminded him of the man he had been once—before war and death and duty had made him wary.

He smiled at the memory of their playful banter, then just as quickly groaned. In the light of day—even with a headache as large as Scotland—he knew he had behaved poorly. A servant clearly hiding in the shadows, and he'd insisted on a kiss. Demanded one, in fact, before he would allow his wound to be dressed. What choice could she have but to comply? And then, when she'd offered a chaste kiss, he'd turned it into something heady and seductive and . . . marvelous.

What had he been thinking? Not of duty or of mission. Certainly not of danger.

The reason, he acknowledged, was simple: loss of blood, laudanum, too much of a fine whiskey, and a woman who slipped past his defenses.

He would have to set it right. *Officer to officer's daughter.* He cringed at the memory of his words. Without them, he could pass everything off as a drunken flirtation, leave her a hefty bit of coin, an affectionate buss on the cheek, and a teasing promise to travel this way again.

But those words had changed the field, forged a bond between them, the same sort of obligation he'd felt when dying men had pressed letters into his hand or whispered messages for their loved ones. He couldn't leave her hiding in the kitchen, vulnerable to rape or misuse. But he couldn't take her with them, not with his obligation to the Crown. And he couldn't promise her he'd return afterward. Who knew the lengths Marietta's enemies would pursue or whether he would survive their next attempt?

The pounding in his head worsened with each twist of reasoning. He couldn't think it through: how to reconcile his old obligations and this new one. How did an officer of honor and principle retract the inherent promise? He didn't, couldn't, wouldn't. And that was the rub. To acknowledge his words required him to honor them.

He could think of only one solution, and it was the coward's path. He could pretend to remember nothing, not their easy conversation nor the arc of attraction between them. Deceit and distance. He knew them well already, but he wished there were another way. He covered his eyes with one hand and groaned again.

"Are you hurting?" Her voice, sultry from sleep, was filled with concern. A cool hand touched his forehead, then withdrew.

"Fletcher." His voice sounded gruff, even to his own ears, and he left his hand over his face, not wanting to see the surprise in her wide dark eyes. "I must speak with Fletcher."

"He's been waiting for you to wake." Her voice was gentle, filled with understanding. "I'll send him to you. If you need anything, there's a bell on the bedside table. Alice should be preparing dinner soon, and I'll bring you a tray when it's ready."

He heard her skirts brush softly against the floor, and he wanted to call her back, even as he let her go. The door opened, and he heard Fletcher's heavy footfalls. He lowered his hand to see Fletcher standing at the foot of his bed.

"Ah, my boy. I feared we had lost you this time. If it weren't for Miss Lucy, you'd be dead and buried." Fletcher nodded his head back toward the closed door. "She simply refused to let you die. Nell says the girl's got the gift of healing in her hands."

"How long?" Colin attempted to push himself up, but a stab of pain stopped him. Fletcher moved to his side, bracing Colin's back and arranging the pillows behind him.

"Five days, if you count today. It's well past noon. And Miss Lucy never left your side. If I were twenty years younger . . ." Fletcher offered with open admiration.

"Should I tell your *wife* you have a tendre for a *scullery maid*?" Colin colored his words with highborn disdain.

Fletcher searched Colin's face intently, then shrugged. "Your brother should be here at any time. I sent for him the morning after we arrived. Two riders, one to the estate, the other to London."

Colin grimaced. "He won't have received either message. My brother's visiting Lady Wilmot at her country house."

"I'll send a rider to Lady Wilmot's straightway." Fletcher set his hand on the door latch. "It's good you'll be alive to meet His Grace. For days, I've searched for just the right words to tell him you were dead. And I didn't like none of 'em."

"What of the others?" Colin called him back. "Marietta? The babe? Bobby?"

"Bobby's shoulder was out of joint, but it's mending nicely." At the table, Fletcher picked up the whiskey and a deep glass. "The babe is a boy. Lungs as big as a moose's and twice as loud. I'm surprised you haven't heard him in your dreams. As for her ladyship . . ."

Colin's stomach clenched as Fletcher poured three fingers of whiskey and held it out. Lifting it to his lips, Colin took a long gulp. "Go on."

Fletcher rubbed a spot on the floor with his shoe. "We buried her yesterday in the churchyard."

Colin leaned back, empty of all emotion. He knew what losing lives in a mission felt like. By the time his older brother Aidan had been called home, Colin was an able leader already commanding his own men. But he could still see Marietta, a book of fashion plates resting on her belly, planning her fall dresses, or hear her laughter as he read to her from the *Lady's Magazine* she had brought. He was glad not to have seen her in death.

"Do you wish to see the boy?"

"Not now." Colin closed his eyes. "I need to think."

"The wet nurse has declared she won't travel alone with three strange men, no matter how much money you offer. So, Nell suggested the scullery maid as a companion."

Colin was suddenly alert. The perfect solution was suspiciously convenient. He regarded Fletcher carefully, watching for his reaction. "And of course Lucy agrees."

Fletcher opened his mouth to speak, then shut it again.

"Speak your mind, man."

"*Lucy* hasn't left your side, boy. Hasn't slept, except in that chair. I doubt she even knows what day it is." Fletcher drew a long breath. "I've known you for better than twenty years. I've fought, starved, bled, and mourned with you, and there's no man I've trusted with my life more than you. I followed you—your men followed you—because you never let us forget that despite the darkness of the war, we could always find a reason to have faith. That for every man or woman who cheated or lied, there were a dozen others who would lend a hand when there was need."

Fletcher stopped abruptly, waiting for Colin to respond. After several seconds of silence, he continued. "But you've let the last months leech all faith out of you. Not just in others but in yourself. And it's made a poorer man of you. Perhaps it's time to remember who you used to be, and become that man again."

The silence grew between them. Colin wanted to object to his old friend's words, but knew they were all too true. Suspicion hadn't been natural to him. It had been a convenient way to stay alive when he'd discovered Octavia's betrayals. But he had no idea how to change or—worse yet—if he even wanted to. Keeping one's distance had its advantages. If you didn't love, you couldn't grieve.

Fletcher rubbed his jaw with his hand and sighed. "Only one door into this building, and I have the key." He patted his pocket. "Bobby and me, we sit with the babe and watch the carriage yard. There's been no trouble, and no questions."

"Where are my pistols?"

Fletcher pulled the case from under the end of the bed and set it beside Colin. "Gun's clean. Padding and powder are fresh." By the time Colin had opened the box, Fletcher was gone, the door pulled shut behind him.

For the next hour, Colin considered Fletcher's criticisms. He had no answers, but he did know one thing. Marietta's death—and the wet nurse's refusal—had changed his options, giving him a way to honor both his promise to the Home Office and his implicit one to Lucy.

Colin was still considering his next steps when Fletcher's voice called, "Dinner," through the door. Fletcher held open the door for Lucy to enter carrying a tray, then withdrew, leaving Colin and Lucy alone.

"I thought gruel might be easy on your stomach. But if you wish for something else, the kitchen is quiet. We've no other quests, and the last stage left an hour ago."

"Gruel will be fine." He looked at her, her dark eyes filled with kindness, and he knew that honesty—or a form of it—would be best. "Fletcher tells me I owe you my life."

"It wasn't your time to die." She placed the tray at the foot of the bed, lay a piece of linen across his chest, then set the tray in his lap. She moved efficiently, but with grace.

"I recall little after my bath, but before that . . . well, I remember enough to know I should apologize. I was hopelessly ill-mannered."

"There's no need. Sickrooms, hospitals, are worlds unto themselves. Just as you can't know who will be brave on the battlefield, you can never predict how a person will respond to pain, fear, or weakness. Most men, in fact, later regret the things they say in a sickroom."

"I regret being like most men."

She laughed, a rich, hearty sound. He lifted the spoon, and she stepped away, closer to the door. She clearly intended to escape when he began to eat.

"Sit and keep me company. If the kitchen is quiet, there's no reason you can't wait for the tray."

She pulled the chair at his bedside back toward the wall before sitting reluctantly.

"I promise not to bite. Besides, if I were to try, you would be back in the kitchen before I could untangle myself from the bedclothes." As he lifted the spoon, he watched her face. "Ah, a smile. I have amused you."

"It's a shame James Gillray is dead. He could have made quite a satirical cartoon of it." Her hands were folded primly, but her voice was teasing.

"Tell me more. It will entertain me while I eat."

"Let's see." She rubbed the lobe of her ear pensively. "'Aristocratic Manners Undressed.' A half-dressed young lord chases a scullery maid down a hall, his bedclothes trailing behind, tripping him. Gillray captures him in mid-fall, arm outstretched toward the fleeing maid. An old woman in a sleeping cap peeks out of an adjacent room to ogle the lord's bare chest."

The gruel warmed his stomach. "But what of the maid? Gillray shows her in full stride, lifting her skirts to reveal two finely turned legs, and dripping soap-suds from her arms."

"Only the reader can see her legs." She shook her head in mock dismay, crossing her ankles out of view. "The young lord's behind her, sliding on the soap-suds."

"True." He grinned. "But look here." He pretended to hold out an engraved print, pointing at an imaginary spot with his spoon. "The suds trail down his chest, and there's a bit of soap on his nose. Perhaps our maid is more complicit than we thought. Look at the expression on his face. I don't think he expected the maid to bolt."

"He is only surprised because he's a lord." She held up her hands, palms facing him, as if refusing to take the imaginary print. "He expected compliance, not rejection."

"And the soap-suds?" Colin lifted the bowl and drank the rest of the broth, watching her all the while.

"He accosted her, and she pushed him away." She turned her nose up slightly to convey conviction.

"Ah, I see." He leaned back into his pillow, and she removed the tray to the bedside table. "But I think your defense of our sweet maid misses one essential point."

"And that is?"

"Soap-suds. Why are there suds if she isn't in the kitchen? He must have been in the bath—and for her to have the suds on her arms, she must have been . . . assisting him."

Lucy shook her head. "I will have to take this up with the ghost of Mr. Gillray—he clearly has misunderstood the maid's predicament when faced with the attentions of a handsome lord." She removed the linen and straightened his bedcovers efficiently.

"Is he handsome?" Colin straightened in interest. Did she see herself in the role of the sudsy maid pursued by the young lord?

"Who?" She lifted the tray to leave.

"The young lord who chases our scullery maid."

"I couldn't say, sir." She pretended to look once more at the print. "I can't see his face for the soap-suds."

Colin watched her leave with regret. He could grow used to a companion with a quick wit and well-turned ankles.

* * *

When she arrived at the kitchen the next morning, Lucy told herself that returning to her dishes was a wise course. She was growing too fond of him, of his quick wit and easy smile. The kitchen offered her a safe and anonymous retreat. Even so, she found herself adding extra soap to the water to make the suds thick.

By early afternoon, three coaches with passengers had come and gone, all eating in the dining hall before they left. Every dish had been used and washed and used again. Washing should have been welcome work, a break from the worry of sitting beside Colin's bed, praying he would live. Instead, each dish seemed like her enemy, keeping her from checking to see that he was still well.

She touched her fingers to her lips. She hadn't expected a simple kiss to create such a complicated web of emotions. And she certainly hadn't expected to want to kiss him again. She returned to the pot, scrubbing absently, while she remembered the feel of his mouth against hers. His hand in her hair.

"I think you've got that pot nice and clean, Lucy." Nell lifted the pot from Lucy's hands and gave it to a towheaded girl at her side. "Peggy will be helping with the dishes until his lordship departs."

"Is something wrong?" Lucy's stomach clenched. The kitchen had been her safe haven.

"Nothing at all." Nell patted Peggy on the shoulder as she led Lucy into a quiet corner. "His lordship has made us a fine proposition."

Lucy stiffened. "A proposition?" She willed her face to remain impassive. Had she misjudged the kind of man he was? From living with her cousin, she'd come to believe that the men of the *ton* were venal and selfish. But Colin, she'd told herself, wasn't a lord as much as he was an officer. And she knew officers—their faults, their prejudices, their shortcomings, but also their virtues. Nell was still talking, and Lucy forced herself to listen.

"I can't see any reason to refuse, but I'll tell him nay if that's what ye be wishing."

Lucy's heart pounded hard in her chest, and her breath felt stiff. She knew how coercive the aristocracy could be. "What does he want?"

"An active man who finds himself bedridden grows bored easily, and bored guests are difficult guests. They complain about the beds, the noise, the food, even the smell of the air."

"Go on." Lucy felt her distrust grow like yeast in a glass of sugar water. She'd been taught from infancy to minimize her risks, to take precautions, to remain safe. She'd been a fool to disregard that training.

Nell held out two pound coins, and Lucy felt her stomach upheave. She'd allowed herself to believe that Colin was an honorable man, but this . . . how could this be honorable?

"He wishes for you to entertain him during the day. And he's provided more than enough to pay both you and Peggy for the next two months. Peggy's da died last month, and she's the eldest of four—I've been hoping to have enough trade to hire her. And this . . ." Nell smiled at the coins.

Lucy looked at Peggy, her thin arms and legs, already doing exactly as Alice told her. "What does he expect me to do?" Peggy's presence made refusal difficult, and she wondered ungenerously if that was what Nell had intended.

"Oh, he's provided a list." Nell held it out. "These things and nothing else. And you may refuse three requests per day. Even better, if he asks for something not on the list, we may keep his coin without any additional obligation."

Lucy read the list. Nothing salacious. Reading aloud. Writing letters. Games involving cards, dice, marbles, or boards, but no wagers. She turned the sheet over to see if there were additional items on the back; then, still suspicious, she held it up to the light to see if other words appeared. Nothing.

Her relief felt like cool water on a hot day. He was exactly who she had believed him to be.

"Mr. Fletcher says his lordship's relations should be here in two, three days at the most." Nell grinned. "And he's already paid us." She pressed one of the pound coins in Lucy's hand.

Lucy turned the coin over. No scullery maid would refuse so much money for a few days' attention to a convalescent. But she still felt vaguely uncomfortable, as if there were a larger game at play, and she didn't know its rules.

Even so, she pocketed the coin. "What harm can come of it?"

"That's what I thought." Nell patted her on the back. "Go on up now. And take that basket: I've collected some games and books from the public rooms."

Lucy picked up the basket and headed toward the guest lodgings. She hoped Colin grew less appealing with familiarity. Otherwise the harm might be to her heart.

Fletcher was standing at the door when Lucy arrived, basket in tow. Fletcher spoke loudly enough that Colin could hear each word perfectly.

"Thank heavens that you agreed, Miss Lucy, or I might have killed him by nightfall. Morose and moody, he is, and no cheering him."

"Then perhaps we can distract him." She tilted the basket so only Fletcher could see its contents. "See anything he likes?"

"Ah, yes, miss. This." The coachman smiled broadly as he pointed.

Lucy laughed out loud. "This should be interesting."

From his bed, Colin strained to see what Fletcher had picked. "Why are you talking to Fletcher when I'm the one who is paying for your time?" Colin had made the agreement with Nell, he told himself, because he needed to know Lucy better before he could consider taking her with them as Jennie's companion. But, in truth, all day he had missed Lucy's teasing tongue and her quick wit. He'd even tried to amuse himself by making absurd statements and predicting what she would say in response. But none of his imagined retorts surprised and delighted him as much as hers did. The game had only made him want her company more.

"Fletcher indicates that you like Fox and Geese." Her cheeks were still flushed from the heat of the kitchen.

"I last played when I was a boy." He shifted toward the center of the bed, hoping she would sit beside him. Instead, she placed the basket on the bed and pulled a chair forward.

"Fletcher chose it first off, so I would wager—if we were allowed to wager—that it's your favorite." Few people teased him as regularly, and successfully, as Lucy, and it made him feel whole in a way he hadn't felt in months.

"Let me see what's in that basket." Colin began to rummage, pulling out dominoes, card decks, marbles, and dice. Near the bottom, he discovered two double-sided board games. "Backgammon on the front, chess on the back, and this one pairs checkers with Fox and Geese." Under the games were four small books.

"Horace Walpole's *Castle of Otranto*. Know anything about it?"

"It's a ghost story. Terrifying, especially if you read it by candlelight."

"Then you'll have to read it to me by candlelight." With satisfaction, he watched her cheeks flush a slightly deeper crimson.

"Our agreement is to keep you company *during the day*." She turned her nose up at his suggestion, establishing the boundaries of their flirtation, if a flirtation it was.

"I suppose no *Otranto* then—I would hate not to find the terrifying bits terrifying." He turned back to the basket, his mood already improving. "Let's see: three more. Thucydides's *History of the Peloponnesian War* or part four of *A History of the Buccaneers of America*."

"Does the Thucydides start with volume one?" She opened the book to its title page.

"What? No pirates?" Colin felt lighter in her presence, less burdened by the past and his choices.

"I prefer my history to be ancient. Besides, I refuse to read any books except from the beginning. In the camps, books circulated from hand to hand, but one could rarely read all the volumes or read them in the right order. Half the time, the volume I'd be reading would end abruptly, and I could never find the next volume. What's our last option?"

He picked up a battered book with no spine and opened to the title page. "It's in Spanish. *El ingenioso hidalgo don Quixote de la Mancha*." He spoke the words with an almost perfect accent.

"It sounds like you can read that yourself, or I can read it to you. In Lisbon, one could easily find interesting things to read, if one was willing to translate."

He opened *Quixote* to the first page, "I picked up a smattering of whatever language I needed. Spanish, Italian, French, Portuguese, a bit of German to converse with the Prussians, Austrians, and Swedes. Usually I learned just enough of one language to pretend to be a native speaker of one of the others."

"I liked *Quixote*, especially during the wars." She took the book out of his hands and let her finger run down its missing spine. He watched the movement jealously.

"Why?"

"Quixote believes in chivalry, in doing good deeds, in restoring justice to the world. But he is a bit mad, and he doesn't see anything as it truly is. As long as he lives in his imagined chivalric world, he's happy. He defeats a giant threatening the countryside because he doesn't realize the giant is really a windmill. But when he is cured, he sees the world as it really is, making him sad and isolated. With no dreams to sustain him, he dies."

"Perhaps we'll read *Otranto* instead. *Quixote* sounds a bit melancholy."

She tilted her head in memory. "Perhaps, but it's also thoughtful and funny. Why would one want to live in a world devoid of hope or dreams? If all you have is a stark reality, would it not be better to live in a dream world, where at least you believe you are doing good?"

"Does my nurse tilt at windmills, then?"

She looked up at the ceiling before answering. "Probably. If my only possible reality was stark and ugly, I'd rather cling to the beautiful dream. And you?"

"Like Quixote after his cure, I see the stark ugliness and retreat from it."

Her face grew solemn with concern; then, shaking it off, she smiled brilliantly. "Enough of that, sir. I know you didn't bring me from the kitchen for philosophical conversation." She pulled Fox and Geese out of the pile on the bed. "I believe, instead, you wished to challenge my skill at herding geese."

"Fletcher will tell you I'm an exceptionally wily fox, outwitting unsuspecting geese at every step."

"I've already seen that for myself." She held up his list of activities. "Or I would still be in the kitchen . . . with my soap-suds."

He felt his expression move from surprise to shock, to amusement and a sort of triumph. But she made no comment, only set out marbles on the cross-shaped grid.

The day passed so companionably that Colin could almost forget how he had come to be there, at a rural inn, gunshot and waiting for his elder brother's help. The acuteness of his failure faded in Lucy's laughter, and his pleasure in her company was as sweet as it was unexpected.

During a particularly competitive game of backgammon, he told Lucy how his elder brother Benjamin had spent afternoon after afternoon teaching him strategy, until he'd grown skilled enough to beat his next oldest brother Aidan, who before then had never lost and afterward never won again. He had been eight and Aidan twelve. Lucy clapped with delight, praising his younger self with real enthusiasm—then just as enthusiastically trounced him without mercy.

As they played their way through a dozen games, he observed with interest the trajectory of her mind, learning—as he had suspected already—that she was a sharp and formidable adversary.

In only another day or two, he would have to take up his responsibilities, Aidan would arrive, and Colin would have to deliver the infant to his relations. But until then, he allowed himself the time to heal, and the babe the time to grow strong and hardy. Like the hours before a battle when soldiers would draw together all their strength, it was a waiting game. But this time, while he waited, he had the sustained companionship of the most interesting woman he'd ever known. For now, he was Quixote, holding on to a beautiful dream.

When night finally fell, Nell's boys brought up an extra lantern, and Lucy read *Castle of Otranto* to him. But after the third supernatural episode, she was too afraid to leave his room to return across the darkened courtyard to her own. She pulled in a second chair from the adjoining drawing room and, tucking her feet up, she fell asleep by his side, returning to her room before he awoke in the early light of day.

* * *

When Lucy returned the next morning before breakfast, she was horrified to find Colin dressed in his trousers, shirt, waistcoat, and cravat, on his way to find her.

"Where do you think you are going, sir?" She let her tone convey all her dismay and concern. Fletcher—that traitor—would pay if Colin fell or overexerted himself.

"*We* are going. I believe games with balls are on your list. Yesterday, I looked out the window into the garden and saw a fine bowling lawn."

"No, no games with balls." Lucy looked out the window and grimaced. The bowling alley was plainly visible. She should have realized that Colin was not a man willing to rest long in bed and spoken to Nell in advance about keeping Colin from it.

"I believe that marbles are balls, so by extension, either bowling is on the list or balls are just especially large marbles. I'll leave you to choose which." He was teasing and playful, obviously feeling well for the first time since the attack.

"Unfortunately, whether balls or marbles, the bowling alley is in the family garden. Guests aren't allowed there," she explained, without any hope it would make a difference. He was charming and headstrong, this patient of hers.

"Nell has graciously allowed me to purchase the garden for the afternoon," he gloated. "She says I'm her favorite guest."

"If by favorite, you mean most lucrative, then yes."

"Ah, unkind, my sweet. But true. At least when my brother arrives, we will have occupants to fill all the rooms I've reserved."

Lucy had noticed that the inn was especially empty, but she hadn't realized why. Gratitude warmed her belly. By letting all the rooms, Colin had unknowingly protected her from her cousin's men.

"No one enjoys losing sleep when an infant cries in the night," Colin continued expansively. "I'm just ensuring that all Nell's guests have a good night's sleep—at other inns. Now, help me down the stairs."

"It is still too early for you to be roaming about—much less play a game of lawn bowls. Your wound isn't fully knit yet."

"Sweet nurse, I was shot more than a week ago. Men returned to the battlefield with less convalescence than I've had."

"Wellington's adjutants made those decisions, not me. And *you* only awoke day before yesterday. Besides, a walk isn't on your list." She crossed her arms across her chest and stared at him. "I can refuse to do it."

"Refuse all you like. I can walk on my own." From the edge of the bed, he pushed himself up, his face paling only slightly. "I'm feeling quite well."

"You are a stubborn, difficult man." She tucked her shoulder under his arm to support his weight and protect him from falling.

"Says the nurse who refused to let me die." He curled his arm around her, then pulled her closer to his side, whether for support or amusement she didn't know.

"I'm reconsidering the wisdom of that position." She held the waistband of his pants to hold him up as she had the night they first met. "If you are foolish enough to break open my carefully sewn stitches, I might just call down St. Peter to carry you away."

"At least you think I belong with the saints. That's something at least," Colin led her out of the room and into the hall. "I was sure you had me for a reprobate and a sinner."

"I'm sure St. Peter can deliver you to whatever place you are bound," Lucy retorted, pleased that, despite his wound, his mind remained agile and quick.

"Ah, but you tuck so nicely under my arm, and you fit so

perfectly next to my side. Perhaps I just want you next to me, caustic wit and all."

"When you are well, I will make you regret that comment." Lucy felt the warmth of a blush bloom on her cheeks.

"Could you make me regret it now?" He gave her a slow wink. "I might still die, and I'd hate to miss that pleasure."

Colin loved taunting her, watching the way her mind leapt to the next retort, seeing occasionally, as now, a blush bloom on her cheeks. He wished he had been less narrow in his list of what activities she could expect to do. Now that he'd begun to anticipate the turn of her mind, he wanted more of her. He wanted to hear all her witty rejoinders and participate in all her thoughtful debates. He wanted to know about her past and her hopes for the future, and, most importantly, whether he could beat her at bowls.

Since that first night, when he'd pressed her for a kiss, he'd told himself that his behavior and her acquiescence was merely an aberration. He wouldn't have felt so drawn to her had he been completely sober and well. He even explained away his compulsion to tease her as merely a welcome escape from boredom. But none of that explained how happy he felt when she tucked herself, like a good nurse, under his arm. He must remind himself not to grow too attached.

But he set aside that reminder as soon as they left the lodge to walk through the carriage yard to the garden door. Lucy looked fearful, holding him more tightly, anxious—he supposed—that he would fall on the graveled drive. Her concern touched and warmed him.

Of course, once they were in the garden with its verdant grass paths, she relaxed and slipped immediately out from under his arm. Little harm could come to him here, save for grass stains if he fell. He breathed deeply the cool breeze, pulling the air into the lowest quarter of his lungs. His side pinched, but not badly.

Beyond them on the wide green, a narrow alley of close-mown grass held several hand-sized balls and, at some distance away, the target, a smaller ball of a different color called a jack.

"Well, look at that. The jack is already in place. A nice distance for the target, don't you think? Or should we reset it."

Her eyes measured the distance, then she sighed loudly.

"After you, my lady," he offered with expansive gallantry, but also watching for her reaction. There was none, not even the startled surprise he would have expected from a servant.

She knelt, picking her way through the balls.

He picked up his first ball. The wound in his side ached only slightly. He let the ball bounce in his hand a few times to feel its weight and shape, then bowled it down the alley—badly. His ball stopped twelve inches from the jack. "I used to be better than this." He picked up his second ball.

"This is a very bad idea. You may feel well now, but think of all the movements you are making: leaning over, lifting a weight, twisting as you pull your arm back, then driving your arm forward against the resistance of the ball. All those are things you haven't done since before you were shot."

"And I'm having a very good time doing them. The day is splendid. I'm in a garden with a delightful woman, and I'm alive to play a game of lawn bowls. Play with me, Lucy. If I die tomorrow I will have had this last exceptional day. Wouldn't Quixote approve?"

"Yes, he would," she said grudgingly, picking up one of the other balls. Her bowl arched beautifully, knocking his off the green and curving to rest less than an inch from the jack. "Beat that."

"Why, my sweet, you never told me you are a shark at lawn bowls."

"I have many talents you have not yet discovered," she said archly, and his stomach flipped at her slight smile.

"Oh, but I would like to discover them, Lucy. I would like to discover every one."

She pressed her lips together, trying not to laugh, and bowled again, placing another ball within an inch of the jack, setting her balls in such a way that by the end of the match, she had beaten him roundly.

He stood looking at the balls, "Tell me, Lucy, what do you value most in a friend—honesty, bravery, or circumspection?"

"I understand that men turn philosophical after a gunshot, but discussing the meaning of life is not on your list." She looked at the jack and threw her ball. "Why do you ask?"

"I need a distraction to ensure I win."

"Ah, then pick a better question, because I value most a friend who has all three." Her ball swung wide, stopped far beyond the jack and Colin's balls.

"Brilliant. My strategy is already working!" Colin pitched his ball. It came to rest perfectly in a small space between his last ball and the jack. "I would choose honesty."

She looked up, regarding his face carefully. "Honesty is the least trustworthy of the virtues."

Colin heard her words with dismay, and he threw his next ball far too short. Octavia had told him much the same thing: "*Ah, but my sweet, it is not in the nature of man to tell the truth. You lie to yourself every time you lie with me.*" But when he turned to Lucy, he made sure he was smiling. "Explain, dear lady. Are you saying that you would wish to have a friend who lied to you?"

"Honesty depends on the context. To keep a friend's confidences sometimes requires that one lie or, at the least, dissemble, to other friends or acquaintances. Even to say, 'I cannot say,' sometimes is a betrayal." She flung her ball hard, sending one of his balls far off the field. "That is why I would not have honesty without it being accompanied by circumspection and bravery."

Not like Octavia, not like her at all. He breathed in deeply, feeling the air calm in his lungs. "Your turn."

She looked at the bowling ground with confusion. "I just threw there." She pointed at her last ball and said with a certain pride. "The one closest to the jack."

"I meant it's your turn to ask a question." He bowled through, moving her ball away from the jack several inches.

She grimaced, then threw short, setting her ball precisely where Colin would need to throw to gain the match. "I seem to lack imagination. I can't think of any questions."

"Ah, see I have the advantage here. I was at a party recently where one matchmaking mama insisted we all 'make our confession' by answering a series of thirty-six questions she'd hand-lettered on long sheets of paper and tucked with a pencil under our dinner plates." He threw a deft curve, avoiding the obstacle and placing his ball between hers and the jack.

"Thirty-six? That sounds dreadful—and time-consuming. Were you able to finish before the fish or did you have to write through dessert?" She considered the playing field, and chose the direct route, hitting the ball she'd bowled to thwart him back toward the jack. But he enjoyed her growl of dismay when her throw hit its target off-center, sending both her balls toward opposite edges of the alley.

"It was only dreadful if you answered honestly. Since I wished for all the mothers in her circle to have their daughters give me a wide berth, I gave answers no mother could love."

"Like what?"

"To the question 'Do you believe in working for money and marrying for love?' I answered with an unequivocal 'Marriage is the province of fools unless the woman and dowry are equally handsome.' To the question, 'What do you consider the most beautiful thing in nature?' I responded, 'My horse crossing the finish line before the pack.' To 'What is your favorite piece of poetry?' I declaimed loudly, 'O good ale comes and good ale goes, good ale makes me sell my hose, sell my hose and pawn my shoes, good ale keeps my heart from sinking.' That's Bobby Burns, by the way."

"I recognized him." A small smile creased the corners of her mouth. "It was a popular song in the camps, except the Highland regiments insisted we sing it with the Scottish words."

Leaving him at the end of the alley, Lucy stood before the jack, assessing the distances between their balls and the target. "Your bowls are clearly closest. That's one match to me, and one to you. But before we decide to break the tie, I'd like you to rest a little. There's a seat behind the fruit trees where the walls join." Without waiting for his answer, she disappeared into the shadows.

The stone seat was sheltered in an alcove, invisible from the inn itself or the attached two-story wing where his party lodged. Thick ivy hung down the garden wall on either side of the enclosure, giving it the feel of a grotto.

"Were you successful in frightening the mothers away?" She sat first, then patted the bench beside her. "There's plenty of room for you."

"Ah, yes." He settled in next to her, feeling the side of his leg touch hers from hip to knee. "I doubt if any of them would allow their daughters to sit with me in a secluded grotto."

"Not that secluded." She patted the wall beside her head. "This wall, on the other side, forms part of the mews. What other questions were part of the game?"

"What? No answers of your own?" Colin pretended horror. "Who, my dear lady, is your favorite living orator?

Your favorite hero and heroine of fiction? Your favorite proverb? Your favorite animal? Color? Flower? I can go on."

"None of those seems so terrible." She patted his knee in commiseration.

"Ah, but you haven't heard the more personal ones: 'Have you ever been in love, and how often? Briefly describe your ideal man or woman. What is your idea of the greatest earthly happiness? The greatest misery?'" He groaned. "And worst yet, 'Do you believe in love at first sight?'" He heard the words as they left his mouth.

Her hand was still on his knee, her scent—rose water— filled his lungs. It would be so easy to pull her into his arms. He turned his face toward hers to find she was examining him intently. Her eyes so dark were unreadable, her lips— oh, those lips!—tempted him. He looked at his shoes, but he could still feel her warmth where their legs touched.

"Do you?" Her voice was soft, even a whisper.

"Do I what?" He turned back to her and saw the uplift of her chin. Then she was kissing him. Her lips pressed firmly on his, not with the sweet gentleness that began their first kiss, but with a pent-up passion that caught him off-guard. Her passion called to his, and he did not resist.

He felt her body turn into his, her arms curl around his neck. And then he was holding her, her chest rising and falling against his. He knew he should stop. An officer to an officer's daughter, but that phrase had little sway over the desire growing at the pit of his stomach. Her mouth ravaged his, and he met her, stroke for stroke, each pushing the other higher, until his breathing, increasingly ragged, caught against the stitches in his side. The swift flash of pain called him back to himself with an unwanted speed.

He set her back from him, searching her face. "I did not intend . . ."

"I did." Her voice was firm. "Your family will arrive soon, and when they do, I will return to my place in the kitchen. But before we part, I wanted a kiss to remember you by."

"And if I'm not satisfied that this was my best possible kiss—to remember me by, that is?" He pushed a lock of hair away from her face, letting his fingers trace the line of her forehead, her cheek, then her jaw.

"We could try again, if you prefer." She pressed her lips against his again. He welcomed them once more, but this time with more deliberation, more consideration, teasing and tempting her with each touch of his lips. He ran his hand down her back, cupping her bottom and pulling her body into his more closely. A long time later, when he set her back, they were both gasping.

"That will make a very nice memory." Her eyes smiled at his. "Thank you. Have we had a sufficient break to play another round, or do you wish to return to your room to rest?

"Could I have a third option? Remain in this alcove until I've kissed you senseless?"

Pensively, she placed her hand on his cheek, a lover's touch, not a nurse's, and looked into his face, as if she were memorizing each part. Then, she pulled away. "We both know it wouldn't be wise." She stood and held out her hand. "Come. I should return you to your room before you over-exert yourself. I'll read you another terrifying scene from *Castle of Otranto*."

"At the risk of sounding like a petulant child, I don't want to go back to my room. My afternoon with a delightful woman in a garden isn't yet over. We have a tie to break."

Two hours later, however, having lost the tie, Colin began to feel the truth of Lucy's warning in his throbbing side and in the painful numbness running down his leg.

When he stumbled on his last throw, he'd expected Lucy's

recrimination. But she'd only offered a patient sigh and curled up against his side once more. "We'll go slowly this time. Walk as you find it comfortable, and I'll match my pace to yours."

At the courtyard, she hesitated again, and this time, Colin noticed how she surveyed the carriage yard before stepping into view, and how she tucked her face into the protection of his chest to keep herself from being seen. He wondered why he hadn't noticed it before—but he had, he realized. He'd simply assumed she tried to fade into the walls because she was beautiful and wanted to be overlooked. Now he had to wonder what other reasons led her to hide in the kitchen.

Fletcher met them at the entrance to the rear lodge, and taking Lucy's place, he practically carried Colin to his room, dumping him unceremoniously into a chair. "Of course you ignored Miss Lucy when she said you shouldn't overdo, and now your face looks the color of paste."

Colin tightened his eyes against a new wave of pain. He made no objection as Fletcher stripped off his loose pantaloons and his smock top and hoisted him into the bed.

Then he felt her hands, smooth and cool, against his skin, and the tender caress of a cool washcloth against his waist. "The wound in back is still holding closed, but you've pulled open the wound in front, and it's weeping. It will be all right—I promise. But you need to let it mend." She brushed back his hair from his eyes, but he kept them shut. She touched him more when he wasn't watching her, and he wanted the comfort.

He heard the clink of the whiskey bottle and felt the press of a glass into his hand. He opened his eyes to see her watching him carefully. She held the glass to his lips, but he took the glass from her hand, considering if he would drink or bear the pain.

"I've put in enough laudanum to make you sleep soundly.

But I'll be here—in my chair." She pressed her hand to his forehead.

"I'm sorry, Lucy. I felt so well this morning."

"You wounded muscle as well as skin. While the wounds might knit in two weeks, it will take two, perhaps three, months before they no longer pain you. Don't be surprised: as much as it hurts tonight, it will very likely hurt twice as much tomorrow.

"Isn't that always the way of things?" he contributed grimly.

"With gunshots and stubborn men, yes, it is. Drink and sleep. I'll be by your side."

He drank the whiskey down, and in minutes he felt the laudanum and her presence soothe his senses into sleep.

It was dark out, very dark. The moon had waned to a sliver.

Below, in the carriage yard, she could hear men's voices, demanding entrance. She looked for a place to hide. She turned the lamp down low. Perhaps they wouldn't search the room of a sick lord. Perhaps she could hide under the bed, or slip into the drawing room, then into the next bedroom while they searched for her.

He was sound asleep. She'd given him more laudanum when he'd awakened last, wanting to give his body more time to heal.

After their days of games, she had intended to ask him for protection, an officer's daughter to an officer. But after their kiss in the garden, she needed to reconsider if she would propose it. Now, even if she wished to ask him, he would not awaken in time.

"Down here, down here." She could hear Josiah's voice sounding conciliatory and strained. The sounds of footsteps grew closer.

She moved to the adjoining door. She put her hand on the knob, but it wouldn't turn. Stuck or locked. She was trapped. Her heart pounded hard. Without thinking, she moved back to her chair, as if being near to Colin could protect her.

The door to the hall opened, and Josiah entered with two lamps, followed by a tall man with dark hair. Not her cousin, nor Ox, nor any of the men she had seen in the stable yard asking questions. Perhaps she might still be safe.

"Lucy, trim that lamp. The duke is here to see his brother." Josiah placed his two lamps in the corners by the door and on the other side of the bed. With the lamp at her side fully aglow, the light in the small room was almost sufficient. Her relief made her almost faint, and she clenched the back of the chair for stability.

Behind the dark-haired man stood a slender woman with nut-brown hair and another fair-haired man farther back. The family resemblance between the duke and Colin was unmistakable.

Forster sat on the side of the bed and called to Colin. He seemed unsettled to see his brother so wan in the light of the lamps. The shadows from the placement of the lamps accentuated the hollows in Colin's cheeks.

"Where is the surgeon? When was he last here?" Forster demanded, his gaze never leaving his brother's face. He touched Colin's arm, then his forehead, gently. He let his hand rest at the center of Colin's chest above his heart.

Josiah looked at Lucy, hands out to his side, palms up, shoulders raised momentarily, then lowered. A gesture of helplessness.

"Your brother's fever broke four days ago, and he has been improving steadily." She pitched her voice to be reassuring but firm. "But today he tore open one of his wounds. He is sleeping so heavily only because I gave him laudanum some hours ago."

"You are acting on the surgeon's orders?" Forster regarded her, noting her servant's wool and dismissing her in a glance.

"The surgeon would have only bled your brother." She folded her hands behind her back and straightened her spine. "By the time your brother arrived, he had already lost so much blood that I thought further bleeding was unnecessary."

"*You* thought?" Forster stood, using his height and natural authority to cow her. "Who are you?"

"She's Lucy, Your Grace. The scullery maid," Josiah answered helpfully.

"The scullery maid?" Forster turned his glare on Josiah. "You listened to a scullery maid rather than call the local surgeon?"

Josiah was a kind man, unused to opposing his highborn guests. He looked at Lucy for help.

"You, girl, get the surgeon now. And do not return," Forster commanded. "I will not have my brother under a scullery maid's care."

"No." Without thinking, she stepped forward.

"No? No!" Forster growled, raising up slightly on the balls of his feet. "Do you not know who I am?"

Lucy raised her chin and stood her ground, feeling the surge to fight in her stomach and heart. "You are a man who loves his brother. And you are afraid for him. But he will be well. He merely needs to sleep for another couple of hours. I promise."

The slender woman with nut-brown hair came to his side and placed her hand on his elbow, but she spoke directly to Lucy. "What have you done for him?"

Lucy described her methods, how often she had given him laudanum, and each of his symptoms since his gunshot.

"And you believe, even at this point, this surgeon will only bleed him?" the woman asked gently.

"Yes, my lady." Lucy held the gaze of the woman's kind grey eyes. "I do."

"Then, Forster, I believe we should give your brother's nurse a couple of hours to prove if her treatment is good." She reached down to feel Colin's head. "He is not hot, and he seems to be sleeping soundly."

"Only because he has been drugged, Sophia." Forster spoke with a set jaw.

"Aidan." The grey-eyed woman looked into Forster's eyes, but said nothing more. Lucy watched the unspoken argument going on between them.

It wasn't clear who had won until Forster turned to Lucy coldly. "I give you until tomorrow morning before we call the surgeon. He must show improvement by then. However, if my brother dies as a result of this delay, I will have you arrested on charges of murder." He paused. "Are you so confident that he is well that you wish to take such a risk?"

"If you promise not to call the surgeon, I will take the risk, yes." She kept her head held high. She had won or, at least, won Colin another day. She looked back at her patient, still sleeping sounding, and prayed one more day would be enough.

"But I will not have you near him," Forster decreed, turning to Josiah. "Innkeeper, I want this servant locked in her room until we see if my brother will recover. Seth, accompany them. Lock her in and take the key."

The blond man at the back of the room came forward, "Come along, miss." He put his hand on her arm and led her to the door.

In the hall, he pulled the door closed behind them, then dropped her arm. "Besides, the innkeeper's wife says you are in need of sleep yourself. Forster will come round. Once Colin awakens, Forster will be pleased you saved him."

"Please." She stopped walking and looked directly into his eyes. Green eyes, not blue like Colin's. "Keep the duke from calling the surgeon. He has lost a great many more patients than he has saved."

"He might call for the surgeon, but I promise: I will not allow any bleeding." Seth examined her face, then smiled. "But you must also promise me, if I stay with my brother, you will go to sleep."

"If you will stay with him." Her eyes felt wet, both from the fight to protect Colin and from his brother Seth's kindness. She turned away before Seth could notice, and they followed Josiah from the wing, across the courtyard, and up to her room. At the door to her room, Josiah took out the key and handed it to her blond ally, then retreated back down the stairs.

Lucy walked into her room and sat on her bed. Seth leaned his head in. "Besides, Lady Wilmot is on your side. My brother may distrust you, but he will do as she wishes."

Then he was gone, and she heard the key turn and lock. She lay on the bed to consider her possibilities, but she was asleep before Seth had put the key in his pocket.

Chapter Five

The next afternoon, Colin awoke to his brother Seth lounging in the corner at the table, eating a meal that smelled wonderful. He tried to sit up, but his head and side disagreed.

"Why are you here?" Colin growled.

Seth looked up, fork halfway to his mouth. "Ah, the dead awakens. How do you feel?"

Colin slowly tested his various limbs, tensing then releasing muscles in his legs and arms. His body felt heavy, sore. So much wearier than it had before his ill-advised bowling match. "Like I've been run through with a bayonet or a bullet."

"That's the sum of it." Seth cut another bite of pie, then gestured with the empty fork. "Except for the raging duke fighting with your nursemaid as you slept."

Colin remembered Lucy's gentle hands cool on his brow. "Where is she?"

"In her room. Aidan refused to let her near you once he arrived. Only family. Thus me." He stood and stretched. "I should call him; he's been beside himself." Then his expression turned serious. "He is going to hate admitting she was right."

"What do you mean?" Keeping his head still, Colin pushed himself up a bit onto his pillows, then up a bit more, slowly moving himself to a partially seated position.

"It took three days for Fletcher's letter to reach us. You know that Fletcher doesn't like words in the best of times, and when he's distressed, his notes become cryptic. 'Brother shot. Come to Grey Goose Inn, Ellesmere Road north of Shrewsbury.'"

"How long did it take Aidan to determine the shot brother was me?"

"Since I was at the estate and Fletcher only travels with you or me, it was an easy process of elimination. But the ambiguity made Aidan cross. I don't think he slept in the fourteen hours it took us to reach you. Then when we arrived, you were unconscious, the surgeon had never been called, and the scullery maid was playing physician." Seth moved to Colin's side, helping him sit upright.

"She was in the hospitals at Waterloo. I trusted her skill, and her treatment has been good. I was simply a fool yesterday and ignored her advice." Colin tried to breathe to the bottom of his lungs, but stopped when the dull pain in his side began to throb.

"Well, whoever is at fault, the best part was watching." Seth sat in the chair next to the bed and began to pull on his boots, having padded around the room in his stocking feet. "Your nursemaid stood toe to toe with Aidan across your sleeping body and told him she was not going to let the local surgeon bleed you to death."

"I wish I had seen that." But somehow he could imagine it: Lucy, his ministering angel turned warrior.

"As one would expect, Aidan responded with threats suitable to his rank." Seth finished with one boot and began on the other, lifting one foot to reveal a sock in need of darning. "Magistrates. Murder charges. The usual. Lucky for your scullery maid, Sophie is here."

"Why?" Colin tried to raise himself up further, but the muscles in his side refused. Was Lucy really in danger of imprisonment? Or was Seth exaggerating to make a good story?

"In Italy, Sophie and Tom ran in circles which thought bleeding counterproductive." Seth turned serious. "But the maid . . . I like her spunk. Are you interested? Or is the field open?"

Colin growled, surprising even himself. Somehow Lucy had found a way past all his defenses.

"All right, dear brother. I'll find other entertainment." He stood and stomped his boots into place. "Let me get Aidan. He's been making arrangements." Seth slipped from the room before Colin could object.

The door flung open only moments later. Clearly Aidan had the suite of rooms across the hall.

Of the three elder Somerville brothers, Colin had always felt closest to Aidan. Their eldest brother, Aaron, had been an ox of a man, moved by his passions for women, game, and drink, a hard brother from whom the younger boys had hidden when he was in his cups or feeling cruel. None of the brothers had mourned when Aaron died from riding his horse too recklessly after a night of drinking and whoring. The next eldest, Benjamin, had been the diplomat, their advocate, finding ways to protect them from Aaron's more overt cruelties. Benjamin's death in the wars was a tender wound with all. That had left Aidan to be the confidante and the accomplice, the older brother the younger ones could admire and emulate and adore.

Crossing the room in three quick steps, Aidan clasped Colin to his breast. "The last time I was this frightened, you had challenged Aaron to a duel with pistols."

"I was nine." Colin endured a brotherly muss of the hair.

"Aaron would not have cared; he still would have shot you, then blamed you for being foolish." Fussing, Aidan helped Colin arrange his pillows. Then he looked at Colin carefully, checking his color, the temperature of his forehead, his eyes.

"Would you like to inspect my teeth? I am sure they are as good as those of your horses." Colin bared his teeth and opened his mouth wide.

Seth laughed from the doorway. "Colin's personality has not improved with his injuries."

Aidan turned serious, motioning to Seth to shut the door behind Sophia. "Fletcher says the postboy you were carrying from Wrexham to Shrewsbury was part of the robbery. He knocked Bobby from the coach, then hit Fletcher in the head to bring the horses to a stop."

"It wasn't a robbery. Fletcher and I took the regular precautions." Colin turned his hand palm upward, then let it drop. "I thought I was merely an escort."

Aidan nodded. "Even though the infant is not of the parish, we had his birth registered in the local church."

"Your brother intimidated both the local clergy and the magistrates," Sophia added conspiratorially. "He hasn't yet learned that sometimes diplomacy is better than a battering ram."

"In intimidating the local authorities, you have not also had my nurse arrested, have you?" Colin noted that Aidan would not meet his eyes.

"If that woman is a scullery maid, I'm Zeus." Aidan colored. "But I have not had the magistrate take her in."

"Which means what?" Colin pressed for a more direct answer.

"Your brother is unused to a servant refusing him his way. I think it was good for him." Sophia straightened Colin's bedcovers and sat beside him.

Colin smiled at Sophia and met Seth's eyes over her

shoulder. "I imagine that growing up in the camps made her less sympathetic to 'great men' ordering her about."

"I see you have talked to her a great deal." Aidan stood at the window, staring into the courtyard.

"Lying in bed all day staring at the ceiling was not very interesting," Colin averred. "But you haven't answered: have you used your rank to bully her into a jail cell?"

"Aidan compromised by having her locked in her room." Seth leaned back against the wall. Aidan turned from the window to glare at him, but Seth only grinned.

"Oh dear." Colin groaned and rubbed one eyebrow with his thumb. "I would like to see her, to apologize for my brother's arrogance.

"After you rest," Aidan commanded.

"I will rest *after* I speak with Lucy."

Lucy paced. She had spent the day locked in her room. Until the extra wing of the inn had been built, her room had served as a small upstairs sitting room for wealthier visitors or a bedroom when the inn was especially full. Since morning, she had likely paced five miles. It was foolish, but the exertion kept her heart from racing, though it did nothing to keep her mind from considering the various threats she faced.

Ten steps from the door to the window. There, she surveyed the carriage yard for her cousin's men. If they returned, and Colin's family unknowingly revealed where she was, she would have no way to escape. Before the duke had arrived, she had played with the idea of throwing herself on Colin's protection, even offering a part of her fortune for his aid. But the prominence of his family worried her. Did they know her cousin? Would they sympathize with her or Archibald? Few knew of his vindictive rages or his capacity for violence. No, returning to her cousin's house would be far more dangerous than being charged with Colin's murder, even with a man as powerful as Forster wanting to see her hung. Had she been wise, she would have run when the Duke of Forster told her to fetch the surgeon.

Four steps from the window to the bed. Beneath the bed, barely visible, was her valise. The first thing she had done on rising was to pack her few belongings in the one small valise she had been able to take with her when she had run away. She had hidden it, fully packed, in the large declivity of a rotten oak for almost a week before she'd been able to escape Aurelia's house. Big enough to carry a fine dress and slippers to trade and enough money to make it to her destination. Her jewels remained at the back of the hollow, buried in a tin box in the depths of the oak.

When she had planned her initial escape, she had packed with the anticipation of a new life and with the purpose of fulfilling her last promise to her great-aunt. And when she'd traveled the roads, hiding for a time in the crowds of laborers traveling to Manchester to hear Henry Hunt speak at St. Peter's Field, she'd taken on some of their enthusiasm. This morning, however, she packed with a strange sense of loss. Whatever happened with Colin, she had to be ready to run.

On top of the bed lay her knitting. Periodically, she would sit, forcing her mind to focus on mending the household's worn socks and torn sweaters. But in the last hour, she found herself pulling out as many stitches as she put in, and for the sake of the yarn, she put it all aside.

Six steps from the bed to the fireplace. She held her hands out to warm them in the dying fire. A chair was pulled to the side of the grate. For a while she had sat there, keeping her mind busy by tracing the complicated repeating pattern in the wallpaper behind the bed. But when she'd begun imagining faces and other shapes hidden in the pattern, she had determined that pacing was more healthful.

Three steps from the bed to the door. At the door, she

listened for any sounds of approach. If the magistrates arrived, it would mean she had failed and that, despite her best efforts, Colin had died. Surprisingly, the thought of Colin dead evoked the same empty loneliness she had felt when she had lost James.

Strange how an attraction could form so quickly. She felt again the surge of longing his kisses had inspired, a longing that was more than mere physical response. At first she'd admired his humor and bravery in the face of injury, but in the past few days, she'd come to appreciate his willingness to be serious. She realized she would never read *Quixote* the same again.

If his relapse were just a small setback, he should have woken by now. But she remained locked in. And she feared for him.

She shook herself; he would not die. Once Colin awoke, she would no longer be of interest, and she could slip away to the next part of her journey. Only two weeks ago, she had thought it too soon; today she could not leave soon enough.

She began another circuit around the room.

Chapter Six

"We have a meeting this morning with a client, Flute. And I am trying to determine which of our partners would handle the meeting best."

"Who is the client?" Flute scratched his head.

"Archibald Pettegrew, Lord Marner. He inquired about our services in the spring, but decided not to hire us." The man called Charters walked from his ornate French desk to the front of a large wardrobe.

"Ah, I remember him. Petty, vicious man. Had some relative he feared was going to inherit instead of him."

"That would be the one. When last I met with Marner about his troublesome cousin, I gave him a very reasonable price for what he wanted, but he decided to handle the situation himself." Charters opened the wardrobe doors wide, revealing a series of shelves and hooks holding the materials for various costumes.

"Then what does he want with us?"

"Apparently, he handled the situation badly. But, given that he chose not to hire us when we were being reasonable, I think Marner deserves to meet with our less reasonable partner." Charters removed a tan superfine tailcoat with richly detailed red embroidery on the sides, a matching embroidered waistcoat, and tan trousers. He held them up for Flute's approval. "What say you, Flute?

"I always say I like Georges best, ruthless old sod that he is." Flute tucked his large frame into a comfortable cushioned chair in the corner, always fascinated by the process by which his employer transformed from one role to the next. "But he's a desperate man, Marner. Georges will try his patience."

"Even better." Charters set his costume on the ottoman to his right, then began to undress. He removed first the tinted eyeglasses that obscured the true color of his eyes, then the blond wig with its long hair pulled back into a working man's ponytail. He pulled the smock top over his head and removed his wide-legged trousers, then carefully folded both and placed them on a shelf along with his glasses. He hung the wig on a hook nearby. "We still haven't the full story from Marner, and perhaps Georges is the man to frustrate it out of him."

Bare-chested and wearing only his drawers, Charters took a pot of grease from the dressing table and began to remove the makeup that darkened the skin of his face and the back of his hands. As he turned to wash the grease away in the basin, Flute noticed again the long, badly knit scar on his employer's back. The lean muscles formed by fencing had been slashed by a sword tip from his left shoulder to his right hip. Flute wondered again at the circumstances: when would an experienced swordsman like Charters turn his back to an opponent?

"I find it a marvel how you take off one face and put on another." Flute leaned forward to get a better view, as Charters picked up a brush and a pencil. Flute was the only man alive who knew Charters's real face and name. It was a bond between them. The men had survived a shipwreck together, years before when Flute was a loyal subject serving in His Majesty's Navy, and Charters was a headstrong aristocrat, intent on a Grand Tour despite the wars. Flute would have drowned that day, despite his superior strength, had Charters not pulled him, unconscious, to shore.

"It's more of a marvel in the *ton* when people change faces with no makeup at all." Charters stood and turned, having aged his face with lines at the corners of his eyes and mouth. Flute nodded approval.

Charters took a brush and applied a layer of white powder to give his skin the pale complexion of an aging fop. Then he pulled on the ornately tall, heavily powdered wig of George III's generation and struck a pose as Georges. Extending his arm out before him, he waved a handkerchief edged with an ornate lace toward Flute, his audience. When he spoke, the low, cultured accents of his regular speaking voice were gone, replaced by the drawling mannerisms and altered vowels of the fops on the London stage.

"Of all things that belong to a woman, I have an aversion to her heart." Quoting from a popular play by Colley Cibber, he pulled his hand back to rest against his forehead, the lace hanging low in front of his nose. "For when once a woman has given you her heart—you can never get rid of the rest of her body."

Flute applauded, laughing.

"It's a shame you never took to the stage, my lord; you would have made your fame as Lord Foppington." Flute took a small apple from his overcoat pocket and bit into it.

Charters bowed, then turned to put on his costume: a padded potbelly, followed by a linen undershirt, then a waistcoat and tailcoat reminiscent of a more florid time and more excessive styles. Once belonging to a gentleman of some means, the coat was crafted from a tan superfine, but with accents in a rich red embroidery. At the shoulders, sleeves of deep red superfine joined the body of the jacket in circles of red fabric that resembled the shape of epaulets. Each red arm was cuffed in a tan brocade with red embroidery.

From those red shoulders, curving lines of red embroidery extended like tree roots across the chest in rivulets or tendrils. The sort of suit a man obsessed with fashion would wear—even if the fashions were more than a decade old. Finally Charters added the trousers, a form-fitting tan superfine with a red vine trailing down the outside edge of each leg.

"Why, split my windpipe, and strike me dumb!" Flute marveled, himself quoting from the plays.

Georges bowed low. "You *are* a thief, my dear Flute, stealing lines as well as apples."

"Purchased the apple," Flute offered flatly.

"Ah, what sentiment, Flute. Unwilling to steal from that most pretty miss who sells fruit in the market?" Georges struck another pose and stole another line from Cibber: "Don't be in a passion, Flute; far passion is the most unbecahming thing in the warld—to the face."

Flute shrugged his shoulders and took another bite, leaving only the core. Then he ate that as well.

By the time Lord Marner arrived with his trio of country henchmen, Georges was ensconced in the outermost office, a tray of perfume bottles of various shapes and sizes next to an ornate desk set filled with ink, sand, and prepared quills.

A hungry-eyed lad named Wilks, hired for his quick feet and nimble fingers, led Marner's group in.

Georges greeted the group from behind the desk, nodding to Wilks that he could retire. "You will excuse an old man for nat standing. The rain—" He waved his hand, making the lace at his wrist ruffle to the sides. "It pains my old bones mare each day."

"I care nothing for your bones, old or not. I wish to see Mr. Charters."

"Ah, but Lord Marner, he is nat free, nat free at all. A

lady needed his skills, and he is—as the Americans say—a slow poke when it comes to the ladies." Georges laughed at his own joke. "Mr. Charters has asked me to manage whatever affairs you bring to us. Are you lang in town? Are you looking for the best gambling hell? Or another kind of entertainment? Perhaps something more exatic that requires the knowledge of a . . . connoisseur such as myself?" Georges winked provocatively.

"If Charters is 'nat free,'" Marner sneered as he mimicked Georges's pronunciation, "then I will see whoever is above Charters." Marner looked at the door leading to the inside office and started to walk toward it.

Flute stepped in front of the door and leaned back against its frame, crossing his arms.

"I assure you I am every whit as ruthless as my younger partner. In fact, our man Flute here often says we are merely opposite sides of the same coin, though I prefar to think of myself as the mare appealing, mare fashionable side."

"You don't seem much alike to me." Marner turned back from the door.

"Ah, that's because you only focus on the surface, nat the heart, nat the soul. I am the very soul of Charters, and he is only one of my exteriors."

"You are daft, old man," Marner sneered, his face contorting into an angry mask.

"Perhaps, perhaps, I have often wondered if the powder in my wig makes me mare or less clever." He let his tone turn cold. "But I am still your only hope." In an instant his tone shifted to playful again. "But, sit down, sit down. I have all the knowledge of your case here." He waved his hand in a circle before his temple.

Marner looked over his shoulder at his two servants behind Ox. "My cousin—dear girl—has wandered away from my great-aunt's house. Since she returned from the Continent, she hasn't been quite well . . . almost mad sometimes. And we have been unable to find her. I had hopes to do so quietly, before she comes to harm."

Georges squinted at Marner, through a monocle he'd pulled from inside his coat. "Ah, a lady's case is a delicate one and best spoken of in private." His voice turned hard. "Your men can wait outside."

"I prefer them to remain," Marner countered.

"Ah, but you see, I do not." Georges placed one hand on his chest, then turned his attention to a sheaf of paper in front of him and, reading, dipped his pen in the ink. "Mr. Flute, Lord Marner and his men will be going."

Flute stepped forward, his body taut and primed for a fight, and Marner's men shrank back.

Marner looked at Georges, then Flute, then at his men over his shoulder. He nodded at the door, and the two younger ones—field hands with an appetite for adventure— fled. Ox remained.

Flute leaned once more on the door frame. "Mr. Georges, I believe Lord Marner has changed his mind."

Georges looked up, offering a wide smile. "Ah, sir, I see we have come to an understanding. Now the truth, please . . . or follow your men. I am already well versed in the details you shared with Mr. Charters."

"She's been gone for over a month. No one has seen her, and we have been unable to find her."

"Then you have the situation well in hand. You have lost the very thing from which you wished for us to free you." Georges waved his hand with the lace handkerchief. "What more can you want?"

Marner looked at the floor and then at Ox. "We need her signature on some documents. Without that . . . well, if she manages to get to her solicitor's office in London before we find her, all my plans will be ruined."

Georges took a pencil-shaped pumice stone from the outside pocket of his embroidered waistcoat. With sharp deliberate motions, he smoothed a particular spot on his index fingernail, stopped, looked at his nails, then moved to the next nail.

"Before you had her, now you don't." Georges tucked the pumice stone back into its small pocket, then dipped the pen in the ink, and scribbled for a moment. "Yes, it will be more expensive." Georges handed the slip of paper to Marner. "That will be our fee, but you need nat worry. Since we learned that your cousin escaped, our man has been guarding the offices of your great-aunt's solicitor. Your cousin will nat slip past us."

"But what if she does?" Marner crushed the slip into a tiny ball. "I was told there was no way she could stay gone this long."

"Nat by us," Georges corrected quietly.

"What?"

"You were nat told that by us. You even waited to write to us until she'd already been lost for more than two weeks. Had you called upon our services, say, the day you lost her or even the day after, this business would already be concluded."

"I didn't know I needed your help until after I'd lost her." Marner pushed over one of the chairs in fury.

"Now, Marner." Georges spoke with almost preternatural calm, his accent growing flat. "Over a year ago, you approached our firm to address the problem of your cousin. You merely didn't wish to pay our fee."

"And now it's tripled." Marner flung the wadded-up slip at Georges.

The ball landed in the center of the desk in the middle of the papers Georges had laid in front of himself. He brushed it to the floor with a sweep of the lace at his wrist.

"When you first consulted us, we had more flexibility. Now the situation is more complicated and requires more resources. Before, all that was required was a particular slow-working poison we import from abroad. During her lingering death, we would have had ample time to address whatever . . . issues . . . her presence created."

"I tried poison, but she figured it out and bolted." Marner stepped forward, his hands balled into fists.

Georges, unflappable, raised his hands to stop Marner's objection. "Our poison is subtle and unknown, a tasteless teaspoon or two a day until she grew too sick to recover. She had no heirs, no friends in the country, no one would have questioned a lingering illness leading to death. You chose to administer a single dose in a glass of milk."

"It's not my fault she decided to share with the barn cat." Marner scowled.

"You thought you could manage the situation, and you bungled it, lost the girl and, with her, a great many of our possibilities. Her death at this point will draw suspicions." Georges pulled a printed piece of paper from his desk. "So, the question remains: do you wish to employ our firm to locate your cousin and bring her to . . . safety?"

"What's this?" Marner began to read the terms.

"A guarantee. That's what you want, isn't it? Someone to solve your"—Georges waved his lace once more—"problems for you."

"I want you to go to hell."

"Ah, my dear sir, I'm sure that has already been long arranged." Georges shrugged.

"Give me the pen." Marner snatched one of the prepared quills from the desk set and began to sign. Angry, he pressed the pen tip too hard into the paper. It splayed and crushed.

Georges handed him another. When the contract was signed, Georges slipped it into the desk.

"We are now partners. Return to your estate and set about the rumor that you have placed your cousin at a country home to recover her wits."

"But we don't have her. How will we find her if my men quit looking?

"Do as I say. We shall take care of the rest."

Marner turned to leave, with Ox following behind.

"And Marner . . ." Georges paused, waiting until the man looked up into his eyes. "Do not return unless you have some information we can act upon."

At Marner's hotel, the men were dismissed to their other duties. Only Ox accompanied Marner to his rooms.

"He's a bad one, that man. Worse I think than the first," Ox spoke his thoughts aloud.

"But we have no other choices." Marner waved his hand, dismissing Ox's concerns.

"He won't like that you didn't tell him everything," Ox cautioned, looking out the window into the street to see if there were any sign that they had been followed.

"All they have to do is find her." Marner poured himself a glass of claret, but ignored Ox. "Then we'll take over again from there." He walked to his dressing table and began pulling impatiently at his cravat.

"Should we call the men back?" Ox helped himself to a glass, not of the claret, but of the sweeter port. "Or do you wish them to keep looking?"

"We'll spread the rumor as he wishes, but keep looking. If we find her, I don't have to pay his fee."

"He strikes me as the kind of man who always gets his fee." Ox rubbed his chin. "He won't like that."

"I don't care what he likes. I need that girl back before she discovers that we read her a fake will."

After Marner and his men left, Charters took off his costume as Georges and settled in to assess his situation. The revenues were coming in just as he and Flute had hoped. His alliances with the gangs in the hells of London and Manchester were growing stronger. He'd even infiltrated the working-class levelling movements to thwart or aid them when necessary. It would do him no good to encourage a collapse of the aristocracy on the lines of what had happened in France. Not just now. Not when he was about to become a very wealthy man.

The finder's fee for the runaway heiress would be very useful. But he still didn't trust that her cousin would allow him to manage things in his own way. He had few qualms about killing the girl, and even fewer about killing the cousin if he decided to try to wriggle out of their agreement.

The thieves of London were easier. They might try to double-cross you, but they understood completely the consequences if they were unsuccessful. And if enough people experienced the consequences, soon no one was interested in the double-cross.

He looked over the maps of rural London roads. He liked maps: they made the lines of his plans tangible. Fields to hide things in, towns to avoid unless necessary.

The heiress had escaped from a country estate in Shropshire. He put a pin in the map. The cousin believed she had taken the London road, and he had focused his efforts in the southeast for the first two days, before considering she might have gone initially in another direction. Marner had found nothing. He'd also insisted that she knew no one who would help her escape, that all of her clothes remained in her closet, and that she had taken no monies. Not all of those things could be true.

When Charters had heard through his networks that Lady Fairbourne had disappeared, he had sent a pair of men to the area to learn what they could. Though their efforts had been hampered somewhat by the traffic to and from

Manchester for the rallies, his men still had taken only a day to discover something interesting

Two days after the heiress had escaped, a secondhand clothes merchant had traded two servant's dresses for a fine silk dress and a set of embroidered slippers. He put a pin in his map. The woman selling the dress had claimed that her mistress had made her a gift of it. Nothing unusual there. But then the servant had chosen two drab, ill-fitting dresses when others more attractive and better fitting were available. That was thirty miles away. He put a pin in the map. Thirty miles farther from London than her estate. If the cousin were correct, she should have been heading to London to see her solicitors. Her indolent cousin couldn't walk five miles in an afternoon, but a woman who grew up in the army could—and far more than five miles. Thirty in two days would have been easy on the roads, but still manageable off them. She would have known that her cousin wouldn't have considered it because it was the wrong direction. So, a diversion.

The next place close by where she could have caught a stage or found a ride was a stable and inn another ten miles away. Farther north, farther from London. But ten miles safer, in an unexpected direction. There were five inns on that road, all with coaches direct to London. He had men at each inn now, watching for a female servant traveling alone on her way to any station in the general direction of London.

He'd known when the cousin described her as a giddy young miss who didn't know her own mind that there was more to the story. No giddy miss would choose to go so far out of the way when alone and pursued on the roads. No, this miss had either friends helping her or a better head for strategy than her relative. He bet on the latter. If she had friends, then he would let the job go. No need to attract enemies when there was so little money in it.

He'd only agreed to the task because Marner owned a property that fit into his plans. If he didn't pay—and Charters was sure he wouldn't—Marner would be pressed to surrender a large unused plot of land with a well-forested private road, well-maintained but rarely traveled. The next best spot for Charters's purposes was forty miles south. He didn't want the money; he wanted the access. Others would call it blackmail, but either way, it served his other ends.

Chapter Seven

Looking out the window, Lucy heard the key turn in the lock. She flung herself to the fireplace, lifting the poker like a cricket bat. If it were Ox or one of the other men who had been searching for her, she could at least give herself a chance to run. She positioned herself behind the door, ready to strike.

The door opened a crack. "Lucy, girl?"

Lucy set the poker against the wall and stepped to where she could see Alice peering through a polite crack between the door and its frame. "Yes?"

"Ah, there you are. Ye are wanted in the sick lord's room."

"Has his wound turned?" Her stomach twisted, and her throat grew tight. Lucy opened the door wider until she could see Alice holding a tray stacked with the remains of a meal. "He was mending when I left him."

"No, la. He's ate a fine meal this morning." She lifted the tray in confirmation. "Told me to send you to him."

"Thank you. I'll go to him presently."

Alice turned toward the staircase, but stopped briefly before descending. "I think he wished to speak to you without his relations present. He was alone when I left him."

Lucy rushed the four steps to the washbasin, pouring water into the bowl to wash her face and hands.

It was foolish to be pleased. She brushed her hair into an unruly bun before she tucked its curls under her maid's bonnet. She looked at herself in the hand mirror, then smoothed her skirts with her hands.

She wished she had some other dress to wear, but the same grey-blue wool he'd seen every day would have to do. She'd never thought it a dour dress, just a workmanlike one, the kind of dress she imagined servants wore to avoid attention. Of the dresses at the used clothing seller's shop, she'd deliberated traded for the one most likely to make her look unattractive, even buying one that fit so ill that she had to bind her breasts to fit into the bodice and had to wear pads to fill out the waist and hips. She'd needed to change her shape as well as her station to avoid being recognized, but now she lamented that decision.

She thought longingly of the wardrobe of dresses at her great-aunt's house; she'd never been too attached to them, thinking them altogether too fine for an officer's daughter. But now, she wished she could wear just one beautiful gown for him before they parted.

If he was well, she could slip away this afternoon.

"I wish the Home Office had chosen someone else for this escort duty. Colin's been distant for months, and the events of recent days can't have helped." Sophia sat opposite her fiancé, the duke, at a table in the small drawing room between their bedrooms, while Seth paced. The couple maintained the proprieties, but Seth was certain that only one of the beds had been slept in.

On the table lay a portfolio of parliamentary reports. The top one offered an assessment of which nobles were in line to inherit the throne in various petty Habsburg principalities in Europe. The Princess Marietta and her late husband appeared in a lesser branch of one of the genealogical trees.

"Walgrave underestimated the danger," Aidan said with all the casual authority of a duke used to having his words accepted.

"Or he didn't tell Colin," Seth objected "The fact that he gave *you* that report a week ago but not Colin suggests . . ."

"That *I* am a member of the House of Lords." Aidan held the report up, then let it fall on the table. "Nothing in the report indicates any real danger. Yes, the prince was heir to a crown, but until some fairly recent deaths, he wasn't a near enough claimant for anyone to want him or his child dead. In fact, news of the closest heir's death only reached London *after* the attack on the princess."

"Walgrave should be informed about the attack." Seth refused the chair Aidan pushed out, preferring to pace to and from the fireplace.

"A letter should already be on his desk." When Seth raised his own eyebrow, Aidan added, "There's a fast post from the town."

"Whatever the Home Office knew or didn't know, Colin must feel the princess's death strongly." Sophia looked up from her sketchpad, where she was finalizing a series of architectural drawings of the same room from different angles.

"Colin was to protect the child, and, despite the attack, the child is alive." Aidan picked up one of the architectural drawings Sophia had finished and marked a change. "At this point, all that remains is for him to deliver the child to Prinny. I have ample men and resources to ensure that happens without any additional danger to Colin or the child."

"I understand your fear for your brother, but taking responsibility for delivering the child isn't the best course of action." Sophia laid her hand on his elbow.

"Sophie is right." Seth picked up the succession report

and scanned through its pages. "Colin will insist that he must see it through. But—don't glare at me, Aidan, until I finish—that doesn't mean we can't help. You can use your influence to get better information and protection from the Home Office. I can stay here and investigate to determine if the conspiracy drew its highwaymen from local stock."

"Nell would likely welcome the trade," Sophia suggested.

"Nell?" Aidan leaned forward assertively.

"The innkeeper's wife. The midwife." Sophia looked into Aidan's eyes. "Quite charming, she reminds me of my Aunt Clara. But there's something about Lucy she hasn't been willing to tell me."

"Let me confirm: you were talking to the *midwife* about the *scullery maid*?" Aidan shook his head in disbelief.

"Lucy might *work* here as a scullery maid, but I don't believe she *is* one. Something about her bearing, her knowledge, her willingness to oppose you." Sophia picked up a new sheet of paper and began to sketch window curtains, followed by a series of designs for chairs.

"If she did grow up in the camps, then her father was an officer." Seth looked over Sophia's shoulder, tapping one of the designs to show his preference. "Only four or five officers in each regiment were allowed to keep their families with them."

"How long has she been working as a scullery maid?" Aidan asked.

"A bit more than a month," Sophia answered, drawing a chaise longue with similar lines to the chair Seth liked.

"Then we need to find out who she is." Aidan strode to the window and back. "The attack happened not far from here. Any survivors would have come to this inn. She might have been sent here to ensure the attack was successful."

"That would have required knowing Colin's route well in advance of his even leaving London," Sophia countered, still sketching. "Besides, Lucy never helped with the princess or the birth, only with Colin."

Aidan raised one eyebrow in question.

"A new servant seemed suspicious to me as well," Sophia conceded. "More importantly, with her knowledge of plants, she could have killed Colin a dozen ways. No one would have given much thought to the death of a stranger set upon by highwaymen. But she kept him alive. We should be rewarding her, not locking her in her room under threat of hanging."

"Whoever she is, Colin's noticed her in a way that he hasn't noticed anything in months. Not his club, his friends, women. I don't even know if he's been to Hartshorn Hall." Seth took the chair he had earlier refused. He leaned back, his arms behind his head.

"Perhaps Lucy might prove useful, then." Sophia took a shallow bowl from her painting box.

"Even if she is part of the attack on the princess?" Aidan put his hand on Sophia's shoulder as she began to prepare her watercolors. "We know too little of her. I don't like it."

"If she *is* part of the conspiracy, Colin might wish to keep her close, to find out the information she knows." Seth took a pencil and changed the line of one of Sophia's chair legs.

"Then how about this? We stay for a fortnight to ensure Colin's recuperation, with my men guarding the inn as my retinue. Then, when Colin is well enough to travel, we'll send my men out on the roads ahead of him, while Sophia and I return to London to meet with Walgrave. Seth, you will remain here." Aidan gathered up the reports, placed them in a leather portmanteau, and locked its clasp.

Seth rubbed his chin with this thumb and forefinger. "I can let it be known that I've stayed to investigate new agricultural methods and purchase goods for the estate. But I'd rather not meet Colin's highwaymen alone."

"Aidan's men will be needed here and on the road, but I can send you some men from the estate," Sophia offered.

"Perkins is a good man in a fight, if you can spare him. After him, Barkley and Tyrrell."

"I'll send for them by the morning post coach." Sophia took a piece of drawing paper and neatly split it in half to make a piece of stationery, then pushed aside her watercolors to write her note. "And Seth, see what you can discover about Lucy."

"If that's even her name," Aidan interjected, unhappily.

The corridor outside Colin's door was empty. Lucy could hear the voices of his relatives, animated but indistinct, from the drawing room beside her. She hurried past, having no wish to see any of them. It would make it too easy for them to recognize her if they saw her again.

The door to his room was shut, and she almost knocked. But she didn't wish to attract the notice of his family, and if he were sleeping, she didn't wish to wake him. She would rather sit beside him until he awoke on his own, but she couldn't wait for him to rise. She would need to find shelter before dark.

She looked down the hall. Finding no one watching her, she turned the knob, slipped into his room, and eased the door quietly closed behind her. She released the knob slowly to keep the catch from clicking as it returned to its place.

She leaned her back against the shut door and watched him. Illogically, she hoped both that she hadn't disturbed him and that he was already awake. No movement. She sat beside him.

His hair had fallen over one eye, and she lifted a hand to brush it to the side, but stopped. In a sickroom, such ministrations were a kindness; but alone in a bedroom, they were inappropriate and forward. Perhaps if his family were not in the drawing room across the hall or if she knew how deeply he was sleeping, she might risk it, but, as it was, she had to settle for being near him.

She would miss him. She would wonder if he were improving once she'd left. She wished it could be otherwise. He might be the one man still alive who could understand her nightmares. But she had lived too long with her secrets to let them go so easily. And she still had her obligation to her great-aunt to fulfill.

When Colin heard the knob turning, he reached for the loaded pistol he had hidden under the covers at his side. Aidan would have objected, saying he and Seth would be close enough to protect him, but Fletcher had seen the wisdom in such a precaution. The coachman nursed a grudge against the postilion who had hit him in the temple with the butt of a gun.

Colin's hand found the polished wood of the handle. He waited. He timed the click of the primer to match the click of the latch against the door frame.

But it was his Lucy, slipping into the room, her dull grey dress a salve to his spirit. He watched her through lidded eyes, making no movement to indicate he was awake. He didn't wish to underestimate the deviousness of his opponents, even if that meant that his ministering angel had come to kill him.

When she slipped quietly into a chair, the tension in his chest released. He hadn't wanted to believe she was part of whatever scheme Walgrave had gotten him caught up in, but he hadn't forgotten being fooled by Octavia either. Time and again, Lucy proved she was trustworthy.

"Ah, my sweet nurse."

"You are awake."

"Yes, and I have another proposition for you." He opened his eyes and searched her face. "His Grace is insistent that I cannot leave here until I am well. I am equally insistent that I must discharge my obligation to deliver my friend's child safely to its relatives."

"Could your brothers take on that task?" she asked, even though she knew he would say no. She understood his sense of duty.

"No, it's my responsibility. However, the duke will object less if I take along someone who knows about wounds and healing." He paused and took her hand. "Come with me."

"Which way are you going?"

"If I were to say that I'm obligated to keep our route secret, would you trust me?" He held his breath, waiting, hoping she would agree to his offer. He wasn't ready yet to say good-bye. "I can promise to return you here after our journey, and I can pay you well for your time."

"However foolish it might make me, I do trust you. As for returning me here, I only stopped here on my way to somewhere else, and Nell gave me a temporary home." She paused, choosing her words carefully. "If I go with you and you aren't traveling in the direction I need . . . when we are done, will you take me where I need to go?"

He breathed again. He knew she had her own secrets, but she showed no interest in the route. Whatever she was hiding, it likely had nothing to do with Marietta's child. "Certainly, I can take you to your destination—unless you were planning to travel to India or the American states. That would be a bit far in return for the trip I have planned."

She laughed, a light, honeyed sound that he wished to hear again, "I promise I won't take you outside of England."

"England. Not Britain?"

She smiled. "Nor Wales nor Cornwall."

"That seems acceptable." It was almost as if a great weight lifted from her shoulders.

"I should tell you that the child is in danger, and it's my obligation to make sure he remains safe," Colin said, still watching her face intently. "Traveling with us may place you in danger."

"I've seen danger before, and I'm likely safer with you than traveling by the post coach."

"If, when he is home, you wish to remain with the boy, I can negotiate a position for you. Nursery maid or governess. You wouldn't have to return to the kitchen."

"No, I have plans of my own, but I will be in your debt if you see me to my destination." She ignored his offer of money. Another way she was intriguing. And another indication she was not a scullery maid or likely even a servant.

"And your destination is?" He was sure she wouldn't answer, but he wanted to try.

"We are both under constraint: you can't tell me where we are going, and I can't tell you where I need to go. It seems we must trust one another."

"It does. For now, we will keep our own confidences."

"Then I would be happy to be your nurse on a journey to somewhere after which you will accompany me on a journey to somewhere else," she said lightly.

"Tell me: I won't be taking you to a husband . . . or a lover?"

She paused for a long moment before answering, "No husband, no lover."

He'd watched her eyes and knew she had considered lying to him. How he knew, he couldn't say: it was something in the way she'd paused. But she had not told him everything, and he wanted everything.

"But you've had a husband or a lover." He made it a statement, not a question.

She pulled away from him, withdrawing into herself. Her voice when she answered was soft. "Did my desire for a kiss in the garden make me appear a wanton?"

"No! I only wondered how you could have lived in the camps, be so beautiful and still unmarried."

"A fiancé. He's dead."

"In the wars."

"Waterloo." She looked away.

He wasn't sure why he had pressed, why he'd needed to know. He wasn't sure why she had told him, except that somehow between them there was a desire for trust. For the first time in months, he felt that someone might understand what had happened in Brussels, someone who could offer him real absolution. Perhaps he would tell her what he'd done—but not now. Instead, he chose to offer her his own absolution.

"I lost a brother in the wars, and brothers at arms. Whoever your fiancé was, I'm glad he had you with him. There was precious little good, particularly at Waterloo. We all needed a ministering angel." When she looked back at him, her eyes were wet with tears.

"I thought I'd die when he didn't return, and then I didn't." She looked into her lap, and her thumb rubbed a circle in her knee.

"I felt the same way when my brother disappeared," Colin said.

She reached out and touched his face. He touched her hand. They shared the moment, each understanding the other's losses.

Then she dropped her hand and sat back in the chair. "And now I'm here," she said, with a playful shift of voice to change the mood.

"With me." He smiled the same mischievous smile he had offered the first night.

"Yes, with you," she said softly.

"This will be, I think, a very interesting trip."

"But when it's over, you will let me go."

"When it's over, if you ask me to, I will."

"To what exactly have we just agreed?"

"I think we've agreed to be . . . friends." He waited, uncertain, for her response.

"I haven't had a friend in a long time." Her face turned from serious to light. "I would like to be your friend, Colin Somerville."

"Then, *friend*, I do not believe you are a scullery maid." He watched carefully, but her face offered no shock or surprise. Instead, she merely held up her fingers, red and raw, and grinned.

"Do I need soap-suds to convince you?"

"My concerns are real, Lucy. If you are a member of the gentry, and if we are recognized while traveling together, it will create a scandal unless we are betrothed. We've already agreed to keep our own confidences. I simply need to know: should we pretend to be betrothed?"

Her back stiffened. He was right. A member of the gentry, then.

She thought for a while. "That's a great many *ifs*." He noticed with a certain degree of admiration that she had avoided answering the question of whether she was gently born. "*If* I say yes, that we should pretend, will you let me tell my story in my own time?"

"I agree, but only if you promise you *will* tell me." He sought the truth in her eyes.

"Then, yes. *If* I am a member of the gentry and *if* we are seen, it would be best to be betrothed. And yes, I promise to tell you why I'm a scullery maid."

"We should announce our engagement then. I can do upstairs. Will you do downstairs?" Colin reached for the bell beside his bed.

"Wait!" She looked startled for a moment. "If we announce that the scullery maid has become engaged to the duke's brother, it will draw attention from every quarter. We should be honest with your family, telling them that, *if necessary*, we will pretend to be engaged to avoid a scandal—but with everyone else, I should be just a hired nurse."

He caught her hand. "I want you to know, Lucy, if *if necessary* happens, I'll pretend to be engaged all the way to the altar. You saved my life, and we are friends. Whatever your story is, whenever you can tell me, I will believe you and protect you."

Lucy blinked away tears, and she lifted his palm to her cheek. Closing her eyes, she curved her face into his hand. He barely heard her whisper, "Thank you." But when she opened her eyes, they were filled again with mischief.

"Oh, don't worry, *friend*. You won't be trapped into a marriage. I promise to leave you at the altar."

Chapter Eight

Later that afternoon, Nell pulled Lucy into the pantry and shut the door.

"Lucy, girl, why didn't you tell me? I knew it from the first day he was awake, oh, the way he looked at you. But I would have thought . . . well, he made me promise to keep your secret. And of course I will. I wouldn't do nothing to harm you, gel. And now—" Nell brushed tears from her eyes. "This way I won't worry about you when you leave. He's an honorable one, he is. I won't worry at all. I know you'll be cared for."

"So, he told you . . ." Lucy let her words trail off, hoping Nell would tell her explicitly what Colin had said.

"Well, I fair to made him. There he was, telling me he was going to hire you as his nurse." Nell snorted. "I told him everyone knew nurse was just a polite way of saying mistress, and that you were too wellborn for people to think you were his doxy. I stuck my finger in his face, I did, telling him you deserved a proper home and a proper man. Then he confided—oh, Lucy, he spoke so sincere—that you wanted time to tell his family, not just the duke and his fiancée, but the whole lot of brothers and sisters, so you were keeping it a secret until a great party at the ducal mansion the duke holds every Advent."

Lucy felt her stomach fall into her feet. "You will keep our secret then, Nell?"

"Oh, of course, dearie. No one will suspect a thing. I've made such very good excuses." Nell beamed.

Lucy listened as Nell excitedly detailed her morning's work. Once she'd learned of Lucy's engagement to Colin, Nell had moved Lucy's things from her attic room in the main building into the lodge, placing her in the best guest room not already occupied by one of the duke's party. Seth now shared the suite with Colin, less in deference to Lucy's virtue than to Nell's pronouncement that it was bad luck for the newly engaged Lucy to sleep where a woman had died in childbirth. It was all superstition. But Lucy was grateful not to have had to refuse the room.

Of course, Nell insisted that Lucy could no longer work in the kitchen, but when Lucy begged, Nell agreed she would be welcome at the large table where the family and servants ate. She was Nell's fairy tale: the serving girl who had won the love of a handsome lord.

But she felt disappointed somehow. In the kitchen, at least she had felt useful, unlike the endless days of nothing she had endured at her great-aunt's home when she'd returned from the wars. To be sure, she had loved her great-aunt, but of what use was a title with no estate and no tenants to give it purpose?

The rap at her new bedroom door was authoritative, and the Duke of Forster entered without ceremony. Lucy shut the door behind him, without thinking of the proprieties.

He looked at her intently as if seeing her for the first time. "Lady Wilmot asked me to convey her invitation to join her for tea."

"Thank you, Your Grace." She stood her ground, unashamed, as he inspected her from head to toe and back again. "I would be honored." She picked up her shawl.

"My brother tells me you are pretending to be engaged. That he needs you to complete his obligation to the child, but that he is in earnest about the engagement if you are." He stared directly into her eyes, as if waiting for her to turn away. When she didn't, he continued. "What will you take to leave him at the end of this? I can pay you handsomely."

"I have no designs on your brother." Lucy set the shawl back on the chair and folded her hands neatly in front of her. "We have simply become friends."

"In a week?" Forster racked his fingers through his hair.

"Sometimes friendship takes no time at all," Lucy said gently.

"I find that difficult to believe." Forster stood, unmoving, his body taut and predatory.

"You are a different man than your brother." She motioned to the one chair in the room, but he shook his head in refusal.

"I am a man who will protect his brother at all costs." He stepped forward, intentionally close.

"I assure you: Colin needs no protection from me." She stood her ground. "When this is over, I will disappear from his life as quickly as I entered it."

"Good." He turned the chair backward and sat, as if at a negotiation. "How much do you want?"

"I want nothing, Your Grace." She remained standing. "Only safe passage to a destination of my choosing when this is all over. And that your brother has already promised me."

"That's all?"

"That's all."

"Are you his lover?"

"No." She bristled.

"Do you intend to be?

"Were you in the wars, Your Grace?"

"Yes, but I don't see how that . . ."

"In the wars, we all knew that life was fleeting. That the man standing beside you at breakfast might be dead by noon. We knew if one had an opportunity for pleasure, or laughter, or even love, it wasn't to be ignored. Your brother is a kind man, a good man. If he wishes, and if for one brief moment we can give one another happiness, I will not say no."

Aidan was taken off guard. "You would compromise yourself with him."

"I have no designs on him. And I have no intention to marry, so the notion that our liaison—if there is one— would compromise me is irrelevant."

"Where were you?

"In the end, at Waterloo."

"I was called home after Salamanca."

"Then we understand one another," she said.

"Yes, I believe we do." Aidan rose. "My brother is, as you say, a kind, good man, but he's also a soldier. If you decide to stay with him, be very sure that you aren't simply another duty he finds himself obligated to fulfill."

Lucy stood outside the drawing room connecting Lady Wilmot's and the duke's bedrooms. She lifted her hand to knock, then lowered it, then repeated the process—all without actually knocking on the door.

"It helps if you breathe deeply, then knock." Seth lounged against his bedroom door a short distance behind her. "And have courage: I have found few women will actually slam a door in your face, however much they may wish to do so."

"Do many women wish to slam doors in your face?"

Grateful for the delay, Lucy stepped toward him, turning her back to the drawing room door.

"More than you would expect."

"And why, may I ask, do you have such difficult relationships with women?" Lucy asked.

"Because he would rather be planning how to increase my next harvest or how to ditch a field." Sophia had joined them so silently Lucy had not heard the door open. "And by the time he returns home, he has entirely forgotten that he was to escort some girl to a dance or to partner with her in the second half, or even to come to London for a family dinner hosted by the duke."

Seth shrugged and offered a slow smile.

"And then the next day he appears at the particular lady's door, and smiles like that, expecting all to be forgiven," Lucy predicted.

"Even worse, they often forgive him." Sophia stood by Lucy's side.

"It is not my fault women find me charming." Seth winked.

Lucy began to comment, but Sophia placed a hand on her shoulder. "It is not a conversation worth having. Someday, he will forget the wrong woman, and she will slam the door in his face, and I will invite her to tea to celebrate her good sense."

"Aw, Sophie, you know I mean well." Seth hung his head, almost sheepishly, but not quite.

"We are ignoring you, Seth. Go amuse your brother." Sophia took Lucy's arm and led her to the drawing room door. "Come. Sit with me. Your Alice has provided a feast."

"A feast?" Seth stepped forward to join them, but Sophia shut the door firmly behind her.

"There." She brushed both palms across the other. "We have our feast all to ourselves. And we can . . . converse."

"I am not sure why you would wish to converse with a servant," Lucy averred.

"That's the beauty of rank." Sophia grinned. "One can converse with whomever one pleases. But truth be told, I am not a particularly good aristocrat. Until my parents died, I lived in a country parsonage, then after that my uncle raised me in the country with my cousins. I had never even been to London until I married my late husband Tom."

Sophia gestured to the chairs beside a table covered with papers and drawings. A silver tea service sat on its own table to the right. "If I may ask, Lucy, how has a woman of your talents come to be a scullery maid?" She seated herself and began clearing the papers into neat piles to make room for their tea.

"My parents died abroad." Lucy seated herself across from Sophia. "When I returned, I lived with elderly relations until their deaths. I found myself on my own, and Nell was willing to hire me."

"But surely you do not wish to wash dishes for the rest of your life." Sophia raised the teapot in question, and at Lucy's nod, she began to pour. "Have you aspirations?" She handed Lucy her cup.

Lucy let Sophia pour her own cup before answering. "The duke believes I aspire to marry his brother." She watched for Sophia's reaction. Would Sophia bluster? Retract or defend her question? Or coldly and politely inform Lucy that she would be an unsuitable match?

Sophia set her cup down. As the corners of her mouth rose, she pressed her lips together and covered her mouth with her hand. But it was no use—she burst out in hearty laughter. "Oh, my." She shook her head, looking down; then she raised her eyes to Lucy's. "When he fails, he fails spectacularly." She lifted her teacup in a mock toast. "To Forster, who often seems to have left his diplomacy at the Treaty of Paris."

Lucy toasted as well, letting her tea cup clink softly against Sophia's. "Men like the duke do not often need diplomacy."

"Forster has needed his diplomacy a great deal in the last year." Sophia held out a platter with small cakes and sandwiches. "But that is my story. And, I would like to know yours."

Lucy felt her stomach clench. "I have little else to say."

"Then I will make it easier," Sophia asked. "If you could do any one thing, what would you do?"

Lucy looked toward the ceiling, thinking. "When I was in the war, I collected recipes. Remedies for burns, for fever, for stopping bleeding, anything that might help save a life or alleviate suffering. I thought someday I might print a book of the best, most reliable cures, and distribute it in places where there was no ready physician or where the physician's fees are too dear."

"What would you call it?" Sophia bit into a slice of carrot cake.

"Call it?" Lucy questioned, swirling the cream in her tea with a teaspoon.

"Yes, you must have thought of a title." Sophia encouraged. "*Every woman her own physician*?"

"'Physician' suggests that the book would help diagnose illnesses. I would wish only to provide treatments for those illnesses," Lucy explained. "I suppose it would need the word apothecary or pharmacy. Perhaps the *Family Pharmacy*? Or maybe *Herbal Medicine*?"

"I like both of those. And your name?" Sophia sipped her tea. "Would you use your own? Is it just Lucy? Or short for something? Lucinda? Lucille?"

Lucy paused on the cusp of giving her real name. Though she liked Lady Wilmot, Lucy knew very little about her. Better to be circumspect than be disappointed if her ladyship turned out to be something other than the gracious companion she appeared to be. "I think perhaps just 'A Nurse from the Peninsular Wars.' That allows me to indicate I know something of healing while remaining anonymous."

"That seems reasonable." Lady Wilmot offered her another cake. "I made much the same decision recently when I published a book on botany for girls. I called myself Mrs. Teachwell."

"Was the book *your* aspiration, Lady Wilmot?" Lucy found herself intrigued.

"Call me Sophia. I have so few women whom I would call friend, and I think we find each other's company congenial." Sophia smiled shyly at her, then rustled through the sheets of paper on the table. "My book grew out of an intellectual partnership I shared with my late husband, so I would not call it an aspiration."

"But this." Sophia handed Lucy several colored architectural drawings of a large hall. "This is the plan for how I would like to refashion an unused gallery in the ducal mansion. I would like to form a salon. I had one in Italy, but it was purely intellectual, focusing on books and art and politics, all very heady. But I would like this salon to be more useful, a place where its members help one another, where each of us could contribute her skills to a common purpose."

"Of us?" Lucy repeated, oddly touched. Like Lady Wilmot, she could not remember a time when she had had another woman as a friend. She began to examine the drawings: warm colors on the walls and furniture, a large fireplace on one side, long windows on the other.

"We would add bookcases along these walls." Sophia pointed. "If it's to be a useful salon, we must have a robust library. I've already given a preliminary list to a bookseller—Constance Vassa at The African's Daughter—but I am limited by my own interests in botany. Perhaps you could advise me on the more medical books."

"The *Materia Medica* lists all the pharmaceutical properties of the plants and dosages." Pleased to be included, Lucy answered without thinking, then she bit her lip. "The doctor in the camp hospital always raged that he needed better books. I learned from him."

Sophia nodded as she poured another cup of tea. "I have spoken to the local surgeon. Had he known Colin was the brother of a duke—he assured me—he would have come to his aid immediately. His preferred treatment regimen relies first on bleeding, then he administers a mixture of calomel and camphor, alternated every four hours with opium. Do you know how those work?"

"Calomel—it's a mercury compound—causes vomiting, while camphor causes sweating," Lucy answered slowly, not knowing if Sophia needed her explanation or if this were some sort of test. "Together with bleeding, the idea goes, the treatment releases harmful pressures in the body. Then the opium stops the diarrhea and gives the patient some relief from the cycle of purging."

Sophia met Lucy's eyes, her face an unreadable mask. "Colin indicated that the bullet carried fabric into the wound and you dug the threads out. But the surgeon assured me that he often leaves them in. Like the rope that led Theseus out of the Minotaur's maze, he said, the threads give the poison a way out of the body."

Lucy's cheeks flushed with surprise and anger, and she clenched her hands under the table. She had thought Lady Wilmot understood and approved of her methods. "That treatment would have killed him," she said, keeping her voice level, her eyes on the tea service.

"I know." Sophia spoke in almost a whisper. Looking up, Lucy could see that her eyes brimmed with tears. "Had you not been here, we would have lost Colin, and not the way he has been lost these last months, but truly and irrevocably." Sophia wiped her cheek with the back of her hand. "As I see it, we owe you a debt, Lucy, and one we cannot easily repay. So, whether you *aspire* to Colin or not, you will always have a place with us. The ducal manor is quite large, or there are other properties if you would wish to have a place of your own."

"But you do not know me. I could be a murderer, a thief, a . . ."

Sophia lifted her hand to stop Lucy's sentence. "Nell, who is a woman of good sense, holds you in great esteem. Colin, who does not use the word lightly, tells me you are his friend. My salon could use someone like you, someone who knows how to doctor wounds and treat illnesses—and who isn't afraid to stand her ground when she knows she's right."

While Lucy and Sophia shared tea, Colin and his brothers met to plan the next stage of Colin's journey. Fletcher would carry the plan to London for Walgrave's approval, then return to Shropshire with the Home Office's response. That alone would allow Colin to rest for a week. A dozen of Aidan's best men, old soldiers who worked for him in various capacities, already filled the house, watching the child under the guise of card games, whittling contests, and other entertainments.

Aidan had brought a large folding map of the southern shires from Shropshire to London in the west and the coast in the south. That, combined with Colin's individual county maps, gave them a fairly clear vision of the best routes to the Royal Family.

"I still think that we should call for more help from my estate. My men can escort you safely to London."

"Few people question why a duke needs such a large retinue, but no one will believe a duke's brother needs so many men. Besides, even when they are serving you, your men attract attention, and attention is exactly what Prinny wants to avoid," Colin objected, thinking of the document Walgrave had given him from the prince regent.

"Let me understand you. You would rather not ask for help and end up dead?" Aidan glowered.

"I've already agreed to stay here for a fortnight while you mother me. But I can change my mind." Colin glowered back.

Seth, ever the peacemaker, tapped the map with his finger, drawing the men's attention away from their growing stalemate. "To get the babe to Prinny most quickly, London would be the best route. Birmingham to Stratford, then through Oxfordshire to London. Let Aidan's men travel the roads before you to ward off trouble. Depending on how often you stop, the trip would take two, maybe three, days."

"If the highwaymen were, as we suspect, assassins, then they will redouble their efforts to keep the child from his relatives." Colin stared at the ceiling. "A post road will allow too many opportunities to be waylaid before we can reach Kensington or Windsor or even Buckingham."

"Circumspection is the key. They will expect you to bolt for London, so do something else," Aidan counseled. "Recuperate here for another week. Seth and I will watch over the child while my men secure the roads ahead of you."

"We will move in stages. A long run on the road followed by a day or two somewhere safe. The days when we aren't traveling will allow me to recuperate and make me better able to protect the child on the days when we are, and your men will have ample time to ensure the next stretch of road is secure. As for our route, we give London a wide berth, not using any road leading directly there."

"That sounds good. And we will also set up a little diversion. If we position the carriages carefully, all someone watching would be able to see would be one man and one woman entering a carriage with two postboys and a coachman. Sophia and I, pretending to be you, will set out at breakneck speeds for London in my third-best carriage, while you and Lucy travel in ducal comfort in some other direction."

"Two postboys?" Colin questioned.

"Of course," Seth agreed, smiling. "From a distance and in the right clothes, the wet nurse will make a fine boy."

Colin leaned forward to trace a line on the map with his finger. "First, we stop here." He tapped a spot in the countryside near Wolverhampton.

"That's certainly out of the way." Seth looked at the surrounding towns. "What's there?"

"An old manor house, known to local residents and a narrow circle in the Home Office, but long ago removed from any map," Colin explained. "It's remote, well appointed, and, other than a gatekeeper, empty. It will be a comfortable haven until Aidan notifies us that the next part of our route is ready to be traveled."

"Depending on what I can discover in London and what Seth can find out here locally, you could be there three, four days." Aidan calculated the lengths of the roads. "Then what?"

"We double back to the Bath road." Colin traced the route with his finger. "Then follow it from Kiddermister, through Worcester, Upton, and Gloucester to stay here." Colin tapped a point east of Gloucester.

Aidan straightened in surprise and rolled back on his heels. "Are you certain Hartshorn Hall is a wise decision?"

"We will be welcomed, and Lady Emmeline would not breathe a word of our presence. The babe will be safe there, as safe as anywhere."

"It isn't the babe I'm considering. Or whether Lady Emmeline can be trusted." Aidan stared hard at Colin.

"It's a trip I've needed to make." Colin shrugged off Aidan's questions. "Besides, it's our best option in that direction."

Aidan and Seth met eyes, wordlessly agreeing not to pursue the topic. Seth turned back to the map.

"Well, then, after that, you'll want to take the road down to Winchester. That will let you come up to London from the south, rather than the north." Seth marked the route with a pencil. "That should give you an element of surprise."

"Have you considered delivering the babe either to Prinny's royal palace at Brighton or the royal family's residence at Kew? No one would find it surprising for an extra detachment of men to be stationed at either one." Aidan identified the location of each royal residence with a circle, then drew in a route of well-traveled roads to each from Winchester. "Any of these routes would offer the safety you need, and the guards to support any further movement of the child. I could consult with Walgrave to see which path best suits the Home Office's plans."

Colin nodded agreement. "So, it's Wolverhampton, then Em's, then wherever the Home Office determines we should go."

"What will you tell her?" Seth asked quietly.

"Her?" Colin scowled. "Lady Emmeline or Lucy?"

"Both," Aidan interjected with clear frustration.

"Lady Emmeline will understand. Lucy won't ask."

"Are you sure you can trust her?" Aidan pressed, his scowl conveying the full extent of his dismay.

Colin stared Aidan down. "Lucy's not part of this. She's in some trouble, but this isn't it."

Chapter Nine

The morning at Hartshorn Hall had been filled with rain, trapping Lady Emmeline Hartley in the drawing room with her cousin and her cousin's unwelcome house party. She had tried to make an early escape, claiming obligations to visit several of the estate's tenants. But the rain had begun to fall in heavy sheets before she had even been able to reach the stables. She had grudgingly accepted her fate: a day with Stella and her vapid friends.

"When can we expect your betrothed, Emmeline?" Stella demanded archly, tapping her closed fan against her palm. "I was surprised not to find him here already. Did he not promise to visit this week?"

Standing at the long west window watching the rain fall, Emmeline pretended not to hear. The window glass reflected her cousin's image only indistinctly. But she knew too well the proud set of Stella's shoulders and the haughty lift of her chin. As usual, her cousin hoped to embarrass her.

At least her cousin's guests were occupied with games. Emmeline had called for tables for whist and faro when she had realized Stella's houseguests could not take their anticipated expedition.

She would have to respond, or Stella would simply

repeat the question in different words, louder and louder, until she had the attention of everyone in the room.

"Somerville had some pressing business that could not be postponed." Em turned away from the window, reaching for her cane as she turned. Though she could usually walk without aid, the change in the weather always made the old injury in her leg ache. "But I am sure he will regret it if he arrives after your party returns to London."

"I promised my friends that we would have fine hunting and pleasant weather, but if this rain continues we will have little reason to remain." Stella had little patience when her desires were thwarted. "Our excursions have all had to be cancelled or postponed. Had Somerville been on time, we could have held a lovely engagement dinner to entertain my guests."

"Certainly, Somerville was inconsiderate not to weigh more thoroughly the imposition he would create for your party by not arriving as expected." Em hoped that Stella had not grown more attuned to irony.

"Yes, his absence causes a tremendous inconvenience." Stella pouted. "Without him, we have no justification for a banquet of that size and variety."

The door to the hall opened, and Em's butler, Jeffreys, stood inside it. He raised his forefinger to indicate he needed an audience.

"Well, perhaps it is for the best." Em nodded to Jeffreys, then walked with Stella slowly toward the door. "Cook has not yet forgiven us for the last impromptu banquet you held for your guests. She had to empty the larder, hire four additional cooks, and purchase the entire weekly produce of two market towns to serve the menu you designed."

"As if Cook's feelings or preferences are any of my concern." Stella lifted her nose and toyed with one of the long tendrils that hung elegantly from her lower neck. "That menu was the perfect complement to the costume ball. It was the talk of the *ton* for weeks."

"No, certainly, the pleasure of you and your guests is always the estate's first priority." Em reached the door. "I simply would regret if Cook poisoned us all for imposing too much on her."

"Your ladyship is needed downstairs." Jeffreys held the door open.

"I say, Em, you would think you were yourself a servant as much time as you spend in the kitchen." Stella snapped the fan in her hand once more and turned back to her guests.

Em limped through the doorway and waited as Jeffreys shut the door. "The footman who delivered tea indicated that your cousin was growing petulant."

"And you were waiting to save me, as usual. Thank you."

Jeffreys held out his arm, and Em leaned heavily on it as they descended the stairs. Once her father's valet, Jeffreys had taken over the management of the house, after the accident that had left Em lame and killed her mother.

"I find myself less patient with each visit. She interrupted my breakfast this morning, demanding to review my management of the accounts." Em released Jeffreys's arm and removed the estate office key from beneath the knob on her cane. "Now that she has borne a son, she finds it impossible to believe that the estate will not pass to him on my father's death."

Jeffreys shook his head as he handed Em into an overstuffed Louis Seize armchair with a curving back. "After all these years, I should have grown used to your cousin's capacity for self-deception."

"It is enough to make me wish my father would marry his French mistress and produce a son." Em stretched her leg out, and Jeffreys lifted it onto an overstuffed round ottoman.

"But a son would make no difference in the disposition

of the estate." Jeffreys brought her a wool lap-blanket and wrapped it around her legs. "I was witness to your grandfather's will myself—and to your father's."

"Stella cannot imagine that my father would bequeath the estate to any but a male heir. And yet, my father has asked me to be kind to her. Therefore, until he dies, I will have to endure her visits with as much graciousness as I can muster." Em closed her eyes against the ache in her leg.

"Perhaps it is time to marry, my dear—share the burden of the estate." Jeffreys stoked the fire and set a pile of Minerva Press novels beside her. "Your father might return from France if there were grandchildren to spoil."

"You know my father will never return—you want the grandchildren for yourself." Em leaned into the chair's thick cushioned back. "I might close my eyes for a while, Jeffreys. Would you send Bess to me?"

"Of course, your ladyship. And if your cousin wishes to find you, I will tell her you are in the stables."

Chapter Ten

Colin spent much of the next five days sleeping or pretending to sleep. It was easier than coping with the loving presence of his two brothers and Sophia. When he was awake, they hovered in his room, tormenting him with their constant ministrations.

Most frustrating, Lucy only visited his room when he called for her, and each time she seemed increasingly distant. After their days of constant companionship, he felt her absence like a missing limb, and he wanted to bring back those fleeting days of closeness. Their conversations, playful and serious by turns, had formed an intimacy between them, an intellectual tie he'd never expected to find with a woman.

But he was uncertain what to make of the physical attraction between them. In the garden, she had made it clear that she desired him, but since then, she had treated him only as a nurse would a patient. Had she been serious when she said she only wanted a kiss as a remembrance of their time together? Would she object if, on the road, he tried to kiss her again? If he insisted on a kiss, would he ruin their easy camaraderie, making their journey together miserable? Or could their bodies be as engaged as their minds?

On the sixth day, Colin awoke, intent to leave and soon, even if it meant breaking his promise to Aidan. It took him no time to convince Alice, who brought him his breakfast, to carry a note to Lucy.

When Lucy arrived, he patted the bed beside him and held out his hand. She took it, but when he pulled her toward him, encouraging her to sit on the bed, she resisted.

"It wouldn't do."

He let her hand fall, and she pulled the chair toward the bed.

"Lucy, what harm can come of sitting beside me? The door is shut."

She looked at the door, the chair, his hand, and, shrugging, sat on the bed.

"I have decided to leave tomorrow."

"So soon?" She looked intently at his face, searching— he knew—for signs of pain. He refused to let her see how much his wound still ached.

"I thought you had agreed to another week's convalescence."

"I will rest during the carriage ride." He smiled reassuringly.

"Given the attack here, I imagine you don't wish to stop on the road, if it can be avoided."

"You imagine correctly." He reached out and carefully trailed his fingers down the line of her chin. She did not object. "We will stop tomorrow night at a friend's hunting lodge."

"I assume the lodge is uninhabited at this season."

"Yes. We will have the place to ourselves."

"Then I'll make a basket." She started to rise, but he stopped her.

"No, ask *Nell* to make us a basket. She believes we are engaged, so you should act like my fiancée. Ask her for enough food to get six of us to our destination and to feed us for a day or two. We will take the ducal coach—it's larger and more comfortable. But I need your help to manage our escape."

"An escape, is it?" She grinned, leaning forward. "I love escapes. Will we do it by cover of night? Or will we escape at noon, but lock your family in their rooms so that they are only able to yell at us from their bedroom windows as we ride away?"

"I do like the idea of locking my brothers in their rooms, but it might be best if I simply tell Aidan we are leaving. He will object, but if we have all the pieces in place, he will have trouble stopping us." He reached out his hand, and she took it.

"Truthfully, if your brother wishes for you to stay, he will succeed." She met his eyes with the straightforward honesty he'd come to expect. "You are still weak, and he is a duke. But I don't imagine he will refuse."

"Why? Do you think he's grown tired of playing nurse-maid and is aching to return to London?" he asked playfully, but his words covered a twinge of hurt.

"No. I can't imagine your brother has thought of anything but your welfare since he heard you were wounded." She looked pensive. "I never had siblings, only my parents and then my fiancée, and I grew up on battlefields, so the term 'brotherly love' never meant much to me. But I saw the look on your brother's face when he thought you were dying and the look when he realized you wouldn't." She patted his hand. "I'm happy to manage the provisions and the people, but I think you might be surprised at how helpful your brother might be, especially when he realizes this is something you need to do."

"Since you recommend it, I will ask for his help in leaving," he said solemnly. "But if you prove wrong and I am trapped in this bed, in this room, for another week, I'm going to expect concessions." He offered her a slow smile and a cavalier wink, waiting to see how she would respond. If they were to be friends, so be it. But would she agree to be something more, even if only for a little while?

"Concessions. I'm not sure I know what you mean."

He started to speak, then stopped, then stammered over some syllables for a moment, trying to think of how to broach the subject.

"Hmmm. Do you mean like the kiss you insisted I give before you would allow your wound to be dressed?" She smiled a little daringly, and his heart melted. "Or the kiss I stole from you in the garden?"

"Yes, like those, if of course you are interested." He caught his breath and held it, hoping and fearing she would agree.

"I suppose I would need to think on it. Perhaps I would even want some concessions of my own." And she slipped from the room before he could even ask what those concessions might be.

After she gave the cook instructions on how to prepare the baskets for their trip and gave Fletcher the message to prepare to leave, Lucy retired to her room. She called for a bath, and Nell, all smiles, had given her the key to the bathing room reserved for the wealthiest guests (and Nell).

As Lucy lay in the hot water, she found her thoughts turning to her great-aunt, and the house she would not return to, a house with running water and heated baths. She would not fool herself that she wasn't grateful to be traveling with Colin. It would hide her better than any other course she could have chosen.

He was a kind, honest man, and she regretted she could not be forthcoming in return. At least not yet—or perhaps ever. What would it feel like to ride across the country with him? Could she resist him under such close quarters?

Would she want to? If "Lucy" were going to disappear at the end of their journey, why shouldn't she enjoy the pleasure of his company in the meanwhile? In any liaison, she would be betraying no future husband, for she never intended to marry, and the husband she had intended was already dead.

No, the only possible problem would be crossing paths with Colin in society. But even that was unlikely. His brother was a duke. He traveled in circles above hers and, she prayed, above her cousin's.

After her bath, she returned to her room—directly above Colin's, an exact replica of his.

She imagined, as she lay in bed above him, that she lay in bed with him instead. She thought of his kisses, and she touched her fingers to her lips, remembering. She remembered his breath in her hair, his lips against her neck, the tickle of his whiskers grown into a pleasantly rough stubble during his convalescence.

She imagined Colin's hands, the elegant strength she'd felt when she'd held them during his sickness. She already longed again for his touch, his hand on her breast, his mouth on hers. She could imagine exactly how Colin's hand would feel on her belly, her thighs, her buttocks because James had touched her in all those places. But she didn't long for James's roughened hands. James had smelled of leather, of gun oil, of lineament, and though he never came to her without as much of a bath as he could manage in the camps, he'd always smelled of war. Colin smelled of—she realized with a half laugh—soap. One of the finer soaps, probably French milled, with just a hint of spice. This man smelled of culture, of ballrooms, of clean sheets—of peace.

The next morning, Lucy rose early, having dreamed of Colin through the night. As soon as she had learned that they were to begin their journey, she had washed both of her dresses, wishing to set out in fresh, clean clothes. She had cut out the makeshift pocket that had held her great-aunt's papers and placed it to the side, where it would not be harmed. It took only a few minutes to sew it back in place and put on her dress for the journey.

Aurelia had not confided in her what the letter said, and Lucy had not asked, only promised to deliver it as soon as she could. Even so, it had already been three months since her great-aunt's unexpectedly sudden death. But she would fulfill her obligation soon: Colin had already promised to take her where she needed to go.

Lost in her own thoughts, she didn't hear the latch click as the door to the shared drawing room opened. And she turned almost into Colin's arms.

He set her back, smiling. "The carriage will be ready within the hour."

"I feel that I must make a confession to you, before we go." She watched his face turn from playful to severe.

"I wish to hear all your confessions."

"It's a small one, really. My given name isn't Lucy. It's a pet name, what my father always called me when I was growing up in the camps and the men adopted it. But Lucy is the name I gave soldiers to hold when they had no one else to remember, as I held their hands. . . ." She blinked away unexpected tears.

Colin's face held only compassion. "When they died."
She nodded.

"Then, is it a name you wish to remember or to forget?" He folded her into his arms.

"I'm more myself when I'm Lucy," she whispered into his chest.

"Then Lucy it is. My angel, my star . . ." He set her back and looked dismayed as he examined her clothes. ". . . in unsuitable clothes. Is there a clothier in the neighborhood?"

"My clothes are adequate, I think, to our travels." His

question reminded her that she had not fully revealed the extent of her troubles, and she felt the same pang of panic that she'd felt each time she'd seen Oaf in the stable yard changing his horse for another leg of his search. She turned away from Colin, so he could not see her face.

"But they are not adequate, if we must claim an engagement."

"It would be easier for you to dress down than for me to dress to your station."

"I'm no better than a lord's younger brother."

"But a lord's younger brother is far superior to a scullery maid." She felt her spine stiffen. "And I have only clothes a servant would wear."

He clasped her shoulders and pulled her to him, her back to his chest, hugging her close but without kissing, just letting his breath warm her neck. He whispered in her hair, laughing. "Well, my lady, I will solve this problem of clothes." He began a line of kisses from her ear to her shoulder, and she tilted her head to let him kiss her neck thoroughly. She felt his body tense; then she heard it too: the crying of a baby.

"Go."

And he was gone.

She leaned for a moment against the wall, catching her breath. Just the slightest touch, and she wanted him to touch her again. It would be a long day.

The baby's cries had been nothing more than a call for food, and Colin only embarrassed the wet nurse as he rushed into the room without warning. He turned his back and retreated quickly, pulling the door behind him. Then he leaned back against the door to catch his breath—slowly. To do otherwise—to extend his lungs fully at the bottom—only made his side ache.

He had refused further laudanum. He would need to keep his wits about him as they traveled—and that wasn't going to be easy with Lucy so near him in the carriage. She was already a distraction, the memory of her kisses never far from his mind.

He was about to return to Lucy's room when he heard heavy footsteps running up the stairs. Seth burst into the hallway.

"I heard . . ." He stopped abruptly when he saw Colin outside Jennie's door.

"He's hungry."

"Ah! The carriage is ready, and Fletcher and Bobby are already aboard." Seth looked carefully at Colin's face. "Aidan is settling up with the landlord. If you intend to set out today, you should slip into the carriage before he returns. Otherwise, he'll take one look at how pale you are and call for the militia to guard the child."

"Pale?" Colin pushed himself away from the wall.

"You look so ill it calls to mind that poem Benjamin used to recite whenever we were lovesick." Seth grinned. *"Why so pale and wan, fond lover, prithee why so pale?"*

"I remember." Colin took his brother's arm to descend the stairs, then filled in the rest of the stanza. *"Will, when looking well can't move her, looking ill prevail? Prithee why so pale."*

"Perhaps when you are well, your pretty nurse will discover what a dreadful ogre you are." Seth supported Colin's weight to the bottom of the stairs. "And that will open the field to me."

"Luckily for me, you won't be with us on the road to tempt her." Colin dropped his brother's arm as they approached the door to the courtyard.

"On the excuse of the ladies, Fletcher has set out the stairs." Seth opened the door wide. "If you think to fall as you go up, fall to the right—that direction is out of the view of the main tavern."

Just three short steps. Colin told himself. Only three. Seth had already positioned himself to the right of the steps as a precaution.

"Can I offer you my hand, dear lady?" Seth gallantly held up his arm.

"Why, dear sir, how kind," Colin replied in a falsetto, but he took Seth's outstretched arm and made his way up the stairs and into the carriage. Taking his position at the far door of the carriage, he lowered the window to take advantage of the breeze.

Unlike the weathered carriage he had borrowed to transport Marietta, Aidan's ducal carriage was made for comfort. Thick cushioned pads for the seats and backs of an extra depth accommodated his brother's long limbs. Aidan had even had a cushioned box made to fit the space between the seats, ostensibly to aid in playing cards on the road. Colin positioned it in the well in front of him, against the far door, converting his portion of the carriage into a chaise longue. Colin suspected (and hoped to test his theory with Lucy) that the box could serve a more erotic purpose.

It was a shame, in fact, that the wet nurse couldn't ride in a separate carriage with the infant. What was the use of a long carriage ride if one couldn't make the hours pass discovering the pleasures of Lucy's body as he had already discovered the pleasures of her mind? Her kisses delighted him like nothing else. His obsession with her made little sense, but then so little had for so long.

And a woman who had made love in the camps would appreciate the richly cushioned privacy of the ducal carriage. He wished he had known her then, in the camps, wished he could have competed with her fiancé for her affections. He imagined her in her sober blue dress meeting him for a tryst during one of the endless sieges. Imagined kissing away her fears as he took his leave to complete a mission or to fight in an engagement.

But his reverie took a sober turn. *Had* he known her fiancé? Had they fought alongside one another? Was he one of the men whose passing Colin had mourned? A man whose body Colin had helped to bury? He offered up a promise to a fallen brother in arms. *Whatever happens between us, I won't let her return to being a scullery maid. When we part, if we part, she will be well cared for.*

"Oh, la. Look at this." Jennie peered into the carriage with awe. Dressed as a field hand, with a smock top and full gathered pants, Jennie had tied her hair up under a straw hat. "I only rode in a carriage once, but then I sat on the outside back on top of the luggage. But this time . . . to be inside . . ." She turned away, and Colin lost the end of her sentence.

A moment later, Seth handed Lucy into the carriage, and Colin patted the seat beside him. But Lucy chose instead the backward-facing seat. He raised his eyebrow in question.

"As your nurse, I need to be able to watch you, to see when you tire . . ." Lucy began to explain.

"Here, Lucy." Seth held out the baby's rush basket. Lucy placed the rush basket on the forward-facing seat to Colin's right.

Colin kept himself pulled into the opposite corner, at a distance from the babe.

"I'm not convinced traveling so soon and with so little protection is the best solution." Aidan stood outside the open window beside Colin's door, wearing his least ducal clothing. "But it is your mission, not mine. I still believe you should accept more help."

Colin bristled slightly. "I have already accepted a great deal more help than I think would please Prinny. And as you said yourself earlier, it's a good plan."

"Of course it is." Sophia, wearing a drab servant's dress,

joined them and opened the door to offer Colin a proper goodbye. "Your brother simply wishes he could do more."

"I will send you news as I find it." Aidan put his hand on Colin's shoulder, and Colin covered his hand with his own.

"Can three play this game?" Seth patted Colin's knee. "Don't die, brother. Aidan will never forgive me for siding with you, if you do." Seth closed the door, then called back through the window. "And, Lucy, remember: you can always call on me when you tire of his moods."

Colin rolled the glass window up, while Lucy laughed.

Chapter Eleven

A mile from the tavern, in a secluded portion of road, Fletcher pulled the carriage to a stop, allowing Jennie to move inside the carriage. Jennie hopped in quickly, then pulled the basket into her side and peeked below the cloth covering the baby from view. "'E's sleepin'," she said with satisfaction. Any name they gave the infant would be only temporary, so they had told Jennie to pick a name she found appealing. Jennie had tried a dozen and rejected them before she decided on Sweet William, the name of her favorite flower.

"Well, I have somewhat 'ere to pass the time." Jennie fidgeted herself into a comfortable position before reaching into her knitting bag. Instead of the thick wool she had been knitting before, she produced three issues of the *Lady's Magazine*. "Any time a lodger leaves magazines, Nell lets me have 'em."

Colin stiffened and drew himself in more tightly. He said nothing, but from the look of pained recognition that passed fleetingly across his face, Lucy assumed the magazines must have been Marietta's.

"My lord, would you read to us?" Jennie turned to a page

marked near the back of one. "Even though it's a magazine for ladies, there is natural science and history and . . ."

"You wouldn't happen to have a *Sporting Magazine* in there would you?"

Jennie looked stricken. "None of the lodgers ever leaves those."

"I wonder why!" Lucy hoped to lighten Colin's mood. "Do you think sportsmen can't actually read?" But the joke fell flat.

Jennie held out the issue, open to an article on traveling in Europe.

Colin paled, but slowly held out his hand. A man who does his duty, even when it pains him, Lucy realized, even when he could snub a servant to avoid the discomfort. He looked at the title and read silently the first paragraph. "I have already read this one. Would it be acceptable, Jennie, to choose something else?"

"Oh, yes, sir." Jennie smiled broadly, at his consideration of her opinion. Another man of his rank and family would have merely chosen a different article.

"Given his wound, it will tire his lordship to read to us," Lucy intervened. "But perhaps we could solve the enigmas?"

"Yes, ma'am." Jennie nodded enthusiastically. "I like puzzles."

Colin handed the magazine back to Lucy, mouthing, *Thank you,* when the wet nurse buried her face in the pages.

"Then find some for us to solve together," Lucy instructed Jennie gently.

Jennie found the enigmas, rejected them all, and began searching through the other issues for better ones.

Lucy leaned forward as if to check on William in his basket, but took the chance to whisper in Colin's ear. "Have you already worked the enigmas?"

"No." He tilted his head to whisper in hers, brushing an

escaped curl back from her face, then tucking it behind her ear. She felt the sweetness of his touch in a tingle down her neck and spine. Then his hand was gone, and he leaned back against the seat. "She preferred the travel memoirs, or discussing court news: who was visiting whom, what marriages were expected, whose fortunes were on the ascent and whose were on the decline."

"Sounds dreadful." Lucy grimaced. She lifted the blanket, saw that William was still fast asleep, then leaned back in her seat.

He raised an eyebrow at her comment.

"I suppose it would be different if you knew the persons being discussed, but without that"—she shrugged—"it's all rather . . . vapid, don't you think?"

He smiled, that slow, knowing smile that made her heart warm. "But sometimes useful as information."

"If one were a Machiavel, intending to use that knowledge to gain or wield power." Lucy regarded him carefully, noting how the corner of his mouth tightened when his wound was hurting or how it twitched with amusement when he tried to hide a smile. "Are you a Machiavel, my lord, gaining information to profit from it?"

"Ah, a bluestocking after all!" Colin winked.

She was saved from response by Jennie's declaration that she'd found the best set of puzzles. Jennie held out the section for Colin's inspection. "Are these acceptable, my lord? Some of them look hard."

Colin took the issue from her hand with a kind smile. "I'm sure your choices will be fine. Should I begin?"

Jennie blushed. "Oh, yes, sir, of course, sir." Lucy was certain that, had they been standing, Jennie would have offered at least half a dozen curtsies.

Colin swept the blond hair from his eyes, "Let's see. Ah, here. Name a popular author in two syllables. First syllable is a valued metal. Second syllable is the second half of a worker of molten iron."

Jennie beamed. "Oh! I know the second word. Blacksmith. The second syllable would be just smith. But I don't know no poets, 'cept Bobby Burns."

"Well, let's think of valued metals . . ." Lucy prompted, avoiding Colin's eyes as he hummed softly the first bar of "O Good Ale."

"Silver, gold, copper. . . . Must be gold. It's the only metal with a one-syllable name." Jennie chewed on the nail of her index finger. "Gold-smith. Do you think that's right?"

"Goldsmith is a poet, so that's likely the solution." Colin looked at the cover of the magazine. "This is June. Do you have the July issue for the answers?"

Jennie's face fell. "No, sir, I only have the three, January, March, and June. We won't have answers to any of the puzzles."

"Then we will simply decide if we are right." Lucy patted Jennie's arm.

"Can we do that, miss?" Jennie looked distressed.

"Well, certainly, as long as our answer meets the criteria the original puzzle provides," Lucy reassured her.

Jennie squinted into the distance, thinking, then smiled broadly. "That seems fair."

"And let's make it more interesting, shall we?" Colin suggested. "We'll make it a contest. If I win . . ."

Jennie looked down at her hands, her knitting stopped. "I have nothing to offer, sir, but the cakes that Alice gave me as a present."

"But those are yours, Jennie," Lucy interceded, sending Colin a threatening glare. "No, we shall be a team, the two of us against Lord Somerville, and I will pay any penalty if we lose."

"Any penalty?" Colin's eyes grew bright with amusement and something else.

"Any penalty, if we lose." Lucy caught his eyes and the intention in them, but she turned to Jennie. "And we shan't lose, Jennie, shall we?"

"No, miss, we shan't. I am terrible good at puzzles."

"Then let's see." Lucy avoided looking anywhere but at Jennie. "Shall we do flowers, desserts, trees, vegetables, or towns? Jennie, you choose."

"Flowers, miss."

"The first enigma is 'a lady's name.'"

"Rose," Jennie answered without hesitation.

"Excellent. Your turn, Somerville." Lucy allowed herself to meet his eyes. Blue. Bottomless.

He offered her a slow smile and another wink. "Ah, this should be easy."

"Rose was not typical," Lucy warned, shaking her head as she silently read over the list. "Perhaps we should work one together before you begin."

"No, just read the first," Colin said smugly. "I'm sure I can decipher it."

"Well, then, here it is. 'An article of food and a vessel.'" Lucy raised her own eyebrow in challenge.

"Hmmm." Colin put his hand to his chin and frowned.

"Would you like me to read it again?" Lucy grinned at Jennie.

"No. But can you give me a hint. Food covers considerable ground. And I've never played *these* games before." Colin let the emphasis fall on the word *these*.

Lucy rolled her eyes at him, then turned to Jennie. "Do we wish to allow Somerville a hint?"

"Of course, miss." Jennie's hands moved in a steady rhythm, as she knitted a blanket for William. "But we get a hint to hold in reserve as well."

"That seems only fair," Colin conceded. "I like to hold things in reserve. What is my hint?"

"The food is something that comes from a cow." Lucy gave him a bright, devious smile.

"Milkweed!" Somerville announced proudly.

"No, sir," Jennie corrected, her attention focused on her knitting and not on her companions. "'Weed' is not a vessel."

"Cowslip?" Colin proposed with a shrug, letting his gaze rake across Lucy's body.

"Have you no better answers, Somerville?" Lucy shook her head, both at the answer and at his sensual invitation. "Jennie, can you solve it?"

"Oh, yes, miss." Jennie finished another row and shifted her yarn. "Buttercup."

"Excellent, Jennie. Now it's your turn. Here's the clue: 'Part of the body, a consonant, and comfort.'"

"Why couldn't I get that one?" Colin raised his hand in mock exasperation. "I'm good at body parts."

Both Lucy and Jennie ignored him.

"That's easy. Heartsease." Jennie beamed at her good luck. "My mother used to grow them each spring."

"Can I have an easier one?" Somerville leaned forward to take the magazine, but Lucy held it out of his grasp. Even so, his hand brushed her knee and lingered.

"How about this one?" She moved her leg out of his reach. "'Vessels and a vowel.'"

"Let's see. Vessels. Vessels are ships, so my possibilities are boat, canoe, bark, dinghy. . . ." He counted off the words on his fingers.

"It's a flower," Lucy reminded him. "Remember: they make the puzzles backward. They have a word, then they create the enigma for it. So, start from the flower names, not the clue. What flowers have names of vessels in them?"

Colin began to list flowers randomly. "Violet, rose, woodbine, clematis, poppy, cornflower, pansy, sunflower, iris."

Jennie snickered.

"Would you like to concede, sir?" Lucy offered, placing

her hand on his leg, and feeling a surge of warmth in her belly.

"Concede?" He looked at her hand, then met her eyes. "Why?"

"You named the flower, but did not realize you had the answer." Lucy removed her hand to her lap.

"How do you know I named it?" Colin objected. "We have no solutions."

"Yes, sir, but both Miss Lucy and I have washed dishes," Jennie interjected.

He thought back over his list. Which flower could also be a dish? Dishes. Pans. Pans plus a vowel to be a flower. "Pansy? Surely not! That's silly. . . ."

"Yes, it's a vessel and a vowel," Lucy indulged him, patting his leg as if he were an obedient dog. "Would you prefer some other game?"

"Perhaps." Colin rubbed his face with one hand. "What do they offer?"

"Anagrams," Jennie read aloud the next section heading. "The category is painters and sculptors."

"Then let's do those." Colin brushed his hair back from his forehead. "My experience with flowers seems to be sadly lacking. But I get to choose for you." He held his hand out for the magazine. "Here, this one is perfect: 'I call my angel O." He mouthed, My angel, to Lucy.

Jennie produced a slip of paper from her reticule and a stub of a pencil and began to tease out words from the riddle. Within minutes, however, her face turned an awkward green. "Oh dear, Miss Lucy, I feel somewhat ill."

"Put the paper away, and look out of the window." Lucy reached in her bag and pulled out a small handkerchief. In it was a handful of freshly picked peppermint leaves. "Chew on this, but don't swallow. It should help to soothe your stomach."

Lucy turned her attention wholly to the wet nurse,

leaving Colin to wonder what painter's name could be made from *I call my angel O.*

It had been hell with a queasy Jennie in the carriage.

They had tried everything. Sit facing forward. Sit facing backward. Windows open, windows closed. Beside the window, in the middle, beside the other window. Nothing worked.

She apologized profusely and constantly. Then, when William awoke, she felt uncomfortable feeding him with Colin present. Since they could not stop the carriage safely, Colin covered his face with a handkerchief and turned his body to face the wall. Within minutes, his side ached.

Finally, miraculously, Jennie had fallen asleep.

Since neither he nor Lucy wished to risk waking her, neither spoke.

Lucy had ended up where she had begun—across from him, facing back. And he'd spent the last two hours watching her with lidded eyes, and imagining the best way to remove her clothes. But he'd learned one thing at least during their ride: Lucy's tenderness to others was as natural to her as his own stubbornness was to him.

Chapter Twelve

The hunting lodge was more than three hundred years old, a survivor of the Catholic suppression. During the Commonwealth, the hereditary owners had been killed and the house seized by the government; during the Restoration it had been bestowed on one of the king's favorites, who had never taken up residence, and then passed through the hands of several of his heirs without one even investigating the property. Eventually, in the last generation, the father of one of Colin's associates had won it in a bet.

Lucy had suggested—and Fletcher and Bobby had agreed—that, for the porter's sake, she and Colin should pretend to be lovers, a man and his mistress, escaped to the country for a tryst. It was a situation entirely to his liking. He would have to—for the sake of the ruse—keep her close. And he already knew he couldn't get enough of her, of her bright mind or the feel of her lips.

Before they approached the caretaker's gate, Jennie moved back to the outside seat with Fletcher. Inside the carriage, they covered the sleeping infant's basket with a blanket.

Finally, he was alone with Lucy, but with no time to enjoy the privacy. "We need enough of a distraction that he lets us pass by quickly without discovering the child. Could you set the basket under your skirt a little to hide it from view?"

"Would this do?" She moved toward him, then crawled into his lap, her legs on either side of his hips. She pulled her skirt free so that it covered their legs, then undid the pins in her hair, so that it fell around her face in heavy curls.

He felt himself stiffen and hoped she would not notice. "I suppose we can make it work." He cleared his throat. "But, when he stops us, turn your face away from his lamp, as if you wish not to be recognized. That will protect you from view."

When the gatekeeper came to the carriage door, Lucy turned her face away, but began kissing his neck on the far side, mumbling in an accent he had not heard, but which sounded decidedly lower class. "Come on, guv, ya promised Ivy a bit o' fun."

She began to unbutton his shirt, laughing as if she were drunk. He groaned without thinking.

The gatekeeper turned away quickly, opened the gate, and let them through.

Lucy looked up, smiling, then slid off his lap onto the seat beside him. "I doubt if he'll bother us now. Did you see the look of horror on his face?"

"I doubt if we will see him all week. And if we do, I find it hard to believe he will dare look either of us in the eye."

"Perfect. Exactly what we wanted."

They waited in the carriage while Fletcher and Bobby lit the lamps in the entry; then they hurried Jennie and William through the door. Colin was tired, but wished not to show it. The first priority was to settle the baby safely into his new lodgings.

In the middle of the house, hidden in the twists of the

staircase, was a well-appointed priest hole, exceptional for its size. One entered a small room large enough for two men to sleep comfortably, and then climbed a ladder to a platform wide enough for a third man as well. With rock walls, the hiding place was silent, conveying sound neither from the house nor to it.

For security's sake, Colin decided that it would be best for Jennie and her charge to spend their nights secure in the hole, safe from any intruders. To enter the hole, one walked into the back of the large fireplace in the main hall. Once a fire was lit and the stones warmed with the heat, the hole was impossible to enter. A moderate fire gave the hiding priest warmth, but a larger fire or one maintained too long would suffocate anyone in the hiding place. Colin showed Jennie the escape route and made her practice the trick until Fletcher and Bobby returned from one of the bedrooms with several blankets to make a soft mattress. As soon as they set the blankets onto the platform, making Jennie and the baby a safe haven, Jennie climbed the ladder, and they passed William up to her. Fletcher and Bobby took the bottom portion of the room.

But that decision had pleasant consequences. Once the door was sealed behind their companions, Colin and Lucy would not be interrupted easily. Often, Colin and his men stayed in the two priest holes, invisible to anyone chancing on the lodge. But to give their story of being lovers credence, he'd decided to make use of the bedrooms.

With their companions settled for the night, Colin raised the lantern to show Lucy the way to their rooms on the second floor. The walk was dark, and she tucked herself under his arm, both to share the lantern and to give him more stability on the stairs. Somehow, she seemed to know when his side ached.

"I've chosen rooms at the end of this hall. They share an interior door, but as long as the porter stays in his lodge, we should have little need for additional subterfuge. But we should leave the inner door unlocked, in case you or I have need of the other."

He opened the door and showed her the accommodations. A hearty fire—lit by Fletcher—burned warm in the gate. Lucy's bag sat on a low bench near the dressing table. The fire was the only light.

"Let me take off my overcoat, then I'll light your lanterns." But as he reached his arm back to release it from the coat, his face—even in the near darkness of the room—blanched white.

"There's no need. Besides, you are in pain. Let me help you." Lucy began to help him remove his coat, and his thoughts turned to the last time she had removed his clothes. "Let me care for you while we're here. A field nurse for a wounded soldier."

"All this way, I was desperate to move, to get out of the carriage, but now, I find I'm already worn." His voice carried his frustration. "Yet I have no desire for more sleep. All I've done for the last week is sleep."

She looked around the room. "I have an idea. Rest here." She pulled the chaise in front of the fire and led him to it. Following her instruction, he collapsed into the chaise.

She pulled an armchair to his side and took his hand in hers. They sat before the embers of the fire for some time, talking at first, but soon lapsing in a companionable silence. At some point, Lucy came to lie in front on him on the chaise. Her back against his chest, they lay next to one another watching the fire and commenting irregularly on their past lives. They focused primarily on their shared experiences on the Continent, not the war itself, but more human things, the taste of bread from the portable iron stoves, the color of the water in winter, the sound of the troops waking in the morning.

He'd wished to sleep, but he found himself unwilling to

give up these moments of peace. He'd had so little peace since Brussels, but he pushed the thoughts aside. He would not let anything ruin this respite.

She had fallen asleep before him, and he lay behind her, smelling the hint of her soap, the scent of lemons, and he wondered how she found lemons out of season.

Chapter Thirteen

The next morning, he awoke when the sun was already high in the sky. Lucy had at some point covered him with a blanket and drawn the curtains tight, but he could see a strong line of bright sun on the floor beneath the curtains.

His side ached, but somewhat less than it had the day before. He moved gingerly, testing how far he could reach without pain. His shirt untucked, he adjusted his braces. The motion made his wound ache, but not with the breath-stealing pain as it had before. He regarded his coat but thought better of putting it or his boots on. Luckily, he still wore his socks—or his feet would simply have to be cold.

He knew the house well, so he could have found the kitchen without trouble. But the smell of bread baking led him easily on. He arrived in time to see Lucy, her hair tucked unsuccessfully into a maid's bonnet, using a peel to remove two loaves of bread from an oven built into the fireplace.

Fletcher and Bobby were seated at one end of a large harvest table, eating a small feast: eggs, a portion of ham, cheese, apples, and pears.

"Did we bring this much food with us? I would have expected the larders to be empty."

"They were." Lucy set the bread on the table. "When you said we'd be here for a day or two, I remembered how easy it was to miscalculate the length of a siege."

He raised an eyebrow.

Lucy shrugged. "I asked Nell to include some staples."

"What staples?"

She motioned at the smaller basket—"Flour, leavening, sugar, salt, coffee"—then at the larger—"fruit, eggs, milk, cheese, butter, ham, and beer."

"I'm afraid to know how much my portion of the bill was. It was likely exorbitant."

"Yes." She smiled, a dazzling smile that caught his breath. "But we won't starve."

Colin began to object, to say he hadn't brought her along to act the servant. But Fletcher interrupted him.

"You could do worse, sir. These are some of the best eggs I have had in some time."

Bobby chimed in. "And the bread, sir. Have some of the bread. And Miss Lucy says there will be biscuits later— with red currants, oats, and walnuts. Never tasted such a thing, but if Miss Lucy bakes it . . ." The boy grinned at Lucy adoringly.

"You should be careful, Bobby. If Cook discovers you've been unfaithful to her cooking, you might lose your kitchen privileges." Colin took an empty chair to Fletcher's right, as Lucy uncovered a plate set aside for him. "Where's Jennie?"

Fletcher answered first, "In the priest's hole with William. Girl says she feels safest there, a little warm cave of her own."

"Bobby took her a tray about an hour ago," Lucy added. "We decided you needed sleep more than food."

Fletcher pushed the loaf of bread across the table. "And

don't be worrying: the porter knows to guard the front gate now that you are having a 'house party.'" Fletcher winked at Lucy, and she flung an apple at him, which he caught deftly. "And me and Bobby have been walking the back and side all morning."

Colin took his first bite, then another. "If this is the sort of food you had during a siege, I wish I'd been with your regiment. Ours was hard tack and soda water." He liked the flush at her cheeks each time they complimented her. Who had valued her so little that easy compliments had such an effect? "I'm thinking of a walk in the gardens this afternoon. Care to walk with me?"

Before Lucy could answer, Fletcher raised his voice two octaves, teasing Colin with glee. "Oh, my dear sir, however can I repay the compliment of your company? I would be delighted, just delighted to stroll through the garden, clinging to your strong powerful arm. Perhaps I might even trip a little over some small twig so that you might have to crush me to your manly chest to keep me from falling and doing myself harm."

Lucy picked up another apple, letting it bounce in the palm of her hand threateningly.

"I don't mean you, miss. I'm only mimicking the young ladies 'his lordship' seems to attract—empty-headed things not worth the cost of their clothing."

Lucy leaned forward on the table, one arm bent forward in front of her body, the other holding the apple up to her mouth. She took a bite, the red flesh crunching beneath her teeth. Colin found himself unable to look away. "And does his lordship like such women?" She took another bite, meeting Colin's eyes as she ran her tongue across her lips to catch the juice of the apple.

Bobby answered quickly, "Only the pretty ones, miss. But none were as pretty as you, nor as smart."

Neither Bobby nor Fletcher seemed aware of the sensual dance between her and Colin. She looked like the temptress Eve in the garden, and Colin wished to follow her into any sin. She took one last bite; then she tossed the half-eaten apple to him. He caught it easily, then met her eyes and, with deliberate care, finished it. She did not look away.

Chapter Fourteen

The man known in the underworld as Charters sat planning his next move, and the next, and the one after that—moves as far out as his mind could strategize them. It was a complicated game, like chess but with money, commodities, and people as his pieces. Pawns, all of them—even the queen. He laid it all out, strategies and tactics, but never tactics without strategy.

He'd suffered a setback in the Wilmot affair, but the papers he'd sought had not been found by anyone else either. He had to assume after so many months that he was safe, his secret covered by the blood of the men he had killed. Lady Wilmot was safe from him as well, her alliance with Forster too dangerous a challenge.

He rubbed a coin between his fingers, a commemorative medal recognizing participation in some charity benefit. This one had been his brother's. A medal for wasting the estate's money in some foolish scheme or other. The outlay would have been acceptable if it had led to something: a new ally, a perception of generosity that could be taken advantage of later. But no, his brother had smiled on everyone indiscriminately, calling it *noblesse oblige*.

He liked the feel of the edge of the medal against his

fingers. It was a shame that the blood from his brother's body had long worn away. He'd enjoyed the reminder of how easily he'd deceived his family and the sheriff into believing his brother's death a tragic accident. He'd mourned well, he thought. Cain to his brother's Abel.

But for now, he waited. Over the last several weeks, his new crew of reprobates, thieves, and murderers had sold the forged banknotes they'd printed. His forging operation had allowed him to extend his reach into the deepest corners of the London hells. He could now count among his allies a range of criminals with skills he did not have himself. If he wished to manage the criminal world, he had made tremendous inroads.

With the money from his forging enterprise, he had generated enough capital to buy the shipping partnership he'd needed. Now, he—or rather, one of his identities—held controlling interest in a fine merchant fleet. He laughed to himself. Others might find it a bad time to go into shipping, but he'd found it a lucrative proposition. The time to advance was when all others were in retreat.

From his first attempt in shipping, he had garnered enough profit to open a tavern and a small gaming establishment for sailors and wharf men. He'd named it the Blue Heron. Run by his trusted lieutenant Flute and specializing in games of chance, the enterprise was already turning a nice profit.

He moved a nautical chart to the top of the papers in front of him. He'd drawn a line from London to Lisbon. A week ago, his favorite ship, the *Clytemnestra*, had left, carrying beads and textiles. Today or tomorrow, at Lisbon, his cargo would be moved from the British *Clytemnestra* to a ship with an indeterminate nationality. Some would call it a privateer, but he preferred to think of it as a ship of international trade.

He drew another line from Lisbon to Benguela, one of

the states of Nouvelle-Guinèe on the southeastern coast of Africa. At Benguela, his beads and textiles would be sold to Portuguese slavers. Since the British had voted to abolish the slave trade a dozen years ago, he wouldn't risk being caught with human cargo. But no law kept him from providing the slavers with the goods they needed to purchase slaves in the African interior or prohibited him from buying goods produced by slaves. It was a precious distinction, he knew, but one that suited his moral code.

He drew another line, this time from Brazil, tracing the route of the Portuguese ships coming to meet his in Benguela. When the slavers arrived from Brazil, his captain would buy their goods: cocoa, sugar, and coffee. The British Navy loved cocoa, treating it as an alternative to rum.

While waiting for the Portuguese to arrive from Brazil, his captain had orders to buy other cargo: cannabis and opium. He looked to the right of Nouvelle-Guinèe to the country on its western border: Ethiopia. Comprising most of the center of the southern African continent and extending as far to the western coast, Ethiopia had proved the bane of Napoleon, tempting his soldiers with cannabis.

He drew a final line on the map, from Lisbon around the southern coast of England and Cornwall to Wales. The *Clytemnestra* would travel to the Welsh coast, where another of his identities had rented a rural estate with a fine isolated cove, protected from observation. There, he could move the cargo quietly.

But his lease was up at the end of the year—and he would need another secluded cove to land his goods.

Marner's land.

He needed to find the heiress, then find a way to end up with that piece of land. But he had three months yet to work it out.

Chapter Fifteen

With the porter watching the front entrance, and Fletcher and Bobby alternating between walking the grounds and guarding Jennie, Colin positioned himself to watch the other approaches to the house. He didn't explain the measures to Lucy, and she didn't ask, grown used—he assumed—to not knowing why or how or when from her years in the camps.

He chose as his watch station the weapons room at the end of the second floor. It gave him full vistas of the back and side of the house.

Overlooking the west yard where the kitchen garden still grew under the keeper's care, he could look through one large window and a smaller round one. Overlooking the back yard into the wilderness, he could watch from two large windows or from the four petal-shaped ones. With leaded glass, each of the four petals opened individually to allow a breeze through—or a gun for protection. At each set of windows, he had set up a stool to lean against and a pair of loaded pistols on a short table.

When Lucy arrived with tea, the weapons room was empty, and she took the occasion to investigate.

The room stored the guns and other sporting equipment a group of hunters might need for a week's retreat. A large cabinet held the small guns, each with its own case and loading kit; on the wall hung the larger guns alongside each one's powder horn. The drawers of a short cabinet below held powder and paper-wrapped cartridges in carefully labeled sections.

The room held more than forty firearms. It read as a history of British weaponry, or at least British weaponry from the American and Napoleonic Wars. She named the guns as she recognized them: a breech-loading Ferguson rifle from the American Wars; Paget carbines from the light cavalry in the Waterloo campaigns; muskets from the East India Company.

She stopped before the six Baker rifles, muzzle-loading, each one accompanied by horns of fine-grain gun powder and a supply of paper-wrapped cartridges. She ran her fingers across the fine wood graining of the closest rifle. She remembered James, his green uniform for the Ninety-fifth Rifle Regiment scuffed and dirty, carefully cleaning his Baker. She turned away from the memory.

On the opposite wall were the swords and other weapons, and in between were the more historic pieces: a suit of armor, beaten and rusted (or at least she hoped it was rust); a battle-axe; and other weapons dating as far back as the Middle Ages.

Well, if we grow bored, we could start a war with the local farmers. She returned to the wall of swords, picking up a light cavalry officer's sword, much like the one of her father's she'd had to leave behind at her great-aunt's house.

She held the sword up before her face. *En garde.* She was caught for a moment in a memory of her father, during one of the endless sieges of her youth, wearing the leather reinforced overalls of undress, calling her his "little swordsman" as they danced around one another. She could still hear his instruction: "Body upright! Head up! Shoulder easy. Wrist opposed to the sword. That's it. Turn your left side in. Now thrust. Good girl. Watch for the counter-thrust. Keep the pommel in line with your temple. Good girl. Now again." Instinctively she took her stance, thrust, and parried, pretending once more she was fencing with her father.

At the sound of footsteps, she replaced the sword. But when they left the hunting lodge, if she could, she'd take one of the pistols and some powder with her.

Colin smiled when he saw her.

"I thought you might be hungry. I brought you the last bits of Alice's fruitcake and some tea," she said.

"I am. Just a moment, and I'll make us a seat."

He pulled a game table from against the wall behind his watch station, then two chairs. He positioned the whole thing where he could still survey the lawn. She met him at the table, placing the tray nearest the seat he held out for her. She tried not to notice how well his leggings fit his form.

He bowed as if they were at a ball. "May I offer you a seat, my lady?"

She laughed. "Why, thank you, kind sir." She offered him her best deep curtsy.

He took her hand and lifted her out of the curtsy. Then, holding her hand out in front of him as if he were leading her into a dance, he directed her into the chair.

"Had I known we were to be so formal, I would have found a way to make weak lemonade and brought up some pieces of yesterday's bread with a thin veneer of butter," she said, pouring the tea into two mismatched cups.

"And I would have braved the crowds at Almack's to bring it to you." He lifted his cup to her in salute.

"I fear you would have had trouble finding me, dear sir. You forget: scullery maids would be in the kitchen."

"Ah, no, my lady, you are an officer's daughter whose beauty and graciousness on the fields of battle have attracted the attention of all London. The patronesses have sent me with this voucher." He pretended to withdraw a piece of paper from his pocket, and held it out for her. "To honor your service to the men of England on the fields of Waterloo."

She blushed, pretending to take it. "Am I to be Cinderella then? Wiping the soap off my hands and waiting for my fairy godmother to transform my working dress into a ball gown?"

He looked at her with unfeigned desire. "Has she not already arrived? Are you not the most beautiful woman in the whole assembly rooms? Your dress sparkles with the light of a thousand stars—to suit your nature. Lucy—Lucia, saint of light—opposite faces of the same coin."

"Well, in that case, if we were at a ball, you would find me standing in front of a window, hoping to get even the faintest hint of a breeze. Or in the garden with my abigail, trying to escape the crush." She placed his cup on a saucer and handed it across the table.

"No, you'll be at a table in the gallery, fending off your suitors, while I"—he reached out and broke off a piece of Alice's cake—"will be enjoying the refreshments." He drank his tea.

"You would leave me with a dozen suitors?"

"Yes, but you are bored. You have seen me at the refreshment table, and you are waiting for me to approach and ask you to dance."

"Ah, I see. I suppose I am also holding the next dance open for you."

"Of course. Our eyes have met across the room, and I have signaled I will come to you. What piece are the musicians playing tonight? I don't recognize it."

"Ah, I think it's . . . no, it can't be. . . . I believe, sir, they are playing a waltz. Scandalous." She lifted her chin and turned her face slightly away from him as if mortified.

"Dance with me."

She raised her wrist to consult an imaginary dance card. "Oh dear, I've made a mistake, I fear that this dance is already taken . . . by one of the men actually paying attention to me, not just watching me from the safety of the refreshments table."

He stood and stepped to her side of the table. He held his hand out. "Dance with me."

"If you insist." She offered her hand, and he held it while she rose.

"I do." He held her hand out formally as he led her into the large open space in the center of the room. Then he turned to face her.

"To what are we dancing?" She felt the warmth of his hand on her waist. She'd waltzed at the ball at Lady Richmond's before Waterloo, in a dress borrowed from one of the British families in Belgium.

James had been with her, dancing every dance, softly repeating the beats of the steps under his breath. She'd thought it sweet, the look of such concentration on his face. He'd kissed her before he'd left with the rest of the men in his regiment. The last time she'd seen him alive.

"Mozart. Can't you hear it?" His voice drew him back to the present. She opened her eyes, and that glittering ballroom of long ago disappeared in the gentle arms of the man before her. Colin, not James. This was a new memory, one to cherish for the rest of her life.

He began to sing in a rich baritone, a wordless tune. *Da-da-dada, da-da-dada, da-da-da.*

She listened to his voice run gently over the melody. She closed her eyes and just listened, the smoothness of his voice, his sense of the pitch and time of the song. She knew it, one of the country songs drawn from Mozart's works.

His hand began to lead her in the dance, moving her body by the slight pressure of his palm when he wanted her to move backward, of his fingers when he wanted her to move forward. He led firmly but gently. He was an easy dancer, in control, his every intention conveyed by the silent guidance of his fingers.

It was an elegant movement, not too slow not too fast. Just enough to focus on the feel of his hands, the closeness of his body, the clean scent of him.

They waltzed around the square of the room, learning the rhythm of each other's bodies. She expected him to falter either in the singing or in the dance, but he did not. In each, he was consummate.

Halfway around, he began also to turn them with each set of steps. Then he began to turn her in his arms, twirling her out, then stepping to meet her in the turn. Turning her out, meeting her again.

He never missed a step. But she felt his arm tense against its own weight, and she saw his face grow pale.

"You grow tired," she said, watching his face. "Perhaps we can finish our dance another time."

His eyes met hers, determined, and he shook his head.

He spun her away from him and back. As he drew the song to a close, he spun her out one last time, and as the song ended, he stepped closer, pulling her tight against his chest.

She paused for a moment looking up into his face, seeing his unconcealed desire. She wanted him to kiss her, wanted to feel the warmth of his lips against her own. Her belly tightened with expectation. But she was his nurse. She pulled away, never dropping his hand, and led him back to his chair.

"I see, dear sir, that you are an experienced dancer."

"How else would I have the most beautiful woman in the room all to myself without raising the ire of her guardians?"

"So, you have done this before?" She refilled his teacup and watched his face regain its color.

"Never to such good success, and never before left so much alone by the other dancers. I like this place: no one cuts in."

"Then we will have to dance here again."

"We will."

She placed the largest piece of fruitcake on the plate. "Butter?"

"No. Let's save it for the stale bread you promised me." He watched her eyes focus out the window and her expression turn from playful to pensive. "What is that faraway look, my sweet? Do I need to be more attentive to keep your interest?" He reached across the table to touch her hand.

"I was just thinking that I can't remember when I've ever had such a lovely time." She brought her eyes back to his. "I'm storing up memories, you see, of you, for a cold day when we have parted, and I find myself lonely."

"There's no reason to store them up, my star. I have promised to stay with you until you send me away."

Chapter Sixteen

Later that afternoon, after she finished preparing food for their dinner, Lucy set up several cushions in a corner of the weapons room to be near Colin as he watched. She had brought several possibilities from the lodge's meager library, and she spent the next hour reading him another set of chapters from *Castle of Otranto*.

> *"Tell me, what reason did the Princess give thee for making her escape? Thy life depends on thy answer."*
> *"She told me," replied Theodore, "that she was on the brink of destruction, and that if she could not escape from the castle, she was in danger in a few moments of being made miserable for ever."*

"Stop," Colin ordered.

Lucy froze.

Colin peered out the window, a movement near the trees drawing his attention. While he watched, two men left the shadows of the wood to stand at the edge of the yard. Their faces were obscured, whether from distance or disguise.

"Stay here. Men in the garden." He picked up his pistols as he ran from the room.

Fletcher was sitting in the hall, carving a piece of wood, looking every inch the part of the bored servant dragged to the country.

"Men in the yard. Protect William."

Fletcher moved with surprising speed for a man in his sixties, toward the secret entrance to the priest hole.

Colin slipped out of the house using the kitchen entrance. The door had the most protected entrance, a hedgerow separating the main yard from what had once been a kitchen garden. He tried to keep out of sight, using the trees of the yard and the hedges of the garden to obscure his progress. He walked only on the grass, not on the stone paths themselves, to keep his movements from being heard. One pistol in his hand, the other tucked in the waist of his pants at his front.

He looked over his shoulder at the gallery window to gauge how distant he was from where he had spotted the intruder. Lucy had moved from the window into the dark of the room. Good.

The lodge was set in the middle of a clearing, woods on all sides. From the house to the woods in any direction was not more than the length of the ducal carriage, but the carriage was in the stables, hidden from view. He had only a few more steps before he would have to leave the protection of the kitchen garden's high hedges.

There had been two men, he was sure of it, with kerchiefs around their faces. Even if they were only poachers, the penalty for poaching could be death. So even if they had nothing to do with the Marietta affair, they could still be dangerous if challenged. As Colin grew closer, he could hear their voices.

"Got me a boy, Jock. No livery, but well fed by the look of him." The first intruder—stocky and bearded—held Bobby by the neck. "What do you want me to do with him?"

"Bring him here. The house was supposed to be empty.

If there's a boy, there's likely others." The second intruder—
a tall man with red hair—stared at the house. "We might
need a little bribery."

Colin moved to where he could see Bobby through a less
densely leaved portion of the hedge. He appeared unhurt,
but he was being pulled along by a large bearded man with
a stocky build and a broad torso. As they walked past on the
other side of the hedge, Colin could see that the man had
two pistols, one strapped to his belt, the other pressed to the
side of Bobby's head. He couldn't see the second man.

"Quit strugglin, boy, or I might lose my grip on this trigger, and then your friends wou'd be clearing up bits o' your
brain from now till Whitsunday," the bearded man threatened.

Bobby quit struggling as he and the bearded man moved
out of sight. *If we live through this*, Colin thought, *I'll teach
Bobby some tricks to use next time.* Next time. He hoped
they would have a next time.

The two men were in front of him on the house side of
the kitchen garden, some distance from the house. Before
him, the paths came to a cross. There the path down the side
of the kitchen garden intersected with the path coming from
the main portion of the house. From that intersection, the
main path extended through the kitchen garden to the
woods on one side, and across the back of the house to
the woods on the other.

As he crossed the intersection, he could be seen down
the long main path. If he could just pass the break in the
hedge without being seen, he could circle behind them.
Having found Bobby, they might now expect opposition
from the house, but not likely from the forest they had just
left. The hedge on his side of the opening, however, was
dense, and he couldn't get a clear view of whether the men
were still close by or had moved farther away. He could
stick his head around the edge and hope no one would see,

or he could just leap across the path. He risked exposure either way.

He chose the path of greater discretion. He tucked his head around the side just enough to see down the opening. He saw nothing. He leapt across. Nothing. He moved forward again, gauging his movements in relation to the windows of the house.

At the end of the hedge, he would be at the bottom of the kitchen garden and could turn into the main yard some distance from the woods. But he would be farther from where he'd seen the men with Bobby.

Unfortunately, at the next intersection, he found the first poacher waiting for him, Bobby before him with a pistol to his head. Before he could respond, the second poacher came from behind him and, pulling his arms back, restrained him. The flash of pain made his eyes see white. He wanted to struggle, but he would not risk Bobby, at least not twice on the same mission.

"This isn't my land." Colin would have to rely on his wits, though he knew from their position, they could be seen easily from the lodge windows. "I'm here on the largesse of the landowner. I have no concern with whatever game you trap or take. Let the boy return to the house."

"He saw my face," the bearded man objected and pressed the pistol against Bobby's temple.

"He's a boy," Colin soothed. If the men were assassins, he needed to discover it.

"A boy's as good a witness as any other in a trial for transportation or execution," the man restraining him said.

"We are guests at the lodge," Colin said, hoping he was giving Fletcher time to protect the child. "Here for a day or two, then home. We have no reason to be concerned with your business."

"But we have reason to be concerned with yours."

"In what way?" Colin waited to hear that these were the men who had attacked them before.

"The lodge has a fine set of plate and weapons, or so we've heard. We'd like them . . . all of them. That means, you see, it's unfortunate that you and the boy decided to visit here this week," the bearded man explained. "Gives us no choice."

Moving his pistol from Bobby's head, the robber leveled his gun at Colin. Colin realized he'd failed once more. Now, they would all die.

If he were lucky, Fletcher would be in the priest hole with Jennie and the babe. But Lucy was unprotected, and she wouldn't have time to hide. He hadn't shown her the second hole or how to get into it.

He prayed she had ignored him and gone to hide with Fletcher. And he prayed that the men wouldn't start a fire in the main hall. It would be a cool night. A small fire was no danger, but a blazing one would heat the rooms behind it and suffocate those hiding in the priest hole.

He felt despair and a bone-deep regret. Why hadn't he seized his opportunity to take Lucy to his bed and show her the pleasure he could offer?

He started to struggle, but stopped. If she were watching, at least she would see him die bravely and know to hide. If she could. If she had time.

As in the carriage, the gun leveled at him was too close to miss. All he needed to do was stand still while the ball dropped and ignited. A gun cracked, and he waited to feel the ball. But instead, the poacher flinched, sending a second shot humming past Colin's head. The poacher fell to the ground, writhing in pain and releasing Bobby.

"Run!" he cried, as he twisted from the second poacher's grasp and began to fight him.

Another shot rang out, and he heard the bore of the bullet pass him by. Another shot fired soon after. How Fletcher was reloading that fast, he didn't know, but he also didn't care. All he needed was to give Bobby time to get to safety and dissuade the robbers—by whatever means.

Another shot. And another. From the numbers of shots fired, it sounded like the house held a full party, and each one was standing in a window shooting.

Thank God for Fletcher, though he'd given him a direct order to protect Jennie and William. He could hardly regret him disobeying it, but he'd have to berate him for choosing Colin's safety over Jennie and the infant's.

He twisted the second poacher's arm until he felt it dislocate. The poacher began to howl in pain. Then Colin knocked him behind the head, felling the big lug to the ground, unconscious.

He had only a few minutes. He called to Bobby, who was hiding in the trees, to get a rope from the carriage. They tied the poachers tightly. There was no way to deliver them to the local magistrate without revealing their presence, but Fletcher could drive the men to the porter's lodge, and from there, the porter could deliver them to the appropriate liaison of the Home Office. The men might not die—because that would attract too much attention—but Colin was sure that they would find themselves on the next boat of transported criminals and poor.

Fletcher came from the house accompanied by Bobby. "Is this all of them, sir?"

"Yes, I believe so. They didn't sound like they had any more accomplices.

"Should we check the woods?" Fletcher searched the first poacher's pockets.

"Yes. Or at least the remainder of the grounds," Colin directed. "We now at least know that violence unrelated to the child is possible, even here so far into the woods."

"Aye." Fletcher began to walk away to collect the porter. But Colin called him back. The older man never liked compliments or compensation. But saving his life was too great an obligation to leave unnoticed.

"Fletcher, that was a great shot. I'm not sure I could have made it. And not from the distance of the house, with a rifle unused for months."

"What shot?" Fletcher looked confused. "I made sure Miss Jennie was locked up and safe, then I came running to help you when I heard the firing."

Colin looked back at the house. From the angle, the shot had to come from the second floor. At one of the petal windows, he saw a reflection and the bore of a gun sticking out unobtrusively.

"Can you handle these men?"

"Sure, especially as trussed as you have left them for me."

"Then I must check on Lucy." He walked, then ran to the house, fearing what he might find and wondering how she had made the shot.

When he arrived back in the gunroom, Lucy was seated at the table where they had enjoyed tea the day before. Her forehead rested, wearily, against her hand.

A row of rifles lay on the floor, each one having been shot to protect him. A long rifle, nearly six feet in length, was supported on a low table, propped by books to create the appropriate angle. She looked serious, severe, and worn to exhaustion.

"Is he dead?"

"No, just wounded. He should live."

"I didn't want to kill him." She looked pleadingly into his eyes. "But you and Bobby were in danger."

"They would have killed us." He hugged her to his side as she buried her face in his clothes. "Where did you learn to shoot like that?"

She was silent for some minutes before she answered. But then she pulled back from his side and wrapped her arms around her chest. "I learned to shoot my mother's pistol when I was young, perhaps seven or eight. And since I had a talent for it, my father taught me to fire a flintlock when I was nine or ten. I became a curiosity. The men in the regiment treated me as a sort of mascot; they taught me tricks . . . how to shoot a penny in the air. Periodically, they would even make a little money off it, betting the new recruits that they couldn't outshoot me. During the sieges, the men practiced firing. In part, it was to remind those behind the walls that the troops were outside, waiting."

"To make the inhabitants fearful."

She nodded, one hand absently rubbing a circle in her elbow. "The men had rifled most of the guns to increase their accuracy, but it was still almost always a surprise to see what they hit. During the sieges it became almost a sort of game between the battalions, to see what one could hit at increasingly impossible distances. But as the sieges wore on, the men decided it would be amusing to teach me to shoot long distances."

"That doesn't explain today. That wasn't the shooting of someone taught to fire for amusement."

"No." She nodded agreement. "But at Badajoz, we shared the camp with the Ninety-fifth Regiment."

"Ah, the sharpshooters." Aidan had served at Badajoz; her story would be easy to confirm, if Colin wished.

"They had Bakers." She pointed to the rifles on the floor. "They took longer to load than the muskets, but they were far more accurate and at greater distances. The riflemen in the Ninety-fifth could shoot a man off the city walls. One day, they staged a competition with my father's men. The hospital was quiet, so I went to watch. It was pretty, in a way: the green uniforms of the sharpshooters—the French called them 'grasshoppers'—next to the scarlet of the infantry. The men were laughing, setting up more and more distant targets. At some point, one of my father's men joked that any man could shoot as well as the grasshoppers with a good Baker at his side. Somehow the bet was amended to be 'any woman.' At some point, I can't remember quite how, my father's men wagered the grasshoppers that the nurse could shoot a flag flying from the battlements. The grasshoppers took the bet."

"I see where this is going. The wagers went high."

"Mostly for whiskey and tobacco," she explained.

"But I'm sure some money also passed hands."

"Of course." Her eyes focused on some point in the distance. "The grasshoppers were very accommodating. They loaded the rifle, told me how it aimed, explained all the tricks of shooting it. It was a calm day, so I didn't have to think about wind, only distance and how much the ball would drop before it hit. I hit the target. That's how I met my fiancé."

"He was one of the sharpshooters?"

She nodded, losing herself in memory. "It was his gun that I shot. Of course he took the credit for being a fine teacher. After that, I learned a great deal more about how to shoot. Later, he gave me my own gun. Sometimes we had intruders in the camps during engagements. There were always some who thought to steal or attack the hospital tent when the fighting moved a distance away. It was important to know how to defend oneself. I kept it under my shirt in the hospital tent, to protect the camp when the fighting had moved ahead of us. Sometimes, if the colonel needed a particularly tough shot, he'd call on me. I thought I'd never have to do that again." Her hands and voice began to shake.

"I'm glad you could. My life depended on it . . . possibly all our lives." He kissed her hair and stroked her back, until Fletcher called for him from the stairs.

She closed her eyes, then opened them and met his gaze. "Tonight."

"What about tonight?

"I don't want to sleep alone."

He stroked her hair. "If you do not wish to, my darling, you won't."

For dinner that evening, Fletcher and Bobby wished to hold a celebration, and Jennie even ventured from her retreat.

Bobby was recounting how he had stumbled across the men and been captured, both men praising Lucy's unexpected skill. "You saved us all, Miss Lucy," Bobby kept repeating, as if still surprised by the fact that he was alive. "You should have seen it, Jennie, both men on the ground, one bleeding something fierce. She saved us all." Jennie and Bobby—separated in age by only a handful of years—had grown into close confidants in the past few days, Bobby spending most of his time, when he wasn't on watch, in the priest hole with her, both telling stories to while away the time.

But with each recounting of the day's adventures, Lucy's face grew more and more haunted. And when Jennie and Bobby declared they would wash the evening's dishes, Lucy withdrew early.

As Jennie and Bobby began to clear the table, Fletcher—drawing upon their years of silent communication in the camps—had motioned with his eyes that Colin should follow her. But Colin had shaken his head slightly, refusing the suggestion. She was shaken and distraught, and he did not wish to impose on her. Even so, he could not keep his thoughts from turning to her, to her plea that she not sleep alone. By the end of the evening, when he was finally able to retire, his body was taut with desire.

Yet when he reached their bedrooms, no light shown from below her door to show she had waited for him, and the door adjoining their rooms was shut.

His side was mending well, testimony in part to Lucy's

skill. Though it still ached, the wounds had knit firmly closed. He stripped to his drawers, chest uncovered, and lay in bed, hands behind his head, trying to distract himself by reviewing the next steps in their plans to move William to Brighton.

When the moon was high in the night sky, he head Lucy cry out in alarm. He was through the door adjoining their rooms in an instant. From the light at the window, he could see that she was in the throes of a nightmare.

She whimpered, a plaintive sound, and called out the word, "No!" followed by a mournful moan and tears.

He moved to her side and, kneeling beside her bed, called her name, brushing the hair from her face, wiping the tears from her cheeks.

She sat up, startled, her eyes wide, her hands out before her as if deflecting a blow. Still not yet fully awake, she remained trapped in the violence of her dream.

He stood and sat on the bed beside her. Pulling her in against his chest, he cooed her name gently. Slowly, her body relaxed against his as she wakened. For several moments, she breathed into the circle of his arms; then, lifting her face to regard him, she searched his eyes.

He kissed her forehead, her hair, her temple, kissing away her fears and replacing them with desire. He brushed his hand over her hair. "I'm here. You are safe."

At the word *safe*, she seemed to make a decision. He could almost see it in her face. She pressed her lips against his softly, then firmly, then with greater passion. He met each change with equal fervor.

Raising one hand, she cupped the back of his head with her hand, holding his lips to hers. It was dark enough that he could not see her body in the depth of the bed, but with his hand, he could follow the line of her body, from her shoulders to her side, down to the curve of her hip. The curve of her hip. He realized it in an instant. All he felt were curves, not the square form he'd spent his last weeks imagining undressing.

He drew his hand back up, tracing the flare of her hips, the narrowness of her waist, the full swell of her breasts. Such efforts to conceal her shape suggested her troubles were more severe than he had realized, but he would think on it tomorrow. Tonight he would simply delight in the unexpected gift of her.

She tightened her fingers in his hair, pulling a handful of it slightly, just enough for a pleasurable tingle to travel down his spine; then she moved her hand slightly and repeated the action. Soon, all of his scalp and neck felt live with sensation. Her other hand caressed his shoulder to his chest, then slipped under his arm to his back, pulling his body closer to hers. She opened her mouth to his, teasing his lower lip with her tongue.

He set her away, just slightly, and looked into her eyes. "Yes?"

She turned her bottom lip under her upper teeth, then whispered, "Yes." He leaned into her mouth, pressing his lips against hers. He sucked her full bottom lip until he pulled the sweet edge of it between his teeth. Her lips opened, allowing him to trace her lips, then her teeth, with his tongue. She mirrored his actions, in a delightful game of give and take.

Caressing her body from hips to breast, he stopped to cup her breast with his hand, raising it slightly as he bent his head. He teased her breast with his tongue and teeth, biting the thin material of her shift and pulling it gently across the responsive skin.

At the middle of her chest, three small bows held her shift closed over her breasts. He pulled the first loose, then the second, then the third. Slipping his hand under the open bodice of the cotton, he felt her flesh, cool against his palm.

Such sweet skin, soft and clean, smiling of roses and of lemons.

She mirrored his actions, letting her hands drink in the feel of his skin at his chest and shoulders. Her caresses felt like cool fire, then only like fire when she leaned down to kiss his chest, trailing a line of lips and tongue from his collarbone to his navel, then lower. She brushed her hair—unbound—against his chest, using its silky length to caress and tease him. The sensation was exquisite. In the darkness, he closed his eyes, focusing on each spot where her body met his, feeling her moving down his body. Each inch lower tested his control, but he reveled in the sensations, at her pleasure in his body. He began to touch her once more, but she pushed his hand away. She tugged at his linen drawers, and he felt the first button release, then the second, freeing him from the restraint of his clothes. The moon at the window yielded a soft half light, and he watched her face. Her eyes closed, she focused on the explorations of her fingers.

Then she drew him fully out from beneath his drawers. With one hand, she gathered him—shaft and balls together—while, with the other, she began a slow tantalizing pattern, around and up and down. He allowed himself the pleasure for a moment, then put his hand on hers, stopping her.

"My turn," he whispered into her hair. He loosened the remaining fabric of her shift, and pushed it down from her shoulders to her waist. Leaning down, he took each breast in turn into his mouth. Ample breasts, filling his palm. He kissed a line from one areola to the other. Next, carefully avoiding the most sensitive spots, he nuzzled the skin between her breasts, using the light day's growth of hair on his cheeks to stimulate her skin. The sounds of her pleasure—soft moans, whispered encouragements—only made him wish to please her more. Never had he been so focused on the slow exploration of a woman's body. An accomplished lover, he had learned early where to touch to bring a woman the greatest pleasure. But now, with Lucy, he found he wanted to know how each inch of her skin responded, a complicated dance where he alternated the greatest pleasures with lesser ones, pushing her to her limits, only to pull back and let her passion subside, before beginning the pattern again with other sensitive spots. He wanted not just to bring her to climax but to prolong the journey itself. He made a sort of pilgrimage of her body, intent on touching, kissing, caressing each inch of skin.

With one foot still on the floor, he took only a minute to stand, let his drawers fall to the floor, then return to her. He leaned her back and tugged her shift out from under her hips, using her slight rise in assisting him as an occasion to press his palm against the sensitive join of her body. She gasped in pleasure. Her legs now free of the bedclothes and her shift, he left one hand's subtle pressure at her mound and used the other to skim the skin from her feet to her thighs, first on one leg then the next. He kept the pressure building at his palm, a rhythmic pulse, until she rose up and pulled him to her, drawing his body down to hers, raising her hips to meet his weight.

"I want you, on me, inside me."

Her words aroused him even further, tightening his body to its limits. But he still held himself back, taking his position at her entrance and pressing shallowly in, then withdrawing, only to press again.

She groaned in frustration, moving her hands from their caress at his back to grasp his buttocks, and pull him firmly against her body, grinding herself against his thickened flesh.

"Now," she whispered into his hair. "Please."

And he pushed himself into her slowly, drawing out each sensation until he was embedded in her warm heat to his hilt. Then he began his dance again, stoking her pleasure with firm thrusts, her hips joining him a game of parry and thrust. He felt her hips rise farther, her inner muscles clenching him more and more tightly, but he held himself back, waiting on her to find her release, wanting nothing more than to chase away her dreams and give her the richest pleasure he could offer. With each stroke, he made her his, claiming her most intimate places. He wanted to possess her thoroughly, wanted to make her never able to look on another man without wishing that man were him, wanted to make her shatter in his arms over and over and over again.

He increased his pace, the power of his thrusts, and she met each one. He had intended for this claiming to be slow, gentle, but the course of their passion had been too long denied, and she held him tighter and tighter against her hips, her fingers clenching his buttocks insistently.

He felt her tighten, and tighten, and then she was his. He met her in the climax of their passion, both breaking together into a mindless oblivion where there was only sensation.

Sometime later, his body still pressing down on hers, he tried to shift his weight, but she pressed her hips against him. "Stay."

At the word, his body tightened once more, urging him to take her again. She returned her hands to his buttocks and pressed down as she raised her hips to rub against him. "When you touch me, I can forget. Help me forget."

He pushed into her once more, and she smiled at the sensation. "Yes, that's perfect. More."

He met her eyes, and much as he would have liked to continue, he withdrew. "I did not expect. I'm sorry, Lucy, but I took no precautions. I will of course care for you and . . ."

She put her hand to his lips and covered his mouth. "I am barren. My fiancée and I . . . for years in the camps, we . . ." She shrugged. "I have long ago come to accept it."

He kissed her lips gently, to take away the sorrow in her

voice. "I would still care for you . . . and any child . . . my child."

"Don't wish for the impossible, Colin. I learned that long ago." She brushed the hair back from his face, then replaced her hands on his buttocks and pressed him into her body. "But we can enjoy the situation. What man doesn't want a mistress who will never inconvenience him with children? Who will never turn him away in his passion because she grows too large for pleasure?"

At the thought of Lucy, big with his child, Colin's passion bloomed fully, and he responded to the insistence of his hips with ardor.

"See: already you comprehend the benefits. I can feel you harden inside me. And I am ready for you again."

He didn't correct her, just let her take pleasure in his body. The light from the window had grown more insistent, and he could now see more of her. But he wanted to see all of her.

He held her hips against his and rolled her on top of him. "Then take your pleasure, my lady. I am here to serve. See me as your concubine, for you are already the master of me."

She laughed, a rich delighted sound. And she sat up on his hips, revealing her breasts and belly to his sight. "I've always wanted . . ." She blushed.

He was puzzled for only a moment. "To be on top?"

"James preferred . . . we . . . How can I be shy when . . . ?" She clenched her muscles, and he moaned.

"If that is shyness, I beg you to be more coy, my lady." She laughed again. "So, let me see if I understand. Your James liked it best when you were beneath him."

"Always."

"Always?"

"Always."

"Well, then I see that I have the great good fortune of introducing you to many new and delightful pleasures."

"Many?"

"Many. And we begin now."

Lucy had used the word *mistress* to gauge Colin's expectations. She would not marry; no man of rank wanted a wife who had lived in the camps as a man's lover. Perhaps had she and James married, had she been a wife, but some—like Archibald—would always call her wanton. But mistress to such a man as Colin? (No, she corrected herself, to Colin, only to him.) It held a certain appeal. She wondered if he would wait for her, wait for her to complete her aunt's plans; then, when her obligations to her aunt were done, perhaps she might seek him out. Perhaps her life might not be devoid of passion.

She splayed her fingers on his chest, lifting herself up, then pressing down on his firmness. His hands guided her hips as they rose and settled, then began again. His eyes watching her made her shy, but as his hands sought her breasts, pressing them up against her chest and then rolling her most sensitive spots between his fingers, she grew bolder. James had been kind but narrow in his passions, and Lucy had always wondered what pleasures they might be missing. But Colin, equally kind, seemed only to want her pleasure, in whatever form or position it took. She gave herself over to the sensation, to the sight of him, to the feel of his hands on her body, of his thighs between hers, of his kisses.

Their release came more quickly, sating and completing them. She collapsed onto his chest, and he ran his hand gently down her back until they both fell asleep.

Chapter Seventeen

"Porter and I turned the poachers over to your brother's men four miles away, then we returned by the back way." Fletcher watched the house over Colin's shoulder as he spoke.

"That was wise, but it shouldn't make any difference. The porter makes regular trips through town. No one would find it unusual to see him in town, even not on his regular day." Colin placed his hand on Fletcher's shoulder. "And the men?"

"Tied up tight and covered with hay. No one saw them." Fletcher held out a note. "Walgrave sent a message saying that they would be dealt with. What does that mean?"

Colin read the note himself. "Apparently, the Home Office will determine whether the men are poachers with incredibly bad luck or part of the plot against William. Either way, we don't want to ask questions."

"What do you think of Miss Lucy? That was some fine shooting," Fletcher mused. "Some of the best I've ever seen."

"Yes." For the first time it gave him pause. She had used her skills to protect him and Bobby—this was the second time she had saved his life. He knew he should be suspicious, but he needed, wanted, to trust that she was what she said . . . an officer's daughter fallen on hard times.

But he'd have to remember her skill with the weapon, and he'd have to learn what other skills she might have.

"Are you as good with a pistol as with a rifle?"

He walked around the gun room, touching the various weapons in the room absently.

"Yes. Why?"

"You learned that in the camp?"

She looked at him quizzically, but not suspiciously. "Were there no families in your regiment?"

"No." He told himself it wasn't a lie. His regiment had been tasked with missions on which no families would have been allowed. "I'm surprised I never heard of you, a girl sharpshooter in Wellington's army."

"I was not a member of Wellington's army, and I was a well-kept secret."

She answered easily, perhaps because she was speaking of a past that seemed far away. She walked to the wall and tested several rapiers. The way she held the blade suggested experience.

"Did they teach you to fence?" With Aidan's connections, he could readily check her story, if he needed to.

"Fencing requires no bullets, so it was a good defense. And it required agility, not necessarily strength."

"Are you as good as you are with a gun?"

"You won't believe me if I tell you," she averred, teasing him.

"You could show me."

She laughed. "I suppose I could. But you must make it worth my while."

"A bet?"

"One that makes it worth winning." She smiled as she

turned to the wall once more, picking up swords and testing their weight and balance. He watched as she pushed the tip of the blade into the floor. She let it bend into a half-circle, then released the pressure to feel it spring back straight. She discarded several, not liking the temper of the blades.

"But, my lady, you are certain to lose."

"Ah, such confidence." She narrowed her selection to two.

"My confidence is well merited, I assure you. I grew up among brothers noted for their skill at the blade, and by my majority, none could beat me."

"Then what is your wager? It must be something I want very badly."

"Whoever loses must do the other's bidding for the rest of the day . . . and night."

"That sounds like a game one would want to lose."

"Who said that losing should be distasteful, if the winner and the loser can both find joy in the game?"

"I prefer to win." She turned to the wall and removed her overdress, leaving only a heavy cotton shift and pantaloons.

"Is that how you dressed when they taught you?" Colin's body grew taut with desire.

"No, then I dressed as I usually did." She removed her shoes and stockings, and set them neatly to the side. She flexed and pointed her feet.

"Usually?"

"As a boy."

"Boy?"

"Yes, boy." She looked at him as if he were dim. "There was an incident. The men in the battalion decided that they couldn't always be present to protect me, so they determined I should dress as a boy. My father and mother agreed. But, after that, it was easy to insist that I learn all the skills that a boy would learn. To be convincing in my disguise, you understand."

"Of course. One must be convincing in any disguise." As

soon as he said the words, he wondered how much of her behavior was a disguise. She was in trouble, on the run. How much was she pretending? At least, he believed, the passion between them was honest—but then he'd believed that and been wrong before. "How long did you keep this disguise up?"

She chose a blade and faced him. "Are you going to use your own blade or one of these?"

"My own." She had avoided answering his question, but for now, he was willing to let the truth come out. The truth always came out.

"I suppose I should see the size of your blade, then."

He choked, then laughed. "I suppose I should give you a demonstration."

"I would like that." She looked his body up and down, then ran her tongue across her slightly opened lips. "After we fence."

He groaned. "You are a sweet torment." He walked to the wall where he had hung his sword and lifted it from its scabbard. He held it upright before him, point to the floor, his hands on the hilt.

"Hmmm. That will do nicely." She let the entendre hang in the air between them. She lifted the blade to her face and took her stance. "*En garde*, sir."

"First, how do we know who wins?" He made a wide circle around her, watching her feet, her hands, the tip of her blade.

"First blood." She smiled.

"No. Something else. I won't draw your blood."

"Why not, sir? I would draw yours, just as I shot that man in the garden. When necessary, we can do a great many things we do not expect we would do." Her voice grew sad and hard.

"But it's not necessary here."

She lunged. He parried. She danced away. He moved

toward her. She stepped in, then back. She played well, thoughtfully, letting her stamina balance his power.

But then abruptly she changed the rules of the game. She backed away from him, giving herself some distance from his parries. Then she lowered the arm that did not hold the sword. She placed her hand on her breasts, and then, meeting his eyes, she drew her hand across her breasts, down the flat of her stomach, and back up the side of her hips. He felt passion rise suddenly, and his movements slowed as he watched her seduction.

With her hand back at her breasts, she pulled the drawstring at her bodice. The material released just enough to reveal the soft curves of the tops of her breasts.

He lowered his sword in surprise, and she lunged, tapping his sword out of his hands.

"I win."

He crossed the room in two steps and pulled her into his arms.

Morning broke through the window, and Colin was still at her side. As he lay on his back, his arm held her around her shoulders as she curled into his chest. She did not move for a few moments, enjoying the lean power of his muscles, the firm definition of his chest and arms.

"Good morning, sleepy head." He turned his head to kiss her forehead.

"Have you been awake long?" She rolled up on her elbow and traced imaginary figures on his chest with her fingers.

"Long enough to write a poem to commemorate our liaison last night."

"A poem?"

"Yes, even an old soldier can have hidden talents."

"Then recite it for me."

"I would prefer to polish it up a bit. I can give you a

demonstration though—but you must be a good audience. Do you promise?"

She grew warm at the hungry look in his eyes. "Yes."

"Good. It begins with a long section detailing the many beauties of your body." He took a single finger and oh-so-lightly traced the path of his description. "Starting with the fire in your eyes, then the subtlety of your nose, the welcome of your lips, the impertinence of your chin, the elegance of your neck." At the base of her throat, he opened his hand, one finger becoming five, each one skimming, tantalizing her flesh. "At your breasts, I consider how dizzying their beauty is for one who has been long alone." He began to draw circles with his fingers, across the plain of her chest above her breast, then slowly moved to tease each soft mound, until he joined his lips and tongue in the play, moving slowly and deliberately from one breast's peak to the next. "And I rejoice in their soft generosity, allowing me to take my fill." His head bowed over her breasts. He took the bud of her flesh between his lips and the ridge of his teeth, sending a thrill of heat through her body as he pulled gently.

She arched into his mouth.

Then, as his tongue flicked and his mouth sucked, his hand moved lower, across the plane of her stomach in a provocative series of narrow circles. "At this point in the poem, I quote John Donne."

In one quick motion, he rose above her. Then, opening her thighs, he settled between them. His sex, fully aroused, pressed at the opening of her body.

"'License my roving hands and let them go.' Let's see, the next part of that line is 'before . . . behind . . . between . . .'"

And as he said each word, his hands followed the direction. At *before*, he placed both hands on the flat of her stomach, then, using the barest touch of his fingertips, raked up and back, stopping at her breasts to hold each one to his mouth for a deep kiss. At *behind*, he brought his hands back down her belly and slipped his hands under her buttocks and squeezed them with a rich pressure. At *between*, he drew his hands down, and let them palm her inner thighs from her hips to her knees and back. Then he pressed his fingers into her swollen lower lips and, parting them, used his thumb to rub circles as his forefinger sought the darkness of her warm heat. He remained there for several minutes, slowly stoking her desire, until she moaned his name.

"Oh, I seem to have become distracted. . . . Do you wish to hear the rest?"

She nodded, biting her lower lip, and arching her hips into his hands.

"Oh, no, if I am giving you my words, you must give me yours." He increased the pressure slightly on her flesh, pushing his finger farther into the heat of her body. "Is that a yes? Or a no?"

"Yes" she breathed between strokes. "Please, yes."

"Let's see: we've done *before, behind, between*. Ah, yes next is *above*." He removed his hand and fingers, and she cried out in frustration. He moved from his position between her knees and stretched out over her body, giving her the satisfaction of his weight settling against her breasts, belly, and thighs. "For *below*, there is just one possibility, my sweet. He pressed his erect sex against her entrance. "Do you wish me to complete the poem?"

She opened her eyes and gazed directly into his. "Yes, now."

And he obliged her, first slowly, then more insistently, until they both found the poem's completion together.

"I've never liked poetry as much as I have this morning," she said afterward.

"I will have to recite it again for you, if you wish.

"I wish."

Sometime later, she turned toward him, her face intent.

"What? So serious. I would have thought I'd loved every serious thought from your head."

"How long do you think we will remain here?"

He grew suddenly alert. "Why, my angel?"

"Because I was wondering how many more poems you could recite to me before we have to move on."

He smiled, once more reminding himself that she was not a threat. "As many as you wish. . . . I could recite poetry to you ten times a day if you wish."

"Really? You know that many poems?"

"If I don't already know them, we can discover new ones. Or we can repeat your favorites as you wish."

"I would like that."

Chapter Eighteen

"Porter says that the market is an easy hour, and the road well marked once you get off these lands." Fletcher checked the leads from the porter's horse to his seat "A big market for hereabouts anyway—should be easy to lose ourselves in the crowds. How much should we buy?"

"At least enough to get us to another market day. Having no news from Aidan, we should settle in."

Fletcher lifted his chin toward the house, where Jennie stood with William in her arms, in close conversation with Bobby. "Become right friends, those two. Like sister and brother. But at least 'e's the one sleeping on that hard cot in the priest hole, and not me. Last night I overheard her telling him how to tell if a girl has a tendre for you."

"What did Bobby say?" Colin lifted an empty basket into the wagon bed behind Fletcher's seat.

"He told her how to catch frogs in running water."

Colin laughed. "I thought he was yet a bit young for girls."

Fletcher shrugged. "He's still horse mad, but that will change. A year, two, and he'll be grateful for her advice. She's a smart one. If Prinny lets her stay with William, it will change her prospects."

"William will need a nurse for some time yet, so it

should not be difficult finding Jennie a place in the royal household." Colin thought of the document given to him by Prinny. "I will ensure that it happens."

"Do you want anything from the market? I have requests from both Miss Lucy and Jennie."

Bobby ran to Aidan's side. "Jennie would like to come with us, sir. She needs more yarn, and Lucy has agreed to look after William."

"You can't choose the yarn for her?"

"I suppose I could, sir." Bobby sent a downcast look toward Jennie.

"It might be best if the gel were to come. She and Bobby could fill our baskets at the market, and I could listen at the tavern for any news. With the gap in their ages and the bossing way she treats him, they will appear to be brother and sister."

Bobby, not waiting for Aidan's agreement, waved to Jennie, and she rushed to the wagon, William in her arms.

"Oh, thank you, sir. I couldn't stand the thought of being in the priest hole all day without Bobby to entertain me. William should sleep for most the time we're gone. He's just been fed and changed." She watched as Fletcher and Bobby took their seats in the wagon, then, without warning, thrust William in Colin's hands. "You'll find him an easy baby."

Colin saw the amused glances pass between Fletcher and Bobby as he held the babe out from his body and stared at Jennie's retreating form. As soon as Jennie had hopped into the back, Fletcher pulled out of the yard, leaving Colin holding a baby, feet dangling, before him.

William began to squirm restively. And by the time Colin arrived in the kitchen to give Lucy his charge, William was fully awake. And angry.

Lucy, however, had her hands in flour, rolling out dough for a pie. "I can't take him now. You will have to hold him until I have this in the oven."

The baby wailed. His cries were ear piercing.

"Can I finish the pie for you, instead?"

"If you take too long, we'll miss the proper temperature for a pie, and then we won't have anything but bitter apples to eat until the others return from market. So, no. Have you never held a babe before?"

"I had younger brothers."

"Did you make them cry as well?"

"No more than they made me." Colin shifted the baby in his hands. "And I'm not making him cry."

"Was he crying when Jennie gave him to you?" Lucy rolled her eyes. "I meant when they were infants. How old were you when your youngest brother was born?"

Colin grew quiet, trying to remember. "Six or seven. But I had almost nothing to do with either Clive or Charles. Their mother died in childbirth, and from then on, we had nannies and governesses. My father was unwilling to lose another wife when, I suspect, he didn't like the trouble of wives much anyway." William's cries grew more insistent.

"So you have never had occasion to soothe an infant?" she asked. "Stop holding him like he's a dirty puppy you are trying to give a servant. Pull him back into your chest. Let him hear your heart. And give him a little bounce. You've seen Jennie do it. Mimic." She pushed back a wayward curl with her lower arm, brushing flour across her forehead in the process.

He followed her instructions, and the babe quieted—but only for a moment. "How do you have experience with babes if you grew up in the camps?"

"I am beginning to wonder what war you fought in. Pace evenly while you bounce him." Her gaze grew distant, as she rolled out the dough. "I was eighteen when Wellington retreated behind the Lines at Torres Vedras, bringing with us the Portuguese who did not retreat into the hills. Two hundred thousand Portuguese. My mother died that year, offering aid to the sick among the refugees. It was so cold. My father had intended to leave us in Lisbon, but after her death, we two did not wish to be apart."

"Not even the British government knew Wellington had built the Lines. One of the men I served under said it was the most efficient use of funds in the whole war." It took a little practice: bouncing, walking, holding the baby to his heart. The babe's cries were less frequent, though no less angry.

"Well, that's somewhat better. But he knows you don't like holding him," Lucy assessed, as she transferred the dough to a pie plate.

"How can he know that?"

"Oh, he knows. Think of something else, of something that isn't a screaming infant." Lucy patted the dough into place. "So if you were not with the army at Lisbon, where were you?"

"Everywhere and nowhere . . . until shortly before Waterloo, when I returned to my troops."

"Ah, I understand. Like now, your obligations were not always on the field."

"Correct." Since the boy seemed to like bouncing, he bounced William a little higher, but that had the opposite effect of what he'd intended. The baby renewed his screams.

Lucy shook her head. "And you had to respond flexibly to whatever circumstances you encountered?"

"Yes."

"And were you good at your job?"

"I like to think so."

"What skills did it require?"

"Creativity, resourcefulness, persistence."

"Ah, good. Then find a way to keep him from crying."

"How?

"Be creative, resourceful, and persistent. I'm sure you will think of something. But if you can't soothe him, you'll need to take him to scream somewhere else until I'm finished here. His cries echo too loudly off the stone floor and walls. At least take him over to the garden door. Perhaps the air will please him."

He opened the door to the kitchen garden and let the baby feel the fresh air on his face. But the baby only renewed his screams. "He doesn't like fresh air."

"Try shifting your weight from side to side." Lucy quickly and efficiently pared the skins from a pile of late apples.

"Bounce, heart, pace, air, shift weight," he mocked. "I can lead troops into battle, negotiate for supplies with local farmers, carry messages that, if intercepted, could get me killed, but I can't escort a single pregnant woman safely to London or soothe a screaming baby." By the end, his words were solemn. "Perhaps he hates me because his mother is dead."

"Perhaps you are holding him against a pin," Lucy suggested practically. "And from his birth, the only mother he has known is Jennie."

Shifting his weight from side to side made the wound in his side ache, but he wouldn't tell her, wouldn't admit that he couldn't solve the problem of one small screaming baby. To ease the pressure on his side, he shifted his hand to cradle the baby's head and turn the baby on his belly. In response, William splayed his tiny limbs out across Colin's lower arm. In the new position—his body fitting between the bend of Colin's elbow and his palm—William stopped screaming.

Colin moved just his lower arm from the elbow, in and out, giving the movement a little bounce. The boy cooed and wriggled.

"That's good." Lucy turned toward him, surprised. "How did you figure that out?

"It's how I would actually hold a dirty puppy."

The laughter from the opposite side of the kitchen, at their backs, caught them both off guard. Lucy grabbed the paring knife beside her bowl of peeled fruit. Colin angled his back to the wall, a defensive posture, but one undercut by the presence of William, who was now sleeping in his arms.

"I called your name several times, but the baby has strong lungs. At the same time, I wouldn't have missed the sight of you so . . . domesticated. Need some help with that little one, brother?"

The man in the doorway was strikingly beautiful, resembling the duke more than Colin, but somehow too pretty, too perfect in his features. Lucy looked to Colin, who crossed the room and hugged his brother with one arm. Somehow only Colin made her ache with longing.

"No, I think I've sorted it out now. He merely wants to see where my feet are going." Colin turned to make introductions. "Lucy, my younger brother Edmund. He's a rake and a gambler, so beware his charms. Edmund, my fiancée, Lucy."

Lucy shook her head. "I assume if you are here, then you know about the pretense of our engagement . . . Edmund, if I may?"

"Of course, sweet lady, you may." He offered a deep bow, then walked to the harvest table and began picking out choice pieces of fruit to eat. "And if you are not in truth engaged to my brother, we might wish to know one another better."

Lucy shook her head, amused, and batted his hand away from the apples, but Colin scowled.

"Why are you here, Edmund?"

Edmund raked the hand not holding a piece of fruit through his thick black hair. "His Grace sent me. Apparently Seth has been trying to find this place for two days, but has been thwarted by its seclusion. Since I already knew how to get here, I was an obvious courier."

Lucy pinched the edges of the upper crust to seal its edges, and Edmund rounded the table to open the heavy oven door built into the stone fireplace.

Colin tilted his head. "We will discuss later how you already knew about this place. For now, should I assume it is safe to move?"

"The roads to your next stop have been well-guarded with Aidan's band of former soldiers for more than three days. You should have no troubles. In fact, if you leave in the hour, you could arrive before evening. Your letter announcing your arrival is already in the appropriate hands."

"We cannot leave today: Fletcher, Bobby, and the baby's nurse have all gone to market."

"I encountered them on the road here. Fletcher needs only a wide space in the road to turn around. They should be here shortly." Edmund turned to Lucy. "If the pie is not yet baked by the time you depart, I will stay and take it out of the oven for you."

"I'm sure that will be a great condescension on your part."

"Ah, yes, and if the pie needs to be eaten, I will bear that burden as well."

"I will gather my things." Lucy washed and dried her hands. "I'm sure you have plans to discuss."

"Don't you wish to take William with you?"

"No, he seems to be quite happy with you." She looked directly into Colin's eyes "If you have need of me, I will be in my room."

Lucy packed her few belongings in her bag. The last few days had been sweet, an idyll in which she had grown to trust Colin, grown to enjoy his humor, his seriousness, and his caresses.

It would be harder to leave him now. It was already hard enough not to tell him her troubles. But he had troubles of his own. Perhaps when his obligation to William was done, perhaps then she might see what was possible between them. For now, however, she had her promise to her aunt, he had his to the child. To this point, being together benefited them both, but soon, they would have no reason to remain together. And then she would have to decide.

She wished she could confide fully in Colin, but every time she had thought to raise the question, some obstacle had interfered: the arrival of his brothers at the tavern, the presence of Jennie in the carriage, the threat of the poachers, and now the arrival of his brother Edmund.

And she'd come to believe that the interruptions might have been for good reason. Colin was a man of complications. He was gentle and kind with her, but he was also clearly a good officer and ruthless in dealing with threats, given the way that he managed protecting William and the fact that he had thought nothing of engaging the poachers alone.

The hardness in him didn't surprise her. He'd told her that he'd killed. What man who was still alive after the battle of Waterloo hadn't?

But there was something more to his face when he confided in her. Something that made her wish she could bring back the laughing man she'd nursed.

In the carriage, Colin had ample time to consider his next steps. They would not arrive at Hartshorn Hall until sometime after nine, but in the summer months, the sun would not have yet set. Much later than that and it would be dark and too dangerous to travel, at least with his cargo.

Aidan had sent his note ahead to Em. Even if Sam were unaware of his message's meaning, Em would understand. Em always understood.

His heart clutched. He'd refused to consider Em a complication to his plan, even when Aidan had brought it up. But how long had it been since he'd seen her last? Two? Three months? But she would be there. She was always there. She'd been his best friend from almost their first meeting.

And then there was Lucy. He looked across the carriage at her, her face calm in sleep. She had found a way past almost all his defenses with her gentle eyes and kind heart. That made her dangerous. Until the end of this mission, at least, he would have to be more cautious. Then he would confess all and hope that, when she knew what he had done, she wouldn't walk away.

But could he really confess all when the truth was something he couldn't admit even to himself, except in those hours before dawn when he woke sweating to the phantom smell of Octavia's perfume? It didn't matter that his orders had been clear. He had loved Octavia and he had killed her.

Chapter Nineteen

Lady Emmeline Hartley held Colin's letter before her, decoding it onto a sheet of scrap paper to her left. She'd known from the cover that she should read it slant: Colin had written her address in his second hand.

In childhood, both she and Colin had developed multiple writing hands, a neat copperplate for general correspondence, and two others, one a household italic, and the other, a completely different copperplate hand. They used the second copperplate only with each other, and only in conjunction with a code they had developed long ago.

She'd known for years of his work for the war office and later for the home department. When he'd returned from the wars, she'd demanded all of his stories, and he'd spared her none of them. He'd told the stories so readily that at first she'd thought him to have come through the wars unscathed. Until Brussels. After that, his demeanor had changed: her loyal, kind, old friend had become reclusive and diffident. He'd shown up unannounced, not merely sad, but haunted, and she knew he'd done something terrible. But each time she'd asked, he'd turned away, his face a grim mask.

She'd intended on his next visit to offer her own secrets in exchange for his, secrets he might very well find unacceptable in other women, but which he would forgive in her. Yet even as certain as she was of his forgiveness, she'd held back: she hated to sacrifice even a small portion of his good regard. Colin had been her only true friend for her whole life.

Decoded, Colin's message spoke of refuge, secrets, and something more significant: a woman named Lucy he asked her to welcome.

His arrival and stay needed to remain a closely guarded secret. There would be little trouble there. She kept a small staff at Hartshorn Hall even when her stepbrother Sam was in residence as now. And the servants were used to the house being used for private political meetings.

The only problem could be Stella, who came and went as she pleased. Luckily, Stella had left disgruntled only that morning.

Rooms for three, one in the nursery, and two sturdy footmen to guard a child.

The house would be ready.

Chapter Twenty

Lucy would have liked to watch the countryside as they traveled. She had seen so little of England since her return after Waterloo, only the post road from London to her aunt's home and the roads she had taken on her escape. But she'd given the window seat to Jennie, hoping that the air from the open window and Lucy's supply of peppermint leaves—replenished from the porter's garden—would ease the girl's uneasy stomach.

As a result, Lucy had spent the trip seated in the middle of the carriage, facing backward. Colin and Jennie faced her, looking forward, and William's basket sat in between them and across from her. With Jennie so miserable, it seemed unkind to converse playfully with Colin, so the lovers subsisted on long glances and private smiles. Several hours into the trip, however, Colin had rested his knee against hers and left it there, solid and comforting, for the better part of the afternoon.

She took his touch as a reminder that she was not completely alone in the world. As soon as they had a private moment at their destination, she resolved to tell him her story and ask for his help in fulfilling her aunt's commission.

She'd grown to trust Colin in the past weeks, and she knew he would help, if she asked it of him.

A mile from their destination, Fletcher—according to plan—stopped the carriage, and Jennie, dressed once more as a stable boy, climbed up beside Bobby. The moment the carriage door shut behind Jennie, Colin held out his hand. "Take my seat. You have been looking longingly at the windows since we left this morning. I anticipate you haven't seen much scenery."

"Not much, but there's no need to move. Jennie's window will serve as well as yours." She rose, but stumbled as the carriage began to move. Colin took the opportunity to pull her down into his lap.

"But on this side, you will have the best view as we approach the hall."

"Your wound," Lucy countered, but he silenced her objections with kisses to her neck. She placed her palms on his cheeks and turned his face up to hers. She kissed him deeply

"My wound heals better with kisses, sweet star. But I wish for you to enjoy the landscape." Holding her into his chest, he gently pushed William's basket toward the opposite door, then sitting her beside him, he slid closer to William's basket.

"That was deftly done." Lucy pulled the curtains apart to their widest extent. "Watch with me."

He angled Lucy's back into his chest and wrapped his arms around her. "Together is best, though I fear Hartshorn Hall will not afford us the same privacy we have enjoyed these past few days." He nuzzled her neck, his warm breath sending lovely sensations up her spine. He stopped, pointing her gaze out of the window. "But for now, you must watch: I wish to hear your reactions as we arrive."

She rested against him, sighing. "As you wish."

The forest outside her window was thick with oak, sweet

chestnut, and beech, alongside evergreen pines, firs, and spruces. Though it was not yet fully evening, deer lifted their heads from the verges, and more than one rabbit hid in the underbrush. But what Lucy noticed most were the birds, so many different varieties, most of which—having grown up on the Continent—she could not name.

"On the other side of this bend, the forest ends, and you should see Hartshorn Hall."

The carriage turned once, then twice in a tight switchback, and the land opened up in front of them past the forest edge.

Lucy gasped in pleasure. "It's a castle!" She laughed, examining its square turreted corners and its crenelated walls. "Not a real one, it can't be!"

"Well, the building itself is quite real, and the castle equally so. You can place your hand on its walls to see it is not an illusion," Colin mocked, pulling her more tightly against him.

"I mean *real* as in a castle built in the Middle Ages."

"Then no, it is not real. Lady Emmeline's great-grandfather was obsessed with the glorious history of his ancestors and, displeased that they had no castle remaining, he built one. He was, however, enough of a pragmatist to ensure all the conveniences were present—or at least the conveniences of a hundred years ago. I loved it here as a boy—Sam Barnwell, Lady Emmeline's stepbrother, and I went to Harrow together. It's always been a second home to me."

In the distance, a petite woman in a riding habit with a dog by her side stood next to a tall man in livery.

"That's Lady Emmeline and Jeffreys. Don't mistake Jeffreys: he has been Em's butler, estate manager, and trusted advisor since her father ran off to the Continent to live with his French mistress." Colin's voice turned hard.

"You don't like her father." Lucy caressed his hand where it rested on her belly.

Colin paused long before answering. "When Em was six, she was badly hurt in a carriage accident that killed her mother and elder sisters. But instead of caring for Em, her father ran away. He's never come back."

"Tell me the story. I would hate to make a misstep in the home of your friends."

"It's horrific. Em's sisters wished to return home early from a visit, and her mother accommodated them. It was almost a full day after the accident before Em's father realized something was wrong. By the time they found Em, she had spent two moonless nights, both legs broken, trapped in an overturned carriage, with the bodies of her mother and sisters."

"Poor child." Lucy shook her head in sympathy, wondering at what grit it took for a child to overcome such an experience.

"For years she refused to travel in any carriage, and later, she would only travel distances that allowed her to go and return before nightfall. On the rare occasions that she agreed to remain somewhere overnight, she would inevitably awaken screaming. And nothing helped . . . until she found Bess."

"Bess?"

"Her dog. With Bess by her side, Em is her natural self, vibrant and charming and confident. She runs the estate better than her father ever dreamed of doing." Colin's voice was proud.

"How old is Bess?" Lucy asked gently.

"Not so old, yet. But Jeffreys, Sam, and I already fear what will happen to Em when Bess dies. But don't tell her you know." Colin kissed her neck one last time. "She would skin me alive. And you would miss me."

As the carriage slowed to a stop, Colin shifted to put a respectable distance between them.

* * *

At the estate office door, Colin and Lucy played the part of guests just arrived, acting as a distraction while Jeffreys directed Fletcher and the carriage boys to unload the carriage directly into his office. From there, Jennie and Bobby used the servant's stairway to whisk William to the nursery.

Em flung herself into Colin's arms. "It's been too long, you devil. You promised to come for Stella's house party, but you abandoned me, and I had to entertain her witless crowd alone!"

"I'm certain you have concocted an appropriate penance." Colin offered a formal half bow.

"Concocted is right—you will see." Em, grinning extended both hands to Lucy in greeting. Colin offered the introductions, giving no explanation of his relationship to Lucy. At Em's side was Bess, a big black dog with a white ruff, white feet, and a white blaze at her chest.

"What a beautiful animal! I've never seen one like her." Lucy held out her hand, palm toward her body, for the big animal to sniff. "What breed is she?"

"A St. John's water dog from Newfoundland. I won her in a bet from the Earl of Malmesbury, who has brought them to England. He raises them in his kennel." Em scratched Bess between the ears.

"Malmesbury is usually picky about who gets one of his water dogs," Colin baited.

Em batted playfully at Colin's arm. "I was very persuasive."

"Oh, yes, persuasive. Tell Lucy what persuasive means."

"Well," Em laughed, "I simply refused to give her back. When I went to the kennel to see the pups, Bess stayed at the back of the stall. All the other pups came forward, but she hung back. I bet Malmesbury that I could get her to come to me."

"What did you do?" Lucy asked, intrigued.

Colin leaned in conspiratorially. "Knowing Em, she secretly tied Bess to the back of the kennel, then untied the lead to win the bet."

Em glared at Colin. "I did not, though"—she shrugged her shoulders—"that's close. In any event, Bess has been beside me ever since. I took her to Malmesbury a couple of months ago to be bred, and her litter is all black with white noses just like their mother. Malmesbury's already chosen his pups, so the rest are mine." The dog lifted its head to nuzzle Em's hand. "She's my good luck charm. I always get a rabbit when Queen Bess comes along."

"Queen Bess?"

Em looked sheepish and pleased all at once. "She rules the estate, so I thought she should have an appropriate name. If you'd like, I can show you Bess's pups."

The three followed Fletcher and the carriage, as it moved toward the stable yard.

Though there were stray dogs aplenty on the battle trail, Lucy had never been allowed to keep one. Most would stay, then disappear, likely killed. Lucy had especially loved one, a scraggly brown dog with a broken leg. She'd begged the doctor to set the leg, but he'd refused, so she'd torn up her shift, made bandages, and done the job herself. The dog had followed her around the camp until its leg was healed, but soon after the splints were gone, he'd disappeared, and she'd missed him for years. But the doctor had noticed her, her skill, and her instincts, and from then she'd been allowed to help with the wounded.

Em's pups were black, roly-poly balls of fur. Crawling over one another in a tumble of paws, they reached the front of the stable quickly. The stable gate had been removed and replaced with a low fence, so that Bess could enter and leave freely. The great dog leapt over the barricade and stood proudly behind her pups.

"Oh, they are adorable!" Lucy bent down and stuck her

fingers between the fence slats. The pups licked and gnawed on her fingers.

"I know. I can't imagine how I'm going to part with them. But they're spoken for, their new homes approved by Malmesbury himself. I'm keeping two: the one with no markings, and the headstrong one over there." Em pointed at the pup gnawing on his brother's leg.

"How did you choose?" Lucy scratched the white belly of a pup that had rolled over beneath her fingers.

"The all-black one reminds me of Bess when she was a pup, all good-humor and deviousness. And the headstrong one seems oddly most devoted to Bess: he watches her constantly and misses her most when she isn't in the stable yard. I'd held one back for you, Colin—the best of them in fact—but then you didn't come when expected."

"Guilty as charged, Em." Colin lifted his hands out to his sides. "What did you do with my pup?"

"He's still here, the sleek one Lucy is scratching. He already shows the instincts to make a fine hunter." Em turned to Jeffreys, who approached from the house, leaving Colin and Lucy to play with Bess's pups.

Colin stepped into the stable and picked up the white-bellied pup with a thick white ruff. Holding him up, Colin looked the pup in the eyes. The pup looked soberly back.

"You really do hold babies and puppies alike. Give him to me." Lucy held out her hands, and Colin gave her the animal. Immediately, she snuggled the puppy to her bosom, and he began to lick her chin and face. Lucy giggled, a light, young sound that lifted Colin's spirits. "Are you a clever pup? Are you? Of course you are." And the pup licked her on the nose.

Em returned to Colin's side. "Your companions are well settled in the nursery, and we have locked the servants' stairway as well as the stairway from the family wing. Your man

Fletcher has one key." She held out a heavy iron key. "Here is the only other."

Colin stuck the key in the side of his boot, then leaned forward to kiss Em's cheek. "Thank you."

"Of course." Em looked seriously into Colin's face. "Is this part of the business from before?"

"No, but it's important," Colin responded with equal seriousness.

Lucy watched as the two shared a private communication. Em made a motion with her hand, and Colin nodded. Suddenly, Lucy felt ill at ease. Something in the manner of the two toward one another made her feel like an interloper. But then the moment passed, and Colin's face shifted to a playful pose.

"So how much will it cost me to buy my dog back?"

"You will find Malmesbury unwilling to negotiate. He was quite smitten." Em laughed. "Losing the pup might simply be your punishment for broken promises."

Em had graciously had a bath drawn for Lucy before dinner, and Lucy had luxuriated in the hot water until it became warm, then tepid. She had pulled herself from the tub unwillingly. The maid who had accompanied the hot water also brought fine linen towels and a heavy brocaded dressing gown, suitable to the season, scented with rose water.

Wrapped in the luxurious gown, Lucy reviewed her two choices for what dress to wear to dinner: the worn blue wool and an equally worn grey muslin, neither fitting her figure. Now that Colin had discovered how she had altered her shape, it seemed foolish—at least while she was in the safety of his company—to continue the ruse. But she had no other options. Having seen Em and her closeness to

Colin, she wished suddenly that she had not refused his offer of new clothes so decisively.

It would have to be the grey, she realized. The wool was wholly unsuited for a dinner at a country manor. Though faded and worn, the grey still showed signs of having been a fine walking dress once long ago.

Her decision was interrupted by a rap at the door. "Miss? It's Dot. Lady Hartley has sent me to you. May I enter?"

She started to call out that there was no need. But having been a servant herself, she would at least open the door to send the maid away. At the door she found not one maid, but three. The first—a broad-faced, flaxen-haired cherub— carried over her arm a pile of underclothes, and the two maids behind each held dresses over their outstretched arms.

"Lady Hartley thought after such a long trip, you might have no clothes fresh enough for dinner."

Lucy did not correct Em's polite fiction. It was a generous kindness—as were the dresses. She stepped back from the door to let the maids enter.

"Lady Hartley believed this one might suit you best." The maid held up a frock of deep crimson satin, with puffed sleeves and a narrow fluted ruffle at its base. Edged in delicate white lace, the bodice was demurely low, cupping each breast individually. "The two of you are of a size and shape, so it ought to fit nicely."

The dress was simple, but elegant—the kind of dress she would have commissioned herself from a modiste. "Then I will try that one first."

"Very good, miss." The maids set to work. Two hung the remaining dresses, eight by the count of them: a riding habit, two morning dresses, two walking dresses, two evening dresses, and a ball gown. Lucy determined to object later.

As she sat to have her hair dressed, the maid—Dot— chatted familiarly, happy if Lucy offered an occasional *um* or *ah*. As Dot worked, Lucy wondered if Colin would find her transformation appealing, or if he'd prefer her as he had found her? A lowly servant.

"And of course Mrs. Cane—her ladyship's cousin—was quite frustrated to find that she and her party had to leave before Lady Hartley's beau arrived. Her guests were growing restive when the rain came unexpectedly and ended their enjoyment of the country. She told me she had been planning the menu for Lady Hartley's engagement party for months."

In the expert hands of Dot, Lucy watched her hair transform from a mess of curls into an elegant chignon with tendrils framing her face.

"It was to have ten courses—though Cook told me she would have refused to prepare it. Cook calls Mrs. Cane a worthless spendthrift, but I think an engagement party would have been lovely. Do you think we will have one now that you have arrived?"

It took a moment for Lucy to register that Dot had stopped her long narrative and was waiting for her to respond.

"Dot, I was thinking that my hair has never looked lovelier, and I missed your question," Lucy said diplomatically.

"Do you really like it, miss?"

"Yes, Dot, it makes me look . . ." Lucy's voice trailed off in thought.

"Beautiful, miss. That it does. No, I was saying that I thought the party Mrs. Cane had planned was just the sort of celebration Lady Hartley deserves after all these years of waiting."

The information registered slowly, leaving Lucy wishing that she had paid closer attention. "Certainly it is difficult to wait on an expected good."

Dot patted her shoulder. "That is exactly my position. Do you think we'll have the engagement announcement this week then?" Dot asked, putting the final touches on Lucy's hair. "I was saying in fact just the other day to one of Mrs. Cane's friends that a short engagement is always best. Why, Mrs. Cane only knew her husband for . . ."

Dot's voice faded into the background once more, leaving Lucy with an uncomfortable twist in her gut.

Chapter Twenty-One

Em was on the terrace, where Colin expected her to be.

But before climbing the four stairs, he stopped and knelt beside Bess, lying at the base of the stairs. He scratched the big black dog behind the ears. "Always watching out for our lady Em, aren't you, girl?" Bess shifted her head to move his fingers to a better spot. As he petted the great dog, he watched Em stand on the terrace, lost in thought.

She was looking out over the stone wall, into the garden and wilderness beyond. In childhood they had made a game of it, the private hand signal that meant *Meet me at the parapet*—their word for the raised portion of the terrace, where the land fell off abruptly below and some distant generation of ancestor had built a stone wall to keep residents from falling. It was the most private public space near the house. A bend in the terrace protected one from view, but at the same time gave a full prospect. If one stood just right, as they did now, they were hidden from view, except from the most distant part of the garden, which they could see fully. There was only one approach from the house that they could not see, and it was almost never used. It had become a ritual between them; if either wished to talk or escape, they would find this spot on the terrace.

Seeing her now, the light on her hair, the curve of her smile, Colin took it in, knowing things were already shifting between them.

He realized with a start that, though her face and form were as familiar to him as his own, he'd never noticed how her eyes mirrored the rich green of the evergreens or how her hair—straight and thick—was the same lustrous black as the crows. Somehow he'd simply expected her to be there whenever he returned, and she always had been. He should have seen her better before now.

She did not turn as he approached, and he leaned onto the ledge next to her, their elbows touching. They looked out together, silently.

As always, the silence was companionable between them, and as always, she spoke first. "I remember the first time we met here. We were seven or eight." She did not look at him, only stared at a distant spot in the garden.

"Seven." He watched the garden with her.

"Seven then. Stella had hatched some plan for mischief, and she had tricked me into the garden so that I would take the blame for it. She hadn't been here long, and I hadn't yet learned not to trust her. But you always knew when she was up to no good." Her shoulder leaned against the side of his arm, comfortably.

"I lured you away from the garden with new pencils and paper."

"And we drew until sunset, imagining worlds and dragons and crusading knights."

"You were never satisfied with being the damsel in distress."

"She won't be either, you know, but I think she'll be good for you."

"What do you mean?"

"I've seen the way you look at her and the way she looks at you. You aren't certain of her yet, but you will be."

Em reached into her pocket and pulled out a folded paper. She put it on the ledge in front of them, holding it down with her hand. It sat between them, but he didn't reach for it. He knew what it was. A child's drawing, in two hands. Their betrothal promise from all those years ago.

"I tried to give this back to you last time." Her voice was soft. "But you refused."

"I wasn't ready. You are always my dream of sanity in a world gone mad."

"Oh, fiddle. More like just another nightmare. But I was right: it's time. Past time. I suppose we should do this right." She picked the drawing up and turned toward him. She stood only chest high, so she had to look up into his face. She paused. Looking down at her, he realized her hand was shaking. He took her hand in his.

She looked up and breathed deeply once before speaking. "Colin Somerville, I release you from our childhood promises."

He brushed the hair back from her face. "Not all of them, Em."

She tucked the strand behind her ear, and laughed, a soft, self-deprecating agreement. "No, not all. You still must be my dear friend. And you must always save a waltz for me. Promise."

He suddenly felt the loss of her in the center of his chest. "I never meant to hurt you, Em. Will this break your heart?"

"Arrogant, aren't you?" She shook her head in mock dismay. "No, you're too late; my heart's already been broken." And she laughed again. It sounded just like Em's laugh, but he heard it differently. He wondered how he'd never seen it before—the fleeting sadness, the hasty smile.

"What? Who?" Colin pressed her for an answer.

"Not now. But sometime—when you have this all sorted out. I'll tell you then. And you can advise me what to do next." She brushed her cheek with the back of her hand. "But you must keep it all a secret."

"Anything." Colin listened more closely now, regretting that he had not listened well in all his visits for the past few years. If he had, things might now have been different between them.

"Always so hasty," she chided lovingly. "You should hear what my story is first."

He stiffened in hurt. "Have I ever done anything to make you question my loyalty?"

"No, never. You've been my dearest friend, my one constant. But I'm thinking I might like to travel, me and Bess. You know how difficult that might be for me. I would need an escort to the Continent."

"Wouldn't Jeffreys or Sam have some objection?"

She turned away from the garden and toward him. She lifted her hand to his shoulder, then gently cupped one side of his face with her hand. "I've been too long on the shelf, Colin. I've only had my way this long because everyone believed that you and I would eventually marry. I have my own funds; I'm of age. And in the last several months I find that this place has grown uncomfortably small."

She let her arm fall to her side; then she picked up the paper from the ledge. She handed the paper to him.

He held back from taking it. Marriage to Em had always been a possibility, but somehow it had seemed wrong to marry her when he was so damaged. But she was damaged too, and he hadn't known. Perhaps if he had realized . . . but now there was Lucy. From the moment he'd met her, she'd figured in his plans.

He unfolded the sheet and saw what he expected: a sketch of two horses and two riders, a turreted tower in the distance, and a dragon lying dead on its side. "I don't want to take this."

"But that was the promise. When one of us decided to

marry another, we would tear this into pieces and scatter it to the wind. I saw the way you look at her. You've decided."

He couldn't object. "Keep it. Send it to me if you ever need my help."

"Still trying to be the knight in shining armor," Em chided.

"No, he's long since dead. His armor is bloodied and can't be cleaned."

Abruptly, she tore the paper in half, one knight and a turret on one side, another and the body of the dragon on the other. But instead of scattering the pieces, she held out half to him. "If either needs the other, this will be our promise . . . of friendship and of succor."

He nodded, taking the paper from her hand—a slender white hand, so different from Lucy's tanned, calloused one. He folded the sheet and placed it in his breast pocket.

"Don't let her get away, Colin." She kissed him softly on the cheek. Turning back to the garden, she leaned her stom aoh against the stone wall, making it impossible for him to see her face.

He placed his arm around her shoulders and drew her against his body. He leaned over and kissed her hair. She leaned her body into his side, rested there for a moment, then pulled away.

She stepped out of the circle of his arm, looked up into his face once more as if for the last time, then walked away. He let her go and took her place looking out over the garden.

Lucy caught a sob in her hand, then turned swiftly away. She had to escape before she was seen. Lucy had thought to walk on the terrace before dinner and, if she saw Em, to thank her for the loan of the lovely dinner dress. But she hadn't expected to chance upon Em and Colin in the middle of a tryst. When Lady Emmeline brushed Colin's cheek with her hand, then kissed his cheek, she had felt her heart drop into her belly. Sorrow, anger, regret, and—she had to admit—jealousy filled her stomach, all in one complicated dish.

She fled down the nearest garden path, a long avenue with thick evergreen hedges on either side. But there was no exit, no quick retreat into another part of the garden. Nothing, but a long unbroken row of green.

He wasn't hers, she repeated to herself. He had never been hers. She had even insisted that she didn't want him. All she'd wanted was a safe passage and some pleasure before she disappeared into a new life. Why, then, had it hurt so much to see him with another woman? No, seeing him with Em shouldn't matter. But the ache in the center of her chest and at the pit of her belly told her it did.

Suddenly, Dot's words became clear. The maid's idle chatter had been about Colin. The realization took her breath. He was the expected beau, the one with whom Lady Emmeline had a longtime understanding. Why, then, had he told her he had no fiancée? That he would marry her? And worse yet, why—on so little evidence—had she believed him?

It had been empty chivalry all along. A sickbed romance turned into a passionate affair, but not one that had touched his heart.

Knowing the playing field, she had to decide what campaign she would begin.

She knew how to fight other sorts of campaigns, campaigns where a man's life depended on how attentive and knowledgeable she was: how to stitch up a bayonet wound, how to slow the bleeding from a severed limb. But this sort of game—where one had to hold one's heart safe, to win with smiles and strategies—she would not play.

As Lady Arabella Lucia Fairbourne, she had the means

and the position to compete for his affections. But, as Lucy the officer's daughter, she couldn't. Wouldn't. In her heart, she wasn't an aristocrat, just an officer's daughter, one whose character and strength had been forged in battles, not in the *ton*.

She would give him up, heart and soul together. She would not falter in her resolve. But she would not again seek his bed with such abandon. No, if she did, she would be betraying both herself and Lady Emmeline.

At the entrance into the hedged walk, Em saw Lucy, already dressed for dinner, walking away briskly. From the set of her shoulders and her position on the path, Lucy must have seen Em and Colin together.

Em started to follow Lucy, then stopped.

If Lucy rejected Colin, then Em could avoid the embarrassment of a broken engagement. She could avoid Stella's ridicule and keep Colin for herself. All she had to do was . . . nothing. Return to the house. Let Lucy interpret the scene on the terrace as she would. And if the budding romance between Lucy and Colin withered . . .

She didn't even have to be brave: all she had to do was walk away. She looked back over her shoulder toward the terrace, where Colin stood obscured from view. Much as she might later regret it, she'd already released Colin even before he'd arrived with Lucy.

No, she might engage in activities that would destroy her reputation if she were caught, but she could never destroy Colin's as well. From the moment that she'd taken Adam's hand and let him show her the world beyond her estate, she had known that new knowledge would come with sacrifice. She simply hadn't known the sacrifice would be her heart.

She called out to Lucy, who paused, glancing back at

the house. "Wait for me. There's something I must discuss with you."

Lucy wished she hadn't turned; she wished she'd slipped back into the house rather than run toward the garden. It was a tactical error, and, because of it, she would have to face Em, the woman she had so deeply, if unknowingly, wronged.

For Em's sake, she wouldn't reveal that Colin, the man Em so obviously loved, was unfaithful. Perhaps, Lucy shrugged mentally, Em even knew and didn't care. Some women cared little if a man sought other women, so long as he returned at the end of each affair.

But to bring his new lover to the house of his betrothed, even if to keep William safe, suggested a cruelty she would not have believed in Colin's character. It was something her cousin would do . . . or rather had done, keeping a mistress in London even when his wife was in residence, and seducing the maids in his own household. Everyone knew that more than one of the children in the village had been born of such liaisons.

But Lucy had believed Colin a man of honor, perhaps the one man with whom she could share her secrets. At least, she comforted herself, she hadn't told him her own, not fully.

Now, she realized just how little she knew of him. How could she have thought she knew the man simply because he reminded her of other men she had loved?

Em, walking slowly, had almost caught up to her, an inscrutable look on her face. What did Em know? Was she coming to warn her off or, worse, explain the rules of their relationship? Lucy's heart was heavy with regret and sorrow. And the memory of his kiss on her lips tasted of gall.

She had only just realized she'd fallen in love with him, and now to find . . . She stopped the thought, just as she stopped her tears with the back of her hand.

By the time Em reached her, Lucy was—at least—no longer crying. Growing up in hospitals, she'd learned quickly to conceal her emotions; no wounded soldier waiting for a doctor to amputate his leg needed a weeping nurse.

She was surprised when Em took her arm, clearly expecting them to walk arm in arm like bosom friends. They were close in height and build, the only difference being that Em's hair was straight. Lucy had to wonder if she fit a type that Colin liked. Had she not hidden her figure with pads, he would have found them similar all along.

"It seems Colin hasn't explained to you about our betrothal. I've chastised him already."

"Please, Lady Emmeline, no explanation is necessary. I'm simply Somerville's nurse, ensuring that he does not fall ill. But he is well on his way to recovery and very soon will have no need of a nurse."

"Lucy. Stop. I've known Colin almost my whole life. I know his nature, his character, even the kinds of women he prefers in his bed."

Lucy's heart caught. Em spoke with a gentle generosity, a woman who had been wronged but had learned to accept it.

"He's told you about his lovers?" Lucy prayed silently that Colin hadn't confessed his affair with her.

"Well, he didn't wish to, but I insisted. Women are so disadvantaged in being kept unaware of such things. For a man his age, there haven't been many, not as you might expect. He kept a mistress for several years, a girl from his father's estate who had been sent away for a liaison with one of the guests. She had been forced to submit, and Colin didn't like her suffering for it. But that was some time ago;

she's a milliner now. Lovely hats. Besides, how was I to learn anything without someone to tell me? He even taught me to kiss when we were, oh, sixteen, I think."

"He what?" Lucy felt disoriented.

"Oh, I threatened him into it." Em laughed gently at the memory.

"Threatened?" Something had gone awry in the conversation, and Lucy couldn't quite identify what.

"Of course we had to be careful about it, or we would have been married straightaway."

Mistresses. Hats. Kissing. Em related it all as if it had no real significance. Nothing Em was saying made any sort of reasonable sense.

"Which leads to the betrothal." Em said with finality.

"Lady Emmeline, please. This is none of my concern."

Em stopped in the middle of the path and faced Lucy, studying her face steadily for several seconds. "No," Em said softly, "it is exactly your concern." She spoke deliberately, her eyes never leaving Lucy's. "Listen to me: Colin and I, we are not betrothed, nor have we ever been. It's been a game between us. Because it matters to you, I will tell you the truth of it. But you must promise to keep our secret. Stella would make my life quite miserable, if she knew."

"Stella?"

"My cousin. Mrs. Cane. We grew up here together, but she and I . . ." Em's voice slowed as she chose her words. ". . . are not close. She's married now, quite well, with a family of her own. But, for a long time now, it's only been the expected announcement of a betrothal with Colin that has kept her at bay."

"At bay?"

"Oh, dear, that's a complicated story." Em led Lucy down the garden path toward the wilderness, again arm in arm. "In short, though, *this* estate is a freehold from my maternal grandfather's estate, held in trust for me by my father, the earl. But because Stella lived here with us after my uncle, the previous earl, died, she cannot be convinced that this estate is not part of the entail."

"Won't her confusion cause trouble for you in Chancery when your father dies?"

"No. The lands were not part of my mother's settlement, and she died long before my grandfather." At the end of the hedgerow stood a long low bench, and Em gestured for Lucy to sit. "Even so, my grandfather consulted with the best legal advisors to ensure that the lands will be mine. But Stella resents not being lady of the manor—or rather she resents me being such a bad one."

Lucy marveled at Em's easy banter. Clearly she'd misjudged everything she'd seen. Bess jumped up on the bench and curled up against Em's back.

"But as to the betrothal. Colin remained here a great deal before and after the wars. He and my stepbrother had been friends at Eton, and after Colin's mother died, he came here for holidays. He was always my defender against Stella's cruelties. So, when she announced that I was so ugly no one would ever marry me, Colin, honorable then as now, declared that he intended to marry me when I turned twenty-five."

"Why would she say that?" Lucy looked closely at Em's face, green eyes in a faultless complexion, an engaging smile. There was no hint of malice in her story, merely a reporting of truth.

"I have a scar along my jawline." Em traced a nearly invisible white line from her ear to the tip of her chin. "Carriage accident. It's faded now, but when I was young, it was impossible to ignore. Pink and angry. Of course, at nine, I was very sensitive to it."

The two women sat silently, Em regarding her hands.

Em spoke first. "Before Colin went to Brussels, I almost let my thoughts turn to marrying him. But he came back so changed, and by then I found myself changed as well."

Em stood, snapping her fingers for Bess to join her.

"He's a good man, an honorable man. And I believe he already loves you. Don't let him go unless you are quite certain he isn't the man for you."

As Em walked away, Bess positioned herself between her mistress and any objects that she might trip or fall on. Em's limp was more pronounced than it had been earlier in the day, and Lucy wondered how much pain her childhood injuries still caused her.

Lucy knew she should follow, knew she should make her way to the drawing room where the guests would assemble for dinner, but she needed a moment to sort through all she had learned.

She fingered the red silk. Why hadn't she chosen one of the less striking dresses? She'd been so delighted to be able to wear a beautiful dress for Colin, but the joy had gone out of it. Only an hour ago, she had dressed to please him, anticipating the wide smile, the appreciative glances. Even with Em's reassurances, the last thing Lucy wanted was to appear to be encouraging their liaison.

She was already grown too fond of him. Otherwise, she would not have felt such hurt and disappointment when she'd thought him engaged. If she were set on leaving him after this trip, then she needed to protect her heart, however impossible that might be to do.

She had also grown frustrated with the way their stories had changed without notice. First, they had been engaged, then they had been a man and his mistress, and here they were only a man and his nurse. In the last two weeks, the stories had made her less and less important to him, as he had grown more and more important to her.

Em had placed them in rooms with an adjoining door. When Lucy retired early, she would make sure the door was locked.

Chapter Twenty-Two

The next day, Lucy remained in her room until she thought it impossible for anyone to remain in the morning room. But when she arrived, dressed in the most demure of Em's loaned walking dresses, Colin was waiting.

He set down the report he was reading and smiled broadly. "You are as beautiful this morning in green as you were last night in red."

She did not answer, but he seemed not to notice. "Em's gone out for her ride, but I wanted to see you. I kept myself busy." He gestured at the reports lying in piles on the table. "It seems that we might not wait here long after all. The duke and Lady Wilmot will be joining us this afternoon or tomorrow, and we will leave with them."

She deliberately chose a seat far from him. "Ah."

His face changed from puzzlement to concern. "I must apologize. I should have considered how it might appear to you—my friendship with Em. When Em told me about your conversation yesterday, I should have come to you immediately. But Em has always been better with words, and I thought she would have explained it best. But you deserved better than that. Can you forgive me?"

Suddenly she wished there were not a river of table between them, but she also could not breach it. Her feelings were still too raw, her heart too engaged. But if she were to tell him her reservations, this would be the time. They were in a safe place, alone, as they would not be when his family arrived.

She took a deep breath. "Colin, I should tell you . . ."

In the distance, a single pistol fired. They both stopped, listening. Another shot fired, and Colin pushed his chair away from the table, his hands flat on the table as he listened, visibly counting the seconds. At the third shot, he paled. "It's Em. Something's wrong." He raced from the room with Lucy hard at his heels.

At the stable yard, Sam and Jeffreys were already on their horses, riding hard in the direction from which the shots had been fired. The stable master and his boys were hitching two fast horses to a low wagon. Another stable boy was filling the back with blankets. A fourth shot fired.

"No one's a better horseman than Em. She always carries two pistols loaded and two additional cartridges already packed. The first three shots told us she was in trouble. The gap between shots was designed to give the men time to mount their horses—the last shot confirmed the direction they were to ride."

"Go to her, Colin." She put her hand on his elbow.

"No." He shook off her touch, brushing his hair back with both hands. "Sam and Jeffreys are more than capable. If there's trouble, my obligation is here." He looked up to the nursery window where Fletcher nodded, a rifle already visible in the gap of the casement.

Two more shots sounded in quick succession, and the stable master threw himself onto the wagon seat and began to drive, hard.

It felt like hours, but it was probably no more than ten

minutes all told. Over the hill, the horsemen came into view, then the wagon, moving more slowly, but still at a good pace. Em's horse followed behind—riderless.

Colin ran forward to meet them as they entered the stable yard, and Lucy saw the two riders shake their heads, silently conveying that the news was not good.

The wagon pulled in front of her, and Em was in the back, weeping, the broken body of Bess in her lap.

Colin rushed to her side to take the dog, but she refused. "No! She saved me. I wouldn't have seen the trap, but she did. If she hadn't run under the horse, I'd be dead. But . . ." She buried her face in the bloody side of the animal. Bess cried out in pain.

The stable master took his pistol from his belt. "My lady, let me have Bess. She's in pain, miss."

"No! Colin, please don't put her down. Please," Emmeline wept.

"It's for the best, my lord. You can see from here—the leg. It's bent and split."

"Em." Colin spoke low but firmly.

She turned on him ferociously. "No. No. No. She can't die."

Colin looked at Lucy. In other circumstances, it would have made her heart leap that he'd turned to her for help, but she couldn't bear being the one who broke Em's heart. "Em, Lucy stitched me up. Perhaps she could look at Bess."

Em looked at Lucy with hope.

"I will look, Em," Lucy offered. "Do you know how badly she is hurt?"

"I don't know. The leg. Bess . . . she saved me." Her voice trailed off.

"Do you trust me? If I look at her and tell you we cannot help Bess, will you believe me?"

Em bit her lip, but nodded yes. "But you will try to help her?" The dog whimpered in distress.

"If I can. I need a table somewhere clean."

"The kitchen. If Cook objects, I'll buy her a new table."

The cook—a Mrs. Adams—took one look at Em, covered with dirt and crying and motioned to the maids to clear the harvest table.

"I don't want to wash the whole dog. But I need the leg to be clean. Is it possible to have some warm water?" Lucy took an apron from the stool beside the table.

Colin started to give the order, but Cook had already moved to set the water on the fire. "What else do you need?"

Lucy pressed her fingers to the middle of her forehead and closed her eyes. "Ice to cool the leg and slow the bleeding. Whatever medicines they have . . . some laudanum to ease the dog's pain, needles, silk thread—the finest available— if I can sew it up. And Fletcher. Tell Fletcher I need four sticks, whittled smooth for splints, and some heavy linen to tie them together."

Colin took charge, sending servants to gather the tools she needed. "Now what?"

"There's a nerve here." She demonstrated the location in the dog's shoulder. "Press it until it relieves her pain."

"How will I know?"

"You'll know." She began unwrapping the bloody petticoat from Bess's leg, Em held the dog's head, cooing to her and promising her the next piece of marrow from the biggest bone she could find. The pressure on the nerve calmed the dog, but Lucy also thought that the dog knew that Em was in distress and didn't wish to upset her more.

Lucy carefully dripped warm water along the line of the wound. She had seen worse, but then most of the worse she had seen had not lived to heal from their wounds. The bone was visible down the long strip of the lower leg, and clearly broken. The dog was panting.

"Here's the laudanum, miss." Jeffreys was at her side. Handing her the drug, he moved to hold Em's shoulders. Though his position was comforting, from the look he gave Lucy over Em's shoulders, she knew he would pull Em away if necessary.

"This is risky, Em. I don't know how much laudanum I can give her to make her sleep without killing her. But I need to try. If I try to set the leg with her awake, she won't understand that I'm hurting her to help. But I can't guarantee she'll wake up either."

"Try. You have to try. I'll understand if she doesn't wake up because you were trying to help her."

She'd given a grown man forty drops of laudanum over two hours to ease his pain. She tried to calculate the differential between a man and a very large dog. She gave the dog four drops, and waited, then another four.

Bess fell asleep and her body relaxed slightly. Lucy hoped not for the last time.

Em wept harder into Jeffrey's chest. "Is she dead?"

Lucy placed her hand over Bess's heart. "No, she's still alive, but we need to work quickly."

She began giving instructions to Cook, whose own eyes were wet with tears, and to Colin. Em she left stroking the dog's head and whispering in Bess's ear, Jeffreys a gentle presence behind her. Periodically Em would look up to meet Lucy's eyes and mouth the single word, *Please*.

She had no idea how to save Bess.

"We have the ice, miss." The stable master brought her a long slab about a thumb's length thick and roughly the length of the dog's leg.

"That's good. Let's rest her leg on it. But try not to put too much pressure on the shoulder."

Cook placed a thick piece of flannel over the ice and under the leg, then folded a blanket and slipped it gently under Bess's body as Colin held the dog up slightly. With the blanket, Bess's shoulder and leg were even with the rest of her body.

Lucy soaked the silk thread in a plate of lavender water, hoping it would help protect the wound from putrefying.

She first investigated the bone. The break was a clean one, and she set the ends against one another, hoping it would knit. Then she pulled the muscles and flesh back around it. She sewed from the inside out in layers, first making small stitches to pull the muscle back into place, then covering it with the outer flesh. Colin helped her by bathing the area in lavender water, keeping it cleaned as best he could from blood. The ligaments were still attached and the arteries intact, so there was hope.

At the point of impact, the flesh was gone, and what was left was hanging in tatters. She was sure the dog would never walk on the leg again. She worked from the least injured point to the most injured, working to cover the bone and muscles as best she could. In some cases she had to stretch the skin where portions were missing, and she could only hope the stitches would hold.

By the time she'd finished sewing, Fletcher had carved four splints out of soft wood to hold the leg in place and cut twine and soft leather straps to make them hold together. She'd known he was the man for the task. Having been on the battlefield, he'd seen the often ingenious solutions the doctors had created.

The splint was in place, but the dog was still sleeping. She felt the dog's chest, nothing. And her heart sank. She felt again, but the dog's thick ruff got in the way.

"Do you have a mirror or a piece of clear glass?

Cook offered her a glass goblet.

She held the glass at the dog's nose and waited. The glass fogged enough to show the animal was still alive. Lucy slumped with relief against the table.

Colin pulled her to him, and she leaned exhausted against the firm security of his chest.

Em looked up with hope.

"She's still alive, Em, but . . ." Lucy couldn't finish the sentence.

"No, buts." Em raised her chin. "She's alive. That's all that matters. That's enough hope for me."

Chapter Twenty-Three

"It was a damn man trap." Sam spit out the words, his face mottled red with anger. "Hidden on the path on the other side of a hill she jumps, it was set in such a way that by the time Em saw it, she would be airborne and unable to avoid it. Em's right. If her horse had landed into the trap at the speed they were riding, it would have killed them both."

"Who do you think would do such a thing?" Colin watched Sam's and Jeffrey's faces. Aidan, who had arrived early that morning with Lady Wilmot, stood at his side.

"After Peterloo, the list has grown disturbingly long: disgruntled Levellers wanting revenge for the death of a friend or relative; criminal gangs taking advantage of the current political climate; and subversive Tories wanting to force greater constraints on the general liberty by whatever means necessary," Aidan said. "The prime minister is already saying that he will call for more restrictive legislation in this next session, and though the Whigs will oppose it, I fear we will lose."

"But her ladyship is uniformly liked in the county, respected for her work with the poor and for her care of her tenants." Jeffreys shrugged, shaking his head in disbelief. "I can't imagine who would wish to harm her."

"Aidan has a point: this might not be directed at Em specifically, just at the estate," Colin suggested quietly. "Sam, are you sure Em was the target?"

Sam shook his head in frustration, the muscles in his neck bulging. "I don't know, but I have my suspicions, and when I find the culprit, I'll beat him to a pulp. I've stood idly by for too long." He fisted his hands at his sides. "I'll be in the stables."

"What does he mean?" Colin looked to Jeffreys. The butler's face was inscrutable.

"If you require me, sir, I will be with her ladyship, watching over Queen Bess." Jeffreys turned sharply and walked away.

Chapter Twenty-Four

Lucy was in the morning room, staring out of the window. She'd stayed with Em through the night, measuring out the laudanum to keep Bess alive, asleep, and out of pain. Her hope was to keep Bess asleep or at least drowsy until the wound knit enough that the dog wouldn't tear at it.

She'd only left her patient's side when Lady Wilmot had relieved her shortly after she and the duke had arrived. But she still couldn't sleep.

Hartshorn Hall had become a house of mourning. None of the servants believed Bess would survive, and most completed their work with tears wet on their cheeks. Lucy contrasted the servants' affection for Em and Bess with the hatred her aunt's servants felt for Lord Marner. When she fulfilled her obligation to her aunt, she would see what could be done to free the oldest servants—the ones most loyal to her aunt—from Marner's employ. Soon, after Colin delivered William to his relatives, she would be able to put her plan into effect. But this was not the time to talk to Colin about her troubles, not when Em's pressed heavily on his mind.

"Lucy." Em stood at the door, the pup that Lucy had played with the first night of their visit at her feet, a line of red ribbon tied around his neck as a lead. "Jeffreys is with Bess. I wanted to thank you. But I couldn't think of anything that would convey how much. . . ." Em's voice trailed off.

"I need no thanks. Bess's recovery will be enough."

"You said you'd never had a dog." Em brushed back a tear. "I thought, if you would like one of Bess's pups, this one is the best of the litter."

"I thought he was promised to Malmesbury."

"When Malmesbury hears how you saved Bess, he won't argue. But if you want something else . . ."

"No." Lucy knelt and held out her hands to the pup. He ran to her, his red lead trailing behind him. She picked him up and nuzzled him. "I've always wanted a dog, a companion like Bess is to you. But"—she handed the pup back to Em—"I have some promises I must keep, and I can't take him with me."

"If you want him, he's yours. You can leave him with me, and whenever you return, he will be waiting."

Lucy held her hands out for the pup, holding him to her chest. "Then I want him. And I already know what I'll call him. Boatswain, after Lord Byron's Newfoundland dog."

"Why?" Em laughed. "That's an odd name for a dog."

"I always thought I would want a dog like Byron's, one who 'possessed beauty without vanity, strength without insolence, and courage without ferocity.'"

"Then, Boatswain, it is."

On the second day, Bess's leg was already beginning to knit well enough that Lucy could feel some hope. Sam and Aidan had built a hard-bottomed litter for the dog, then filled it with pillows and blankets, allowing Em to have

Bess by her side at all times. And the whole group had spent the morning entertaining Em with faro.

Lucy took her opportunity as banker to watch the interplay among them all. Em and Sam spent most of their time watching Bess. Sophia and Aidan watched each other, and Colin—she had to admit—seemed to notice only her.

She pulled a card from the bank and laid it out on the green. Colin met her eyes; then, seeing that the others were focused on the display of the cards, he let his eyes caress her body. She felt her cheeks grow hot.

Sophia bet first. "Aidan has been encouraging me to open my own salon. After the troubles we faced this fall, I'm not interested in something frivolous or purely intellectual. I would like to create a salon where each woman can be useful, where we can to contribute our talents to help each other and those around us."

"Only women?" Sam objected, waiting for his turn. "I'm pretty useful in my own way. I made Bess her litter."

"I suppose we could admit some men." Sophia smiled at Aidan, who met her eyes, then turned back to his cards. "Like the ancient muses, I'd like for us to inspire each other. I thought we could call it the Muses' Salon—a play on the idea of muses as inspiration and of museum, the place where we meet. As for my skills, I can draw, and I know plants, their seasons, and their medicinal properties. In that way, Lucy and I share some interests, and Lucy has—I think—already joined my endeavor. The Muses' Salon's first muse."

"Second muse. You are the first, darling." Aidan placed his hand over Sophia's, the heat in his glance visible to all.

"I can attest that Lucy has the gift of healing." Colin stood up and playfully pulled at his shirt. "Anyone want to see her work?"

"NO!" Em, Lucy, and Sophia answered in unison. Colin, playing dejected, sat back down.

Lucy was grateful for Sophia's gracious compliment—it hid her response to Colin under a demure blush. "I'm not sure I would qualify as an inspiration to anyone. I simply know battlefield medicine . . . how to sew a wound, how to stop bleeding, how to ease a man's death. So, unless one of you is shot . . ."

Sophia lifted her reticule to the table and withdrew a small lady's pistol. "I've carried this with me since my child was kidnapped."

"I suppose, then, we shouldn't cheat at cards," Em observed wryly, placing a penny on one card to reverse her bet. "I'd like to join your salon, Sophia, but I haven't any skills, other than perhaps offering advice on breeding stock."

"Em has at least three talents to contribute." Colin placed his bet, then leaned back in his chair, smugly.

Lucy paid careful attention to Colin's manner, his interplay with Em. As Em had said, she could see no signs that the two were anything other than old and dear friends. Nothing about his relationship with Em seemed to be an obstacle to their continued liaison.

"First, animals trust her. That's why she rides better than any man, even when she lets Stella bully her into using a sidesaddle."

"That's true. She can hardly go out without some lost or hungry animal coming out of the brush to greet her." Sam tossed his bet to land expertly on the card he wanted. "And if you are in trouble and there's a horse about, Em is the one to go for help."

"Second, she has an amazing ear for music, voices, anything tonal. Don't play tricks on her thinking you can get away with it by disguising your voice," Colin said. "Believe me—I know."

"And the third?" Sophia began to tally the bets.

"I'll let Em reveal that in her own time." Colin leaned back smugly, as Em shook her head in irritation.

"Colin says you can shoot and fence, Lucy." Em changed the subject deftly.

"I learned to protect myself, yes." Lucy wondered what else Colin had revealed and how much.

"Could you teach us how to protect ourselves?" Sophia asked, and Em nodded her agreement.

"I would be honored," Lucy replied quietly, touched by how easily the two women offered their fears and friendship. When Lady Wilmot first had mentioned the idea of her salon, Lucy not been certain she could participate, but realizing that Colin was in fact free, she reconsidered the possibility. The idea of friends—women friends—who would support and aid her was all too appealing.

The group played until early evening, when—Em having beaten them all roundly—they broke to dress for dinner.

Chapter Twenty-Five

The knock on Lucy's adjoining door some time later was not unexpected. She had felt the heat in Colin's gaze all afternoon.

But Colin, when she opened the door, wore the face of a soldier, not of her lover. She stepped back to allow him into her room, but he did not enter.

"The letter I have been waiting on has arrived. We leave early in the morning for a hard day's travel. I have healed sufficiently that I do not need for you to accompany us. But I have not forgotten our bargain. If you would rather remain here, I will return and take you to your destination. Of course, it might be that your path coincides with ours—if you trust me enough to confide in me." His voice teased, but not his eyes.

"My obligations take me to London—to Mayfair and the City."

"I didn't expect you to tell me." He brushed the side of her face with the backs of his fingertips. "I thought perhaps you regretted our time together."

"No." She took his hand and kissed his palm. "The misunderstanding over your engagement set me back, but now that I understand, I would prefer to travel with you than wait."

He kissed her deeply. "Then pack some pretty dresses. Perhaps I can show you a little of London when I take you there."

Colin had not lied. It was a hard day's travel, made worse because he rode outside with Fletcher, leaving Lucy to manage Jennie's indisposition alone. William, at least, was an easy traveler.

After two hours, they took a short stop in Chipping Norton to change horses, then once more headed west, then south, then west again. Outside Oxford, they left the main road to travel to a deserted manor house some miles out of the way.

"We will be here for about an hour." He handed Jennie down. "You might wish to stretch your legs, I've arranged to have a light repast set in the drawing room. We will not stop again for any length of time until we reach our destination."

At the porch of the house, Edmund stood with another man, and Colin hurried to them, carrying William's basket and placing it inside the door. Though Edmund offered a brief wave, he did not approach her, nor did either man introduce her to their third companion.

She would have been hurt—the slight was significant—but she knew the looks of such men, focused on some mission she was not allowed to know about until it was all over. For so much of her life, she had accepted that being excluded from important plans was simply the way of things. But having seen the way that the duke included Sophia in his considerations, she had grown discontented. If she were to marry, she wanted that sort of bond. She saw glimpses of the possibility with Colin—but only glimpses.

She looked over at Colin, who was holding up a map for the others to look at, and she had to wonder exactly whom he was working for. He didn't have the demeanor of a mercenary, but many men had turned to private employment after the wars.

Colin was at her side before she realized it. "Go inside. Our next steps have been carefully orchestrated."

The house was so silent that she was stunned to find the drawing room filled with people. Screens stood in front of each window, blocking the view outside. In one corner stood five women, dressed identically as maids. Opposite them were five men dressed as young gentlemen about town. At the table itself stood a dozen men, former soldiers by their carriage and bearing. And beside the door in a great pile were five rush baskets like William's.

But Jennie was nowhere to be seen; neither were Fletcher and Bobby.

Lucy stood alone near the baskets, waiting and watching. No one looked at her.

When the trio entered, each man went to a different group. Edmund and the third man matched the women with men, while Colin paired the former soldiers, handing one man a sheet of paper and a portion of a map. Then Colin led two of the men to the door and shook their hands in parting, Edmund and the stranger followed them out.

Over the next hour, Lucy sat on the stairs in the entry and watched. Every ten minutes, a black closed carriage with no distinguishing marks pulled up to the house's porte cochere. And each time, the man and woman, suddenly appearing very much like lovers, entered the carriage with a basket. Two of the former soldiers took their places at the front and back, with a driver and a postboy between them.

* * *

When all the carriages were gone, Colin held out his hand to help her from her seat. "We have been asked to remain here until all of the carriages make their way to their destinations. Some have longer journeys than the others. I assumed you would wish to remain with me." He pulled her into his arms and kissed her thoroughly.

"When can I know who William is?"

"I suppose I can tell you now." He took her by the hand and led her up the stairs. "His mother was an English Catholic heiress sent to convent school on the Continent. There, she met and fell in love with one of King George's various Habsburg cousins. When Marietta returned to England, the cousin followed, smitten, either with her or with her wealth. Perhaps both."

"Let's pretend it was both." Lucy curled her arm through his.

"Let's." He chuckled against her hair. "The cousin was a strong political ally and fifth in line to rule a significant kingdom, though at the time no one expected him to ever ascend to the throne, and if he did, not for at least another twenty years. George supported the marriage, though he counseled secrecy. But as of this summer, all those who stood between Marietta's husband and the throne are now dead—as is he."

"So, sweet William is in line to rule?" Lucy said with amazement. "I never expected the secret to be one involving the stability of nations."

"It's exactly that. William's uncle had not known of the marriage, and since William's father's death, the uncle has believed himself the legitimate king. He has not been happy to become merely a regent. But King George was immensely fond of his cousin and has vowed that young

William will live to ascend his throne. However, the king had wished not to offer his explicit protection until William was safe with him."

"Then, the attack on your carriage was an attempt to thwart the birth of the legitimate heir." Lucy's voice grew soft in realization.

"So much safer for the mother to never deliver."

The quiet extended for some time between them. Colin escorted her to her room and opened the door.

She looked into the room, lit only by a single candle, the curtains drawn tight. "I suppose this portion of our agreement is concluded."

"Yes. But not my promise to you. I will take you wherever you need to go, and I will stay with you until you send me away."

"Then it seems we have more time together."

And she pulled him through the door and into her arms.

In the night, Lucy had nightmares. But Colin held her to his bosom, and, as she had done for him when he was feverish, he sang to her softly. Sang until the lines on her face had softened, and she fell into a dreamless sleep. And he kept watch over her, sleeping, listening to her breath, wanting to keep her beside him.

He knew she still didn't trust him fully. Sometimes, on the road, she had looked threatened, glancing over her shoulder at the hedgerows as if great arms were going to reach out and pull her into their depths. When he asked her to confide in him, she refused, over and over. But now, with his obligation to Prinny done, he would discover her secrets.

Several hours later, he felt her awaken.

She curled into his arm and began to speak, her hand tracing circles on his chest.

"Living in England after Waterloo had seemed like a strange dream. There was no artillery fire in the distance, no night lit by flames. For months, I had trouble sleeping in the quiet of the countryside. Like tonight, I would awaken screaming."

"I imagine our dreams are much the same. The call to arms, the waving banner, the men rushing forward, the crush of battle, being lost in the smoke of gunpowder. Enemies on every side, my men falling around me, and the noise: guns firing, the spin of bullets, the impact of the cannonballs as they hit and explode, the flying shrapnel."

"No, for me all the noise is distant, but threatening. Where I am, the battle is already over, and the fields are covered with blood and bodies, and parts of bodies. Dead men without limbs stand in battle rank calling for me to save them. The wounded are groaning, begging me for help, for water, for death. The smell of blood is so pungent I can taste it on my tongue. The scavengers are already in the field—vultures, jackals, flies—townspeople stealing men's valuables, even the very epaulets on their uniforms. I try to find my father, and James, but there is no way left to identify which bodies are theirs."

He drew her closer into his chest and brushed her hair with his lips.

"When I woke, my great-aunt would always be there, holding me, stroking my hair—just as you did. She would repeat to me, 'This will pass. This will pass.' Then she would ask me to describe my dreams. She said it would take the sting out, that looking at them in the daylight would allow me to see what my mind refused to forget. It helped."

"In my dreams, I search as well." His voice was heavy with sorrow. "But I also dream of those I killed. Men, women, those who would have harmed my men, England. At the time, I believed I was on the side of right and justice. But the war is over, and I still have the dreams."

She tilted her head to kiss his jaw, then his neck. Comforting kisses. She put her hand on his cheek and spoke gently.

"My aunt was right: eventually, life does go on, whether one wants it to or not. And we forgive ourselves for living when so many didn't. But you can't blame yourself for those you killed. I know it's not much comfort, but you were being a good soldier. Eventually, this will pass."

He kissed her forehead and pressed his cheek into her hair. For a long time, he did not speak, wanting to hold on to her words, to her absolution. "When I was first back, I hated to hear lambs bleating. They sounded too much like the cries of the dying. But eventually the lambs sounded just like lambs. Then, one day I took joy at a sunrise without feeling guilty I had lived to see it; another day, I went on a horse ride and didn't wonder once how well my horse could turn or run under ambush."

Still lying on his shoulder, she shook her head in agreement. "One day, I watched some horsemen ride off to a hunt, and I didn't find myself wondering how many would return. And eventually I awoke one morning and I found that I had not dreamed of James in a week, then in a month, and finally when I did dream of him, I didn't wake up crying."

"He would have wanted for you to live without him. If he loved you . . ."

"He did love me, from almost the first moment we met." Her eyes filled with tears.

"Then he would have wanted you to have this as well." And he turned her on her back, and kissed her from her lips to her toes.

* * *

Hours later, still lying in his arms, Lucy asked the questions she knew he needed to answer. "Tell me about Benjamin and Octavia." She caressed the side of his head with long strokes.

He closed his eyes, breathed several times, then opened them. "Benjamin was my second eldest brother. Older than Aidan. He was ambushed with a group of other officers who were carrying orders to various divisions. Only two survived, but none of the bodies were returned to the regiment. Perhaps if I'd seen his body, I wouldn't have this feeling that he's alive. But if he were alive, he would have come home by now."

"And Octavia? Who was she? A lover, fiancée, wife?"

"A devil."

She touched his chin and turned his face to her. "And a lover."

"Yes. Nothing about her was real, but I only learned that after I'd fallen in love with her. When I met her, I was young, and her attentions were flattering. She was vibrant and witty, and her company was much sought after. But she chose me. I fell in love with her before the end of our second dance."

"She picked you because you were young—because she thought she could manipulate you."

"Yes. I believe that is true." He swallowed once, then twice. "When I discovered she was selling secrets to all parties and I informed my superior officers in Belgium, they refused to let me break it off with her. For months, my job was to take her to bed and pretend to confide in her the false information they gave me. And then when she was no longer of any use, it became my job to silence her."

"They should have given that job to someone else."

"She asked for me specifically, when she was under arrest in Belgium, living in the same house where she had welcomed all her lovers. I think she believed I would not harm her or that I would help her escape."

"Or she knew it was only a matter of time before some-one came to kill her and she wanted it to be someone who had genuinely loved her."

"So the fact that I'm capable of smothering my lover doesn't give you pause." He stared at his hands, rubbing the back of one hand with his opposite thumb.

She didn't answer. The silence grew long between them before she spoke again.

"There was a young soldier, French. His wounds were not so grave that he would not have lived if I had tended his wounds. But Englishmen were also wounded, and I was or-dered to let him wait. I clasped his hand and promised I would return, that he would not die before I could take care of his wounds. He asked me to mail a letter to his fiancée if he died. But I refused, telling him to wait, that I would return." She felt her throat close with tears, and she waited until she could speak without crying.

"He bled to death, from a wound I could have sewn up in ten minutes. He could have lived a long and happy life with the girl he loved. But I followed orders—and I wasn't even a soldier. I could have chosen not to. I could have chosen to save him. So you see: I murdered him just as if I'd put a pillow over his face." She turned his face toward hers, laying both of her hands alongside his cheeks. "How can I judge you for the decision to follow orders? You saved other lives. Other men who will live long and happy lives with the girls they loved because of what you did. And you chose a kind way for her to die. You didn't tie her to a chair and beat a confession, or give her poison, or garrote her. No, you let her fall asleep and not awaken. You gave her more peace than she gave thousands of others."

He kissed her fingers again, and this time looked into her

face. "Your great-aunt was right—sometimes you need to see the nightmare in the light of day. Do you forgive me?"

"If you need forgiveness, and if mine is sufficient. Is that why saving William mattered so much?"

"In part."

"I've meant to tell you: Nell said that Marietta had a weak heart. She would not have survived her labor, even without the bullet wound. It wasn't your fault, love; it wasn't your fault."

They lay in silence for a time, until Lucy sat up and stretched. "I suppose we must get up. Soon, Fletcher will send Jennie up to see if we are alive."

"No fears of that: we have the whole house to ourselves." Colin reached to pull her back into the bed, but she pulled away from him.

"What do you mean? Where is Jennie? William?"

Colin sat up, apologetic. "I thought you understood. It was a kind of shell game, except none of the shells had anything under them. While we were making a show of loading five identical carriages, Jennie and William were secreted away in the back of a gypsy's caravan. Edmund, Walgrave, and Aidan's formidable former foot soldiers guarded the baby inside, while Fletcher and Bobby and Jennie sat on the outside, dressed as a family of vagabonds."

"But I would have at least wanted to wish them well." She stiffened visibly. "I'd grown fond of them. Did you think I wouldn't care what happened to them?"

"It was important to give the appearance, even to the other participants in the ruse, that one of those couples was given the actual baby. You played that role for us."

"So Fletcher, Bobby, Jennie, they all knew the plan."

"Yes."

"But it never occurred to you that I might wish to know, might have been able to play the part. Did you even realize that you were treating me differently from everyone else, even though I've been beside you this whole time?"

He looked surprised, then dismayed.

She backed away from him, pulling her dressing gown over her shoulders, until she stood at the bedside. "No, I was just a pawn in a bigger game. I lied for you, shot men for you, risked my life for you, and confided my deepest regrets to you, and not one of those things earned even a bit of your trust."

"That's not fair, Lucy." Colin held his hand out in supplication. "My obligation was to the Crown."

"And as we know, you take those obligations very seriously." And, not having a brick at hand, she flung the pillow in his face.

An hour later, Colin was saddling a horse when Lucy came to meet him in the yard. She held a shawl tightly around her shoulders, as if it could protect her from her heart breaking. She watched silently, hoping he could not tell that she had been crying.

"I thought I would retrieve the carriage Walgrave and Edmund left in a deserted barn about five miles away. I'll be back in a couple of hours. Then I can take you to London as I promised."

She said nothing, simply stood staring at him. She didn't trust her words not to betray her. How could she still want to be with him, still crave his touch, when he gave more consideration to a twelve-year-old postboy and a sixteen-year-old wet nurse. Like him, she had lived through the wars, but it seemed to make no difference in whom he trusted. No, she was thankful she hadn't told him her woes.

He adjusted the saddle, then spoke again. "Lucy, I'm not used to having to think of another person before I make decisions, and yes, I have treated you as a chess piece. But it was a mistake. I know you aren't Octavia, that you aren't going to betray me, but I still treated you as if you were. Can you forgive me?"

He stood, his arms slightly out from his sides, waiting. "Let me take you to London, show you the sights. You don't even have to tell me what you need to do, but I will take you anywhere you need to go."

"Is there another horse?" She looked past him into the stables.

"Of course. We would need a pair to drive the carriage to London."

"Then I think I'd like to ride."

By the time Lucy had changed into the riding habit Em had loaned her, Colin had saddled the other bay. He helped her mount. She hadn't ridden astride since before she returned to England, and it took her a few minutes to remember her seat. But after that, she found the wind on her face a comfort.

They rode in silence, Lucy trying to sort out her own mind.

Everything she knew about Colin said that he was an honorable man—one who always kept his word—but what if his neglect of her opinion wasn't simply an oversight? What if, without realizing it, he felt constrained by his repeated promise to stay with her as long as she wanted him?

She didn't want to let him go, but she didn't want him to be trapped by his words if he had reconsidered them. Aidan's warning rung in her memory. She had to find a way to release him if he wished to be free. Without that, she would never know if he had chosen her or if circumstances had made the decision for him.

Chapter Twenty-Six

Colin looked up at the red stone boardinghouse on the very edge of Mayfair in Marylebone. "I don't understand why you won't stay at the ducal mansion, or at Sophia's."

"Because we haven't decided what we will do." She held her reticule before her and her small valise.

"You have decided. I am accepting your decision." He raked his hand through his hair. "But not to meet again for a fortnight seems unreasonable."

"Nothing about this affair has been *reasonable*, Colin. That's why I want the two weeks, enough time for our heads to balance our hearts. For you—for us—to weigh our duties against our desires."

"All I've ever known is duty, Lucy. Perhaps it's time for me to choose desire."

"And if you still feel the same in two weeks, then you will know . . . as will I."

"If you are worried about how we will live, I have some land, a house. It's nothing like the ducal mansion, but it could be a home, if you were there."

"I promise: I have not thought once about how we would live. I have only thought about whether you—we—can be happy together. Even in the camps, my parents delighted in each other. If—*on reflection*—we both determine we still wish to be together, then we will meet at noon at the British Museum. But if one of us arrives and the other is not there, then we agree to let the other go. No pursuit, no recrimination. Only a grateful acceptance of the time we had together."

He pulled her against him and kissed her as if for the last time. "I will be there, Lucy. Nothing could keep me away. I was broken before I found you, but with you, I can be whole. I love you, Lucy. I always will. And if you don't love me, I can love you enough for the both of us."

She met him in a kiss that held her soul. But she could not say the words yet, not when she didn't know whether he would truly return to her. She pressed her fingers to his lips and smiled.

Colin watched her walk away, the warmth of her fingers still a ghost on his lips.

Chapter Twenty-Seven

From the safety of a milliner's shop, Lucy watched the street in front of her solicitor's office. She'd paid the woman a tuppence for the privilege. She'd hoped the milliner—a wan woman with gnarled fingers—would be talkative, but she learned little besides the difficulty of acquiring good ostrich feathers. She didn't know if her cousin knew of the codicil she carried to her aunt's will, or even if he knew that their aunt had changed solicitors. But it seemed wise to be cautious.

Once she delivered Aurelia's papers, she could think of her own life and how Colin might—if he wished—figure in it. Unfortunately, as yet, Lucy had been unable to deliver Aurelia's letter to Sir Cecil Grandison. The barrister had been out of town when Lucy had first arrived in London; then, for the last two days, he had missed her visit, having been called unexpectedly to Whitehall. Even though Grandison's wife, Calista, was gracious, Lucy had been reticent to leave the letter. Aurelia had insisted that Lucy deliver the letter into Grandison's hand. But Calista had promised that Grandison would be present the next afternoon, and Lucy had made an appointment to meet him then. Soon, she thought with relief, her obligation would be met.

Watching through the milliner's window, Lucy noted each person who walked by. In the better part of an hour, none looked like any of the men she'd seen with Oaf in Nell's stable yards. Nor did anyone else appear to be watching the solicitor's. She couldn't wait forever, so she slipped from the milliner's shop and crossed the street.

The door rang a bell as she entered. But the outer office was empty. Several standing desks with stools lined the room, but no clerks worked at them. The hair rose on the back of her neck, and she turned to slip out again, wishing—not for the first time that week—that she'd told Colin her troubles and her plans, and brought him with her. But she would meet him again in only two days. The thought warmed the inside of her chest.

Before she could leave, a portly man with red hair and an ill-buttoned waistcoat emerged from the back of the offices. "Ah, madam, we are here." He waved his thick hands as he approached. "Big case in Chancery today, and the clerks have gone to record the proceedings. But we are here."

Lucy could not avoid thinking that *he* was quite large enough to be a *we*.

"Are you our client already? Or do you need our services?"

"I am already a client—or at least I'm a client of sorts."

"Then, come, come." He held open the low gate that led through the clerk's room to a sitting area. "Our new partner, Mr. Rose, will assist you."

The man's warm smile eased her trepidations somewhat, but the ghostly emptiness of the main office still made her wary. But, she told herself, she'd been anxious for months—ever since the barn cat had drunk from her milk and then sickened and died.

"This way."

* * *

The new partner, a bony man of indeterminate age, stood to greet her. Save for a disconcerting crop of white hair at one temple, Mr. Rose could have been thirty or fifty or half a dozen ages in-between. His skin was drawn taut across the bones of his face, making him appear formidable, though his smile seemed genuine.

At her introduction, Mr. Rose briefly looked uncomfortable. "I am glad you came on a day when the office is not busy. We have had several inquiries as to your location."

She unconsciously looked over her shoulder.

"There now, it's safe here. And we will provide you with an escort to your lodgings. I might not appear considerable, but I assure you I can be deadly with an umbrella." He chuckled to himself, as he retrieved a copy of her aunt's will.

When he had it in hand, she produced her copy of the codicil her aunt had drafted.

"Ah, yes, this is very helpful indeed. It clarifies some ambiguity that might have caused trouble in Chancery. But of course that would only have mattered if someone were to dispute her will. With this, however, your aunt's will is quite clear: you inherit her settlement. Quite a tidy sum of two thousand pounds per annum, the bulk of which . . ."

"I'm aware of the bequest. Your partner Godfrey read us the will shortly after my aunt's death."

"Godfrey?" Mr. Rose's skin pursed at the edges of his eyes. "I have only recently purchased a share in this firm, so I am perhaps unaware of all the former partners." He shook off the question. "But in any event, the funds are payable quarterly. I show that you have already received the last two disbursements."

"I have not."

Mr. Rose grew confused. "But I have the receipts here." He unfolded two slips of paper and smoothed them out for her inspection.

"Neither of those receipts bears my signature. But I have

suspicions of where the money has gone. From this point on, you are not to disburse any more funds to the estate. I wish for all monies to be made available here." She handed him a slip of paper with the bank address.

"Then there is the situation with your aunt's estate itself."

"Those should be addressed to my cousin."

Mr. Rose tilted his head to look at her through one eye. "Certainly, many young women of your station allow male relatives to manage their concerns. But do you not wish at least to know what expectations you may have from the income of the estate?"

Suddenly suspicious, Lucy sat back in her chair, "Yes, of course you are right. Please do go over the details with me."

An hour later, Lucy understood more fully why her cousin wanted her dead. And she understood why she would need powerful allies to stay out of danger. But until she knew Colin's decision, until she knew in what capacity to make the request, she would have to wait to approach them.

She signed the papers as Mr. Rose handed them to her. All of them precautions to ensure her aunt's final wishes would be fulfilled, whether she lived to see them or not.

At the end, Mr. Rose picked up his umbrella and walked her to the street. "Are you certain I cannot escort you to your lodgings?"

"No, thank you. It is too far. But I will return tomorrow to sign the other papers."

"I will have them ready." He raised his umbrella to call for a hackney, and a carriage driver waved to them from the other side of the street. "Ah, there. That's convenient."

"Until tomorrow." She shook his hand; then, after waiting for a free space between the carriages, she crossed the street. At the carriage, she asked for Hanover Square. From there, she would walk to Bond Street to catch another hackney or simply walk back to her rooms.

"Safer to enter from this side, miss." The carriage driver motioned her to the sidewalk side and held open the door.

Curtains drawn, the interior was dark, too dark to see. She didn't see the second occupant of the carriage until the coachman had already handed her in. She started to back out. But the carriage driver pushed her forward. Before she could call for help, a hand pulled her to the seat and covered her mouth. The carriage driver climbed beside her—not a carriage driver then—and between the men, they tried to force her mouth open, but she held her teeth and lips clenched.

"I knows a solution to this." And he pinched her nostrils tight. "Now we wait."

She held her breath as long as she could. But when she tried to breathe through her teeth, jaw still clenched, they poured laudanum onto her gums. She felt the numbness travel across her mouth and down her throat. More laudanum, and more, until she felt nothing.

"My dear, lift your head. Yes, there." An older man with a lisp gave her a drink of water, cool on her throat. "You'll feel nauseous for a bit, but this should help."

"Why are you helping me?" She tried to focus her eyes, but found that it just made her head reel.

"Your cousin thinks he can outwit us, even though we had an agreement. He wants you dead. Therefore, we want you alive . . . for now, at least."

"Who is we?"

"Ah, today *we* are your friends, tomorrow . . ." He lifted his hands to the ceiling. "Tomorrow, we might be your executioners. It all depends on fate and whether she smiles on you."

"I can pay you. My great-aunt left me money. I have friends, if you could take me to them."

"Ah, my pretty miss. Do not lie to me. Your cousin has already told us: you have no money, no friends, no one who will miss you after your death."

"He is wrong."

"Then who, pretty miss, will notice you are dead? To whom could we take you?"

"Lord Colin Somerville," she offered more confidently than she felt. "Or Lady Wilmot. Or Lady Emmeline Hartley. Any of them would take me in. Any would miss me if I were dead."

The old man went still. "Ah, then, my pretty miss, we have more than one reason to keep you alive."

Chapter Twenty-Eight

"I'll have a whiskey, my good man." The drunk weaved and stumbled.

"A whiskey?" Flute polished a glass with a damp rag.

"For my liver. Keeps it strong." The drunk leaned up against the man to his right, a sailor who had been boasting of his share in the cargo of a ship recently come to port. The sailor pushed him aside, and the drunk almost fell to the floor.

Flute glared. "Go away now, old man. Whiskey isn't free."

The old man cursed him, but stumbled to the door and into the night.

Hours later, Flute closed the bar.

Though Flute enjoyed the bustle, the customers, the news they carried him from the wharfs and the surrounding neighborhoods, he felt the deep quiet of the empty bar as a comforting calm. He'd already sent Bertie to bed an hour ago, after the boy had wiped the tables, swept the floors, and checked all the corners for drunks and stragglers. Flute had adopted the ginger-haired ten-year-old when he'd returned to England, taking him from an orphanage in Manchester.

It was an act of kindness to Bertie's father, an officer who'd pushed Flute out of the way of a falling mast, only to die himself below it, leaving his wife and son destitute. Flute enjoyed telling Bertie stories of his father, of the vagaries of the sea, but he paid every month for Bertie to be a private scholar at Mr. Neal's Mathematical School in Dorset Street, learning trigonometry and surveying. The Crown might have no concern for the orphaned children of the men who'd served her, but Flute at least didn't forget his obligations. He'd even given the boy a room of his own, a closet at the back of the kitchen. Warm in winter, it was more than Bertie had at the orphanage.

Heading to the back of the bar, Flute turned down all the lights in the wall sconces as he passed, leaving a path of growing darkness behind him. At the back of the linen closet, a door opened onto a long stairwell. As Flute ascended the stairs, he could hear the muted rumble of voices in the gambling hell above his tavern, then the stairway grew silent again as he entered the attics. He and Charters owned the whole block, and the attic was their private passageway from one building to the next, from one enterprise to another.

At the middle building, Flute descended the stairs and entered the series of rooms they used as their offices.

"What did you gain last night when you stole from my customers?" he growled when he found Charters.

"What do you mean?" Charters looked up from the map he was sticking pins in.

Flute didn't argue. "The drunk. I know it was you."

"How?" Charters sounded genuinely surprised.

"I know the ways you stand when you take on a different voice, the way you bunch your clothes to make your body appear misshapen. No one else would notice. You take too much care to appear unremarkable, but I know. If you steal from our customers again, I'll beat you silly."

"Ah, but the man had been such a braggart." Charters lifted his hands in half apology. "I thought he deserved a comeuppance."

"The Blue Heron needs to be above reproach. You know that. No thieving in the bar—just in the hell above. A safe place to make them foolhardy. Give me back your haul, and I'll tell him he dropped it on the floor."

Charters laughed. "Not many men would threaten me."

"Not many men like you," Flute rejoined.

"True." Charters nodded his acceptance. "It's on the table. Just banknotes—and not even as many as he bragged of having. By the way, there's a woman in my room."

"So? I don't remark on your habits." Flute picked up the young sailor's pocket watch and wallet and put them both in the deep pockets sewn into the lining of his jacket. He would send out a message on the wharfs for the sailor to retrieve his belongings.

"Not a doxy. Marner's cousin. We caught her this afternoon."

"What's you going to do with her? Kill her?"

"No. Hide her until we get our money. Perhaps now that we have her, we'll find out what his game is. We meet with him tomorrow, show him the woman. If his answers don't satisfy me, tomorrow you will take her to this address." Charters held out a piece of paper.

Flute looked at the address and scowled. "There?"

"Yes."

"Wouldn't it be kinder to kill her outright? A nice drowning perhaps? Send her there, and she's good as dead anyways."

"Perhaps, but I need time. She's given us some information we need to pursue. And we can't keep her here."

"You know best." Flute shrugged. "I'm thinking of taking the apple girl to a play."

* * *

Marner was angry. Charters could tell by the way his jaw twitched as he stood there silent. But the man had learned that Charters preferred civil discourse in his business dealings, and he was attempting to control his rage.

"How am I to believe you've found her?"

Charters swirled the whiskey in his glass, then sniffed, filling his nostrils with the aroma. "I have alliances, connections, and—unlike you—I pay those who help me promptly. I find it makes my affiliates willing to preference my requests over those of others. If you wish to take the woman with you, you know my fee."

Marner stiffened and clenched one of his hands into a fist. "That's a bloody lot for a fortnight's work. I don't have that much on hand."

"I'm happy to give you whatever time you need to raise the funds. Until then, however, your cousin remains with me."

"With you?" Marner stepped forward, threateningly. Flute raised his eyes from his woodcarving and met Marner's. Marner stepped back. Without the protection of his men, he was more manageable. "But I have plans. Plans that require her to be at my home."

"I'm certain I could help you effect those plans." Charters traced the thick raised scar on the back of his hand.

"No, I'll not be paying more to you than what you already claim."

"It is no more than the price we indicated when you called on us before. Georges had you sign a contract I believe." Charters pulled a page from the top of his desk. "Ah, yes, here it is."

Marner ignored the exchange. "I want to see her . . . alone. I have questions only she can answer."

"She's asleep, drugged."

"I still want to see her."

Charters nodded to Flute. Flute rose, slipping the carving he was working on into his pocket. "This way."

"Five minutes, Flute, no more," Charters directed, then turned back to the pile of correspondence on his desk.

Flute led Marner down the hall and opened the door to a large bedroom kept by Charters. The room was well appointed but understated, the pieces all good, but not fine. A low couch fronted a dressing table and wardrobe at the front of the room, and at the back a tester bed stood next to a washstand and pot cabinet. On the washstand, on top of an embroidered piece of linen, stood a pitcher of fresh water in a basin. In front of it stood a jar of laudanum and an empty glass. A low fire burned in the grate, keeping the chill from the room.

Flute let Marner proceed him, then stepped into the room behind him. The woman lay on the bed, on her back, arms by her sides, legs extended straight. Her fashionable grey walking dress was smoothed out around her. To the side of the bed, on a table, sat her bonnet, its ribbons carefully extended over the edge. It was as if she had lain down for a short nap, smoothing her skirts to avoid wrinkles. Her only movement was the shallow rise and fall of her chest.

"I said alone," Marner sneered.

"She's too far down. She won't answer, and if she does, she won't make no sense." Flute stood in the narrow doorway, easily filling it with his height and girth.

"*I* make that determination." Marner glared again. "Out." He pointed toward the door; then, he pulled a chair to the side of the bed and sat.

Flute stepped outside the room, shutting the door behind him. He knew five minutes: it was enough time to smooth out the neck of his most recent carving, a giraffe. He'd based it on a print hung in the window of the bookseller's shop below. The apple girl had told him how much she liked the engraving, and he was going to surprise her with the carving when he visited her stall in the morning. He leaned into the door, hoping to hear what Marner asked the woman, but he couldn't hear any words. No surprise. The girl had been carefully drugged, enough to keep her asleep, not enough to kill her.

He'd finished the first smoothing stroke when he grew uneasy. He slipped the giraffe in his pocket and quietly opened the door enough to see in.

Flute took in the details in an instant. Marner had moved the washing basin to the chair. The woman's right arm was extended off the side of the bed, her wrist and arm below her elbow in the washing basin, the water red with her blood. Marner himself had moved to the opposite side of the bed, followed by a trail of blood. He had just cut open the woman's sleeve. In his hand a knife dripping blood. He picked up the woman's arm and moved to make a cut.

Howling for Charters, Flute ran at Marner, knocking him into the wall beside the bed. Marner let go of the knife and Flute kicked it aside as he lifted the smaller man off his feet. His first hit left Marner dazed, the second unconscious. Flute threw him to the side and turned to the woman.

Charters was already there, lifting her arm from the water. "Fool. He cut down her arm, not across it. Good to kill her, but it looks like murder, not suicide." Charters lost his working-class accent, slipping into the educated tones of his youth. He pulled the embroidered cloth off the wash-stand and pressed it against the wound, drying the back of the arm with the ends.

Blood dripped onto the floor. Bertie, having followed Charters, stood in the doorway, watching, waiting.

"He missed the artery, but the cut is deep. And from the looks of his knife"—he nodded to the blade on the floor—"it may well fester."

Charters ripped the wide ribbons from her bonnet. "Lift the linen, and hold the wound closed."

Flute put his hands on either side of the long cut and,

pressing his fingers in, pushed the skin together. Blood oozed from the length of the wound.

"I can sew it. Used to help the ship's physician sew up the men who were wounded or lost limbs." Flute turned to Bertie. "Some silk thread from the milliner's, Bertie, and call for the men as you go."

Bertie ran from the room, and Flute heard the door slam behind him.

"Think she'll die?" Flute looked at the blood in the basin and on the floor, so much blood.

"Not if we can help it. Any magistrate who views the body will know it was not suicide. At least you stopped him before he cut the other arm."

Charters pressed his hand over the wound, trying to reduce the flow of blood. But blood seeped through between his fingers. "The blood's not easing. We'll need to burn it."

"I know. Be ready to hold her still." Charters picked up the knife and walked to the fire, leaving Flute to open up the bandage. He held the knife in the fire, turning the blade from one side to the next, until it glowed red. He walked quickly back. Flute pressed his hand against her chest, holding her against the bed.

Charters pressed the hot blade against the cut, searing the flesh. Still unconscious, Lucy cried out, throwing her head back with the pain, then she fell back against the pillow. The smell of burnt flesh and blood filled the room.

Bertie stood quietly in the doorway, holding thread and a needle, looking sick. Behind him, two of the men Charters hired to manage unruly gamblers waited for instruction.

Flute held out his hand, and the boy approached. "Don't worry, Bertie. She won't remember feeling it." Flute ruffled the boy's hair, then took the needle and thread. "She'll only think it was a bad dream."

As Flute threaded the needle, Charters motioned for the men to carry Marner away. "Lock him in the empty storage room, until our employers decide what to do with him. Then bring us some of those new linen cloths from the dining room and a bottle of whiskey." The men nodded and dragged Marner by his arms out of the room. Charters moved the basin back to the washstand, allowing Flute to sit before the woman's arm.

Charters pulled another chair from the wall and held the arm steady for Flute to work.

Flute began to make small stitches, working his way slowly down the long cut.

Charters occasionally wiped away the blood oozing from the stitches. "That's fine work, Flute, as good as any lady's embroidery."

"The Doc was a tidy man, insistent on keeping a clean line. He liked to show off his best ones. The less visible the scar was in the end, the happier he was."

The woman began to moan and pull against her arm. Charters poured a trickle of laudanum into her mouth, then covered her mouth and nose, forcing her to swallow.

When Flute was done, Charters folded a cloth into a bandage and pressed it against the wound, and reused the bonnet ribbons to tie it to the arm.

They stood back and watched her sleep fitfully.

"Do you think he thought she'd bleed to death before we noticed?"

"I don't know. By cutting her here, he may be trying to implicate us in her death. Then he gets what he wants: her dead, and our bill unpaid." Charters moved the chair back to the wall. "But I look forward to asking him what he thought he was doing. Bring his knife. Wrap your knuckles while I change my clothes."

Marner returned to his estate by night, wanting no one to see his face. A bruise grew along his chin and brow where

Flute had struck him. His side hurt, inhalation painful where the big man had hit him over and over. One hand was throbbing where his two outside fingers were surely broken. His plan—imagined in the spur of the moment—hadn't accounted for the cold anger he had seen in Charters's face.

After the initial beating, Charters had left him lying on the floor, his head and belly aching from where the old sailor Flute had struck and kicked him. When he'd heard the door unlock, he had feared that Charters would be the one to let him out, and he'd been pleased to see that the aging fop Georges had come to free him.

But then the fop had stepped aside to allow two large men to enter the room. The men had pulled him from the floor and seated him in a chair that the aging fop had pulled into the room behind them. Then, taking another chair and turning it round, the fop had seated himself, letting the silence draw out between them.

After a long silence, Marner had thought Georges was going to question him. But instead, he'd pulled that blasted piece of pumice from his pocket and begun to sharpen and smooth his nails. After the fourth nail, Georges spoke, never looking up from the pumice.

"My employer is nat pleased that you thought to injure your cousin while she was under his protection."

"Protection?" Marner started to rise, but the two men pulled him back. "I hired you to find her. You had no right to keep her from me. You. Work. For. Me," he spat. He was a lord. They wouldn't dare push him too far.

"Ah, but that is where you have it wrong. *We* work for those who pay us. Had you paid your bill, then chosen to slice her ladyship up, we would have provided you with a comfortable arena to do so. We might have even provided you with better tools. But you haven't. So until that time that your account is paid, we are our own agents, free to work as we please, for whom we please. At this moment, it pleases us to help you understand the limits of our relationship." The fop nodded to Flute, and the pain had begun. Searing pain that had made him more than once lose consciousness.

Each time he'd awoken, they'd begun again.

By the end he would have answered any question, but they didn't ask any. Only made him hurt. Then made him hurt some more.

Chapter Twenty-Nine

"Lucy promised to meet me today at noon at the British Museum. But she wasn't there." Colin felt frantic and was doing a terrible job of hiding it.

"From the first, she said she would leave when William was safe. He's safe. She's gone. Perhaps it's for the best." Aidan spoke the words gently.

"I went to her boardinghouse to see if I could find her there. The landlady remembered me. Lucy's rent is paid through the end of the month, but she hasn't been to her rooms for several days. The landlady let me into her room, and everything was there. Her dresses, her valise, everything." Colin paced to the other side of the room. "Something's wrong. I know it."

"How do you know it? Has she not merely done what she said she would do?" Aidan insisted. "When I spoke with her at the inn, she suggested that she intended only to have an affair."

"That was at the inn." Colin remembered the unspoken promise in her eyes, the touch of her hand on his cheek. But she hadn't said anything. Aidan would say her gestures only signaled goodbye. He rubbed behind his ear, trying to come up with an argument Aidan would entertain. "The puppy.

She might have decided she didn't want me, but she wouldn't abandon Boatswain."

"Well, that's an unexpected argument." Aidan shook his head in disbelief. "Are you certain?"

"I'm certain."

"Colin, you are my brother." Aidan placed his hand on Colin's shoulder. "I would move heaven and earth to find Lucy, if doing so would make you happy. But we have nowhere to start. Not even her real name. Do you know anything that would help us?"

Colin shook his head ruefully.

Fletcher coughed for attention. "If I may offer, Your Grace. We do know something."

"What?" both brothers asked in unison.

"I've never known a woman who could shoot as she did," the old sergeant said firmly.

"Yes, Aidan!" Colin grasped the detail like a drowning man would a piece of driftwood. "You were at Badajoz. Did you ever hear of an officer's daughter who served in the hospitals and was a sharpshooter? She would have been seventeen or eighteen."

Aidan scratched his forehead. "The hospitals were at Llerena, about forty-five miles away, but there was constant movement between the two. She could well have been at Badajoz for some of the siege. But the Allies were twenty-seven thousand strong there. Was her father with the Ninety-fifth?"

"No, her fiancé was. Her father was in the light cavalry." Colin rubbed the inside of one hand with his opposite thumb. "See, we aren't completely without information."

"Badajoz." Aidan shook his head. "I still have nightmares about it sometimes. So many lives were lost, and then the Allied troops pillaged the city. For three days, it was a rout, shameful, inhumane. No one could control the men.

A seventeen-year-old English girl at Badajoz. Her father must have been mad."

"She dressed as a boy," Colin added helpfully.

"So, we could be looking for a boy or a girl." Aidan brushed his hair back in frustration. "Do you at least know where her father died?"

"Waterloo, as did her fiancée."

"Over fifty thousand men were killed, wounded or lost in action at Waterloo." Aidan walked to the window and looked into the garden, where Sophia and her children were playing croquet. "You do realize that none of this is terribly helpful."

"I know. But she didn't leave me. I know it was her plan. I know it looks like she changed her mind, but I can't believe she left me, at least not of her own free will." Colin threw himself into a chair and buried his face in his hands.

Seth and Aidan watched him silently, then, meeting each other's eyes, raised their hands in helplessness.

Seth said quietly, "When I was first trying to discover who our mystery nurse might be, I heard about a missing heiress in the next county over. She'd been missing for several weeks—from the description, it sounded like our scullery maid. Apparently the heiress was found wandering the countryside out of her wits. The family was reportedly grief-stricken and put her into an asylum, hoping she'd recover."

"So it could be Lucy?" Colin raised his head from his hands.

"Probably not," Seth replied.

"Why not?"

"Because Lucy was with you at Em's when I heard the reports that the heiress had been found," Seth countered gently.

"But something about it felt right?" Aidan interpreted.

"Yes," Seth pushed his thumbs into his waistband. "Your

run-of-the-mill heiress wouldn't hide in the kitchen of an inn, but one who grew up in the camps wouldn't have been afraid of work or dishes."

"And you can't shake the feeling that the heiress might have been Lucy." Colin leaned forward, hopefully.

"I couldn't at the time—and I still can't."

"Then perhaps you should investigate," Aidan directed. "Ride back to the Newfords'. Find out who the heiress's family was. Then track down anything you can about their mad relative. And see if Nell will give you any more information now that Lucy has disappeared. As for me, I think I know whom I might ask about the sharpshooting."

The banquet hall was full, a dinner for Prinny about to commence. Colin and Aidan found General Hampton in the corner regaling a group of MPs with stories of his latest fox hunt. The general had enjoyed his years since Waterloo, growing happy and fat.

"My boy, glad to see you!" He slapped Aidan's back firmly. "I haven't seen you since that night when . . ." His voice trailed off as he saw Lady Wilmot.

"My brother Colin Somerville; and my fiancée, Sophia, Lady Wilmot."

"Welcome, welcome! I'm happy you could accept the invitation."

"We have a question about one of the officers under your command, or who we believe might have been under your command."

"Give me the name, and I'll tell you what I can. But I have only a few moments. I'm to offer some good words about Prinny once he arrives."

"We haven't the name. That's the problem. We are looking for an officer who reared his daughter in the camps and taught her to shoot and fence. She was at Badajoz, and we believe her fiancé was in the Ninety-fifth."

Hampton grew solemn, distant. "I'm afraid I can't help you after all, my boy."

Colin pushed forward. "She disappeared last week, and we fear she might be in danger."

"But you don't know her name."

"I knew her as Lucy."

Hampton picked up his pocket watch and checked the time. "I cannot help you. A girl who could shoot at Badajoz? That would have been dreadful for morale."

Colin started to object, but Aidan held out his hand for him to be quiet.

"Are you saying that there was no girl, or that she would have been kept a secret? Even now, a secret?"

"If there had been such a girl, then Wellington would have wanted to make sure that no one knew."

Chapter Thirty

She wasn't sure where she was. She couldn't open her eyes. She could move her fingers. She pressed the tip of her thumb to her forefinger and felt only numbness. Drugged. She fought to remember.

She groaned. A rough hand touched her face.

"She's waking up."

She heard indistinct voices. A calloused hand forced open her mouth. Bitter liquid dripped on her tongue. She knew the taste. More laudanum. She tried to spit it out, but the hand shut her mouth and held it closed.

Her limbs began to float, as the darkness enveloped her.

She was cold. The wall against her back was uneven stone, dank with mold. She'd been set in a corner, her neck crooked painfully against the side wall.

Her arms felt heavy; they hung at her sides, hands against her thighs. Under her fingers, she felt a coarse woven fabric. She moved her fingers, feeling for the edges. A thin pallet.

She tried to turn her head to the room, but bile rose in her throat. Nausea. Too much laudanum.

Slowly. She could turn her head if she moved it slowly.

The room was dark, but the air smelled of unwashed bodies. She could make out the sounds of two, or more, people sleeping. She held her own breath and tried to count the noises made by the other sleepers. At least two.

With effort, she could move her left hand. Beside the pallet was a thin folded blanket. She had enough strength in her hand to pull it into her lap, then with concentration, she lifted her right hand to help her left hand stretch it across her lap. Exhausted, she let her hand fall back to her side.

Her fingers felt the floor. Wood, old and much marred. Her fingers could trace its deep groves. Her left hand found a lidded chamber pot to her right. With the laudanum she had been given, she had little need of it.

One of the sleepers grunted and rolled over in the dark. Were they also captives or her captors?

She waited, listening.

She slept again.

She awoke sometime later. The transit of the moon now offered a weak half-light. The sleepers still slept. How much could she move without waking them?

She tried to move her legs. One of her legs was tied. She leaned forward and felt a shackle on her ankle. The thick fetters were bolted to the wall inches below her feet. The chain measured no more than three spans of her hand. Enough to stand and no more. No hope of escape.

Colin. She thought of the last time she'd seen him. She'd touched his face and looked into his eyes. He'd clasped her hand in his, kissed the inside of her palm. She'd intended the moment to signal her commitment to him. But, with her gone, he would think she had meant goodbye. He wouldn't look for her.

She was alone. She would have cried, but she couldn't.

She hunched down onto the floor, facing the wall. She pulled the blanket up from her lap over her shoulder. She curled her knees into her belly as protection, against her invisible foes. She struggled against sleep, but it came against her will.

She woke again. It was morning, but what morning she did not know. Her right forearm throbbed with pain. It was bandaged. She didn't remember hurting herself. She was afraid to take off the bandage. That was at least clean, and she didn't wish to see what they might replace it with.

She pushed herself partway up and examined her cell. A long, thin room in the upper level of the building. Tree limbs moved with the breeze outside the window.

The window had no glass, just an opening to the outdoors. The cold would be unbearable in another week or two when fall finally set in. The fireplace looked long unused, no cinders or ashes on the stone hearth. The other occupants were gone. Three other pallets stuffed with straw lay on the floor, each one near a shackle bolted to the wall near the floor. Dirty linens and blankets were piled high in the corner to her right. A prison or an asylum. She blinked away tears.

Footsteps, heavy, approached her cell. A key scraped in the lock. She lay down as quickly as she could. She forced her eyes closed, wanting to watch, to see who her captors were.

Footsteps approached and stopped near her. She made her breath shallow and even. A thin hand grasped her shoulder and shook.

"Wake up. Time to eat."

She pretended to be just awakening, her movements slow and languid. It was easy to do. There was still so much drug in her body.

"Open yer eyes."

She complied but kept them deliberately unfocused.

"Ah, too drugged still. Lucky they didn't kill yer with it. But yer's safe now. As long as ye abide by the rules, yer'll be treated fairly. They says yer a wild one. Need to keep ye close so ye don't harm yerself agin. Do as I says, and yer'll do fine. We keep an orderly house here. Understand?"

Lucy nodded. A linen-covered tray sat on the floor behind the woman. She leaned down and helped Lucy sit up.

"I'm Smith. I watch the lodgers. Yer name is Sally. Doesn't matter what yer name was afore. It's Sally now. Matron likes her lodgers all meek and easy. She won't ken well to arguing about why yer here. Your relatives pay her well to keep ya, and she won't like to find yer isn't crazy. Best be a bit melancholy and grateful."

Lucy nodded again.

Suddenly, from her right, the pile of blankets moved, and thin arms grabbed at the tray. Lucy recoiled instinctively.

"No, Moll. That's Sally's." Smith pushed the tray toward Lucy. Then she took a piece of dried bread from her apron pocket. "Here's a treat."

The pile transformed to an emaciated woman with large eyes and a dirty face. So tiny one could think her a child except for her hair, almost completely grey, and the lines on her face. Smith tossed the bread, and Moll with surprising speed, caught it, and retreated to her corner. Her back to the walls, she squatted, gnawing the bread with suspicious eyes.

Lucy looked at her with dread. Was this what she was to become? Old, mad, and alone?

"Ah, don't fear her, luv. Just keep yer distance," Smith said plainly. "Moll's long past human. Acts like one of those African monkeys in the Royal Menagerie. If we let her into the garden, she climbs whatever is nearby. Last time, she took to the matron's rose trellis. Thorns in her hands and feet, and never noticed. Cold don't faze her. She breaks the window fast as we replace it."

Smith uncovered the tray, revealing a bowl of oats and some cheese. "Yer family is paying dear for yer meals. Few gets this much."

She needed to learn the rules of the place, to appear compliant. It was her only hope of escape. If she tried to escape and failed, there would be no second chance.

"This is yer room. You share it with Moll, Dinah, and sometimes with Rebecca when she's offended the matron. Dinah works in the yard, Rebecca in the kitchen. Moll, well, she keeps here most days."

The nurse held out a spoonful of oats. The smell reminded her of mornings in the camp, the sunlight on the walls of Lisbon. James and her father welcoming her to the fire, smiling. She drifted.

"No, gel. You must eat. It'll help with whatever they gave you."

She opened her mouth, and Smith fed her like an infant. She slept again.

She woke in the night. Moll stood in front of the window, swaying. The moon was almost full. Moll held one arm outstretched through the window, reaching for something. She moaned and hummed. The tune hung at the edges of Lucy's memory.

She slept. Moll's moans became the moans of the wounded. Blood and fire powder. Limbs without bodies. The noise of the cannon. Her own cries rang in her ears.

"Wake up. Wake up, gel. Yer dreamin. Wake up."

Smith shook her awake, then bathed her face with cold water. "There, there. Just a dream. Nothing to be a-feared of. Smith is here." Her tones were even and soothing, like the voice of a mother with a frightened child.

Sometime later, she awoke to screaming—this time not her own. The woman called Rebecca was struggling against two large men who dragged her into the room from the hall.

"You should know better than to offend the matron."

The woman was wailing, weeping, screaming, fighting them with all her might.

The men who smelled of the stables threw Rebecca to the floor, pressing her face into the pallet, one man's knee in her back. "She'll need air soon. But at least she's quiet now." The second man laughed as he locked the shackles on her legs; then they dragged her to her feet and shackled her arms high above her head. The man cursed as she bit his arm, and he slapped her hard, then crushed her face into the corner.

The first man groped her breasts from behind. "Want a little of this?" he proposed and lifted Rebecca's skirts, revealing bare legs. He kicked her feet farther apart, and Rebecca struggled against the shackles to close her legs. "Or do you prefer taking your pleasure in the basement?"

"That one has family." The second man walked to the still open door. "And they all end up in the basement eventually, and by the third night, they welcome a bit of company."

"Looks like you have only me for comfort, lass."

Lucy closed her eyes, not wanting to see what would happen next. But Rebecca, rallying, screamed for Smith. And Smith—miraculously—came.

Smith came to rouse her. "Time to see the doctor and meet the matron."

Lucy needed to know what line Rebecca had crossed that had led to her being chained against the wall for two days. When they had finally released her arms, Rebecca had crumpled to the floor, and they had left her, curled up there, still shackled at her feet and smelling of her own urine.

Smith had told her to be meek.

The matron was a well-dressed woman, with a cross at

her neck and a Bible in her hands. A member of one of the reforming societies. Lucy's heart sank.

An older man, hunched and wizened, removed the bandage from her arm. He pressed on the wound to see if it would weep. "Ah, nicely mending. No weeping of the wound. You are lucky, girl. A wound like this could putrefy easily." He watched her eyes for a reaction, and Lucy was careful not to give one. Shaking his head slowly, he latched his medical bag, then spoke to the matron. "If the weather suits, she may walk in the garden three times a day."

"No, she is able in body, if not in mind. She will walk in the garden only if she has completed her chores."

The doctor picked up his bag and left, leaving Lucy standing quietly.

"Your family tells me that you suffer from fits of melancholy and in one of those fits you harmed yourself." The matron's voice was hard and stern.

Lucy kept her gaze at a spot on the floor six inches before her toes.

"While you have been healing, you have been allowed to remain in your room, but now you will go about with the other patients. If you comport yourself well and do your work cheerfully, you may remain with the others. If you do not, you will be confined in your room until your demeanor improves. If your manner is not improved by that correction, then you will be moved to the cellar, where the dark can calm your nerves and promote useful reflection. Do you understand me, Sally?"

Lucy nodded her head, keeping the movement slow and her eyes fixed on the rather elegant carpet.

"If you work cheerfully and well, you will find that we do everything to make our guests comfortable. You will be allowed to wash your face and hands three mornings a week and bathe every two weeks in the warm months, every month in the cold. We will give you flannel to wrap your feet when the days grow colder, and we will change your straw whenever it is wet or dirty. Until we can be sure you will do yourself no more harm, you will be confined to a strait waistcoat after you complete your work. Do you understand me?

Lucy nodded.

"Then you may go. Smith, escort Sally to the kitchen, where she may begin her chores."

She no longer knew what day it was. She had begun to make scratches in the floor next to her pallet to keep track of time, but she hadn't begun her calendar immediately. And any time the matron entertained the local magistrate or her friends, the patients were given laudanum to make them appear placid and content. She never knew how many days she lost. But her scratches numbered twenty-one.

Her routine was unvarying.

She would awaken in the morning. Three times a week, Smith would bring a bowl to her room and let her wash her face and hands. Then Smith would unlock the chain that connected to the metal ring bolted on her ankle. She would go down the stairs with the other women, sit in rows at the tables, and eat a bowl of porridge. Most days, she and the other women were served from a common bowl, but on other days her porridge came to the table already in a bowl. On those days, she ate as little as possible. Sometimes she had to avoid eating on regular days, so that they would not figure out that she knew the pattern. She grew thin.

After breakfast, whether she ate the porridge or not, she would work first in the kitchen, once more a scullery maid. If she were too good at washing, she would never be allowed to do anything else, so she had to work to splash the water on the floor or to bang the pots together loudly enough that the Cook cursed at her clumsiness. Tea was always safe because she ate it in the kitchen, but it was rarely more than a biscuit and cup of tea.

Every other afternoon, she would scrub the floors alone, working her way through the whole house once a week. On the other afternoons she would work in the kitchen garden. Though the days were growing cold, there were late plants to harvest and beds to prepare for spring.

Each day before it grew dark, she would walk in the garden with the other patients, making slow circles around its edges under the watchful gaze of Smith or one of the other nurses. She knew each crack in the garden wall, each place where she might find a handhold. She had looked out each window in the house as she mopped the floors, trying to learn the lay of the land beyond the asylum, trying to find a way out. She hadn't been able yet to find one.

In the evenings, the mistress would read from deportment books or from revivalist sermons while the able-bodied inmates embroidered in the half-dark of the firelight. Lucy found it strange that the matron would read long lists of how to behave at a ball when her audience largely would never have occasion to attend one. The matron would sell the best of their embroidery at a shop in London, so those who were particularly accomplished sewed all day under the matron's watchful eye. Lucy had realized that she would never find a way of escape if she were too accomplished at the needle, so she sewed poorly. Each time she made her stitches uneven or knotted the thread, the matron hit her knuckles hard with a ruler, leaving bruises across the backs of her fingers and hand. But she kept up the illusion until eventually the matron was convinced she lacked the ability to improve, and she was trusted only with the most rudimentary repairs.

While her work was often sloppy, no one could fault her for being disagreeable. In each task, she acted as if she were a bit dim. Meekly apologetic, she never fought back, but instead stood quietly awaiting each blow.

She was afraid, afraid she would have to spend her life here, unremembered, unknown, called by a name that wasn't her own. The worn hands she had been so proud of at Nell's only lent truth to her cousin's tales. No lady would have the hands of a scullery maid.

She learned quickly that it was safest to agree and, when she couldn't simply agree, to say nothing at all. To bow her head and appear contrite. Silence was safety.

The trick was to avoid offending the mistress. Yet this was harder than one might imagine.

The cold made her fingers clumsy, as did lack of food. If she fell asleep at her sewing frame, she awoke to the hard rap of a switch on her fingers and a lecture on the sins of laziness. The cold made the switch ache to her bones, but if she cried out, more punishment followed.

Matron believed that stern discipline would lead her guests to lives of useful domesticity. She'd been told that Lucy was headstrong and lazy, so she did everything to beat both qualities out of her charge. Whether her charge complied from exhaustion or beatings, the matron didn't care.

Moll was howling again and beating her head against the wall. Luckily, since the last time, when Moll had tried to strangle her, they had allowed Lucy to move to another corner of the room, one where Moll couldn't reach her.

"She relives the happy moments does our Molly. She sings to her babe, welcomes her man home. They both died in a fire, and Molly was the only one got out." Smith carried new straw for Moll's bed. "They say she tried to throw herself into the flames, but some cruel man passing by thought it would be better for her to live than die that day. He held her back, and her mind broke with sorrow. She lives in a past that's better than her present. But if I were her, I would too. If I could find a happy moment in the past, instead of this place, I would want to hold on to it. For her, we're the nightmare."

"Will I go mad?" Lucy was afraid even to voice the words.

"If you do, miss, who could blame you—or any of you? I suppose the way to know if you are sane is if you imagine things in your world that you couldn't know, couldn't imagine."

"But can't we imagine anything?"

"That's the problem. How do we tell what's real and what's not? Perhaps we're both sleeping now, and you've dreamed me up because you need a friend."

On the battlefield, or rather in the camps, which were like the battlefield, she'd learned all the things she couldn't do. Save her mother, her father, James.

She'd learned to take each day's gifts as they came, the flight of a triangle of geese in winter, an alpine flower growing amid the snow, the song of frogs by a pond in spring, the scent of grass after a rain. She tried as best she could to remember those things when her senses were blasted by the acrid smoke of powder, the deafening noise of the cannons.

In the asylum, the only gifts were her memories. More and more, as she worked, she lived in a place that was long past.

"Come, come, girls. Mind your work." Matron stood at the edge of the floor Lucy and Rebecca were mopping, holding her switch in her hand. "This passageway will be our visitors' first impression of how well our lodgings are maintained for our guests."

Lucy and Rebecca had been mopping for hours—every floor in a single day. Delegates of the parliamentary committee on asylums were visiting all the private asylums, and Matron had learned that hers was next on their list. Matron was determined that she would have no criticisms of her care.

Lucy's knees and wrists ached, and her fingers were blue from the cold. Cold stone floors, bitterly cold air blowing across the loggia from the garden, and cold water. She flexed her fingers to force some warm blood back into them, but there was no warmth left anywhere in her body.

"Sally, stop dawdling. That corner behind you needs attention."

Lucy backed up, pulling the bucket of freezing water with her. Another five feet, and they would be through. Exhausted, she closed her eyes as she scrubbed, back and forth, both hands on the towel, the way that Matron preferred. Then the towel wouldn't move. She opened her eyes to see Matron's foot, holding the towel firmly in place.

"Do you think, Sally, that you can adequately scrub this floor without watching your work?"

Lucy shook her head meekly as Matron raised her switch. Rebecca tried to move out of the range of Matron's ire, but in doing so, caught her rag under her bucket and tipped it, and its dirty water, onto the floor. And Matron's new black slippers.

Matron screamed for Smith and for the men who dealt with difficult guests. Then she beat Rebecca's back with the switch, punctuating each word with another blow. "We . . . will . . . see . . . if a night or two in the basement doesn't teach you to be less insolent."

But when the men came, Matron sent both Rebecca and Lucy to the basement.

The basement was dark, pitch black. Lucy could hear movement, the sounds of mice—she hoped they were mice—squeaking at the corners of the walls, felt a spider's web trail across her face. Lucy pulled herself into a ball, tucking her feet under the edge of her dress and pulling the fabric under her as much as she could. For the first time at the asylum, she was truly afraid: of the dark, of what lived there, of the men who might choose to visit them, of never being allowed to be Lucy again, of having no place to hide.

Each time the camp had moved, Lucy's father or mother would always find a place for the two women to hide—"just in case," her father had always said. When she was young, it had been a game, but as she grew older she understood more fully what the stakes were if they didn't hide—or if they were found. They had never used the hiding places, until one day—after her mother had died—a battle five miles away had turned into a rout, and an officer had ridden ahead to warn the camps, sounding the alarm as he rode on.

The hiding place she had chosen was in the large rocks at the edge of their camp. Hidden behind brush and twigs, she'd found a declivity under one of the larger boulders big enough for her to crawl under. She'd wrapped herself in a brown wool blanket, and then she'd curled in as far as she could, pulling the blanket over and around her. Behind the brush, she could only see out from a small space close to the ground.

The memory was so clear that she could still feel the cold rock through the wool at her back. She could smell the wool, wool the color of dirt and stone, heavy with the grit of a thousand miles, grit one could never completely beat out of the cloth.

The horses had come first, the beat of their hooves resounding in the ground beside her face. Then the foot soldiers had passed before her, yelling to each other, falling, screaming. Then nothing, but the terrifying silence of the battlefield, where, in protest, even nature refused to speak.

If no one came for her by nightfall, then no one would come. Dead or captured.

Once more, she had heard her father's voice: "If you are ever hiding, Lucy girl, you stay quiet. Close your eyes, and listen. But breathe slow and long, letting your breath take your fear away, so that you can be ready if someone finds you. Friend or foe, you must be ready. If you have a long wait, then sleep when you can, so that if you need to run, you have rest on your side."

She'd waited, forcing her body to calm, to half-sleep. She'd watched the light change, as morning became afternoon and afternoon began to spread into evening.

Eventually she'd heard steps, then a low patterned whistle much like the English nightingale's. Her heart had risen and fallen in the same moment. Their signal, but not her father's pitch.

A pair of boots approached, scuffed and dirty, the bottoms of the trousers sewn with buckskin. One of Wellington's men. But she'd waited. *Caution*, her father's voice reminded her. *Strategy. Don't reveal your intentions until you are ready to act.*

She'd heard her name, pitched low. "Lucy. All's well. It's over. You're safe. We're all safe."

James. The kind-eyed young officer who had begun to smile shyly at her—always respectful James. He'd pulled aside the brush and twigs, and she'd pushed aside the wool blanket, looking up into his broad open face. His wide smile had reassured her that her father was yet alive. He'd sunk onto one knee to help her out, her body stiff from the cramped quarters. His hands in hers had been warm, comforting.

He'd pulled her to her feet, and when she wavered, her feet not quite under her from the hours of inactivity, he'd pulled her into his arms and held her upright. She'd leaned into him, his warmth, strength, kindness. Their mutual relief—at finding themselves still alive—filled the first time they'd touched, giving it an unexpected sweetness and poignancy. He'd kissed the top of her head as she leaned her face into his chest. Then, he'd let her go. He'd picked up the blanket and folded it briskly, then offered her his arm to escort her back to the camp.

Tears welled, and she allowed them to fall. All her losses seemed to lead her to this dark place—and the monsters without.

She'd lost her father and James on the same day. It had seemed ironic even then: they had lived through every battle, only to die in the last.

The battle had been horrific, so many dead, so many wounded, maimed. She'd focused on caring for the wounded, the dying. Hours had passed without her being able to think of anything but the broken body in front of her.

She'd been in the surgery when she received the news of their deaths. She'd just finished bandaging the wounds of a young sergeant when the room had grown silent as it always did when Wellington and his adjutants entered the tent. But this time had been different. She'd known from the moment that Wellington approached and took her hands in his. She'd heard the words, received her father's pistol and sword from a young officer. She'd felt the grief, waves of grief, but she had stood, without crumbling, an officer's daughter to the last.

Then another young man—one of James's men— stepped forward. Only a bit younger than she was, he held out a piece of folded oil cloth, and she knew what was inside. James had written her a letter and carried it in his boot, another "just in case." She took it and laid it with her father's effects. She shook each officer's hand as he offered words of condolence. It had seemed like an endless stream of officers and condolences. She'd heard each one as if from a great distance. Then she'd listened as they outlined the plans to return her home, nodded to the officer who'd volunteered to ensure her safe return to her family. From their faces, she knew they grieved with her: her father had been well-regarded, well-loved, and they had all, in some fashion or other, seen her grow up. In some way, she was each officer's daughter.

Her father's body had been brought to her later, delivered to the camp because he was an officer and because his men knew she waited for him. He looked as he had in life, but pale, killed by a bullet to the chest, the kind of wound that would have killed him almost instantly.

Her lover's body she never saw. His men said they wished for her to remember him in life. And she knew what that meant, that what remained had been too damaged to bring back.

She'd read James's letter in the wagon back to Lisbon. It had been brief,

Lucy, I do not have the words to tell you what you already know. Before I met you, I loved honor and country, nothing else, not even life. Those were a soldier's loves, and my life a soldier's life. But then your soft smile and kind words conquered my warrior's heart, and from that moment I have fought for honor and country out of my love for you. I had hoped we would grow old in each other's arms, but the gods of war have denied us that dream. But I

have loved you already enough to fill a lifetime.
Good night, my darling. If death brings dreams,
mine will not be of honor or of country, but of you.

She'd carried the letter as James had done, in the lining of her boots. And then once she had it memorized, she didn't need to carry it at all. It was hidden with her other treasures in the base of a rotten oak, already buried as she was.

She laid her head on her arms, folded across her knees, and wept.

That night, she dreamed of Colin loving her, of a bright sun-colored room like the one at her great-aunt's house, of awakening in his arms as he kissed her forehead. And no one disturbed her dreams.

Chapter Thirty-One

After a month, Colin accepted that Lucy had made another choice, one that did not include him. She had simply vanished, and because he had searched for her in every town and kitchen within ten miles of London, he had to acknowledge that she did not want to be found. Even then, he collected her things from the boardinghouse and stored them in a trunk in Sophia's attic. Aidan would have argued for a clean break, but Sophia simply pointed the way to the attic, then gave him a copy of its key. Eventually, he would give the dresses back to Em if she wanted them, but for now, he kept them—a memory he was not yet able to release.

Then he'd taken Dart, his favorite, fastest horse, and ridden to Hartshorn Hall, stopping only to let the horse rest, speaking to no one at the inns, enveloped in a sorrow as black as his overcoat.

Em had welcomed him without question when he'd ridden up alone in the rain, drenched to the bone.

She'd met him in the stable yard, having already called for a small army of groomsmen to unsaddle and brush down his horse. Her eyes had searched his face for only a moment before she put the house into motion, preparing the room he always occupied, drawing a hot bath, sending for dry clothes. Then she had stood beside him as he ensured Dart was dry and fed, holding his hand in hers.

"She didn't come, Em." He turned away, but Em could see his eyes were wet with tears. "I never considered she wouldn't be there. That she didn't want me."

Em had never considered it either. She'd seen Lucy's face, and she had been sure she'd read love there.

She wrapped him in her arms, as he had her so many times in their youth. "She must have had a reason. Wait. Perhaps something delayed her, perhaps she's there even now, hoping you will return."

"I waited a month, Em. I went to every lodging house, tracked out every road. No one had even seen a woman of her description. I went back to the inn where I met her, but no one had seen her since I took her away with me."

"I don't believe it, Colin. Something isn't right."

But he didn't hear her. As she watched, the mask he'd worn since Belgium stiffened back into place. Some might believe it a function of his military training, but she knew better. "No, we made no promises. Even when I told her I loved her, she said nothing. The fortnight's delay was clearly a way to let me go easily. I must accept her decision."

"Stella is here with her usual retinue. But I will make your regrets at dinner. Tell them you have caught cold in the rain."

"No." He clasped her hands in his. "I failed you on Stella's last visit. I will not fail you now."

"Sam has escaped to the cattle markets with his valet." Jeffreys stood at Colin's bedroom door, with a pressed suit over his shoulder. "So, I have taken the liberty of finding you suitable dinner attire out of his closet."

Colin allowed the butler to enter. "Thank you, Jeffreys. I should have considered that the Hall might be entertaining a house party."

"If Lady Em would allow it, I would have put out Stella's guests sometime last week. As usual, they are a vapid lot. Field, stream, and dinner—their only interests."

"How much longer do you anticipate them staying?" The jacket Jeffreys had chosen fit well, if not perfectly. Colin held out his arms for Jeffreys to help him into the waistcoat; he felt a stiffness in his side where the bullet had gone through, but no pain. Lucy's ministrations . . . no, he turned away from the thought.

"I am hoping for rain. That usually sends them packing their bags for drier climes—or London. Last time, I hid all the dice and cards. But this time Mrs. Cane has thwarted me by bringing her own. So, I've been burning the London papers as soon as they arrive, hoping the lot will grow desperate for news of the *ton* and take their leave. I'm sure Lady Em will be grateful to have one friend to bear some of the brunt of Mrs. Cane's pettiness."

"Has Stella been uncivil?" Colin lifted his chin for Jeffreys to arrange his cravat.

"She has grown more so now that she has a son and Lady Em remains unmarried. Lady Em indulges Mrs. Cane and her guests because she believes her father would wish her to be gracious."

"I will do my best to divert Stella from tormenting Em." Colin pulled on the ends of his waistcoat to straighten it.

"May I take away your wet clothes?" Jeffreys held Colin's suit and trousers in his arms.

"Yes, but just a moment." Colin slipped his finger in the inside waistcoat pocket and transferred the ring—Lucy's ring—into his new one. He had been carrying it with him since he'd bought it, and—like her clothes—he was not yet ready to let it go.

Jeffreys held open the dressing room door. "You should find the party gathering in the drawing room."

"I've been waiting to ask you for some time, Mr. Somerville, what your intentions are toward my dear cousin," Stella declaimed loudly enough for the whole company to hear.

The room grew quiet. Stella loved an audience for her performances, and Em kept her in check by not having large dinners unless she knew Stella was in London or Northumbria.

"It seems my dear cousin has lost even your regard," Stella continued, "though I suppose no one can blame you, disfigured as she still is."

Em watched Colin's face, hoping he would not rise to Stella's challenge. She was too far from him to place a warning hand on his arm.

"It's lovely that the scars have faded as they have, and certainly they are not so bad as those on poor Miss Featherstonebaugh. She's retired entirely from society I've heard, and her young man has begged off." She turned to the crowd, who nodded sympathetically. "But I can't complain really. If you have no wish to marry our Em, my son will make a fine lord. It's a foolish thing, letting Em inherit instead of a man fit to manage."

Em had heard the speech many times in recent years, but never at a public dinner. And Colin had never before been present when Stella arrived to "inspect" Em's management on the justification of needing to ensure her son's patrimony. It had made Em wish her father would marry his French mistress and provide Em with a stepbrother who could take over the estates. But it was her father's and her grandfather's wish that Em have the estates after his death, and they had both spent a great deal of money to ensure she would inherit.

Colin's smile widened, and Em's heart sank. It never helped to challenge Stella; she would only find some petty revenge.

Colin turned toward the room and held up his glass as if to toast. Had the room not already been silenced by Stella's cruelties, his presence—honed by his military bearing—would have done so. Even then, he waited for several seconds before he began to speak.

"I had hoped to have this conversation first with Lady Emmeline. But perhaps surrounded by our friends . . ." He paused and looked sharply at Stella. ". . . and family. I should address my intentions. From our childhood, it has been expected that we would marry, though we have never been formally engaged. My time in the wars and this past year have made me reconsider all my commitments, my obligation to Lady Emmeline included."

Em stood taller, preparing for the aftermath of his speech, preparing for the look of victory on Stella's face. But Colin was right: it was time to make their relationship clear.

He walked toward her, all eyes in the room following him until he stood in front of her. She breathed in as he took her hands in his, his strong hands giving her strength.

"Would you, Lady Emmeline Hartley, do me the great of honor of becoming my wife?"

She watched, stunned, as he took a ring from his inner breast pocket. Lucy's ring, not hers. No, not hers.

He knelt on one knee and placed the ring on her finger as she searched his face. She saw nothing but resolve and kindness.

"Say yes, Em." He squeezed her hand.

"Are you sure?" she whispered, aware of their gazes.

He nodded seriously, his hands tight on hers. He rose and held her to her chest, as always a safe refuge. "Say yes," he whispered.

She pulled away, pitching her voice so everyone could hear.

"Then yes, Colin Somerville, yes."

He picked her up and swung her in his arms, as the room cheered. As he put her down, he whispered in her ear, "It was always supposed to be me and you, Em. I know that now."

His smile was wide and sincere. No one, not even Stella, questioned his sincerity.

Chapter Thirty-Two

"Sally, please leave your station and go to the matron's drawing room."

Lucy felt the now familiar panic. She couldn't think of anything she had done to call herself to the matron's attention. She couldn't bear another week confined in the straitjacket and chained to the floor in her room or locked in the darkness of the basement.

But now at least she knew the rules.

"I should wash my face and hands."

"No, miss, she's said to come straightaway. I'm to escort you there and back."

A new torment. Require submission to the rules, then deny her the opportunity to obey them. But the promise of a "back" meant that she might be allowed to return to the kitchen and to her dishes.

Sometimes, when she was washing, she could almost imagine she was still free, washing dishes in Nell's inn. That she had her own room with a real bed and a fire when she wanted one. And friends. She'd been grateful at the time for Nell's kindnesses, but she hadn't realized how much she'd grown to rely on the innkeeper's wife as a friend.

She'd wished now she'd told Nell her story, told Colin. She'd thought at the time she was protecting them and herself, but now she realized that she should have told everyone she met. Then, her disappearance would have made at least one person, any one person, wonder where she had gone and whether her cousin had had anything to do with it. She'd been too reliant on her own resourcefulness, and now she was trapped in a place where her only resource was submission.

She stood in the doorway of the matron's drawing room, curtsying and waiting for the matron to give her permission to enter.

"There you are, Sally. You've received a letter from your family. A messenger waits for your reply. I've laid out your letter, paper, and pen at the desk in the corner."

Lucy moved to the table deliberately, not wishing to indicate how much she had healed, how much stronger she'd grown.

She sat at the desk slowly, then picked up the envelope addressed with her cousin's hand. "Matron?"

"Yes."

"Would you be so kind as to read the letter to me?" At least she could have a witness to this transaction.

"No. Your cousin's instructions were quite explicit. No one is to read the letter but you."

Another trap. "Thank you, mistress." Meek fear was the pose the matron liked best. She held her body to mimic the taut tension that she'd seen in women who expected a blow.

She broke the seal. The matron was watching her, so she paced her reading to suggest a weak or immature mind.

My dearest cousin,

I write today hoping to find you improved and your mind returned to a healthier state. We have so feared that your lapse into madness would not abate. But the matron tells us that with clear discipline and a regulated routine, you are greatly improved and increasingly lucid. Believing her assessment of the state of your mind, I write with a proposal that I am sure you will greet with the same enthusiasm as when you heard it before.

Despite the infirmity of your condition, Mr. Barnes still remains your committed suitor, willing to make you his wife and spend the rest of his life aiding your recovery. As your nearest and only male relative, I have accepted his suit on your behalf. Your recent infirmity gives me this authority, as it has become clear in recent months that you are unable to regulate yourself or your affairs.

If you believe that you have recovered sufficiently to return to your loving family and the arms of your beloved suitor, then we can come to retrieve you at the end of this week. But you know the state of your mind. If you fear that you are not yet sufficiently recovered to accept this kind and generous offer, then you must tell us that, and we will—by your estimation—leave you to the kind offices of the matron who has done so much to aid your recovery. Mr. Barnes is willing to wait until you believe yourself ready to leave the security of Matron's house and become his bride. We eagerly await your answer.

> *Your loving cousin,*
> *Archibald, Lord Marner*

P.S. I have left ample room at the bottom of my page for your reply.

It was masterfully done. To say she was well enough to leave was to agree to the marriage her cousin had arranged. To say she did not wish to marry was to indicate she was not yet ready to leave the madhouse. But if she agreed to leave and later tried to avoid the marriage, then this agreement would be used as an example of her fragile and wayward mind. She would be deemed a lunatic, unable to manage her own funds.

She was trapped.

But she was also surprised. She knew her cousin to be cruel and vindictive and even intelligent, but intelligent in the way of the bully. He had repeatedly underestimated her resolve and her intelligence. But this letter . . . it was clear that he had received advice. And that person, whoever it was, was clever enough to give her pause. The game had shifted, and not in her favor.

She could not even keep the original letter, for he had explicitly indicated the letter was to be returned with his

"Sally, you've been reading the letter for almost a quarter of an hour. Surely you have had time to write a response. I will give you five more minutes. But after that you will need to increase your time in the kitchen to make up for your dilatory behavior."

"Yes, Matron."

The best way would be to refuse. She sat thinking of the ways she could reply, but each time came to a crux she couldn't see around.

Finally, she determined to write briefly.

Dear cousin,

  I am aware of the great condescension Mr.
Barnes makes to my health, but I cannot ask him to
take on such a burden as I may be without seeing
me more recently than our last conversation. I
welcome a visit from you and him, so that we can

*determine the path most conducive to a general
happiness for all.*

> *Your cousin
> Lady Fairbourne*

She sanded the letter to absorb the remaining ink. She unfolded the sheet used as an envelope, then refolded it, making use of the blank back to form the envelope to her message.

"Would you like to read my reply and advise me, Matron?"

"No, no. That's between family. But if you are done, your cousin's man can take your letter." She reached out and rang a bell, and Ox entered the room. He leered at her from his corner by the door.

"Sally has completed her response. You may take it from her."

Ox came nearer and nearer. She remembered the grope of his hands against her body, and she felt the bile rise in her throat.

He snatched the letter from her hand, then leaned down to whisper so only she could hear. "Now we've got you. There's no one able to come between you and his lordship now."

The beer-soaked smell of his clothes, the smell of a man who hadn't bathed in days, the putrid breath, all combined to make her wish to recoil. But she couldn't, wouldn't respond. Any response would attract the ministrations of the matron, so she sat unresponsive, her fingers gripped white in her lap. She felt like a fox cornered by a growling, drooling hound, with his master only yards behind ready to shoot her for her pelt and the glory of killing.

"Do you want me to escort *Sally* back to the kitchen, Matron?" Ox offered sweetly.

"No, sir, we have wasted enough of your time waiting on Sally to write her response. But I will see that she is well cared for until the next time we meet."

Matron rang a bell. The housekeeper arrived to show Ox out, then returned to escort Lucy back to the kitchen and her dishes.

"Oh, and Sally, you've been away from the kitchen for close to an hour. By now, one of the other girls will have completed your chores. We'll have you scrub the floors in the halls until nine tonight for good measure. Next time, perhaps you'll think to mind your time when you have a letter to write. That poor man had to wait on your inability, and that's not the way that a polite lady responds."

She curtsied. "Yes, Matron. As you wish, Matron." And she waited at the door until the housekeeper led her from the room.

Chapter Thirty-Three

"Arabella."

The voice called her by her given name. The name that no one who loved her used.

"Arabella. I know you are awake. Your breathing shifted. The others might not notice, but I'm not a man to trifle with. That cold you feel at your neck is a blade. Open your eyes."

She believed him and opened her eyes. Her vision was blurred. She blinked and tried again. But all she saw were vague shapes.

"You are having trouble focusing your eyes. That's understandable. I arranged last night for you to have a little something to help you sleep very soundly. That way, when we took you from the asylum, you made no objections. Your cousin has hired me to assess whether you should be allowed to return home."

It was a trick.

She remembered Em's words about Bess: "She's alive. That's enough hope for me."

She moved her fingers. She was alive. That would have to be enough hope . . . for now.

"Who are you?" The words came out slow and garbled.

"Who I am is quite irrelevant. But I would recommend

doing exactly as I say. I'm not averse to killing, and your cousin has little concern for keeping you alive."

"The inheritance. He isn't my heir."

"That doesn't matter anymore. All we needed was a sample of your handwriting. Here's the way it will be. You will agree to marry Mr. Barnes. You will have a short season in London, during which you will never reveal that you are being married against your will. If you tell, I will kill whoever you confide in."

"Why would you do that?"

"Because it suits me. Of course, you may also choose to return to the asylum. But if you do, you will never leave. We will publish your obituary. Hold a lovely funeral, private of course. Your cousin will offer some touching words on your unexpected demise. And then we will abandon you—as an unpaid lodger—to the matron's care. The choice is yours."

"That is no choice."

"But, my dear, it is the only one you have."

The next few weeks were confused and confusing. She attended a great many dinners and teas and other events, but before each one, she was forced to eat a portion of a green concoction made with sweet spices, honey, nuts, and candied fruit. Dawamesk, the man who wore lace called it. She had once known what that was, but she couldn't remember.

Every time she ate it, the room filled with color, swirling color, expanding and receding around the objects in her view. If someone were speaking with her, she would grow distracted by the color surrounding their heads like the nimbuses of the saints, but alive and moving. Sometimes the colors sounded like a symphony, and she would have trouble hearing the conversation around her. Sometimes the words that the people spoke to her turned into color, not words at all. Other times, the faces and bodies of the men and women in the room grew distorted: elongated, twisted, or collapsed.

That, coupled with the lace man's threats, made her fearful of talking to anyone for too long or of seeming to engage with any conversation. She believed him when he said he would kill anyone who tried to help her.

The only time that she was allowed not to eat the foul mixture was when visitors came to her cousin's London house. And even then, she had to promise to remain quiet, and she agreed, every time. Her cousin rejoiced in her new demeanor. She'd learned submission as a tactic at the asylum, and she used it again. Her only hope of escape was to appear incapable of it.

But the pose—the longer she practiced it—threatened to become real. She had to create tiny rebellions to keep a sense of self. Asking for books to read, then scratching a line under one word on every a page to tell her story. Moving objects from their expected places.

Luckily, the man with the lace trusted her cousin no more than did she, and he appointed his own men to guard her. Though she knew he was a criminal and a murderer, she felt safer with his cold calculations than with her cousin's unpredictable rages. Her favorite of her jailers was a big silent man who carved her a series of circus animals.

That was how she ended up in a room in the nursery, with bars on the windows and the door firmly locked. But she didn't mind: as long as the door was locked, she was safe.

She was at a ball, dressed in red silk, her cousin watching her carefully from his group of friends. Each dance, her companion was chosen for her, men who trampled her feet, or breathed sour breath into her face, or tried to draw her too close into their arms. Reprobates, drunks, lechers—her cousin's boon companions. And she struggled to keep her face placid and calm. She'd learned at the asylum that the punishment for not being agreeable was a beating.

At each turn around the drawing room, she watched for Colin. And with each turn around the dance floor, she felt her heart sink. He was not there. He had not come for her.

But then suddenly she was in his arms, dancing. When she looked past Colin's shoulder, she saw that he had enchanted them. All the guests at the ball had fallen asleep, slumped over their chairs, leaning against the walls, while she and Colin were twirling in a breathless waltz, through the ballroom, onto the porch, and into his waiting carriage.

Once more, she felt his arms around her, felt the warmth of his caresses, and she fell asleep finally safe, finally home.

The dream always made waking more painful. And each day, if she were allowed, she slept a little longer, wanting to lose herself in that dream.

Chapter Thirty-Four

"Why are we here, Clive?" Colin asked his youngest brother when he saw that the ballroom was already a rout.

"Because Sophia told us to accept, and we do what Sophie says?" Clive posited. "Besides, you should enjoy balls now. As an engaged man, you are happily off every matchmaking mama's list of eligible bachelors, so you can skulk around the margins of the ballroom with impunity. You *are* happily off their lists, aren't you?"

"Of course. What foolishness makes you ask that?"

"The way you have been searching the dance floor, even though we both know that Lady Hartley did not accompany you to London," Clive said soberly, looking around the dance floor as well. "What does she look like?"

"Go away, Clive," Colin growled.

"I was only trying to help."

"Help somewhere else." Colin started his retreat toward the front door, but took only two steps before he was pushed back to his brother's side by another wave of arriving guests. "Too many people."

"Take the stairs there; they lead to the balcony." Clive pushed ahead of him, taking the stairs three at a time. Colin followed, hoping to find an alternative way out. He passed three footmen on his way to the center of the balcony, where Clive already had stationed himself for the best view.

"Clive, have you noticed? Footmen at every door and corner. Is Prinny to be in attendance?" Colin nodded at the two footmen at either end of the balcony.

"That *is* strange. Perhaps it's to make sure the fiancée doesn't wander off. She isn't well known, and there is some talk of incapacity. But Barnes is apparently smitten." Clive leaned over to wave at a classmate from Cambridge. "Look, it's Seymour, back from the colonies."

"I find it hard to believe Barnes could be smitten with anything save a hefty wallet full of cash. Is she wealthy?" he said as he followed the line of Clive's wave, and suddenly he felt as if his lungs couldn't open, as if there was no air to breathe.

She was there, standing below him. He recognized the shape of her face, the line of her body. She was dressed in a dark blue satin, embroidered with tiny rhinestones that glittered in the ballroom lights. The embroidery gave the illusion of stars on a night sky. He felt the nearness of her as a sharp knife in his gut.

"Do you know the woman there in blue?"

"Her? That's the fiancée, Lady something or other. I met her last week."

"Lady?" Colin wondered which detail was more noteworthy: the fact that she was here, that Clive had met her a week ago, or that she was of his class.

"Fairbourne, I think. Yes, that's it. Lady Arabella Fairbourne. Stunning, isn't she?" Clive shook his head. "Shame that she's dim."

Colin felt as if he'd been given the gift of the gods: her name. "She isn't dim. Something is going on. Watch her."

They observed together, shoulder to shoulder. Lucy offered a sweet but vague smile for everyone. She listened far more than she talked. She moved deliberately, with little grace, as if she was thinking about every step.

"You know, you may be right." Clive pushed back from the balcony after several moments of observation. "It's the movement that clinches it, as if she isn't certain where her own feet are."

"Introduce me."

It took almost half an hour to reach her side, and when he did, it was no surprise that her dance card was almost empty. He took the next dance, grateful it was a waltz.

In the middle of the floor, protected by the crush of dancers, he squeezed her hand. "Come into the garden with me."

"The footmen," she whispered low.

"Ah. So it's you they are keeping in, rather than someone else they are keeping out."

She said nothing. He led her gently but firmly in the steps of the dance, and in his arms, she began to relax. She made fewer mistakes, her feet seeming less disjointed from her body.

"After our dance, wait ten minutes, then excuse yourself to the lady's withdrawing room. The one on this floor, to the right of the entrance."

She looked at him with blank eyes, but then her eyes focused on the front entrance, then moved to the right of them.

"Agree."

She nodded just as the waltz ended, and he returned her to her former place, trying to look as bored in her company as possible.

As soon as he returned Lucy to her chaperone, an aged dowager already half asleep, Colin began to evaluate each of his options.

The lady's withdrawing room was at the end of a hallway.

A footman stood at the entrance to that hall. Two more stood at the entrance to the ballroom, with another two at the entrance to the house itself. He counted back in memory: outside, four or five helped guests in and out of their carriages. A frontal assault would be difficult, if not impossible.

The ballroom was on the second floor. Even if she were well, the drop to the ground below one of the windows would be risky to attempt safely, and if she were drugged, as he believed, impossible.

The doors to the terrace—he hurried up the stairs and looked over the ballroom—were also guarded by one or two footmen. Who knew how many servants were in the gardens?

The front door—impossible as it seemed—was his best option.

But he had allies in the ballroom. He simply needed to gather them. First, he needed a female relative, one he could trust to reassure Lucy. Luckily, he knew exactly where to find one: the gaming room.

Ophelia Mason stood at the entrance to the gaming room, gossiping with a small crowd of married women. Her peacock feather plume was as good as a beacon to find her.

Smiling at the women, he pulled Ophelia aside. "I need your help. I'll explain later. At this moment, however, you feel faint and need an escort to the lady's withdrawing room."

"Oooh, intrigue. Whom are we deceiving?"

"The footmen." Colin nodded in their direction.

"Hmm. They are everywhere, aren't they?" Ophelia mused. "I can't understand it. Sidney told me that Prinny is in Brighton."

Before they turned the corner and came into the footman's view, she slumped into his body, whispering, "Like this?"

"Exactly."

He helped her past the footman without garnering a second glance. The footman was looking out into the ballroom, not down the hall itself.

"Lady Fairbourne is in the withdrawing room. Help her into the next room down. It's a study if I remember correctly. I'll be waiting."

"To do what? Debauch the intended? That's not like you, Colin. Besides, she seems a bit dim."

He felt his frustration surge. "I know her; she's not dim. I think she's been drugged."

"Then, dear, she's been drugged for weeks," Ophelia said, then stopped, "Oh, dear, you are serious. Not dim, then? I spoke to her several times in the last month. I regret now not having paid more attention."

"Call her Lucy. Tell her you are bringing her to me."

Lucy entered the withdrawing room, an antechamber with seating and a large mirror. She sat at one of the chairs, hands folded limply in her lap. The mirror reflected her in many colors, but she knew the position: despair. She closed her eyes.

He had come to her, in grey silk, elegant, and danced with her at a crowded ball, just as she had dreamed it. But it couldn't be him.

A hand touched hers, and she opened her eyes, trying to focus them. A woman with kind eyes knelt before her, and the colors wrapped around her.

"I'm Ophelia Mason. We've met before. At Lady Wentworth's ball last week."

The colors turned into flowers. Rosemary for remembrance. Pansies for thoughts. Fennel and columbine. She knew the flowers weren't real. Nothing was real.

"Lucy? Colin said your name is Lucy."

The woman said her name, her real name. The name he called her.

"My cousin Colin Somerville. He says he knows you. Do you know him?"

She nodded.

"Here, let's see if this helps." Ophelia poured cold water from the pitcher onto a linen handkerchief, then pressed it against Lucy's temples. The cold pushed the colors to the edges of the room.

She nodded.

"He wants me to bring you to him. He's in the next room. Will you come with me?"

The woman might not be real, but the cold was real. She could believe in the cold.

"Yes," she whispered, hoping to keep the colors from returning. Ophelia took her arm.

When the door to the study opened, Colin stood before her, his eyes searching hers. Ophelia led her in, and he folded her in his arms.

"Lucy, look at me."

"Do I know you, sir?" she spoke deliberately, making sure to form the words correctly. It was best not to give anything away. If she did, she would awaken in her room with the barred windows and locked doors. No, she had to find a way to make the dream stay.

"Yes. You saved my life." He pressed his lips to hers, gently, but with remembered passion, and she stiffened, then melted into him. "Is that enough to remember me by?"

She pressed her fingers to her temples. "It's not safe. He'll know you've been here. He'll kill you and her."

"My angel, my star. No one is going to kill me, or Ophelia."

"It *is* you." Her vision seemed clearer. "Can you help me? I can't think."

"Can you refuse what they are giving you?"

She shook her head and pushed down her glove. He saw the still-pink scar at her wrist, the marks of restraints, and the bruises.

"Ophelia, get Clive, quickly. He's waiting on the stairs. Then, if you can, find Edmund and Aidan. If a footman asks where Lucy is, tell him Lady Fairbourne is ill in the with-drawing room, and you are finding her a doctor. That should gain us some time."

Clive entered the room with Ophelia, Edmund following behind them.

"Whatever you are planning, brother, you better move quickly," Clive advised. "Marner and Barnes have noticed she is missing from the ballroom and are looking for her."

Edmund stepped forward and saw Lucy, her arm still uncovered. His face blanched. All of the brothers were un-sympathetic to men who beat women, but Edmund felt it most strongly. The woman he loved had also been abused by her relatives.

"Ophelia, walk with Lady Fairbourne around the ball-room. Don't let her drink or eat anything. When you are done, introduce her to Kate, and have her do the same thing, then Ariel. Has Sophia arrived? Or Audrey?"

"If they haven't, I have other friends who will help." Ophelia extended her arm to Lucy, "Come, we will walk to see if some exertion makes you feel better."

"Keep her with you or someone you trust for the next hour," Colin instructed.

Edmund glanced at the clock on the mantel. "The ball ends in an hour, brother. You haven't much time."

"Half an hour, then," he instructed Ophelia and Lucy before they slipped into the hall. "I have a plan, but it's a risky one. And we need the clothes from one of the postboys."

As she walked around the ballroom with Ophelia's friends, the colors receded, and she felt more stable on her feet. But at the same time, she knew better what a danger Colin and the others were taking on themselves. By the time Ophelia escorted her back toward the withdrawing room, then slipped with her into the study, she was shivering with fear.

"We have some clothes for you, and Ophelia is going to help you into them, but you must change quickly. I'll be waiting outside the door."

She leaned into his cheek and whispered, "Don't leave me."

He looked at the clock. "Ophelia, watch at the door."

He began to undress her, forcing himself not to remember the last time he'd held her, the last time he'd untied the strings under her bodice and at her waist. He focused on the ribbon first, untying it just enough to loosen the drawstring. Then he moved to the pins. He loosened the dress enough to slip it off.

He looked at her partially clad and wished to weep, then kill. He'd seen that she'd grown thin, but not how thin.

Within five minutes, Lucy had become a very pretty boy. The postboy's legs were longer than Lucy's, so they used the pins from her dress to fold the pants legs up. Colin had intended to bind her breasts as she had done in the camps, but there was no need. She was already so thin, and the shirt was tight enough that it, with the jacket, did the job suitably well. The only problem had been her hair. Curls and curls down the back of her neck. He'd considered cutting it off, but there was no time. Instead, at Ophelia's suggestion, they made her a turban out of a strip of petticoat to mimic the uniform of Lady Stanford's postboys.

"Lucy." He lifted her chin so his eyes could meet hers. They were filled with fear and exhaustion. "We have one chance. Watch the floor as we leave. Don't look up; don't meet anyone's eyes. Hold on to Ophelia, and whatever happens, don't stop walking."

They took their positions, Colin on one side of Ophelia, Lucy on the other. Ophelia pretended to lean on Lucy, all the while directing her steps. Edmund stood outside the study door, lounging against the wall. "The carriage is first in line. The twins stand ready, as do I."

Lucy's feet were steadier, but she still moved as if she were uncertain. They passed the guard at the end of the hall to the withdrawing room without incident.

They neared the door to the ballroom just as Sophia's two cousins engaged in a loud disagreement and called on the two footmen at the door to adjudicate. Though the footman refused to move, it was enough of a distraction for the three of them to enter the main hallway.

Any time someone approached, Ophelia groaned, and Colin nodded them away. As they had hoped, few paid any attention at all to the servant who appeared to be helping Ophelia walk upright.

When they were almost to the front door, Colin heard his name called. It was Barnes, the fiancé. "Get her out of here," he whispered to Ophelia, then he motioned to his postboy, who was waiting at the door. "Help Mrs. Mason to her carriage." One of the footmen at the door stared at the pair but, to Colin's relief, looked away.

"I say, will she be all right?" Barnes patted Colin's back as if they were old friends. "I've never seen Mrs. Mason discomfited in this way."

"She believes she ate something earlier which didn't agree with her." Colin forced himself to maintain a pose of friendly conversation, even though he wished to bash the man's crooked teeth in.

"I hope not from my table." Barnes pressed his clammy hands together in false consternation.

"That's unlikely. The indisposition has come on her too quickly." Colin had disliked Barnes before for the way his vote went to the highest bidder, all while pretending to vote on conscience. But perversely, Colin hated Barnes now for not caring enough about Lucy to recognize her in the most flimsy disguise. Colin would have recognized Lucy anywhere. "I'm sure a night's sleep will cure Mrs. Mason."

"Barnes!" Edmund called from the ballroom doorway. "We need you to settle a dispute. Cragfield here still believes that Lord Byron authored that novel that came out this summer. You remember the one—*The Vampyre*—but I can't remember the name of the true author."

Barnes turned back to the ballroom, "Polidori, that's the name you want. Polidori."

By the time Barnes turned back to finish his conversation, Colin was gone.

Chapter Thirty-Five

"I see you've lost her again." Charters rolled up his sleeves to throw a dart at a target across the room. "I told you the ball was a dangerous idea."

"I had men watching every door on the first floor," Marner objected.

"Then she must have jumped from an upper window. Are you certain her body isn't lying broken in the rosebushes?" He let the derision fill his tone. "Do you need for me to check?"

"She was helped."

"I thought you said she had no friends".

"Perhaps she's made some during the season," Marner snapped.

"That should not have been possible." Charters aimed and threw, hitting the bull's-eye firmly in the middle. "Did you follow my instructions for events? Someone beside her at all times? Only men who believed in her incapacity dancing with her? The drug timed to make her appear uncertain and, if she spoke, unwell."

"We did everything." Marner paced. "But she's disappeared."

"And what precisely do you wish for me to do about it?" Charters threw another dart with the same result.

"Find her before this unravels."

"I think my partners and I will sit this act out until you provide the funds you already owe us." Charters threw a final dart, splitting the first one.

"I haven't got access to that sort of money until I inherit her portion."

"Then you'll need to find a way to pay our outstanding fee without inheriting the estate. Besides, you had enough blunt to go to the Painted Lady two nights ago, where you won a tidy sum. In fact, you won a full half of what's outstanding to me. We'll take those winnings." Charters leaned back against the wall beside his desk.

"I need that money to pay my accounts."

"We know that you paid one of the girls at the Painted Lady to signal you when Farthingmore had weak hands. I could just as easily go to him. Tell him how you won his yearly income. He's not known as a forgiving loser," Charters threatened. "We don't care what happens to you or to the girl or to your plans. All we care about is our fee. My employer insists that we don't work for free."

Chapter Thirty-Six

She dreamed he came for her at a ball and stole her away into the darkness. She dreamed that she lay all night in his arms, safe. She didn't want to awaken; she didn't want to open her eyes and find that he was gone, that the bed was her own, and that another day of nightmares had begun.

She moved her arm to touch the cuts, now healed into raised pink bands. She had told herself for months that at least she was alive. If she were alive, there was hope. But now . . . perhaps it had been better for her to have died. Because now she had gone mad, and all her senses were complicit. The sheets felt soft, but the room smelled like tansy, rosemary, and bay. Like another sickroom.

"Lucy." A man's voice. His voice. Another indication she was mad. Before, at least she had not heard voices. Just seen colors, and distortion, everywhere she'd looked.

"Lucy. You're safe. Open your eyes. I'm not leaving your side again."

"Yes, you are." A woman's voice, firm but kind. "Sophia needs to dress her wounds, and put salve on her scars. But you can stand in the hall."

"I won't leave until she opens her eyes and sees I'm here and that she's safe."

"If you were in a fairy tale, you would kiss her." A child's voice, young. "It's in a story Sophie read to me. She will know you from your kiss and wake up."

Lucy didn't want to be kissed, not the rough torment she had to endure every day since coming to town. The groping hands, the suffocating embraces, the stench of sweat and drink. At least her cousin was prudish enough to allow nothing further.

She heard a chair creak. Beside her bed. How long had he sat beside her? He put his hand on hers.

"Lucy, come back to me." The kiss when it came was soft, then firm. His mouth opened slightly on hers, and his tongue teased her lips. Gentle, even loving. Soap, he smelled of soap. She breathed more deeply. Soap.

She opened her eyes and looked into his eyes. He broke off the kiss and smiled. His smile. If she were mad, this was a heavenly madness. To have found a safe place in her mind to live when they chained her to the wall like Molly. Perhaps she would stare all night at the moon, imagining it to be his face.

"There. She knows you're here. Now go. Take Lily back to the nursery." Behind him, she could see the kind auburn-haired woman she dreamed had helped her at the ball. And behind her Lady Wilmot, holding the hand of a small dark-haired girl.

"Lucy, you remember my cousin, Ophelia Mason, and Sophia, Lady Wilmot. Remember?" He squeezed her hand in parting, but she held it fast. "And this is Lady Wilmot's daughter, Lily."

She opened her mouth to speak, but said nothing. He leaned down. "What, darling?"

"Am I mad? Or dead?" she whispered.

He did not laugh. Only a sad, gentle look passed over his face. When he spoke, his voice was kinder than she'd ever heard it. "You are neither. You are safe. I will never let them harm you again. Even if I had not the power, you have met my brother, the duke. Already he helps protect you."

Sophia joined Colin, Aidan, and their brothers in the drawing room.

"What can you tell me?"

"I will only tell you if you promise that you will do nothing without your brother's approval."

"Tell me." He glared. "Or I will go look for myself."

"And terrify her?" she said. "What will you do? Challenge someone to a duel, then leave her without protection?"

"You think I would lose."

"I think you have yourself suffered a wound from which you have not fully recovered."

"It's been four months."

"Yes, and you still wince when you pull yourself onto a horse. You don't yet raise your arm to full height. Another month, two, and you will be well, but not now. You might die if you challenge someone. Your brother is a fierce man. Let him pursue this for you. You take care of her."

He agreed, reluctantly.

"It's clear she's been malnourished, whether by choice or intention, I can't tell. She's clearly suspicious of food, but Judith was able to get her to eat by eating from the same plate with her. The bruises on her arms and ankles indicate she's been bound, and I have to say, from the look of them, that's happened repeatedly. She has cuts in both places in various stages of healing. At some point, fairly recently, she's been beaten, but carefully. None of the bruises would show in everyday or evening dress. The scars on her arms are perhaps three months old, fully healed, but still pink and thick.

"She tried to kill herself." His heart fell at the thought.

"I don't think so. What hand does she prefer to use?"

"Left to fence. But that could be just a learned advantage."

"The direction of the cuts only makes sense if her arm were held down and someone else cut it."

"They tried to kill her and make it appear a suicide."

"But then they doctored her wounds. It doesn't make sense. But the cuts have healed. In fact," she said, "I found nothing that won't or hasn't healed . . . in her body at least."

"What do you mean?"

"Until we determine what exactly she has been given, we can't determine whether she will heal fully in mind or if there are some effects of body we cannot see. We need her to talk to us, tell us how the drug made her feel. If I know that, I can consult the *Materia Medica* and try to determine what substances would fit. But there's some good news: whatever it is, she doesn't seem to want it yet. If it were opium, she would be wanting more by now."

"Tell Aidan," he said. "I'll try to get her to talk to me."

"Perhaps I can help." Walgrave stepped through the doorway.

Colin stiffened.

"But, first, the Home Office would like to make a formal apology to Colin." He stretched out his hands, palms up, toward Seth, Sophia, and Aidan. "And to all of you. We had no indication that Lady Marietta was in any danger. No sign that she or her child was at risk." He turned to face Colin directly. "Had we known, we would have sent you with appropriate reserves and support. You would never have been left without protection on a rural road."

"Thank you for telling me," Colin said gracelessly, but Walgrave ignored it.

"I am sure you have heard the latest scandal. After you left Marner's ball, Barnes's fiancée disappeared entirely.

Apparently she has wandered off before, so Marner had footmen at every exterior door . . . to protect her of course."

"Of course." Colin spoke through clenched jaws.

"When he discovered she was gone, he called every one of the footman before him and the company for an interrogation, then after raging at every one of them, he fired the lot without references."

"And . . ."

"One lad—you might have seen him—at the front door, fell at Marner's feet weeping. Apparently, he is the only breadwinner in his family, five children, parents dead, begged not to be let go or at least to be released with a reference. But Marner was unmoved. He even kicked the lad down the front stairs."

"Oh, that is terrible." Judith stood up. "He was at the front door, you say? Aidan, we cannot allow the lad to suffer. We must find him. Certainly, you can find a place for him in your service."

"Not necessary, your ladyship." Walgrave stepped to the window and pulled back the curtains to the front yard. A thin boy about twelve stood waiting beside Walgrave's carriage. "I hired the lad myself. Turns out he is great friends with Marner's cook."

"Stop the pretense, Walgrave. You know we helped Lucy escape, or you would not be here. And you would not have hired a cast-off servant just because he cried—though I am grateful for your foresight." Colin looked out the window. "What does the lad know that we can use?"

Walgrave smiled. "Then I am forgiven?" He held out his arms to embrace Colin.

"It depends on what you know." Colin knocked his arms aside to avoid the embrace, but held out his hand in conciliation. "If it helps, I will be in your debt."

"Good enough." Walgrave took Colin's hand and pulled him into a brotherly embrace. "I would never have forgiven myself if you had died on that road, and from what I understand our missing heiress saved your skin. I owe her for saving your life as much as I owe your family for nearly costing you yours." Walgrave turned to speak to the group. "When Lady Fairbourne was not meeting guests in the drawing room as Barnes's fiancée, she remained locked in her room, and meals would be brought to her on a tray. The boy—Hallett—was often the one tasked with the job, because—despite the appearances at the ball—Marner actually employs few servants in town."

"The point, Walgrave. Or I might forget we have said pax," Colin growled.

"When there were not guests or engagements that required her attendance, Lady Fairbourne was often lucid, and Hallett grew to like her. That's why he did not give the alarm when he realized you were helping her from the ball—and why he did not, even with the threat to his family, give away who had helped her."

"Oh, god." Colin sat down with dismay. "How did he know?"

"They had become friends, of a sort. Hallett knew her face . . . better than any of the other footmen who were hired just for specific events."

"Back to her food, Walgrave," Aidan interrupted. "Clearly someone tampered with it."

"Whatever she was fed, we might have it in the carriage."

"And you could not start with that?"

"Well, it is not as straightforward as you hope. And before we give you the baskets, Hallett has several requests."

"Name them." Aidan stepped forward.

"He fears what Marner will do if he learns Hallett helped

you, so he wants your assurances that his siblings will be safe."

"Do you have them in the carriage as well?" Judith stepped to the window and looked out. Hallett, looking stoic and brave, held the hands of two rail-thin girls with mops of curling blond hair. Two other faces—both boys—looked out of the carriage windows, then disappeared when they saw Judith watching them. "How many and how old?"

"Three sisters and three brothers. The twin boys are the youngest at five, the girls are nine, seven, and six. They have lost all the others."

"I will take them." Judith smoothed her skirts and turned to face her brothers, daring them to oppose her. "If the boy needs assurances that his family will be cared for, then he will have them from me." The group parted as she strode to the door.

"Someday, that boy is going to regret this day," Aidan murmured, and Sophia pushed a hand against his shoulder in jovial correction.

"What else?" Colin demanded.

"Hallett wishes to stay with Lady Fairbourne until she is well. Apparently he made her some promise, but he will not tell me what it is."

"He may stay," Aidan promised.

"Then you might wish to call for some servants to unload what we have stolen from Marner's house—he has left town and closed the house until his return. We did not know what to take, so we took whatever looked interesting."

Within ten minutes, Forster's servants had unloaded seven large baskets of various unguents and salves in small pots, dried herbs and flowers in jars and boxes, and other foodstuffs—as well as tonic waters and other consumables found in Marner's study and the room in which Lucy had been kept. Under the direction of Aidan's valet-cum-butler, Barlow, the baskets had been removed to the kitchen.

"What is this?" Colin lifted a small brown crockery pot. He removed the oil cloth tied around the pot's neck and held it up, so that Aidan could see inside.

"Green marmalade? Butter?" Aidan peered into the jar. "With raisins? Or are those figs? Never seen such a thing." Aidan stuck his finger in and removing some on the tip of his finger sniffed it, then started to taste the slightest bit.

"Wait!" Sophia crossed the room and wiped the green jam from his fingers. She held the towel to her nose, but pulled it away, shaking her head. "Colin, would you fetch your sister?"

"What is it?" Colin growled. "Has she been poisoned? Will she recover?"

"Colin." Sophia spoke firmly, tilting her head toward the door. "Get Judith."

Colin started to argue, then ran through the open door.

"Did you send him away because the news is bad?" Aidan leaned in, speaking low.

"He needs to do something, and I need Judith." Sophia turned back to the concoction. "If this is what I think it is, then it explains Lucy's symptoms, her waking dreams, her pervasive fear. . . ."

She took a butter knife and removed a portion of the jam, then spread it out onto a plate, revealing both nuts and fruits. "What does the label on the pot say?"

"Label?"

"Yes, no herbalist would leave such a decoction un-marked."

"Decoction?"

She waved her hand impatiently. "This . . . some plant boiled down for its essential qualities, then the plant parts strained out. But then all these other elements were added. Is there a label?"

"There is a word, written in wax pencil . . . 'Beautiful Lady'?" Aidan shrugged his shoulders.

"Bella Donna," Judith translated, entering the room with Colin at her heels. "I assume you need me to smell something dreadful and tell you what it is, though—luckily for me—belladonna is largely scentless."

Sophia held out the plate with the green decoction on it.

"I wish I had never confessed my talent for this." Judith leaned forward. "Green—sweet, cloying, but I don't recognize whatever the plant is at the base—hints of orange water . . . and some spice. Not cinnamon." She sniffed again. "Cardamom. The wildflowers smell vaguely of poppies, so if this is a drug, then opium. The fruits are figs, and honey is part of the butter mixture holding it together." Judith pulled back grimacing. "It must taste dreadful, and the other bits are to make it edible."

"Thank you, Judith. That helps a great deal." Sophia turned back to the towel, spreading out the decoction to see its larger ingredients.

"What is it, Sophia?" Colin's words were clipped and hard.

"I have never seen it—what I think it is—but I have read about it. I believe it is a cooked form of hashish called dawamesk, but laced with opium and—from the label—belladonna."

"Sophia," Colin growled. "Tell me. Will she recover?"

"She has not craved it. That was my confusion. Some of her behaviors pointed to opium, but not all." Sophia looked at the ceiling, talking through the various options. "I think Judith is right: this is a mixture of various drugs, along with fruits and spices to make it palatable. But how much of each drug and how much she has consumed over the last month and what other drugs might be present in it . . ."

"Sophia, darling." Aidan placed his hand on her shoulder.

"He knows you will be making a guess, but he needs an answer."

"Oh, yes, of course." Sophia straightened and looked directly into Colin's eyes. "All of the drugs we mentioned in small enough doses work their way out of the body over time. She has been without this mess for several days, and we see no ill effects, or at least not in her body. As for her mind . . . I cannot say. I am sorry."

Colin's body slumped into the news.

"If she shows no improvement in the next week, I will find a home where she will be cared for," Aidan offered gently. "And of course her maintenance will come from the ducal accounts. She will not be abandoned."

"No." Colin straightened. "I will find another way."

Chapter Thirty-Seven

Each morning, he sat beside her bed, asking her to speak again, but each day, she simply clung to his hand.

At a knock at the door, she held his hand more tightly. He might not be real, but if she let go, this particular sweet dream might escape her. The door opened and closed behind him, and she heard a whisper.

"Thank you for coming."

"Your cousins are very convincing, but I would have come for her in any case."

"She's been sleeping heavily for several days, but before that, she'd been drugged. We don't know for how long, but months likely. She doesn't trust us—I don't think she trusts anyone right now."

"Perhaps she'll trust me."

Another face moved into her view. Nell.

Lucy began to cry, tears streaming silently down her face. Now she knew she was mad: everyone who'd cared for her after her great-aunt's death was in the same room. That could only happen in a dream.

"Let him go, girl." Nell brushed her hand across Lucy's forehead, smoothing her hair. "We have a bath ready to be brought in. Let us wash your hair and get you some clean clothes. Then we'll take a walk around the room."

"I'll be right outside the door," he promised.

She let go of his hand, reluctantly.

When Colin returned, the shades had been drawn back to let in the sunlight. Nell sat at the side of the bed, talking of the events at the inn since Lucy had been gone.

"I swear my Mark has grown four inches since you were last with us. He's all arms and legs that one. Not a shirt reaches his wrists or trousers his ankles." Nell smiled at Colin and reached out her hand. "Your man is back, Lucy."

Nell stood, smoothing her skirts, then she picked up the tray. "I'll take this down to the kitchen, and look in on you a bit later."

As Nell passed, he whispered, "Thank you."

Lucy was pale, wearing a shift of laced cotton with sleeves that extended only to her elbows. Her fingers kept rubbing the scar at her wrist as if it hurt and she wished to comfort it. When she saw him looking at her bruises, she tucked her arm under the coverlet.

"No, don't hide it." He took her hand in his. She watched him with wide eyes. And he kissed each finger then turned her wrist upward and kissed the scars.

"Have the effects of the drug receded?"

She nodded, but tentatively, as if any answer might be wrong. What could have happened to make a woman who'd lived through the camps so cautious?

"Can you tell me where you have been? I looked for you, down every street and road, stopped at every inn and wasn't satisfied until I'd seen all the scullery maids. For weeks, Seth and I looked, until Seth had to return to Sophia's estate. But you had vanished, disappeared." He kissed her hand again and put the back of it to his cheek. "I had only just returned to London when Sophia insisted I go to Marner's ball. But I almost didn't go. I would have missed you."

She lifted her hand and brushed his hair back from his forehead, but did not speak.

"You stayed with me when I was wounded, sat beside my bed, and I'll be here for you, Lucy . . . until you wish to speak again."

Lucy was sitting in the sunshine, her chair close enough to the open balcony that she could feel the warmth, but far enough back that no one could see her from the garden. The dream hadn't ended yet: she was still with him, with those who loved her, and she was very careful not to do anything that would make her wake up.

She heard sounds behind her, then a biggish black dog, still a puppy, but bigger, ran to her and nuzzled her legs. She reached down to pet its head, but it pulled back, and sat looking at her, its tail wagging back and forth on the floor.

She held her hand out, and the pup came to her and nuzzled her hand. She began to pet it again, and it wriggled its body until her hand was between his shoulder blades. She scratched the spot, and the dog's tail wagged some more.

Then, without warning, he jumped up, put his paws on her knees, and licked her face.

She felt the wetness, the uncomfortable wetness, a sticky sensation she had only felt one other time before—when Boatswain had licked her face. But Boatswain was a puppy. This animal was almost a dog.

If she were mad, Boatswain would surely be still a puppy, or perhaps she would imagine him like Bess. She couldn't have imagined this, this nipping, growling, barking, tail-wagging half-grown ball of fur.

The dog must be real. But if Boatswain were real, then Colin would be real.

She stood and tried to catch the dog, but he kept jumping close by then away from her, forcing her to chase him around the room.

She tripped and fell, and her hand burned with pain. And she felt it. Not the cushioned, tempered ache of the drugs but real pain. And suddenly the dog was crawling on her, and she felt real dog kisses. And she began to laugh. Then cry, then laugh again.

And then Colin was there, and Em, and Nell, until all of Colin's family had gathered in her room.

And she knew she was not mad.

In the safety of the ducal mansion, protected by Colin and his brothers, Lucy began the slow path back to herself. Sophia had researched each of the drugs they suspected Lucy had been given, then explained to her the effects of each one, and how long it might take for each drug's influence to dissipate. Sophia had also insisted that her susceptibility to the drugs had been aided by her lack of healthful food, and that to recover she would have to eat again, but slowly, her stomach having adjusted to the small portions she'd been allowed to eat.

Each day, then, Cook made small portions of her favorite foods, and Colin sat with her while she ate, fulfilling his promise not to leave her side until she was well again. She realized that one of the ways that the matron had asserted her oppressive rule was by limiting her lodgers' food. Hard work, little food, inadequate sleep, and the threat of punishment—all contributed to keep her lodgers submissive and afraid. Unfortunately, Lucy could not tell Aidan or Walgrave anything about the location of the private asylum. The only accents that could provide any help—the cook's, Smith's, and Matron's—had all come from different parts of England.

She finally felt more observant, more resilient, more capable, more like her old self. But the irony of the situation did not escape her. Hiding from her cousin and his men, she had moved from one confinement to another: she could not venture from the ducal estate, or even walk in the garden without an escort. But she was not confined in any other sense, and she was not denied any need or desire. If she had said she wished to see the lion at the Royal Menagerie, she was certain that the lion tamer would have been paid handsomely to allow a private audience or would have put his lion in a cage and brought it to her. She was free to remain in her room or not, to play with Boatswain, to draw, or embroider, or do none of those things.

And with her freedom came a returning confidence in her observations and in her responses. At dinner, when one of the Somerville men teased her, she teased in return. And when the duke scowled at some frustration or annoyance, she treated him as any other scowling man in her past. She did not assume she was the cause; she simply ignored him. When Aidan came to her—accompanied by Walgrave—with questions about her inheritance and her cousin, she did not hesitate to answer. And when they offered her their resources and their aid, she accepted. She would not again make the mistake of believing she could oppose Marner's power alone.

Chapter Thirty-Eight

On the lawn below the terrace, Hallett seemed never to tire of throwing a ball for Boatswain to fetch. Lucy, her lap covered by a blanket, sat on the terrace steps, watching the two with pleasure. The boy and the dog were always close at hand if she needed them, and she was grateful for their care. But she was growing tired of being the invalid. Another week, she told herself, and she would be fully recovered.

Colin approached the terrace from the garden. Boatswain ran to Colin, and Hallett threw Colin the ball. For several minutes, Colin played the game, and Lucy watched him, admiring the economy and elegance of his movements, the line of his arm, the power of his throws. Colin could pitch the ball farther than Hallett, and the dog had to run farther and faster to catch it. It was a picturesque scene, two men, a dog, and a ball. She could easily imagine it painted by George Stubbs or John Constable. Soon, however, Colin made his way toward her seat on the stairs, and she felt his approach as a spreading warmth in the center of her chest. She smiled as he stood at the foot of the stairs before her.

"I was hoping to find you alone."

"I'm alone enough. In addition to surveilling my visitors,

Hallett is wearing out my dog before dinner." She motioned to the top of the stair beside her. "Would you like to sit?"

He took the seat, then leaned forward, his forearms on his knees. "He's a beautiful dog. I'm glad you have him."

"Em taught him an amazing set of skills. I'm surprised every day at something he already knows how to do." Lucy paused, watching Colin twist his hands before him, rubbing one palm with the opposite thumb. "You're upset."

"I need to speak with you. I have been waiting until you were well, and . . ."

"And now I'm well." She examined his face, but he did not look at her, only stared at Hallett and Boatswain.

"I want you to know that, when you did not meet me at the British Museum, I searched for you, for weeks I searched." He looked at his hands. "But . . ."

"I would have met you, Colin, except my cousin's men found me first. But I loved you, love you. I'll never love anyone else. Only you." She put her hand on his knee, but he did not acknowledge it, only kept twisting his hands. She withdrew her hand.

She looked at him closely, at the dejected way he held his shoulders, at the hang of his head. "Something happened when we were apart. Are you married? Is that why they look away sometimes when I ask where you are?"

"No, not married."

She breathed out in relief.

"But I'm engaged. The banns were already read before I found you. And the wedding is next week. The household leaves tomorrow."

She couldn't catch her breath. She felt immobile, her chest caught mid-breath, her heart frozen. "Who? How?"

"After weeks of searching, I returned to Hartshorn Hall. I needed Em's friendship and consolation. But there was a party. Everyone from the town was there, her family, and she'd waited for me for years." His voice drifted away. Then so softly that she almost didn't hear it. "I believed you didn't want me."

She remembered Em's graciousness, her kindness, and Colin's strength, honesty, integrity. At the least she could do the noble thing, even if it broke her heart a million ways.

"No, Colin, you did right. Em had a prior claim." She shifted her body to face him. "I should have told you from the beginning who I was, my troubles. I should have taken you with me when I was in London. But even though I knew in my heart what kind of man you were, I didn't trust you enough. I was too used to relying on my own ingenuity. But in the end, you saved me. You found a way to free me, to convince me I was not mad, to give me powerful friends. If I have the possibility of a useful life now, I have that possibility because of you."

"I've lain awake every night since I found you, trying to imagine how to set it right, how to break the engagement. If it were any other woman, I would, but . . ." He looked at his hands, the glint of tears in his eyes.

"But it's Em."

"Yes, it's Em." His voice held the finality of his decision. "For my whole life, she's been my constant friend, and I'll care for her until I die."

She put her hand on his and left it there for a long time before she spoke again. "Whenever we are in the same company, I will greet your wife as a dear friend and you as her loving husband. We will sit through meals and dances, and remind ourselves of our obligations. And one day we'll wake up and find that the longing has faded. And sometime after that, we will find it has disappeared entirely."

"Never!"

"Yes, Colin. It will fade. Because it's Em. Because we cannot hurt her."

He rose and offered her his hand. She took it, savoring the feel of his hand in hers.

"You are of course invited to the wedding. But Aidan has arranged a house guard for you, if you wish to remain here."

"Thank you. That's very considerate." She could hear their language becoming more distant.

"I have made some arrangements. I will be gone for some weeks after the wedding. Em wishes to see her father in France, and after that, we will return to Hartshorn Hall. I will not be much in London in the future, but I will, of course, always be at your service. In my stead, Aidan and Walgrave have agreed to act on your behalf, to protect you and resolve the situation with your inheritance. I regret I will be unable to do more."

"Thank you, but you have done more than anyone could expect, particularly under the circumstances."

"You have friends here, Lucy. Real friends. Let them care for you, for my sake."

He took one last look at her face and returned to the house.

She sat back on the stairs, wiping away tears and watching Hallett throw a ball to Boatswain.

Chapter Thirty-Nine

The day of the wedding arrived. The gathering was to be a small one—friends, family, the community near Em's estate, but not the *ton*. Lucy had been invited, and, though it would be painful, she told herself that she needed to attend. She needed to hear the vows and know that he was never going to be hers. When Walgrave had offered to escort her, she had accepted.

She wore a blue-violet day dress, borrowed from Colin's cousin Kate. Her money was not yet her own, her cousin having filed a petition in Chancery declaring that his missing cousin was incompetent. Few knew where she was, and those who did were sworn to silence. Marner's suit put her inheritance at risk, but Aidan, using his status as a duke, had begun to work on her behalf.

Everyone was already seated when she arrived, chatting quietly as they waited.

The church was crowded, but there was a seat in the back row of the church next to a solemn-looking man in a dark red suit. He looked at her with an odd recognition as she slipped into the seat next to him, and she dreaded thinking that he was one of those members of the *ton* she'd met while drugged on dawamesk.

"Lady Lucia Fairbourne? It is Lucia, am I correct?" he whispered. "We met once when your great-aunt was still alive, shortly after you returned from the Continent. She held a party for you, on the lawn, and invited the whole countryside."

"Yes, I remember. But there were so many people there, I'm sorry that I don't recall your name."

"My friends call me Adam."

"And are we to be friends . . . Adam?" He was a handsome man—dark hair, green eyes, his voice cultured. In other circumstances, she would have found him attractive.

"We have much in common, Lady Fairbourne, much more than you imagine. For one," he spoke low, leaning close to her shoulder without touching it, "both of us have come here to end an affair: you with the groom, and I with the bride. We must see them marry"—his voice grew sad—"must we not, to know that our time is over?"

He looked so sincere, and his words fit her motivations so closely that she did not object to his forwardness.

He leaned away from her, sitting upright in his seat. "But we should talk of something else. I was one of your great-aunt's protégés. My father held a living on one of her Irish estates, and she sponsored my education."

"I would never have known from your accent."

"My parents were English, but even so, any hint of my Irish childhood was a necessary loss. Ultimately, though, your aunt grew a bit disappointed in me."

"Why, sir? My great-aunt was rarely disappointed in anyone, other than my cousin, that is."

"Ah, yes, the grasping Archibald. I am pleased to see you escaped his plans. No, I think she hoped I would visit the estate and fall in love with you. But by then I'd already found someone I'd hoped to love."

He looked to the front of the church, and they grew silent together.

A small boy, one of the baker's youngest, tapped Adam on the shoulder, and handed him an envelope. Adam looked at the hand on the envelope and turned white. He broke the seal with his finger and let the contents fall into his palm; a small charm shaped like a mermaid.

He looked surprised, then disbelieving. He carefully unfolded the note that accompanied the trinket, then he spoke quietly to the baker's boy. She watched as he handed the child a shilling, then rose and picked up his hat from the seat beside him.

"Lady Fairbourne, I must be going. I think perhaps my luck is changing." He stepped into the aisle, then turned back to smile at her. "Perhaps yours will change as well."

Some minutes after Adam left, the baker's boy carried a letter to the front of the church, where the Somervilles sat as a group. Aidan stood and took the letter. She watched as he read it, then, holding it open, strode to the back of the church.

He paused as he approached her, both surprised—and not surprised—to see her. "Lady Fairbourne, I would talk to you after . . ." His voice trailed off, and she was surprised at his indecision. It was unlike Aidan, except where his brother was concerned. "Would you please wait here until we can speak?"

"As you wish, Your Grace." She owed him too great a debt to refuse.

Colin stood in the vestibule, talking to one of the Shelton spinsters and the minister. When he first entered, he had seen Lucy in the back row, but he'd forced himself not to look at her. He could not bear her tears. He knew his duty, and he always did it.

The wound in his side barely hurt him anymore, but he knew that till his dying day the puckered scar on his side would remind him of her touch. Even now, the thought of her hands ministering to him was enough to make his body tight with desire and regret. He forced himself to smile at something the minister said, having heard enough to know it was a joke of some kind. He tried to replace the images of Lucy, naked and kissing him, or Lucy, drawing a sword to challenge him, with those of Em, quiet Em. But his mind was unwilling.

Miss Shelton was saying something about Em, and he forced himself to listen. Even if the old woman was a shrew, Em deserved his attention.

"Of course, Miss Emmeline has always pleased us for being everything her father is not. Dependable, concerned with the well-being of her cottagers, trustworthy."

"That's Emmeline for you," he agreed heartily, "Always dependable."

"Well, and of course, you know about her father . . . the absent lord, off in France raising a second family with his French mistress."

"I believe that the proper term is wife." Colin found it strange to be defending the man, but Em would wish him to do so, even if it meant he spread a little lie on her father's behalf.

"Well, in my day, a man didn't marry below his station without repercussions being felt through the whole estate."

"Perhaps that's why her father has not come home. He knows what reception he'll receive. Perhaps it's kinder this way, allowing Em to run the estate."

"He always was a flighty one, running off to the wars though he was the heir presumptive. But I suppose you will take over now. Certainly you and Lady Emmeline will wish to begin a family, and it wouldn't do to have the lady of the manor mucking about in the fields, as Lady Emmeline has often done."

He thought of having children, but none of them looked like Em. Instead, they all had the shape of Lucy's face and her dark curling hair.

The minister saved him by escorting the shrew to her pew.

Colin brushed his hair back from his face and took a deep breath, as Aidan appeared at his side.

Aidan took his arm. "I need to speak with you in private."

"Can it wait? The ceremony is about to begin. Em will be here in just a moment."

But Aidan's grip on his arm was tight, too tight. Colin noticed the thin line of Aidan's mouth.

"What's wrong? Is Em unwell?" He allowed himself to be led to the vestry at the side.

Aidan shut the door behind him.

"A boy brought a note for you, but I thought whatever it was, it could wait. He insisted, so I opened it."

Aidan held out a crumpled piece of paper. "I'm sorry, Colin."

Colin saw the letter was written in Em's most formal hand, the one she reserved for declining invitations and writing letters of condolence. Colin took it, turning his back to read.

> *My oldest, my dearest friend,*
> *I appear to be my father's daughter after all.*
> *Please forgive me.*

No signature. Colin dropped the letter to his side. "Two women running away from me. At least this time there was a note." But his voice held no hint of humor.

"Lucy didn't run," Aidan offered gently, putting his hand

on Colin's shoulder. The two men stood silently for a moment.

"I need to find her, convince her to come back." Colin's voice was quiet, almost a whisper.

"Is that what you wish?" Aidan turned Colin's body toward him by the shoulders. "Because if it is, I will call for my carriage, and we will search for Lady Hartley until we find her. She can't have gone far. But before I do that, consider the great gift Em has given you: the chance to marry Lucy. Can you tell me that your thoughts haven't turned to Lucy even once today? That you haven't wished that somehow, someway you could marry her—instead of Em?"

Colin looked up into his brother's eyes. "I can't."

"Then Em was the wiser of the two of you."

Aidan, Duke of Forster, made the announcement, Colin and Sam standing at his side.

Since a feast had been prepared at the manor and all the neighbors and tenants were already invited, Sam encouraged everyone to join them at the manor house. A neighborhood dinner, he called it, instead of a marriage celebration.

Colin stood stoically at the front of the church, flanked by his brothers, waiting for the church to empty. A line formed of friends who wished to offer their condolence, and Colin, as any good soldier doing his duty, held his shoulders back and his head high. Her heart broke for him.

As the family waited for the line to wend its way past Colin, Walgrave took a seat beside her. Both waited in silence.

Colin never looked at her, and then, when the church was almost empty, he left through the vestry with his brothers.

"Forster has asked me to remain with you until he returns." Walgrave offered her a piece of hard candy. The action, so incongruous with the situation, made her stare, then laugh. "See, hard candy has amazing properties. It can soothe an anxious stomach, improve the breath . . . and make a lady who faces an uncertain future laugh."

She took the candy.

"I imagine you would prefer to return to London rather than attend the festivities . . . a decision that suits me as well. And, besides, Colin's guests are unlikely to remain here past tomorrow in any event. Ah, the great man approaches. I will wait for you in the carriage." Walgrave shook Aidan's hand, then took his leave.

Aidan sat in the row before her so that he could face her. "I am sure that you are as surprised by today's events as the rest of the family. Unfortunately, despite the fact that Lady Hartley compared her behavior to that of her father, my brother believes himself somehow at fault, that somehow he conveyed to Em some reticence or reluctance to marry her, and that in doing so, he forced her to this course of action. It is, in his eyes, a breach of honor, duty, and friendship. I fear that he will respond by denying himself a marriage to the one woman he truly loves. As you will continue in residence at the ducal mansion until, at the least, we can determine that you are no longer in danger from your cousin's machinations, I have suggested that, when he returns to London, he withdraw his lodgings to his club. I hope he will come to the right decision, given time. But until he does, there is no good served by his distressing you."

"May I ask a question that may seem impertinent, given all you have done and continue to do for me?

"Of course." The corner of his mouth twitched momentarily into a sort of smile.

"Some months ago, you wanted nothing more than for me to reject his offer of marriage. Yet today you advise me to wait patiently for such an offer. Why? What changed your mind?"

"I have regretted that conversation many times in the last several months. But Colin is more himself when he is with you than he has been since he left for the wars. Even if I had not come to admire you, your courage, your resilience, these past weeks, I would still wish to do whatever I could to ensure that my brother remains that man."

For the fourth day since their return to London, Colin remained away. Each morning, Lucy hoped to see him, and each evening she went to bed disappointed. She had hoped at least he would appear for the meeting Aidan had called to discuss how to assert her rights over the money and property she had inherited from her great-aunt. But Colin seemed to be holding to the plan he had outlined when he thought he would be married—Aidan and Walgrave would help her, and he would stay away. It hurt to think that he could throw away the gift that Em had given him, but at the same time, Lucy had to consider that he had finally realized—albeit months after her original fortnight deadline—that he did not in fact want to be married to her.

"As I see it, we have two paths, perhaps three." Walgrave folded his long frame into one of the chairs across from Aidan's desk. "Marner claims that in light of his cousin's lunacy, he should be given oversight of her inheritance and lands. As long as Lucy remains missing, there is no bar to his argument. A judge might well give Marner the rights to her properties on the argument that they cannot go unmanaged."

"Can we insist that the court appoint a manager other than Marner, one to be paid out of the estate funds?" Aidan looked over the judgments Walgrave had brought with him.

"Not without revealing that we act on behalf of Lady

Fairbourne. If we do that, any judge of good conscience will demand she appear for a competency hearing. Given that she appeared as incompetent for months in the *ton*, they will likely prevail. If we lose, we might well also have to return her to her family," Walgrave said soberly.

"We can't have that." Aidan marked a passage in one of the documents.

"But if we reveal that she is still in London, she becomes even more of a target." Walgrave continued to outline the problems as he saw them. "As her heir, all Marner has to do is arrange for her to fall victim to some accident."

"I'm not sure I like our options." Sophia put her hand on Lucy's elbow.

"Can we go back several steps?" Lucy felt puzzled. "Marner isn't my heir."

"They say they have a will, in your hand," Walgrave explained.

"*My* will is at my solicitor's. I wrote it and had it witnessed the day they took me." She wrote down the address. "Here."

Aidan took the note and nodded as he read it. "Reputable firm. We should be able to see a copy at the least."

Walgrave scratched his head absently, "If we can show that Marner holds a forged will, using the will already filed with Lucy's solicitor for comparison . . . actually, that might work. It would make the basis of the claim the documents themselves, not Lucy's competence. Of course if we can't demonstrate that Marner's will is a forgery, we are back to the beginning."

"Lucy, who is your beneficiary?" Aidan, sitting on the other side of her, touched her hand.

She blushed. "I wanted someone who would not interfere with my wishes or bend to the will of my cousin. Someone who could not be bribed or threatened. So, I made Colin my heir and executor."

"Brilliant!" Walgrave threw his pencil into the air and caught it. "That's the best news we could have heard. As your heir, Colin has a legal right to make inquiries into the state of your will. We can avoid the issue of competence entirely if Marner's will proves to be forged."

"It's a shame that the Gray's Inn solicitors who read Chancery suits are such a tight-knit bunch," Aidan mused. "It would help if we could get an opinion—privately of course—of the possibilities of our success."

"I used to know Sir Samuel Romilly, but poor chap killed himself last year when his wife died." Walgrave thought aloud. "James Odum is in Ireland. The only other one we might be able to approach is Sir Cecil Grandison, but he's a stickler."

"Grandison?" Lucy was surprised to hear the name. "I was to deliver a letter to him from my great-aunt. But it was with my things at the boardinghouse, and I'm sure they have been long dispersed to the poor or discarded."

Sophia looked up. "No, they haven't been. I don't know why I didn't remember sooner—you could have used the dresses. When you were lost, Colin retrieved your belongings from your boardinghouse. He put them in a trunk in my attic. I'll have my butler, Dodsley, deliver it."

"As your heir, Colin will need to accompany you to meet with Grandison." Aidan did not look up, so she could not see if he were serious or plotting. "While you and Sophia are finding your great-aunt's letter, Walgrave and I will retrieve Colin from his club."

"Then we had better take a mop. Last I heard, he was thoroughly drunk and had been for the better part of a week," Walgrave said, without thinking, then bit his lip, glancing at Lucy.

"Lord spare me from honorable men." Aidan motioned Walgrave to the door.

* * *

Lucy clutched Aurelia's letter to Sir Cecil Grandison in her lap, as she and Colin waited in the solicitor's study.

Colin had said nothing since he had been delivered to the ducal manor by Walgrave and Aidan, freshly bathed and hair still wet. He did not look at her. But the beginning of a bruise on his jawline suggested that he had not returned willingly.

The door opened, and Sir Cecil, preceded by a Scottish white terrier, strode authoritatively into the room.

A portly man of about sixty, Sir Cecil boasted a thick shock of white hair that curled around his ears and across his forehead. He waved them to two Queen Anne chairs. The dog—"Mutt"—sniffed Lucy's shoes, then leapt onto a velvet ottoman, where he scratched in a circle before curling into a white ball. "Ah, Mutt likes you. You must have a dog, my dear."

"Yes, Sir Cecil. A Newfoundland whose dam came from Malmesbury's kennels."

"Ah, great dogs, great dogs. As for me, I prefer the terriers. Ferocious animals, but often underestimated."

"My great-aunt described you in much the same terms, Sir Cecil," Lucy reminisced, and the great man blushed.

"Quite a woman, your aunt. Had I been ten years older, I might have thrown my hat in the ring for her hand, but she had already loved and lost, long before I met her."

"She sent you a letter. It was written shortly before she died." Lucy held out the fat envelope. "I would have delivered it sooner, but I have not been long in London."

She watched as Sir Cecil carefully pried off the sealing wax without damaging the insignia, then let two miniatures fall into his hand along with a small folded packet in paper. "Ah, me. I didn't think she would remember. Thank you, my girl, thank you. When I heard she had died, I feared they might be lost."

The miniatures were in the style popular forty years before. "May I ask who they are?" Lucy ventured, but Sir Cecil was lost in her aunt's letter. He read the pages slowly, turning over the first leaf, then returning to it, reading ahead, then doubling back. As he read, he rubbed his jaw, clean-shaven, with the forefinger and thumb of his hand. Then when he was finally done, he reviewed the envelope carefully.

"Well, my dear, I must assume that you do not know the contents of your aunt's letter."

"Why, sir?" Lucy felt confused, but Grandison did not answer, turning instead to Colin.

"And you, sir." Grandison pointed a thick finger at Colin, one Lucy imagined he used to great effect in the courtroom. "I understand why Lady Fairbourne is here, and certainly I need to discuss her aunt's letter with her. But I do not understand who you are and why you are here—at least in relation to Lady Fairbourne's case."

"Colin Somerville, sir, most recently, an agent of the Home Office." Colin straightened in his chair as he answered. "As to the lady, I am her fiancé."

Lucy bit her tongue and forced herself not to react, other than to nod blandly. But she vowed to kill him later. To use that ruse long after their work together was done and to a man who knew her aunt—it was unconscionable.

"Ah." Grandison relaxed into his chair and regarded them both carefully. "I understand. You may remain." Having dispensed with Colin, Grandison spoke to Lucy. "Now as for your aunt's letter, Lady Fairbourne. Had you known its contents before now, you would either have gone to the magistrate to report a murder or you would have destroyed this piece of damning evidence."

Lucy and Colin responded almost simultaneously.

"Murder?" Lucy tilted her head in question.

"Evidence?" Colin leaned forward in his chair.

"Yes, yes. To both, yes. Your aunt corresponded with me for some years about her growing concerns about your cousin Lord Marner's avarice. After you arrived from the Continent and your aunt discovered the daughter she had always wanted, she wrote to me more frequently. In part, her questions were to ensure that your cousin would have no legal grounds to challenge her will. I helped her on that account—and my colleagues reviewed my work. But the other part of her letters dealt with her growing conviction that your cousin was stealing from the estate accounts. This sheet"—he held up one of the pages of the letter—"details his embezzlements."

"But what about murder?" Colin interjected. "What evidence can a letter hold?"

"Nothing that will prevail in court, unfortunately." Grandison held up the packet of paper. "Your aunt's letter also details a number of illnesses she found suspicious. One evening, she felt unwell and chose not to drink a glass of milk her nephew had sent up to her. The next morning, powder had settled to the bottom of the glass. After that, she was more cautious about what she ate or drank, but in the end, she feared not cautious enough. While, with the portion she has sent me, we can determine what the powder is, we cannot prove—save for your great-aunt's word—that your cousin is responsible. But this list is long, and your aunt was not a fool. Her request is not for herself, but for you, my girl. She asks that I aid you in whatever way I can. And I will, whenever you need my aid—now or in the future."

"Then I would like to tell you my story."

Grandison nodded, and Lucy began to lay out her tale, from the incident with the cat to her first escape, her capture, her second escape, and her current predicament. The old man listened with the patience of one who had spent his life listening to stories. And at the end, he specified in detail exactly what she should do.

During their meeting, Lucy only contained her anger with Colin by focusing on the advice Grandison offered. But once they left the great man's house to walk to their carriage parked on the road, she felt her pent-up anger well up and spill over. So angry was she, that she did not even notice the girl selling apples on the corner or the large man with the pocket knife whittling her an animal from the Royal Menagerie.

Colin handed her in, then gave the driver an address she did not recognize. She waited until he had shut the carriage door before she spoke.

"Of all the arrogant, thoughtless, cruel—yes, cruel—things to do. Being engaged is not a game, Colin Somerville. You can't claim it one week because it suits you, then decide against it the next. It is not a ploy to gather information. I agreed when we first met to the game of it because I never intended to marry, you or anyone. I had no friends in the *ton*. No one who would recognize me and force your hand. But Grandison—he knew my aunt. I've had tea with his wife. He knows my real name—and yours. And yet, you think to, to, to . . ."

"Marry you." Colin spoke with conviction. "I think I'm going to marry you. In front of all our friends, my family, the *ton*, Grandison, his wife—and anyone you wish to invite. Then, after a banquet large enough to leave even Aidan reeling, we're going to take a marriage tour. Anywhere you wish to go, and then we are going to find Em and make sure she is well and happy. And I'm going to thank her for knowing my mind better than I myself did."

She turned her face to the window. For several minutes she watched the city pass by. "You can't play with my heart like this."

"But I'm not playing, dearest." He turned her face to him. "I've spent the last week trying to reconcile my sense of duty with my desires. You would say my head with my heart. But I couldn't somehow wrap my mind around how to do that until this morning, when I saw you again and my heart fell into my shoes. I realized I didn't need to make a choice. I needed to acknowledge that the choice was already long made. Perhaps even from the moment you first agreed to kiss me. So, my darling, my dearest, will you do me the honor of becoming my wife?"

"But Grandison's advice . . ." Lucy shook her head in disbelief.

"Had nothing whatsoever to do with my decision. I'd *already* declared I was your fiancé before Grandison said that the easiest solution was to marry."

She searched his face. In his eyes, she found only sincerity and love. "Then yes, Colin. Yes, I will marry you."

"Then, kiss me, my angel. And forgive me for being a fool." His kiss was tender and sweet, then hungry and skillful.

Chapter Forty

Since marriage would provide Lucy with a new, powerful set of relations and by law make her husband the owner of all her property, everyone agreed that the marriage should take place as soon as possible. But Colin—having promised Lucy a large wedding—was unwilling to deny one to her, though she asserted over and over it didn't matter. Eventually, however, she realized that it mattered to Colin.

They compromised on an estate wedding at Colin's childhood home seven days hence.

Aidan used his influence to speed Colin's application for a special license and sent letters by special rider to his estate to begin the wedding preparations.

In only two days, Colin and Lucy were ready to make the trip to Monmouthshire. As Aidan had some committee meetings that he could not avoid at Whitehall, he and Sophia would follow soon after, with Judith and her menagerie, including Boatswain, in two separate carriages. The other brothers, as well as the Masons, coming as they would be from all across southwestern England, would arrive shortly before the wedding itself.

As an extra precaution for their travel, Colin hired a

carriage of former soldiers to protect their rear. To travel more easily, Lucy wore trousers and boots.

On the second day of travel, Lucy awoke to the sounds of gunfire. The carriage was running fast, too fast.

Colin was kneeling on the floor of the carriage, trying to keep his balance. He was doing something . . . she couldn't figure out what. She clung to the fabric handle next to her head. Still too fast, soon there would be a curve, and then . . .

She looked back at Colin, still kneeling, when suddenly the whole bench of the backward-facing seat lifted from the floor. The open space inside went somewhat below the floor. A space big enough for a person. Her.

Colin held out his hand. "Quickly. In here. We can't let them find you."

She didn't ask questions. She moved. She flung herself to the floor and rolled into the space.

"Whoa, whoa, stop now, whoa." The driver, whose voice she did not recognize, slowed the carriage.

"There's a bolt on the inside. Slide it. It will make it impossible to open this compartment from the outside. Even if they figure out it's hollow, they won't realize the space is big enough for a person."

He put his gun in with her and his knife.

"You'll be unarmed." Lucy searched his face.

"Sometimes it's better to be unarmed," Colin whispered. "Don't come out, not unless I call your name, your *full* name."

"But . . ." Lucy felt helpless.

"No buts, no time." He touched her cheek and shut the bench.

She slid the bolt, just as the carriage stopped completely. Then she heard the carriage door being pulled open roughly.

"Where's the chit? There's supposed to be a chit."

"I'm sorry, my good fellow. . . . Sent the chit to London. No time for virtuous women. Have pressing business at my estate. . . ." Colin's voice sounded strange, distorted.

The other voices argued, but she couldn't make out any of the words. "Out. Get out."

The carriage shifted as Colin stepped out. "I'm unarmed. I have a little money, if that's what you want."

The voices began to argue. The first voice wanted to kill him. The second wanted to deliver him to the man who hired them instead of Lucy. Other voices joined in. She couldn't hear them distinctly. Then there was a shot. And the sound of feet walking away.

Tears sprung to her eyes. What if they had shot Colin? He couldn't die, not after everything. She didn't dare make a sound, but the tears rolled down her face, across her temples and into her hair.

The carriage shifted again. Someone was in the carriage, tapping on the seat top. The tapping followed the board above her, moving from her feet to her head. "Seats are built in. No way to get into them that I can see. He must have been telling the truth. Switched carriages on us."

"I don't know how. We were with them the whole way. Damn."

"What do we do with the carriage?

"It's ours. Spoils of war, and all that. We'll meet our employer for our fee, then take it with us. A little paint, and we can sell it in Manchester."

The hiding place wasn't completely dark. Several drill holes, each about a half an inch in diameter, let in air and a little light. If she needed more air, she could press her face to one of the holes.

But it was still an enclosed space, a dark, small, enclosed

space. She tried not to be frightened, but her heart beat heavy and fast in her chest. As her panic rose, she felt bile on her tongue. No, she had to be calm. She had to be strategic. Otherwise, Marner would win.

She wasn't trapped, she told herself. She had the bolt. At any time she could let herself out. But she was safe, at least for now. Out there was more dangerous than in here. She'd already escaped from Archibald twice. She knew what would happen if she was delivered back to him, especially now that she had made him look a fool.

But if she were to escape again, she would have to pay attention. She might not know where they had been when the carriage was attacked, but at least she could try to remember how to get back to that place. If Colin were wounded and they hadn't brought him with them, she needed to be able to find him. If he were dead, then she prayed she would find his body—she didn't have the heart for another lover lost and never returned.

The carriage began to move.

To keep from panicking, she counted her heartbeats and converted them to minutes. One minute. Five minutes. Twenty minutes. At this pace, that was one mile. At six miles, the carriage slowed, turned a hard left, then stopped. She heard the creak of rusted hinges. A gate perhaps?

The carriage moved forward again, this time slowly. The road was uneven, and the carriage bumped and swayed. Another five hundred heartbeats, and the ground turned to gravel, crunching under the wheels as the carriage stopped. An inn? An estate? Voices met the carriage, but their words were indistinct. The carriage swayed as it was unpacked, then moved very slowly again. The smell of straw and manure told her it was a stable yard. The carriage swayed again as the horses were unhitched, then the carriage was pushed backward into a carriage stall.

Then silence.

She waited, trying to think through it logically. From all the angles, it was clear that she would have to act to save herself—and Colin, if he were still alive.

Her best chance was night, still several hours off. But until then, she should sleep, following her father's advice to conserve her energy for whatever circumstances she encountered.

The sound of men putting animals into their stalls woke her. The light through the drill holes had dimmed. Night, then. She didn't know how much noise the bolt would make unlocking. She felt the lock. It was sticky with grease. But to be safe, she would wait.

Again, she counted her heartbeats. An hour after the last sound she heard, she slid the bolt open and pushed against the lid of her coffin. It moved silently. No creaks. She held it up slightly, heard the sounds of animals more clearly. And crickets. So, they had gone on to the coast. One could only hear the sound of crickets in the southeast. That was at least some information. She tried to remember if Archibald had held properties nearby. And suddenly she knew where they were . . . or had a very good idea.

Clearly, the men had waited to ambush them until they were close enough to a place where they could be easily hidden. But she knew the house, knew how to escape. She tucked the gun—already loaded—into the waistband of her trousers at the back. She stuck the knife in her boot as James had taught her.

If they'd brought Colin with them, he could be any-where in the house. Luckily, it wasn't too large, and most of the lower-floor rooms had a window to the outside. She walked around the perimeter at a distance, keeping to the line of the woods that encroached on the house from all sides.

It didn't take long. She saw him through a window, tied to a chair. Blood was caked on his forehead, on the side of his face, and down the front of his shirt. His clothes were torn, and his head was hanging to the side. From the window, she could see his chest rise and fall, and she almost wept with joy. One of the windows was already open, and she lay her pistol on the sill and climbed through.

He smelled of whiskey, on his shirt, his hands, his hair, his mouth. There was a whiskey stain down his trouser legs. But in the carriage he hadn't been drinking. She'd seen the ploy before: rub yourself with whiskey to appear a drunk. It explained his distorted speech when he'd left the carriage— he'd deliberately slurred his speech.

She used the knife to cut his ropes, waiting to speak until he started to waken. Then she put her hands across his mouth. "Shhh, I'm here. Be quiet."

His eyes when they opened were angry. "You were supposed to wait."

"You were supposed to come for me. But don't worry: I know this place. I know how to get away. Just let me get your hands free. How many men? And where are they?"

"Four. Remember the wine we were carrying for the wedding?"

She nodded while she whittled away at the ropes.

"We'll need to get more."

In a few minutes, she had him free, but he stumbled against her. "Are you drunk or hurt?"

"Just a bit beaten up. I'll be fine."

"Can you ride?"

Since he could not exit easily the way she had come in, she preceded him into the hall. The door to what had been a drawing room was open, and two men lay on the floor snoring. She led him to the back entrance. As she had before, they moved immediately to the line of trees circling the yard, then back into the barn.

Six horses were in stalls.

Colin stumbled to the stall where the two horses from his carriage were housed together. "Help me climb the stall wall." From there, he crawled onto one of the horses' backs. "I'm not going to be able to ride, Lucy. My head is spinning and my vision is blurred. Just hide me here, and go for help."

"Again, what regiment were you in? I'll just tie you to your horse. I'm not letting you go, Colin Somerville, not another time."

The night seemed enchanted, with very little sound. She moved swiftly, tying his feet around the horse's belly and his arms around her neck. Then she let the other horses go and mounted her own.

She waited over and over for one of the men to appear, but they never did. It seemed too easy. She decided that she could cope with something being easy.

The magistrates caught the men, still sleeping off the whiskey and wine they had drunk. They admitted to having sabotaged the coach of Colin's protective guard, then waiting to attack Colin's coach until it was alone on the road. The highwaymen couldn't tell who had hired them, only that he had promised them more than he had paid . . . which was why they had chosen to drink the alcohol they found. And why, though they had been told to destroy the carriage, they had kept it to sell.

"Marner," Lucy declared. "The only man who can repeatedly ruin his own revenge plot by being too stingy to pay for it."

"Lucy." Colin nuzzled her face. "The only woman I ever want to spend another moment with. Marry me, my star, and I'll light up the skies with proof of my love."

The day of the wedding, when the bells rang at the estate chapel, a display of fireworks as brilliant as those on Guy Fawkes Day filled the sky.

Chapter Forty-One

"Explain to me why we are still doing business with him. He lies to us, does not pay us, and tries to leave us the trouble of a body—then, when I finally find the girl, he once again takes matters into his own hands and once again loses her," Flute growled

"He has something I want. A small piece of land, not more than a few acres, but located perfectly for a plan I have in mind."

"But is it hers or his?"

"His. A bequest from an uncle. It's bottom land, not valuable, on a canal. He has owned it for most of his life and ignored it. Ignored the possibilities of that one little piece of land. And I want it. Outright."

"So all of this? The girl, the asylum, the . . ."

"Just a means to an end. I could have bought the land, ut then someone could have wondered why I wanted it. ⸱is way, the line of ownership is muddled, and no one will ⸱k a thing about a piece of property lost in a gambling ⸱rite or who ends up with it in the end." Charters sat down ⸱ desk, prepared to play the devil if necessary. He set ⸱rite knife—a Damascus blade—and Georges' pumice ⸱ plain sight on the desk.

"Bring him in, Flute."

The door opened, and Flute shoved Marner into the room. The man recoiled at the sight of Charters behind his desk.

"It was not wise to try to hide from us, Lord Marner. Now tell me: why should I let you live? Have you anything at all that I might find valuable?"

Marner stood, silently defiant.

"No, I didn't think so. Just a defunct title that dies with you."

"If you kill me, I can't pay you." Marner shuddered.

"Other methods of payment also suit me. Like a slow, painful death, after which no one will ever be able to identify your body. Pieces of you strewn all over the city, an ear here, an eye there. Or perhaps all fed to the hogs on your cousin's estate. Missing but dead. Very dead. Your death will serve as a caution to others who think to take advantage of my . . . good nature."

He took out the knife, played with it in the light, and held it out to Flute. "Would you like to do the honors, Mr. Flute? But slowly—I want him to regret his actions."

"I have a piece of land," Marner blurted out. "It's a prime piece, good for grazing, water adjacent, near the coast."

"Does it have a house?

He looked away. "No. It's a ruin, not habitable. But there's a cottage, small but livable. You could rent it out. There's a tenant there already. . . . You could let her stay, though she pays almost nothing."

"Her?"

"The ward of my uncle who left me the land. I'm not supposed to dislodge her, but if you own the land, there's no violation of the will."

"Let me understand you: you expect me to take a piece of land with a disputed ownership instead of a nice handy pile of money? Is there at least a barn?"

"No . . . a shed, but that's all."

"Then why would I want it?"

"It's worth more than I owe you," Marner argued. "It might be the only way I can ever pay you."

"Fine. I'll take the land."

Marner's hands fumbled about. "If you will give me a piece of paper, I'll write a transfer of deed now."

"No, you will go to the gaming hell below. Mr. Flute will show you to a table. When a white-haired man comes to the table and invites you to play, you will play. And you will lose. You will bet this piece of land, and you will lose. Do you understand?" Charters let the light fall on the decorations in the blade of his knife.

"Yes," Marner stammered in fear.

"Good." Charters picked up the pumice stone and walked toward Marner. He recoiled in fear. "Ah, I see you remember my friend Georges's toy . . . scrapes the skin off so nicely and from such sensitive places. If you think to walk out without playing, Mr. Flute will stop you. If you think to play and win"—Charters tilted his head—"well, that would be foolish. Don't you agree?"

Marner's eyes never left the pumice. "Yes, yes, I agree. I will lose to a white-haired man who invites me to play."

"Excellent. I see we have an agreement."

Marner grew bolder. "After that, you will leave me alone."

"Of course. I will have no use for you."

"I'll be destitute."

Charters turned. "For five years you lived on the largesse of your aunt, waiting for her to die, giving her a little bit of poison every day, watching her grow weaker, spending the estate accounts for your own purposes. But you never set anything aside—no, you expected to inherit, so you were spendthrift and foolish. Then, when your cousin returned from the Continent, you could have dispatched her quickly— you called on me, confided all you had done, then decided you didn't want to spend the money. And now you have nothing. If you are to be destitute, it is not by my hand. Show him to the tables, Flute."

"Have you read the paper yet today?" Aidan held out a barely mussed copy of the *Times*.

Colin looked up from his coffee. "Should I?"

"You might find it interesting. At least, your lady might."

Colin held out his hand. "Any particular page . . . ?"

"Three. Under 'Police.'"

"The magistrate determines that the man threw himself into the river, or fell in a state of intoxication. Nothing was found at the time, the man having no items on his person that would provide his identity. But in recent days, the absence of Lord Marner from his county seat . . ."

"Marner's dead?"

"I viewed the body this morning to be sure. Apparently he lost what few possessions he had left at a gaming hell near London Bridge."

"Then she's safe. Well and truly safe."

Epilogue

"Sir, it's time to return home." Joseph Pastin stood at the doorway of the office, looking in. No one would have been surprised to hear that the man at the desk had very nearly died in battle. One long scar ran from his temple down his cheek and to his chin, a reminder of the sword's tip that had sliced open the once-handsome features. It had missed his eye, but not the edge of his mouth, and the parts had knit together unevenly, joined by a thick, raised scar.

"You never stop watching out for me." When the man smiled, as now, the whole plane of his cheek, from the edge of his mouth to his ear, remained motionless, making him appear either clownish or terrifying, depending on the light.

"No, sir. The prince regent has made it quite clear that I am to take good care of the hero, who died for his country and now spends his afterlife in a hidden office suite, poring over information the way Wellington used to pore over maps. The others left hours ago."

"Well, if no one is here, then you must stop calling me 'sir.' If any man has a right to my name, it's you."

"Then, *Benjamin*, it's time to return home." Pastin had already turned down the lights in the outer offices.

"You won't ever get used to my new name, will you? I

thought we picked Mr. James because you liked the sound of it."

"No, we picked it because it was my grandfather's name, and I thought it would be easy to remember. But I've found I'm too old to change. I've known you as Benjamin for my whole life. Or at least all of my life that's worth remembering."

"I suppose I must get up, but my leg is objecting to this change in weather." Benjamin rose with difficulty, his good leg stiff from lack of exertion. He reached for the cane to steady himself, but began to falter. Joseph reacted quickly. Sliding his arm under Benjamin's, the adjutant pulled his old commander against his body, helping the man to stand until he regained his own feet.

"It was a good day that I recruited you to join my regiment."

"How could I not follow the fair-haired officer who promised to show me the world?"

Joseph helped Benjamin into his greatcoat, then offered him his arm. Benjamin took it. "Have you discovered anything else about Princess Marietta's murder? Anything that might indicate who was behind the assassination or the Levellers' riots?

"No, but I'm certain they are related. I just don't know how yet. I simply hope we can sort it out before one or more of my brothers find themselves in a trouble from which I cannot extricate them. But at the same time, I certainly put Colin in the eye of danger."

"Yet it turned out quite well—I met Lady Fairbourne several years ago when we were still on the Peninsula."

"Her father was a good man. I suppose had I known she was in distress, Colin is exactly the brother I would have sent."

"Are you still sure you are doing the right thing? Letting them believe you are dead?"

"If they know I'm alive, Aidan will refuse to remain lord. And I'll be obligated to marry and provide an heir. And we both know I cannot take that chance. No, it's better this way. And besides, spending my time in this office ensures that I don't scare any children."

Joseph extinguished the lights one by one behind them as they made their way slowly, arm in arm, out of the office and down the hall.

"At least you were able to intervene for Lady Wilmot. Your brother and Walgrave were able to find the planted papers before the magistrates arrived."

"Yes, but I worry. What if that request hadn't come to me, to this office? Would Lady Wilmot be in the Tower even now awaiting execution as a spy and forger?"

"But it didn't happen, sir. All the information that has to do with the security of His Majesty's kingdom comes across your desk. As long as it does, you can look out for them."

"As long as it does, Joe, as long as it does."

Dear Reader,

I thought you might like a little more information on the background to Lucy and Colin's story. I love history and words, and, when I'm not writing, I enjoy mucking around in nineteenth-century magazines to see what I can discover.

Mental Asylums

In 1818, a parliamentary committee visited all of the asylums in England, and the details about Matron's house come from the report of that committee published in 1819. By the standards of that report, Matron's house would actually have been one of the better facilities for the care of the mentally ill, providing fresh straw, flannel in winter, glass in windows, and fresh air (even if that air was accompanied by a strait waistcoat).

Word Games and Enigmas

A staple from the late eighteenth-century through the end of the nineteenth, word games were a common feature of women's magazines and books for women and girls. I have used actual enigmas from nineteenth-century books, though not from the 1819 *Lady's Magazine* itself. Though that periodical had for many years devoted a section of pages to various sorts of games and their solutions, by 1819 it no longer did so.

The question game that Colin attributes to an overly

zealous matchmaking mother is drawn from *The Querist's Album*, published by David Bryce in Glasgow between the late 1860s and 1890. The *Querist's Album* asked players to offer their 'confessions' to thirty-six questions on personal topics, and the questions Colin recounts to Lucy are from that book. My favorite question of the whole list is this: "Is it acceptable for a woman to pop the question?" Until I read the *Querist's Album*, I had no idea that the phrase ("pop the question") or the practice (women asking for men's hand in marriage) dated back so far as the late nineteenth-century.

Dawamesk

I have extrapolated the possible presence of dawamesk in England from various sources. Hemp was praised in botanical and medical books from the sixteenth-century, including William Turner's *New Herball* (1538) and Nicolas Culpeper's *The English Physician* (1652). Further, Robert Burton in his *Anatomy of Melancholy* (1621) recommended marijuana as a treatment for depression.

Additionally, a number of counties in England grew hops during the early nineteenth-century, though the hallucinogenic present in that strain was relatively weak. British trade with African countries that produced the drug was well established; and Napoleon himself—who had brought the plant back to Paris for study in the 1790s—had trouble with his troops experimenting with hashish in Egypt. Given these factors, it's not inconceivable that forms of marijuana, such as dawamesk, made their way into England before the 1840s.

Lucy's symptoms—the vivid colors, the synesthesia, the perception of shapes bending around other objects—all were recorded in Jacques-Joseph Moreau's memoir of using marijuana, published in France in the 1840s.

I hope you enjoyed Lucy and Colin's story, and that you are looking forward to the next book in the Muses' Salon series: *Tempting the Earl*. There, Harrison Walgrave and his estranged wife Olivia must work together to solve the mystery behind some coded letters before Charters kills again.

I'm happy to hear from readers—you can email me at rachael@rachaelmiles.com. For more historical notes on *The Muses' Salon*, or to connect with me on social media, go to my website—rachaelmiles.com—which provides links to Twitter, Facebook, Goodreads, etcetera. While you're there, sign up for my mailing list, and I'll send you an announcement when the next book is coming out.

I'm happy to talk to book clubs and community groups, and my website provides a list of possible topics I could discuss. Drop me a line to set something up.

Happy reading!
Rachael Miles

Keep reading for a sneak peek at
the third book in the Muses' Salon series,

TEMPTING THE EARL,

available in November 2016.

And be sure to read

JILTING THE DUKE,

available now
from Zebra Shout.

The man was still behind her, on the other side of the street, tracking her. Olivia had been lucky to have seen him, or she would have led him straight to her hiding place. Now she needed to go somewhere else—a market, a crowded shop—anywhere to give herself a chance to escape.

But the street was quiet, and the shops too small. Nowhere to hide. She looked in the reflection of a shop glass as she passed. Still there. She forced herself not to increase her pace. If she hurried, he would know she'd seen him.

Ahead at the end of the block, a carriage pulled to her side of the street, and two footmen carrying packages stepped out of a shop. Footmen and packages meant a woman shopping, perhaps more than one.

She looked at the shop's sign, hanging out over the sidewalk. An open book beside a stack of papers and a jar filled with quills. A bookshop and stationer. Her chance.

Olivia gauged the remaining distance between her and the carriage, estimating how long it would take for the woman (she prayed it was a woman) to leave the shop, step into the coach, and for the coach to pull away. The woman hadn't left the shop yet: that gave Olivia more time. Each moment the woman delayed was another moment Olivia had to reach the coach.

The footman opened the door to the shop, and two women, well-dressed and laughing, stepped onto the sidewalk. Olivia clenched her fingers on her worn reticule, holding it close to her belly. Inside, tucked in the lining, she'd hidden the instructions for meeting her informant. Usually she memorized the complicated dance of sign and counter-sign right away, but she'd been distracted, telling herself it wouldn't matter, this once. But if he caught her, if he found the paper, then it *would* matter—because people would die.

It had been six months since she'd penned an essay on the struggles of soldiers returning home and sent it off to be published in the fashionable newspaper *The World*. She hadn't really expected the editor to publish it. If she had, she likely would have chosen a better pseudonym than "An Honest Gentleman." And she certainly hadn't intended to become the banner bearer for the rights of man. But her essay had struck a chord with the British, weary from the wars and the inflation that followed. She'd begun a correspondence with the editor, and soon her essays had started appearing every week. From corruption in Parliament to abuse on the docks, *An Honest Gentleman* brought it all into the light.

But there's no predicting the hand of fate, and soon she was receiving correspondence from all across the land, asking for her help—or rather, *An Honest Gentleman*'s help—in revealing this or that wrong. From one informant in the London hells, she now had more than twenty from across Britain. She'd become—in the Home Office's estimation—the greatest threat to a peaceable England since Napoleon. But no one expected a short, softly rounded woman with a middle-class accent to wield the pen that caused MPs to shudder. And until recently she had thought that her anonymity would protect her.

She was still too far away from the carriage. The women stood outside the bookshop for a moment, their heads bowed in conversation. *Keep talking*, she willed the women, *keep talking*. But they moved slowly to the carriage. A waiting postilion handed each one in.

She glanced in the next shop window as she passed. He was still behind her, tall, menacing. She tamped down her welling panic, feeling her mouth grow wet with nausea. What would she do if he caught her? It was crucial that *An Honest Gentleman's* new essay be published before the next set of debates in Parliament. The information she'd been able to garner from her network suggested that a widely supported bill was being financed by a powerful group of criminals. Her informant tonight had promised to give her the name of the man behind the plot. But she'd never met this informant before—and if she missed their meeting, she might not be able to convince him to agree to another.

Before her, the door to the carriage remained open. The postilion had placed before it a stool with three steps. The footman remained there, waiting. Someone else was in the shop, she realized, and her heart rose.

Instinctively she quickened her pace, then slowed. But it was too late; he'd seen and increased his pace as well. With each long step, he narrowed the distance between them. But he hadn't crossed to her side of the street, not yet at least. The carriage still standing in front of the shop would hide her escape.

Only four more shops and she'd be there.

The footman opened the door again, and a young woman with a brightly colored feather in her hat moved slowly toward the open carriage door. At the carriage, the younger woman stopped before the steps, then held out her hand. The postilion placed it on his shoulder, and she stepped up, then up again. At another time Olivia would have wondered at the young woman's slow movements, but not today. No, all that mattered was reaching the group, the carriage, the shop. And she was so close . . .

The footman opened the shop door once more, letting a fourth woman out, then turned to shut the door behind him. Olivia almost leapt into the space of the closing door. As the door closed, she heard the coachman call out to the postilion to lash the steps on tight. For another minute or two, the carriage would hide her entrance into the shop.

Ranks of bookshelves circled the room, with tables in the middle. At the front of the shop to the right, two women stood on either side of the counter. Both faces were kind.

"I need . . ." She saw the carriage begin to pull away from the sidewalk, and past it, a man crossing the street to the shop. She turned back to the women, who waited for her to finish her sentence. "A man is following me. Can you help?"

Neither woman looked flustered. The one with the almond-shaped eyes pointed her hand toward the back of the store.

"Follow me."

The aristocratic woman in front of the counter turned kind grey eyes to Olivia. "I'll give you time. Go."

Olivia obeyed without thinking.